AOIFE

(EEFA)

MY DEAR, WRITE YOUR STORY!

Sarah Katherine McKelvey Perkins

Table of Contents

Part 1:
Change Me

A novel for young Christian readers to be enjoyed by all

"Battles are fought every day. This is no truer than now. Whether they be spiritual, mental, or physical, we have to watch and remain strong. For all of God's children, our battle is the Lord's. His will is strong; his way is true. The only thing that needs to change is you."

-Sarah K. McKelvey

"If you have accepted Christ as your savior, the next time you go through a trial, get down on your knees and say, 'Father, I trust in you. Please guide me through this and help me to be

patient as you mold me into something better than I was before. I love you, Lord, and I pray that I will love you more every day. I know you love me more than I could ever comprehend. I put my faith and trust in you, let me get how of thy word what I need to hear today. In Jesus' name,

Amen.' Then open the bible and read and hear what God has to say; let him talk and don't do all the talking. Think of every trial as an adventure that Gad takes you on, so you come out better than you were before."

-Sarah McKelvey

Chapter 1:
What is Home?

Dear reader, I would like to take you on a journey with me, but first, I have a question for you to ponder. What is a home for you? Is home a place for you? Is it your family or friends? Is it the people you hold dear? Is it your material possessions? Is it good food? Write down what home means for you and why that is. This helps you to see what makes you tick.

For me, home is a mixture of many things. It's my daddy's hug after a long day. My dad is the Beairclen clan master. I am a half sprite (a large elf-like being) and half human, and my daddy is a large bear. Considering that he adopted me, his big furry hugs are home to me. My little siblings nuzzling me for a hug and wanting to be picked up and held are a constant state of comfort for me. The smell of the woods and tree sap lifts my spirits, while the scent of my mother's cooking, paired with her beautiful smile, makes my mouth water and fills my heart with love. All these things are *home* to me.

What makes you feel safe and loved? What makes *you* feel at *home*?

For years, I have concealed a tale within my mind, and it can stay there no longer. I know not where to exactly begin. This is a tale of my childhood and of my inner self. Hold on tight, we're going in.

The country itself is called Whispherknot. Whisperknot covers nearly a span of a thousand miles. The beings who live within are very diverse; however, most of them are close-knit. The history of Whispherknot goes so far back that if I told you now, there would be no pages left for this story. But I will, for the sake of understanding, give you a short summary of its past and describe its hidden location.

You are familiar, I am sure, with the number of continents in the world. There are seven that you know of: Europe, Asia, South America, North America, Australia, Africa, and Antarctica. But what you do not know is that there are eight. The eighth has been hidden from the world for centuries, isolated and cut off. Where in the world it rests, I cannot reveal as much as I wish to, but its inhabitants permit me to share a bit of knowledge. The continent is a few thousand miles smaller than Australia. It has rivers, lakes, forests, plains, deserts, canyons, and most of all mountains. It is divided into seven countries, each utterly distinct from the others.

The first country I will tell you of is known as Ekland. This beautiful country lies on Mossland's Northern border. Ekland is a land filled with dense forests, beautiful rivers with gushing waterfalls, and vast stretches of crystal deposits that fill its canyons and mountains. These crystals come in all colors under the sun. The crystal is known for its unique ability to capture sunlight in the daytime and glow beautifully at night. The people of Ekland are mostly human, which is rare for Whisperknot, with pockets of dwarves and tree beings. They live in villages along the cliffsides and valleys.

The second country is called the Dearblaria. This country is very elusive and secretive. The people of Dearblaria once played an active part in trading with Mossland and Ekland until Dearblaria felt as if they were betrayed, and now, almost three hundred years later, most seem to have forgotten the country's existence at all. Tucked safely and strategically in a mountain range covered in dense forests and rivers, Dearblaria lives concealed and content to remain so.

The third country is known as the Skiski and is half forests and half plains filled with lakes and streams. This country is a breathtaking fortress. Streams and lakes line the edges of the country, making it impenetrable. Their waters, as deep as the ocean, are filled with nightmarish creatures that lurk in the murky depths, dragging countless souls into the other world. The country's plains, though scattered with trees and boulders, are no less terrifying than the waters that surround them. Underneath these plains lie a maze of caves and canyons that are inhabited by the country's beings. Though these beings may appear friendly and behave as such, they are not to be disturbed, for their vast underground cities also conceal immense dungeons. The plains above their earthly cities are used for farming, and each family has its own plot for herds or plants. The fields vary in size, and often half of the city will work together on its land while the others expand their city and store their goods beneath the earth.

The fourth country, Paula, is named after its first queen and features a peninsula that protrudes into the South Sea. The majority of this country is a plateau, and the rest is covered with mountains. The beings that inhabit this land are tough and resilient. They dwell by the sea, where the land is barren, and raise goats and sheep; the only animals with the skin thick enough to survive the harsh terrain.

The fifth country, Sabatoy, lies barren on the northern edge of the continent, ravaged daily by fierce winds. The rough, unhomely ground is stained red and jagged with rocks. The beings that live here make their homes underground and survive by their own savage will, or so we thought.

The sixth country is called Bawl, nicknamed The Green Wilderness. This country is home to large plains and deep rivers dotted with small patches of trees. The beings that live here are called the Slingbrees and the Capelic. They raise animals and farm their land, all while living under a king, who is always looking for more land, eager to expand his kingdom. This has led to many territorial disputes and skirmishes in Bawl. Countries like Mossland and Ekland are just thankful that they do not border Bawl and don't have to deal with them.

The seventh is my kingdom, Mossland. I was born there. I am writing to you now from somewhere else, and I cannot leave even though I long for home. This kingdom has many different types of beings, from the tiny Firewhip to the towering Great Pine Treebeings. This country has no king anymore. However, Mossland does have a council that oversees every matter that needs tending, except for the pursuit of peace. Our country was, and still is, tired and old and was not prepared for what was to come, and what I, dear reader, am writing to you about.

Chapter 2:
The King's Adviser

Deep within the curious woods of a time-scarred land, in an uncharted continent, lived a creature of grace and mystery. No one knew what he was or where he came from, for he kept his heritage a secret for beings to ponder. The creature secluded himself in the deepest parts of the forest, rarely venturing out unless the stars were at their brightest or something unusual stirred.

For stars, dear reader, delighted the creature so much that it made the creature cry and weep out of joy.

The creature, dear reader, lived in a cave. Well, I can't really say a cave, because it consists of an endless maze of tunnels with huge caverns that opened, ever so often. Streams of cold, pure water ran through many of these tunnels, collecting in a great underground pool that he would sit by on hot days, for the water was ever cold. This endless maze of tunnels stretched from one end of the creature's country to the other. The creature's favorite tunnel, the one where he primarily lived, had holes that let in beams of sunlight, and at the very end was a giant hole that opened right up behind a gorgeous waterfall.

Sunlight, dear reader, was crucial to the creature's love of flowers. He would weed, water, and tend its flowers every day. They were very special to him, for in his country, beside the many children that he adored, they were the only sunlight that seemed to shine.

The creature was wise and vigilant, always making sure that his country was safe. One of his tunnels contained a room that was stocked with enough weapons to furnish an entire army, but no one knew of this for the creature kept all secrets entrusted to him, and most of all—his own. The creature spent long hours writing letters to his friends, acquaintances, and royalty who resided in faraway countries, working to maintain peace between his country and theirs. His country's elders were old and stubborn, primarily concerned with floods and horse thieves, under constant denial about the great big continent that they were a part of. The creature longed to pull his country back to where it had been back in the days of Biro the Stone, King of Mossland.

The creature worked diligently to restore his country, all while pouring his efforts into his words, actions, and writings. His country was stuck, caught up in the past, unwilling to move forward, and a little too comfortable in its stagnant misery. The Queen's tomb stood cold and grey on the eastern banks of Marigold, and the King's remained untouched and forsaken on the western side.

"The people must have a new King—a young King." He said, hopefully.

The Creatures' true name was Theodore Weatherly, though few knew it, and those who did, rarely used it. One night, the creature sat in his study scribbling away in his journal, but an impulsive thought made him stop. He pulled a loose, blank piece of paper from his drawer and wrote these words:

"My heart gushes blood for my country on fire; a fire of hate, of pain, of physical weakness, a debilitating languor."

On starry nights, the creature would climb the hill above his cave, lie down under the stars, and gaze into the heavens, pondering every step of his plan that he had anticipated. After a few hours, he would rise, stretch, then walk around in the woods looking for fire daisies, dragon blossoms, and sprite king crowns—his favorite kinds of flowers. Upon finding a bunch, the creature would ever so gently feel through them until he found one that was too crowded or too small to get enough water or sunlight, then tenderly dig it up to add to his ever-growing collection.

The forest that the creature lived in was serene and diverse. It was in places tightly packed with tree brush, where a multitude of beings lived. For the creature's country was called Mossland, and within the country resided many different individual communities.

The creature lived in the region of Dragonwood Forest between the rivers Marigold and Littlestone. The Country that contains his forest is inhabited by ten main types of beings. If I were to tell you of every being in Mossland, I would have no room for the tale I wish to tell you, dear reader.

The first and quite abundant type of creature in Mossland is the treebeings, who love tightly packed areas of forest and have numerous families. The second, the most jolly and unpredictable type, are the talking bears that live in clans around large areas of rock, wood, caves, and caverns. The third and most stubborn to the rest of the country's inhabitants are the Headbricker Clan, who make a living off rock and woodwork. The fourth and very prosperous are the Rosians or rose people that inhabit parts of the Forest that are less dense. The fifth and largest in size are the giant clans that prefer living close to the headbricker and bear clans. The sixth and second most dainty to the fairies are the butterfly people that live close to the rivers, prairies, and streams. The seventh and mischievous are the fairies that were close relatives to the butterfly people, but are much smaller and do not care where they live, as long as they have a grove of flowers to tend. The eight and most cunning in their minds are the elflings that inhabit the forests along the river Marigold. This clan shares a love for music and woodwork, striving for perfection. The ninth and most lively are the bird clans, quite diverse in families and traits, loving to live alongside the bear clans who tend their gardens diligently. The tenth type of being is quite powerful; these are the large flying serpents who usually live solitary with a large territory of rocky hills, caves, and vast open plains. These ten types of beings are the main ones that made up the Forest and Country in which the creature lived.

The creature, as you can imagine, dear reader, was tenderhearted, graceful, compassionate, and witty, with a touch of timidity. All the other beasts and birds of the wood thought that the creature was very peculiar; however, they never questioned his heart, for they all knew how caring and generous he was. One good deed here, one helping hand there, had multiplied, making him a favorite among many. However, the creature did not like attention, so out of respect, the birds and beasts were sure to give him all the peace and quiet he wanted. He often lived alone and in peaceful solitude for at least two hundred years until his world and the world around him were shaken at its core.

The creature had travelled all over the continent when he was young and had collected rare objects from every country within. He kept these objects safe in a hidden tunnel that only he could find. The only being that knew they existed was Simon Birchbark, who had travelled with him in his youth.

On one especially starry night, the creature ventured farther than he ever had before, seeking the rare dragon blossoms that bloomed beyond the crystal streams of Marigold. The stars burned so brightly that the night almost appeared to be day. The mushrooms and lichens along the sides of the trail glowed all the colors of Noah's rainbow from dark purple to radiant orange. The trail floor was well trodden with roots that bumped out of the earth here and there, littered with leaves and pine straw, and marked with old stones that told where it led to. Along the sides of the path, there were little clearings ever so often, and it was here that patches of flowers thrived with their guardian gnomes. Just as the creature resolved to continue his search tomorrow, he turned to leave and nearly stumbled into his old friend, Simon Birchbark, an ancient tree making his slow way to the annual Councel meeting.

Simon was a treebeing. Treebeings are so incredibly camouflaged that you can't really tell them apart from an ordinary tree, unless they're walking or talking. They vary in size and shape depending on their age and clan. They have legs and arms like beings, while their skin is rough like bark. They have many leaf-covered branches, mostly on their heads and shoulders. One of their favorite things is to add decorations like moss, bird's nests, and vines.

Simon was an oak treebeing that lived in Dragonwood Forest by Marigold stream. He enjoyed taking long walks around the woods with his wolf named Shadow, and he loved spending time with his grandsapplings who lived in Shadowlark meadows. He was also quite fond of the creature who had been his good friend since he was quite young.

"Good day, Simon. Or should I say, 'good night'?" The creature said pleasantly, happy for the companionship on such a pleasant night to soothe his fears of a coming danger.

"'Good day' shall do, you flower-lovin' teddy bear," said Simon, and they both erupted with laughter.

"Stop calling me a teddy bear," the creature replied to Simon, "I'm not a teddy or a bear."

"Well, what should I call you then?" Simon pouted in reply, "You don't have a proper name, and you won't choose one for yourself. And you certainly won't accept any of mine."

"Peace, my old friend," the creature replied with a laugh, "The good Lord will give me one when He sees fit."

"Hopefully sooner than later, flower-lover. Oh, I just remembered why I was out here," Simon recalled. "I was trying to find you so we could go to the High Counsel together, and we'd better hasten."

"After you," the creature said happily.

He liked a good Counsel meeting. And they were off, rather slowly, somewhat due to Simon's age, but mostly so they could take in the beauty of the landscape, because they both love starlit nights. They stopped occasionally, a few times, to admire flowers they encountered, a couple to rest for a bit, and once at a river.

"Theo, have you heard the silent news?" Simon asked nervously, shaking his long mossy beard.

"Only a little," the creature replied, solemnly looking up into the tree's grave complexion.

"Well, I hear it's worse than we've ever imagined," Simon gravely reported, running his rough hand through his beard. "They want nothing but vengeance. Theo, they want war, and I'm afraid they'll have it."

"You can't condemn people on rumors," the creature stated thoughtfully, trying to make sense of it all, for indeed many rumors had come to torment his ears, "However true or timely it seems to the common hear. And if this is boldly true, I have a plan in mind that you will surlily approve of."

"I am aware, old friend," Simon agreed with assurance in his words, "but you need to face reality. This might not end well, even with a well-thought-out plan."

"Oh, I know it won't end well, Simon, but it is happening, isn't it?" The creature replied gravely, "You know as well as I what needs to be done, but we must be quiet."

"I'm glad we're in the same neck of woods," Simon said, then added with a curious smile, "You have someone in mind, don't you?"

"I do," the creature answered, "and I'm sure about what needs to be done, but let us not spoil this beautiful night with unpleasantness when there will be plenty of unpleasant nights to come, but it is not upon us yet."

"Your words are true, and you know far more about this world than an old tree like me ever will. I trust you will make the first move when it's time," Simon stated with confidence.

They walked in silence for a while, each lost in heavy, unpleasant thoughts, as they followed the rough, familiar path under the moonlight, until Simon finally spoke again, this time to lift the mood.

"Let's stop at Marigold, Theodore. I'm rather parched," said Simon, who had changed his whole mood around in hopes of cheering his dear friend up.

Marigold was a river that ran straight through Mossland diagonally. Many villages in Mossland lived along its grassy banks.

"Very well, Simon," the creature replied, shaking his head at being called Theodore, but not about to argue it on such a splendid night. "I suppose I could use a drink as well."

The creature got down on its knees and scooped up some of the crystal-clear water in a large, kaskal leaf that had been lying by the brook, and took small sips, savoring every one.

The night was indeed beautiful. The starlight had made the giant mushrooms and crystal rocks glow different colors. It was an amazing sight to see the entire forest lit up on such an important night. The woods were empty because all the beings were headed to Shadowlark Meadows for the Council meeting. Beings from all over Mossland would be present for the momentous occasion.

Simon, being a tree and a bit less civilized, stepped his large mossy legs right into the brook and drank right up through his toes, smiling with satisfaction.

"Are you done yet?" Simon asked, quite impatiently.

"I'll be done when I'm done, and I won't be rushed." The creature said simply.

Simon sighed and waited silently for a few moments. Then an idea popped into his head. If he teased him, he might hurry up. "Do take your time, Teddy baby, and I'll just be here dozing for a century or two."

"I'll be done right now if and only if you promise not to call me that again," the creature replied, a tad amused and trying hard to look serious.

"Of course, I promise, Fairy-Blossom. Now hurry or we'll miss my grandsapplings, said Simon, pleased that his plan had succeeded.

"You didn't say anything about your grandsapplings being there earlier. If you had, we could have taken my tunnel shortcut," said the creature, starting down the well-trodden path after the rather fast old tree.

"That would have never worked," said Simon in disgust. "Do you remember the last time you shoved me down a hole?"

"You mean a tunnel? A well-cleaned, well-cleared, and mapped tunnel that will come in very handy in the future. I know where they all lead, well, at least most of them. Besides, you used to like tunnel travel," the creature said, breathing hard and trying to keep up with the unusually fast tree.

"That was before I got stuck in one, and before I aged, I suppose," said Simon, using his long legs to take large strides. "That was not fun."

"I got you out, didn't I?" the creature replied, "Plus, you weren't stuck, but twenty minutes?" The creature smiled, remembering the inconvenient event.

"Felt like an hour, though," Simon replied, obviously not too fond of the event. "Have you a poem up your sleeve for such a night, such as this?" Simon asked, changing the conversation.

"I have one, but I doubt it will do this lovely night justice," said the creature, who was quite fond of writing a poem occasionally when he wished to take a break from his work.

"I shall surely want to hear it then," Simon replied, slowing his fast pace so as to hear it well, for he was also quite delighted at changing the topic and getting to hear one of the creature's poems that would take a person to a different land and time.

"Upon the eve of the dance of the sprites

A blessing fell from heaven.

As it passed through the sky

It lit up the stars

And made God's vast heavens glow.

As it passed through the trees

It made the lightning bugs and dragon whips sparkle.

And when it finally touched the earth,

It made the flowers, moss, and lichens glow.

Then it spread to the beasts and the birds alike,

Filling their hearts with heavenly bliss.

Heaven's kiss."

The creature ended, staring off into the distance as if the words had carried him away. Simon's thundering applause, however, brought him back from his faraway stars.

"Brilliant, Theo," Simon praised, believing that it was the Creature's best yet, "I must get me a copy."

"Thank you, Simon," the Creature replied, letting his thoughts slip back to the coming fear.

"You need to read it aloud to everyone at the meeting," Simon exclaimed, "I'll talk to Rowsheen. There's no reason why she wouldn't let you. You know she quite enjoys a good poem."

"I know, old friend. Well, here's a thought. Why don't you do it for me?" the creature replied with a crafty smile, holding his arms behind his back.

Simon caught his intentions and creatively replied, "A poem is from the heart, and should be read by the soul that possesses that heart, no matter how shy or modest."

"You're right, you know. I'm not getting around that, am I?" The creature replied with a laugh, "And much as I dislike admitting it, I've got to do it myself."

"By my dragon's nostrils, you're going to do it," Simon exclaimed, quite pleased with himself.

Chapter 3:
The Council Meeting

As they spoke, the trail widened, and the sounds of countless beings gathered from near and far all rose to their ears in a chorus of laughter, chatter, and merry-making. This was a meeting that almost all beings looked forward to, and some had traveled half a thousand miles or more to attend. The momentous occasion takes place in a different province of Mossland each year, and this year it was to be hosted in the Shadowlark meadows that lie over the river Marigold from Dragonwood.

The meeting always began with reports from every province, delivered by its chief elder, Osgood the Valiant. These announcements were seldom grave, for tidings of a darker nature were reserved for a separate audience before the council on another day.

After the council of elders had given the news, they would ask every province to bring up their annual gifts that would be given to Mossland's neighbors as peace gifts. Then they would respect all who had died with a sweet, mournful song entitled *Bittersweet.*

The Sun rolls in upon our home,
There is no place we'd rather roam.
Here we'll breathe our last,
Here our bones shall be cast.
Here our fathers gave their last,
For our country free 'n vast.
We hope to join them where they are,
Even if it be on a faraway star.

Here our mothers born and bred,
Here they cried with eyes of red.
Here they cherished and loved,
Our sweet country, our beloved.

I'll sing till I breathe my own sweet last,
And give my all to those who've passed.
A tune of love I'll carry,
A song that is quite merry.
A song to our fallen King,
And His beloved Queen.
A song so sad, a song so sweet,
It is forever Bittersweet.

Next would come the country's song entitled *Our Land.* After the Country's tribute would then come the announcements and upcoming events; like which province would host the Autumn celebration. The meeting would end with a poem or song, then the festivities would start. After the sun dipped behind the Western sky, everyone would camp out under the stars with music and crystal lights, and the next day, there would be contests to enter, merchandise to buy, games to play, and food to eat.

"Thank goodness it hasn't started yet," said Simon, scanning the crowd for his beloved grandsapplings.

Suddenly, the creature and Simon were surrounded by an army of giggling, laughing, and bouncing little tree saplings.

"Papa Simon, Uncle Nin, pick us up," the saplings chorused together, pulling and hanging on their arms and legs. Uncle Nin was a nickname the saplings had given the creature when they were very small, and he didn't mind.

"Are all thirty-three of you hooligans here?" asked Simon, between fits of hearty laughter.

"Yes, sir!"

"Yes, sir!"

"YES, SIR!"

"Yes, sir!"

The saplings echoed to the last one dancing about, letting their bunches of leaf curls twirl about.

"Line up, troops, and see if your uncle can remember all of your names," Simon bellowed, bending down to look them in the eyes.

Obediently, the sapling lined up from oldest to youngest, laughing, pushing, and poking all the while. The atmosphere was filled with delight, portraying the essence of joy.

The creature scratched his head, pretending to look confused, then he called off every name, not missing one, "Jubilee, Victory, Dragon-blossom, Brook, Barkbert,

Dragonberry, Spritewing, Starlight, Fireburst, Lilybitt, Cherryblossom, Knight,

Firelight, Grace, Forest, Treasure, Ruth, Streamstone, Rockabeth, Dragonsnap,

Fairyblossom, Nightsky, Angelbreath, Easter, Anne, Fire, Waterfly, Firefly, Chiste, Eric, Tigerwing, Katherine, and our little Simon III."

The saplings clapped, giggled, and danced about once more, loving their exciting game and insisting it be played at least twice a day.

"Run along to your parents," Simon coaxed them, trying to make a stern face but badly failing, "Your Uncle and I must speak with the Lady Rowsheen before the meeting begins." And they were off, running around and through everyone's legs, taking the longest route possible to their exhausted parents, who were enjoying a moment's rest.

"Are you sure about this?" the creature asked, nearly intimidated by the massive crowd.

"Sure, as I grow coconuts," the old tree joked.

"Don't worry. You'll do great. You have a way with words, you know," he added reassuringly.

"All right then. Where's Rowsheen?" the creature wondered, looking around the platform where she was most likely to be.

"I haven't the faintest clue. Oh, wait. There she is!" said Simon, glancing with delight, spotting her talking to her mother, Rosabitt, about ten giant strides away. "A few giant strides away," he approximated.

"Stop that. Do you want to upset the giants? There are a good handful here," the creature scolded. The giants were not overly pleased when their size was presumed as a scale for measurement. Many giants were self-conscious about their size, especially if they were a tall giant clan.

"Sorry," Simon apologized, *"It is good to keep the giants happy,"* he jumbled his thoughts within.

"Rowsheen!" the creature called as he and Simon pushed through the crowd.

Rowsheen was the young Rosian who had been selected to assist the counsel and province elders that year. This was her second year being selected and was not so nervous as last year. She was dressed in formal Rosian attire; this consisted of leaf slacks, knee-length bark boots that were of a very dark grey, a dark leaf shirt with a purple hint tucked into her slacks, a brownish red leather belt containing a sword with gold accents, and a deep red rose petal coat trimmed with lace that buttoned above her belt with gold buttons. The coat nearly dragged the ground behind her with twin elegant wrist guards engraved in silver, and a silver chain necklace that had her family crest wrapped tightly about her throat. She looked so proud to wear the elegant attire of her people on this momentous occasion.

"Simon, Sir, it is so good to see you both," Rowsheen greeted them, then she informed,

"The meeting will be starting as soon as all the elders from the provinces arrive."

Rowsheen was tickled that things were going as planned. She bit her lip and rubbed her hands together as a bit of anxiety showed through. Although Rowsheen was a natural leader, she did not like public speaking and organizing things. She was helping the council and the tree guard as a part of her education. Her parents thought it wise to have her learn public speaking and leadership for her future.

Description of Rowsheen and the Rosian People

In Part I, I would like to describe Rowsheen to you. Rowsheen, dear reader, was a Rosian. A rosian was a being that resembled a rose bush in appearance. Their hair and clothes are traditionally giant petals and leaves, and the color differs from clan to clan. More modern Rosians wear cotton, wool, and leather. Their skin resembles the smooth bark of a greyish color with patches of green lichens and moss. Their arms and legs are often covered with tiny emerald green leaves so closely placed that their skin is unnoticeable between them. Their eyes are often various shades of green, some with a hint of gold or brown. They are of average height for forest beings; most were no more than a giant's waist.

The most common Rosian occupation is guarding Mossland from intruders and protecting the council members. This differs from clan to clan. Many Rosians are writers of history and literature, counsel elders, and mapmakers. Rosians love history and philosophy. The Rosians who lived in the North around Sunspeak prefer to immerse themselves in the essence of music and poetry. The Rosians that lived near the Southern border, however, were less friendly and seemed to enjoy far more rough activities like dragon taming and sword fighting. The Rosians from Blackwood were the majority mapmakers. This clan was by far the most adventurous clan of Rosians the forest had ever known. They traveled all over the forest, scouting out and documenting every trail that existed for their maps, which they remake every year. The Rosians are often associated with being reasonable, as well as organized and efficient.

Rowsheen was a beast creek Rosian. She had dark reddish petals with pale greenish brown eyes. Her father was a farmer and her mother a writer. According to tradition, a young

Rosian would often take on the occupation of one of their parents; however, her father wanted Rowsheen to explore and find a job that would be both fulfilling and enjoyable.

Rowsheen, had no desire to be a writer or a farmer. Her sincere wish was to leave home and join the Rosian treeguard. This was an elite protective force that protected the Northern border from unwanted intruders on all borders, but mainly from Ekland, their northern neighboring kingdom that caused more trouble than many Mosslanders believed they were worth. She longed to join, but was hesitant to ask her parents, fearing that they would worry about her safety.

Back to the Council Meeting

"Hi, Rowsheen," Simon breathed beneath his bushy, mossy beard, "We were wondering if Jewelbith could possibly read his new masterpiece to the prestigious council ceremony?"

"Of course, my lord," Rowsheen replied with a nod. Her happy smile was laced in nervousness about announcing the ceremony. She knew the Creature would do a good job and take some of the spotlight off her, which she appreciated greatly.

The creature was adored throughout all parts of the vast and tangled woodland to the wide-open plains and was known for his delightful writings of lore and valor. Rowsheen politely asked with enthusiasm, "Would you like to close the ceremony with it?"

"I'd love to," the creature took a deep breath, hardly aware of the words releasing from him, then replied, "As long as the high elders do not have something more important in mind."

"They could choose nothing more momentous, my lord," Rowsheen replied politely, "They will be pleased. Please excuse me. My help is needed on the stage."

"You nervous, lightning bolt?" asked Simon, teasing, "You look almost as nervous as Rowsheen. You get to close this prestigious ceremony."

"Pray, you won't torture me, Brother. If Rowsheen can muster up the courage to open the ceremony, surely I can close it," replied the creature, dreading the ordeal for the stage was not his place of choice.

Rowsheen felt her palms grow sweaty and her pulse quicken. Her breathing was light. "LORD, I know you got this!" Rowsheen breathed deeply and then stepped confidently up the stage steps. The drums sounded to attract everyone's attention. Rowsheen opened the ceremony and introduced Elder Mossbeard, the high elder of the year.

The ceremony had started, and Rowsheen stepped off the stage. Her heart was pounding in her chest, and her steps felt as light as air. The ceremony commenced as usual, and Rowsheen felt a sense of pride for going through with it even though she did not want to.

The news was not anything new; the Horseland prairies and Dewberry Meadows were flooded, Blackwood was experiencing a drought and an overrun of dwarfgnomes, Sprites Grove had introduced a new kind of house that was suspended from a tree, Sun's peak/hills was inventing hundreds of new war and escape tactics every year not including new weapons, the Sun's Hills miners were finding new kinds of crystal and metals every day. Sadly, what was not said was the uneasy feeling everyone had about the ancient peace treaty with Ekland to their North that would be expiring in two leprechaun moons. The countries were getting restless, and everyone knew this. After the council meeting, the leaders of the provinces would meet to discuss the issue in secret.

By the time the announcements came, everyone was too restless to keep quiet, so Elder Mossbeard motioned for the drums to sound. Thousands of beings from all over the country packed the great, open plane. All stood at the sounding of the drum to hear the old elder speak. Elder Mossbeard spoke into a horn so the beings way across the field could hear what he had to say.

A young giant named Daniel walked over and stood by Simon and the creature so he could get a better view of the stage. His family had traveled all the way from the Horseland Prairies to attend the momentous ceremony. Daniel was to stay with some of his cousins, instead of heading back to Horseland Prairies after the festivities.

"Say, I haven't seen you in a while, son. Good gracious, you're taller than your father already," Simon addressed Daniel, "Just staying for the festivities or a little longer," Simon winked.

"I'll be staying with some of my cousins for a while, Sir," Daniel replied, looking back at the stage. Simon spotted Rowsheen by the stage. "I wonder what is so interesting by that stage to made you stare so," Simon teased, making Daniel turn dark red.

"I don't think you'll be leaving any time soon." Simon teased him again. "Leave the boy be, Simon," the creature advised, leading Simon by the arm toward the group of elders, "you were once young too."

Description of Daniel Charles Caster (and his people)

Daniel was a giant, and specifically a Horseland giant. Let me define giants, because many souls believe giants to be unfriendly or vicious. Dear reader, it is not so.

Out of all the beings and creatures in the wood, I have found giants to be the most agreeable and pleasant in comparison. There are four types of giants across Mossland. Most Mossland giants prefer to live around the Great River in the East and South and around the plains, where they often tend cattle and horses as well as sheep and goats.

The clan of the Great Giants lives below Blackwood Forest, Eastward. These great giants are the tallest giant clan. They often grow as tall as a pine treebeing. They build houses out of earth and rock along rivers and lakes. They also keep sheep in pens along the riverbanks and enjoy the beauty of nature.

The second giant clan is known as the Huckleberry clan, and lives in Dewberry Meadows, where Marigold ran into the Great River in the South. This is the shortest known giant clan, getting no taller than an oak treebeings' shoulder. They are farmers and take pride in their work. Their houses were usually made of wood and waterproofed with tar, although many prefer underground tunnels and houses below the earth to stay cool in the summer heat.

The third clan of giants was commonly known as the Horseland clan. They live in Horseland prairies in the Southwest along the river's edge. They raised animals like horses, cattle, sheep, goats, and swine, but horses were by far their favorite. Beings come from all over for their livestock, and especially horses, for they were the best horse breeders and trainers that can be found in Mossland.

The fourth giant clan is called the Rock Giants, and they live by Marigold and Sun's peak and were known as the Mountain clan. They were the only giant clan ever to live that far north. They raised goats and sheep. They also quarry stone and precious metals with the headbricker clans. They usually lived alongside the headbrickers in large, stone villages in the snow-laden mountain sides.

Daniel is a Horseland giant. He often lives on a horse and cattle farm on the banks of the Great River. Daniel often visits Leo, his cousin, a Huckleberry giant who lives by the Merigold stream. Most Horseland giants, as you can imagine, prefer horses, but Daniel enjoys raising cows. Daniel loves horses too, but cows are by far his favorite. Someday, he wants to own his own farm for cattle and horses.

Back to the Council Meeting

"I have one more announcement before we close the meeting and the festivities begin. The Whinghums will be coming to Mossland in a few weeks' time that we must entertain them with a joyous welcome. Which province would be willing to host such an event, and is there a noble willing to give of his halls and supply?"

"Simon," the creature beckoned earnestly, "I pray you'd lift me up on your shoulders that I might accept the good elder's proposal."

Simon drew the creature up effortlessly onto his shoulders and motioned to the elders by the stage to get their attention. When this did not work, Simon hollered to them, "Good Elders, I pray you lean your ears!"

"What is your say, good tree?" the elders answered Simon with interest.

"The Creature of the endless tunnels has offered his halls and his supplies to the most noble celebration for the Whinghums in accordance with your request and proposal."

The elders murmured in hushed tones, their words weaving through the air like ancient winds. At last, they turned their eyes to Simon, the mysterious creature still nestled upon his shoulder. Then, with a voice that seemed to carry the weight of ages, one elder stepped forward and spoke. The chosen voice of the now-united council, "The council accepts your most gracious offer, oh noble Creature of the endless tunnels."

The high elder Mossbeared stepped up onto the stage once more and raised his horn to his mouth, "The creature of the endless tunnels has graciously offered to host the momentous celebration of the visiting Whinghums. And lastly, may our country reign forever in unity and peace. LET THE FESTIVITIES BEGIN!" he said loudly before stepping slowly down from the stage.

Description of Whinghums

Whinghums, dear reader, are quite beautiful creatures. Many beings believe them to be angelic, but dear reader, they are far from it, seemingly as flawed as us humans. They have the amazing ability to appear human, but don't let that fool you. They're not. Their quick change in appearance is just a survival instinct. When real humans are near, the Whinghums appear perfectly ordinary, blending in with practiced ease. But the moment the last gaze turns away, their true selves emerge, shimmering hues ripple across their skin as vibrant, radiant wings unfurl in a burst of color. With effortless grace, they take to the skies, unburdened by the charade, free at last to revel in the truth of what they are.

The creature, dear reader, was quite interested in Whinghums. No one could blame him. After being abandoned as a child, a Whinghum flock adopted him for a short time before dropping him off in Mossland to be raised by the old council elders.

The elders called a vote, and of course, everyone agreed. It was decided that the party for the Whinghums' arrival should take place on the next laughing moon, twenty days hence. Then, with all the announcements over, the creature climbed onto the platform, read his poem, and dismissed the meeting. Everyone made their way to the festivities in joyous voices.

Everyone clapped and cheered for the creature, then the festivities began. Well, for all except Flutter and Fragrance, the two fairies who had taken the job of delivering the party invitation to the Whinghums. The Whinghums were not in the country yet, and that was why fairies were sent because they can fly above the trees and even turn invisible in case of possible danger, which the elders anticipated.

Chapter 4:
A Wish

Rowsheen had decided to walk the creature home, as the mouth of the creature's main tunnel opened up not far from the Rosian village by the rocky revenue. Because she had questions, she was sure he could answer. The creature often tutored Rowsheen, Aoife (Eefa), Kate, Leo, and Daniel. He told them many stories and tales from history and taught them mathematics and the art of reading and writing.

Rowsheen, like many of Mossland's inhabitants, was unaware of the conflict simmering just miles from Mossland's border. This was partly because she was only a young teenager, and in part, because she lived thousands of miles from Mossland's border. As many of the young in Mossland, Rowsheen had never met or seen a Whinghum and knew the creature would describe them to her if she asked.

"Sir," Rowsheen called, running up beside the creature as he strolled along towards his tunnels once more. Speed was no longer his gift, but he still loved to talk to the youths.

"Rowsheen," the creature replied, stopping and offering her his arm, smiling, "How much I wish my legs were as fast as they once were. What do I owe this pleasure, young one?"

"I was wondering, Sir, if we could talk as you walk home. My home is close to your tunnels," Rowsheen replied shyly, taking his arm.

"Of course, you can, child, just run along and grad Aoife (Eefa) will you. I have some books and writings for her. I would love the company of you two," the creature replied.

"Of course," Rowsheen replied, running off with a smile. Aoife was dancing with Macintyre, her little brother, who was just a little bear cub. Aoife scooped him up and laughed and danced to the music that the butterfly children were playing. The butterfly children were great musicians and very talented.

Aoife was clad in her usual woodland garb, which was comfortable, practical, yet touched with quiet charm. Brown leggings hugged her legs, paired with a green, knee-length dress whose sleeves brushed her elbows like whispering leaves. Black, high boots, worn from many paths, reached just below her knees. A loose brown belt rested at her waist, supporting a side purse with hidden compartments. Around her forearms, brown leather sleeves concealed twin daggers, ever-ready. She moved like the forest—calm, deliberate, and always watching. Aoife's hair was light red that barely touched her shoulders. That day, she had it twisted up with green ribbons that matched her dress.

The jewelry Aoife (Eefa) wore was quietly peculiar, laced with memory and meaning. Around her neck hung a simple cross, worn smooth with time, gifted long ago by a beloved family member. But what made it unique was the three rings that shared the same chain, each one old and etched with the quiet history of her bloodline. She never wore them on her fingers, too fearful of their loss. They hung close to her heart, where they were safest.

Aoife's eyes were light brown with a hint of green as if she had the reflections embodied in her gaze, and her skin was pale for a being who spent most of her time outdoors. She had her mother's nose, which was larger than some, but it complemented her face beautifully. Aoife had been adopted by Honeysuckle and his family when she was a small child. Honeysuckle was the clan leader of the bears around Merigold.

"Aoife," Rowsheen said, joining her and embracing her with a hug, "The Creature has some writings for you."

"I'm coming," Aoife smiled, giving her little brother one last squeeze and placing him in her mother's arms, "I'll be back. Mama, I'm going with Rowsheen to the Creature's tunnels for some writings of his that he said he'd lend me for school."

"Just be back in an hour," Her mother replied, fixing Aoife's wild red hair, "We're heading home then."

"I will," Aoife replied with a smile. Aoife hooked Rowsheen's arm, and they skipped towards the wood line where the Creature was waiting.

For the creature enjoyed the young generation quite a lot. "What would you like to talk about on such a pleasant night, Rowsheen?"

"What are Whinghums like?" she asked. Her big greenish brown eyes gave away her sincere curiosity.

"Yes," Aoife echoed beside her, "What are they like?"

"Whinghums are magnificent creatures," the creature started setting gaze to somewhere, a distant place within his memories, "but they have their flaws. They shape-shift at will and can deceive many if they wish.

"Interesting, can they shape-shift into you?" Rowsheen interrupted, suddenly looking down at the tips of her boots, blushing with shame that she had interrupted her elder with a slip of the tongue.

Aoife quietly listened intently, all while enjoying the crickets chirping along the side of the path. Aoife loved to read and write, and she was interested in what the creature had to say about the Whinghums. Reading and listening to stories were her favorite pastimes. It allowed her to go on as many adventures as she wished without even leaving home. It opened doors to many new horizons.

"In a way, child, but also very different," he continued, not at all upset at the interruption. "Well, they cannot shape shift into a specific person, but they can shape shift into a version of different beings. It won't look right, though. You may not notice it, but your gut will tell you that something is off. They travel in flocks and migrate to warmer places in times of cold and heat." The creature replied, searching through his vast memory.

Noticing that Rowsheen seemed uninterested in this bit of information, he decided to describe them instead. "They have brightly colored wings and hair. Their bodies grow scales in place of clothing, and they can choose to have human skin when they shape-shift. When in danger, their wings disappear, their hair turns white, and their scales morph into clothes."

"Do they sing and write poems like you?" Aoife asked suddenly as the creature paused, as she hopped across a brook that flowed over the trail on her sturdy legs.

"Oh, yes, child," the creature said, remembering the sweet, angelic songs that they had sung him to sleep with when he was small beneath starlit skies, "They have the most glorious voices you've ever heard."

"Will you sing us one?" Rowsheen asked intently, tucking back a stray rose petal curl that had fallen into her eyes, "Please."

"Why not?" the creature answered, wondering which one to sing and which one he actually remembered all the words to. He finally selected a nursery rhyme that they had sung to him as a lullaby. "I've quite forgotten the tune, but I still remember the words," he replied, clearing his throat.

"May starlight fill your smallest dream

As you lie beneath the heavens vast.

No need to cry,

I'll tell you why,

Your Maker's got you in His eye.

Through the softest breeze,

He whispers through starlight,

His ever-watchful eye,

Around you, his angel-guards.

So always tell your Maker what is in your heart,

Always ask forgiveness when you've done what you should not,

Always remember He is watching over you,

Always dream of starlight, and love your Maker too,"

The creature finished his low, majestic lullaby.

"That was beautiful," Rowsheen commented dreamily, gazing off into the mountainous distance, and added, "I wish even for a mere moment that I was raised by Whinghums, but it is vain to wish; is it not?"

"It is merely mortal to wish and dream not a sin unless it consumes the good and beautiful in life that God has put there for you to enjoy," the creature replied thoughtfully.

"Someday, I truly wish to be as wise as you, dear Creature," Aoife replied, looking ever thoughtful.

"You will," the Creature replied to Aoife, "Wisdom takes learning and experience, but it also takes a willing heart to listen to those around you. You must take in the voices and decide what advice would benefit you and what would not.

Throwing away the trash clings to the best and move forward, always learning and growing. Never stagnant."

"I just want my parents to understand what it was like to be my age. What it was like to dream and wish." Rowsheen added, looking ahead.

So that's what she really wanted to talk about, the creature thought to himself.

"I suppose you want adventure then, child," the creature replied, thinking of his own childhood back to his pleasant carefree days.

"Maybe," Rowsheen sighed, thoughtfully looking to the sky as if for an answer, "I don't really know. The world is so vast and beautiful. There is so much to do here, and so much is expected of me in this life. I would love to protect my country someday if there were even the slightest chance."

"Tell your parents then. Why don't you, child? Family is often more caring and understanding than we give them credit for," the creature advised with an understanding glance, "They'll understand, and if they don't, I'll talk them into it. Just let me know."

"I know, I just don't want to worry them," Rowsheen confessed, "or let them down."

"The Treeguard is a great honor," the creature commented, "they would be very proud of you."

"I agree," Aoife replied with a soft smile, "We'll miss you, but I know you'll do well."

"How about a song to relax you while you build up the courage to tell your parents," the Creature replied, "You know the 'flowers of home.'"

"Yes, I do," Rowsheen replied. With that, he started to sing an old, familiar, merry tune. Aoife joined him, and Rowsheen listened thoughtfully.

Then Rowsheen smiled, remembering the old tune quite well, and sang the second verse.

Then together, they sang the chorus, arriving at the creature's cave just as it ended.

"Well, here we are," whispered the creature, hoping not to break the magical feeling the song had placed upon him, "Let's go see that flower collection of mine; shall we?" he beckoned.

"Oh, yes, please," Rowsheen and Aoife echoed. The Creature had endless rows of flowers and hundreds of different kinds.

The creature gestured to them into follow him as he entered his tunnel entrance way. Rowsheen gazed into the dark hole abyss he had disappeared into, drew a deep breath, and stepped in. She placed her hand against the rough cave wall so she wouldn't bump into anything and followed the faint sound of the creature's footsteps onward.

The cave was wet and cool to the touch and smelled earthy and fresh. After about ten minutes, they noticed the cave began to widen, and objects became gradually clearer. Then, about five minutes later, they stepped into a wide cavern. The roof of the cavern had holes to let in sun, but mostly purposed for starlight. The floor of the cavern was surprisingly smooth, except for an underground stream that flowed gracefully through its center, reflecting the starlight from the tiny holes above.

"Do you think it'll fit everyone?" the creature asked them, walking through the cold stream, hoping this cavern was the right size.

"Oh, yes," answered Rowsheen, startled out of her daydream, eyes just adjusting to the light.

"Come now," the creature beckoned, motioning them to another tunnel, "Let's go see those flowers and get you two home before your parents begin to fret."

They stumbled on down the next tunnel that opened into a beautiful starlit cavern with the most gorgeous flower garden she had ever seen.

"How did he manage to grow such beautiful blossoms under the earth?" Aoife pondered, stroking the leaf of a great, fuzzing plant with bright, radiant, orange flowers that she had never seen before.

"Aoife, Rowsheen," the Creature addressed them, "I'm going to get those papers. Enjoy the flowers. I'll be right back. Do you two want tea?"

"Yes, please," they both replied, wandering through the rows of flowers, mesmerized by all the different kinds.

The creature emerged from his office with a tray of tea and a leather satchel loaded with papers for Aoife. He set the tray down on a stone bench and beckoned them over. After a party of tea and small cakes. Aoife and Rowsheen thanked the Creature for his hospitality and left, enjoying the pleasant starlit night.

Chapter 5:
What Is My Future To Be?

Back from the creature's cave, Rowsheen walked through the fair Rosian village that interwove itself in the forest it occupied, and up the tall, winding stairs to her home above, suspended in the great Mosquito tree. Every step upward, she pondered what she would say to her parents.

"Mother, I'm home," Rowsheen whispered loudly, tiptoeing across the smooth, ancient, cedar floors. Her high, brown knee boots made little sound as she made her way past the cozy, firelit din to the kitchen on the other side.

"We're here, Rosebud," her mother, Roseabit, answered sweetly from her chair in the corner of the kitchen. She thought her mother looked tall and elegant in her corner perch while she read one of her books on herbs.

Her mother spoke, "How was your day, love?"

"My day was very pleasant, Mother," Rowsheen replied, pouring herself a cup of tea from the old steel pot and stirring in a spoon of honey. The spoon made a sharp clanking sound on the porcelain cup. Her father stepped heavily into the room.

"No need to wake the whole village, Treguala," her father teased, wrapping his big, branchy arms around her shoulders.

"Hey, Father," smiled Rowsheen, steadying her cup of tea, then spoke, "could I be like, Treguala? Would you be fine with me joining the treeguard?"

"Why do you want to go?" Rowsheen's father answered pleasantly, "If that be your wish. Go ahead, it's a great career to have and a very honorable occupation."

"I have been speaking with members of the treeguard along Marigold, and they tell me that it is a great and noble feeling to go home at the end of their day and remember that they saved a life that day," Rowsheen explained. "I would love to join such a fulfilling branch of protection for Mossland. The training base is in Monolva, and in two years I will be of proper age to go."

"I think you would make a very fine treeguard, child," Rowsheen's mother beamed, setting her book down on her lap.

"Not the Agua terrain," her father teased, trying to push her towards his favorite branch, then replied, "You will be great, sweetheart. With whatever you choose."

"I can go!!!" Rowsheen hollered, jumping up and down, not caring who in their small village heard her, "Thank you, Mother! Thank you, Father!"

Her joy was nearly uncontainable, and she breathed a sigh of relief to know that her parents were truly content with her chosen path, but what she did not know was that her safe, happy, little world next to the foothills of a great mountain would be turned around and forever changed. Everyone's world was about to change. Rowsheen eagerly prepared for the day she would attend the treeguard training. Her father had taught her basic self-defense techniques to help her in her training. Each day was new and exciting for Rowsheen, and she was confident about her future. Rowsheen's friends, Aoife (Eefa) and Kate, were bright and merry.

They worked a job together for a farmer twice a week, tending his cows and horses. Kate was a butterfly child, tall and fair as any elfin, with a large pair of bright, teardrop-shaped wings that changed their color to match her mood, but they were normally blue to match her eyes. Her outfit today was the same as any day. She wore a multicolored fairy dress of blue, purple, pink, and white that hit nearly four inches above her ankles. Her feet were bare as usual. Her hair was a light brown that nearly fell to her waist, and she preferred to leave it down. Her skin was a pale tan that reflected her delicate nature.

"What do you want to be, Aoife (Eefa)?" Kate asked in her laughing smile that lit up her mischievous, icy-blue eyes.

"I'll be a big, fluffy teddy bear," Aoife (Eefa) answered, scooping an armload of dusty hay and carrying it to one of the horse's stalls. "Come now, we know you have plans," Rowsheen replied, shoveling a scoopful of muck out of the other stall.

"What plans, deary?" Aoife (Eefa) replied, winding up a long, coarse rope to hang on the rough, stable wall.

"Oh, just your plans to become a successful physician or- what was that-a writer was it?" Kate teased, tossing a load of hay in Aoife's face.

"Achu, Achoo," Aoife coughed and sneezed, wiping the dusty hay from her face and shirt.

"I'll die young with you around," Aoife (Eefa) teased before blowing her nose.

"Oh, please," Rowsheen commented, snatching up the rake from where it lay on the ground.

"Okay," Aoife (Eefa) replied, "if she doesn't kill me, I'll morph into a beautiful butterfly and be eaten by tigerwhip."

"I thought you'd choose something more, oh, how do you say... romantic," Kate commented, ducking her head to miss an armload of hay from Aoife (Eefa).

"Okay," Aoife replied, "I'll become a hero and marry a prince."

"Where did the hero part come from?" Rowsheen asked, closing a clean stall tight.

"My pride, of course," Aoife replied, receiving another pile of hay to the face.

Chapter 6:
The Hardest Burden To Bear; Letting Go.

For the next few weeks, the creature could be seen running here and there, and back again, gathering supplies for his celebration. Beings from all over the forest offered their help for the special celebration. Fairies hung flower vines, giants moved boulders and large flat stones to serve as tables and chairs, sprites debated the menu with the bears, and the headbrickers argued about entertainment with the Rosians and Elflings. Finally, the anticipated night arrived. Birds and Fairies gathered at Katherine's Meadow to welcome the Whinghums as they landed and to escort them to the celebration.

"Do you think they're coming soon?" a hummingbird asked, impatiently, "Do you? Do you?"

"Yes, they're coming," answered a blackbird, then whispered to a nightingale, "Hummingbirds are so impatient."

"Well, my good friend," Simon said, congratulating the creature, "you certainly did it. This place looks crazier than a sprite dance."

"Really?" the creature questioned, looking over the chaos in pure disbelief.

"Of course, laddie," Simon bellowed heartily, and added, "Would I ever tell you a fib?"

"When we were a good many moons younger," the creature recalled, "some tree told me there was a patch of crystalhoppers at the end of Noah's rainbow."

"Ha-haa-haa," Simon chuckled, letting his long grey beard shake back and forth, "you fell for that easier than a rockaltrout on a dragonwhip line."

"I walked for hours," the creature whined, "and when I got there, it was just Sean and his shiny coin collection."

"You mean Sean the Leprechaun?" Simon asked, ducking his head as a group of fairies flew past with an oversized bag of glitter dust, "Hold it, Ladies! We don't need...never mind."

The giggling fairies had already dispersed their glitter all over the decorations and flowers.

"Yeah, that's him! Aaaacchhhoo," the creature answered with a sneeze from the glitter and nearly tripping over a pile of flowers that were for decoration, then asked, "Why does he hang out there, anyway?"

"Don't know," Simon replied, scratching his burly beard, "just his thing, I suppose."

"You got to admit, though," Simon boasted, "that was a joke worth remembering."

"Ha, ha!" the creature sarcastically laughed.

"Where's Honeysuckle?" he asked, standing on the main table so he could spot the big bear. "He was supposed to bring the honey barrels."

"I'll go look for 'im," Simon offered, starting for the entrance tunnel and trying not to step on anyone. Then, he turned and called to the youth at hand who were being given every job available to keep them busy, "Daniel! Kate! Come help an old tree!"

"Yes, sir!" they answered in unison, setting down their boxfuls of flower vines and starting after him.

"Now," Simon asked, as they emerged from the long tunnel, "where do you two youngsters suppose that giant teddy bear has got off to?"

"Haven't seen 'im, sir," Daniel answered quietly, brushing his head against the tall tree branches above.

"Speak up, son, I'm a tad deaf," Simon said, scratching his beard.

"He said he hadn't seen 'im yet, sir," Kate answered, loud enough for Simon to hear. Today was an exciting one for her. She was impatient about waiting all day to meet the Whinghums finally.

"Hmm," Simon thought out loud, "Well, no use waiting. Let's head down the trail and see if we meet him down the way."

"Do you think he'll bring Aoife (Eefaa)?" Kate asked, tripping on one of Simon's long roots.

"I reckon that red-haired handful will come when she pleases," Simon answered with a laugh, moving his great limbs onward. Daniel, with his head held high in the trees, started whistling an old marching tune, and the others joined in, half-humming, half-singing the familiar old song.

> *"Rise, son, rise, son,*
> *The day is marching on.*
> *March, son, march, son,*
> *The battle has begun.*
> *Fight son, fight, son,*
> *The enemy is here.*
> *Fight 'til day is dawning,*
> *'Til you see the mountain mist,*
> *'Til they fly surrender's flag,*
> *'Til the sun and moon change shift.*

Rise, son, rise, son,

The day is marching on.

Sing, son, sing, son,

The battle has been won.

March home, my laddie fierce,

March home, my son.

March home, my laddie strong,

The battle has been won.

Go home to your parents,

Your Country, your king,

To your God you owe the victory,

To Him you do sing."

As they were nearing the song's end, they came to the creek and found Honeysuckle carrying the barrels of honey across, one by one. Honeysuckle was a dark, tubby, brown bear that loved his water hole and patch of wood. He had raised Aoife since she was just an infant. Honeysuckle was on the great council, although he did not like to travel.

"You mind lending a branch, old chap?" Honeysuckle asked, rolling another barrel onto the bank, happy to see Simon, "I wasn't about to pull the cart through the water. It could have tipped."

"I thought you two'd need help," Simon replied, moving through the cold, fast-flowing water, "Great Headbricker On Fire! What's all that honey for!?"

"For the honey fountain, of course," Honeysuckle said proudly, "Isn't that right, Aoife?"

"Yes, sir. The bear clan is contributing a large honey fountain for the celebration," Aoife answered. Aoife was a headbricker-elfling mix that Honeysuckle had raised since childhood. The bears called her "Aoife," pronounced (Eee-Fa), a traditional headbricker name for girls, her last name from Honeysuckle being Beairclen.

"Every bear on Firewhip Hill must have given their private stockpile," Simon exclaimed, wondering how they would fit it all in the creature's cave pantry and still have room for any guests.

"Nonsense, ol' boy! I've got another cartload coming. Should be here shortly," Honeysuckle replied, receiving an irritated glare from Simon, and glanced at his pocket watch that hung from a chain around his neck. That watch was a gift to him from a headbricker when he was a cub, and he never let it out of sight.

"Come on, Daniel, help me with the cart. We'll be here all day if we don't get started now," Simon directed, walking backward into the water with his branch arms steadying the front of the cart while Daniel steadied the back.

"Hey, Aoife," Kate called as she waded through the cold stream to help Aoife (Eefa) on the other side.

Kate was a friend who was very dear to Aoife, and she was never bored in her presence.

"Hey, Katie," Aoife (Eefa) called back, as she unloaded a barrel of honey from the old, wooden cart, "How's your day been?"

"Just swell, Aoife," Kate replied, heaving up another barrel, "How about yours. Or can I guess?"

"Well, I've been loading honey almost all morning," she laughed, stepping into the freezing water, "But that's plain obvious."

"I got Rowsheen to tell me about the Whinghums." Relayed Kate, holding her wings higher so they did not dip into the water, "I found her descriptions very interesting."

They had made their way back across the stream for another barrel and were now lifting one to take across. Aoife noticed that the stream was especially cold today. Most of the morning, she spent loading barrels of honey with Honeysuckle. However, what she didn't tell Kate was that Honeysuckle had taken her to the fairies' grove for singing lessons. Kate was a very good friend to Aoife, but she had decided to keep this a secret for a little while.

Aoife did not particularly like large crowds but was just as excited at the chance of meeting the Whinghums as the rest were. She had her thick red hair tied back. She was tired from the work, but grateful and proud of all the help she was able to provide for her family. She was a hard worker and proud of it. She did not shy away from work and put in her full effort.

Kate and Aoife heaved another barrel across. The cold, shallow water was lapping at their knees. The barrels smelled strong of thick clover honey. Shadows from the trees overhead speckled the ground. To the three youths, it was no time at all before the barrels were loaded and they were headed back down the trail to the tunnels. When they got back to the clearing in front of the tunnel, Simon turned to the youths and told them to take the honey to the storage hall. When they were gone, Simon looked at Honeysuckle, and they both exchanged serious looks.

"There's no use telling me," Honeysuckle said, brushing his paws against his furry sides, "I know as well as you that Whinghums don't migrate South for no reason. There's trouble afoot in Ekland and the East lands. I know it even though I wish not to."

"Hush, Honeysuckle," Simon breathed quietly, "Let's go somewhere else to talk."

"Very well," Honeysuckle replied, following Simon through the main tunnel that had been lighted up with torches hung against the walls.

They walked into the tunnel and past all the busy beings to a separate tunnel on the far side of the North wall. They walked on for a few minutes, then stopped when they came to another passageway that led into a spacious room with a stream running through it. The room was round and had stone benches everywhere. Simon walked to a bench by the stream and sat down, and Honeysuckle sat down a few feet away. They sat in silence for a time before Simon spoke up.

"Honeysuckle, we... We need a plan," Simon spoke nervously, "the creature knows what he's doing, but we need something to fall back on."

"We'll get a plan," Honeysuckle reassured him, "You've got to stop stressing yourself, or you'll die young. The Creature won't fail us. He never has. When we were young, he knew what to do, and now he'll find a way."

"Neither of us are young, Suckle," Simon replied, shifting in his seat, "We are not young anymore. How can we protect our own when we're old and grey?"

"Simon," Honeysuckle said, looking him in the eye, "It's not our turn. It's not our job anymore. This time we have a new job. You know it well."

"How can I possibly bear to see my children and grandchildren face what we have feared for centuries?" Simon asked, looking into the dark water that ran past his feet.

"I do not know... but we must," Honeysuckle replied gravely, "It's in our best interest to start training our children for what is coming."

"How could you possibly watch your little Aoife lift a battle axe and walk to the enemy lines!?" Simon asked, knowing full well that Honeysuckle was right.

"That is not a sight I wish to see," Honeysuckle replied, looking up at the ceiling, "But I would feel a lot better if I had taught her how to use it properly."

"Are you proposing that we send our children to Fayatoch?" Simon asked with a nervous shake in his voice.

"My dear Brother," Honeysuckle replied firmly, "There is a time for everything. This is a time for war. Our children must be prepared. The high council is meeting in the twilight hour with the Whinghum queen. We will soon see what will come to pass, but now, Brother, do be merry for the children's sakes."

"I shall do my best to wield a cheerful countenance for the young ones," Simon reassured him. "Shall we not now assist in the preparation?" Honeysuckle asked, motioning for him to follow, "They will be missing us soon."

"After you, old bear," Simon teased, trying to regain his composure.

"Thank you," Honeysuckle replied with a smile.

The two made their way back to the main hall, where everyone was bustling about. Simon spotted Daniel, Aoife, Kate, and Rowsheen moving tables and laughing at each other's jokes. He gave one long, deep sigh, thinking to himself, "It will be hard to let them go. It is their time, and they know it not...how can I bravely kneel to let the children go in my place? They will do well; my job is hardest to bear."

Chapter 7:
The Celebration

"Rowsheen, Aoife, HELP ME," Kate screamed, running straight through the kitchen, her long, straight, brown hair flowing in a wave behind her. She flew past the two of them. Not a split second passed before Daniel ducked as he went, so he did not slam into the low door frames, followed by a broom in his hand.

Rowsheen and Aoife chuckled. "She deserves it," Aoife mused, wiping a smudge of flour off her apron, "she's been at his throat all morning trying to make every little detail perfect."

"Serves her right," Rowsheen continued, washing dough off her hands and brushing a stray rose petal out of her face, "maybe she'll leave him alone from now on."

"Probably not," Aoife replied, making them both laugh till they hit the ground in tears.

"Oh, that soup smells soooo good," Rowsheen said, giving it a good stir all the way to the bottom of the pot. Rowsheen was decked out in her famous work clothes, which consisted of a dark red cloak with grey-green slacks and a black apron over top.

"I'd better go help her," Aoife smiled and shook her head as she untied her apron. Aoife was loyal to her friends even if they did stupid things to get themselves in trouble. She did not know how she would help Kate, though; Daniel was also her good friend.

The children had been working all morning, being ordered around by the adults to clean and decorate. You could say children, but Kate was eighteen, Aoife was seventeen, Daniel was fifteen, and Rowsheen was fifteen and a couple of weeks older than Daniel. They would sound like youths to you, but on this continent, beings grew far older than you would believe if I told you. A being would only be considered a teenager when they reached the age of twenty-five, and in some families, it was far, far older.

The Creature smiled as he heard the children's laughter as they worked. Quietly walking into the main hall, he heard Aoife and Rowsheen talking. They were hanging a welcome banner.

"Aoife," Rowsheen asked, tidying her rose petal curls as was her constant habit and trying to steady a banner while standing on a ladder at the same moment, "Do you ever feel like something big was about to happen or something?"

"I did when I was younger," Aoife answered, hooking the banner up on the other side over the large stone archway, "I always was hoping that something peculiar was about to happen. Something adventurous or out of the ordinary, like something extraordinary." And little did she know her wish would soon be answered. Her whole world was about to change.

"You'll find when you're older that the most extraordinary things come from the most common and ordinary places," the Creature said, walking up to them, "it's not just in the big moments that great things happen, it's consistent little choices and decisions that people make that change the world. Aoife, I do believe that the left side is higher."

"I'll adjust it," Aoife replied with a smile, climbing the ladder placed against the archway.

After the food and decorations were ready, everyone hurried home to dress for the exciting occasion. Everyone except the creature and Simon, who were too busy talking and laughing.

Simon had indeed put on a merry countenance, and he wore it well.

Soon, everyone was arriving in their holiday apparel. The finishing touches were quickly done, and everyone conversed about this or that as they waited for the Whinghums to arrive. The food was brought out by the youths and set on tables. The food's pleasant aroma rose to people's noses, making their mouths water.

Suddenly, the trumpet blared, announcing the Whinghums' arrival. Everyone rose and faced the entrance tunnel. Out of the tunnel's mouth marched the Whinghum guards that stood in perfect formation. Next came Queen Oona (Ooo-Na) with her bodyguards on either side. The high council moved forward in a very controlled manner, and the guards parted for their Queen, who went to meet the high council. When the council, the elders, and the Queen were about five feet apart, the council bowed, and the Queen made a curtsey.

"We welcome your majesty with the highest honor," spoke the chief elder Mossbeard, "It is a privilege to be in thine presence once more. We have made a holiday for this rare occasion and pray that you and your people will attend."

"We are grateful for your hospitality, my lord," Queen Oona spoke with an odd grin, "and my people and I would be delighted to attend your holiday."

The chief elder turned to his understudy, who gave a nod in reply, "Let the festivities begin!" he announced. The chief elder Mossbeard extended his hand to Queen Oona, who accepted it with a smile. The chief elder led her to a large table covered with plates of food and gave her a seat at his right hand. The guards broke formation and laid down their armor in a separate room before joining the festivities.

While that was going on, the rest of the Whinghums that had been waiting in the tunnel poured into the dining hall, being about three hundred in number. They were greeted warmly by the Mossland's people, who were doing everything in their power to help them enjoy themselves.

Chapter 8:
A Meeting at Twilight

After the festivities, everyone walked home under the light of a laughing moon. The Whinghums had set up camp in a large clearing beside Marigold, West of the creature's tunnels as all the beings of the land slumbered with sweet dreams the counsel elders, tribal chiefs, judges, governors, tribal elders, generals, clan leaders, captains, Queen Oona, and the Whinghum generals made their way to the creature's tunnels for a twilight meeting.

The tunnels were lit by torches that showed the way to the Council chamber; the same chamber Simon and Honeysuckle had spoken in before the celebration. The stream that passed through the room's center reflected the torchlight.

Silently, everyone chose a bench and waited. The room was uncomfortably silent, which was odd, for there were over two hundred beings present in the round stone room. Having never been present at the twilight meeting.

The youths and children of the clan chieftains, elders, and generals were stowed in a room out of the way with Shaun, the youngest clan leader, to watch them and make sure no one got in trouble. The room was decked with wooden benches and tables. All the youths and children sat in silence. They were nervous. They could tell that something wasn't right.

Aoife bit her lip as she jotted down some thoughts in her journal. She felt anxious to know what was going on. Daniel sat not too far away, looking determined and angry. His hands were clasped as fists in front of him, and his face was red. Aoife could feel his energy without looking in his direction. She knew that more than anything, he wanted to be in the council chamber and hear what was being said.

Shaun, the headbricker clan leader and Aoife's cousin, in charge of keeping an eye on them, noticed Daniel's silent anger and frustration.

"Son," the addressed him quietly, "it's their business to know what's going on, and ours to trust their decisions."

"AM I NOT A MAN!" Daniel shouted, standing tall and towering over everyone present. The usual quiet and reserved youth voiced his frustration, "It's my country too! Isn't this next war mine to fight in? Am I not worthy to know what will become of us? What becomes of me and my future? And the future of my family and friends?" Daniel passionately faced Shaun with a fire in his eyes.

"Son, I don't blame you or your intentions," Shaun replied with a sigh, "If I were you and your age again, I would want to know as well. You can go. Just stay quiet and remember you may hear more than you wanted to know. Sometimes not knowing is far better than knowing. You will understand that someday."

Daniel nodded, his fists were still clenched, and his jaw was tight. He was determined to know what was going on despite Shaun's warning. With a deep breath, Daniel walked past Shaun and silently out the door, closing it softly behind him. Danial walked quickly and silently down the corridor to the large red cedar door with cold iron hinges. There was a part in the wood that cast a soft ray of light on the stone tunnel floor. His heart pounded within his chest and rattled in his ears. His heart sounded so loud to him that he was sure that they would be able to hear him.

Softly as he could, Daniel knelt on the cold stone floor and peered through the part in the cedar door.

The high counsel elder Mossbeard walked to the center of the room and stood on a large boulder amid the stream and spoke, "Brothers, Sisters, and Friends, we have always been aware of conflict beyond our borders, and now we must prepare for it to come to us. Queen Oona has come to inform us of the coming conflict, and we are forever grateful."

With that, Queen Oona rose from her bench a few feet from the stream. She lifted her skirts as she stepped into the cool stream and made her way to the center rock. She stepped lightly and gracefully as she went through the water and mounted the stone steps leading up to the rock. She paused for a moment and took a deep breath, then spoke.

"Ekland and the Eastern territories are restless and bloodthirsty. King Stephen is a madman," she coldly spoke.

The Creature felt as if the words she spoke were daggers plunged deeply in his heart and soul. King Stephen was once a young boy who sat at his feet and learned from him. He was wise for his young age and well-versed in how to run a country. The Creature missed him and could not imagine anyone calling him a madman. Queen Oona continued, "He is gathering his allies and declaring a census of his people. I spoke with him two moons ago, and he was adamant about war. Thinking he had persuaded me to join his ranks, he said that he was planning a war to build himself a continent-wide empire and offered me a portion of the land and spoil. When I asked him how he would accomplish this feat, he said that he would not attack for seven years until he could build a big enough army and store enough food and ammunition to support his war. I do not, however, believe that this madman will wait seven years to launch his army. We must prepare for the worst, but I speak not in grave tones, for this country can be fortified, allies gathered, and troops prepared easily and quickly. War is coming, and we will be triumphant!"

The Creature listened in horror and wondered how she could speak in a calm tone about war as if she just loved to hear herself speak. Every word fell like cold stones on his heart. He felt choked up inside. The great war that had ended so many years ago could not repeat itself. He was too old to fight as he once was.

She ended her fine speech with an elegant bow as if she were proud of herself and took a step back so the high elder Mossbeard could speak, "Brothers and Sisters, we have up to seven years before we must meet King Stephen's force. But until then, we must use our time wisely. I have asked several beings of high knowledge to offer a strategy. Brother Honeysuckle, chief of the bear clan, will speak first."

Honeysuckle made his way to the rock and spoke, turning himself around every now and then to look into every face, "As a father, I will first consider our youth. I believe the most prudent course of action with the time available is to send our youth to Fayatoch. The monks there will train them in return for our goods. We can take them down the Great River to Kadaspin and put them on ships to Fayatoch. They should reach Fayatoch in two weeks' time by sea, and they will be out of harm's way. I suggest the children be sent fifty at a time, so they do not draw the attention of spies. I know my words speak haste, but I do believe that it is a prudent and necessary action to take." Honeysuckle stopped and glanced at the high elder Mossbeard, who looked as troubled as he did angry. Mossbeard was not known for taking serious action and most often pushed new ideas aside as if afraid to try anything new.

"Whoever agrees to these notions, please rise," the high elder Mossbeard bellowed. He reluctantly nodded his approval of the proposal.

Everyone except the headbrickers who were present rose, amounting to seventy-five percent of all present.

The high elder Mossbeard faced the headbricker clan and said, "Please state your opposition, my lords."

The head clan chieftain arose and spoke, "I understand the need for movement, but I'm not sure this is the best course of action. We raise our children to fight when they're younglings, and as much as I people trust her majesty, we're not even sure that this so-called seven years wasn't made up to fool us. I now don't mean to be the only negative voice, but me and me people are going underground if this goes south, and anyone is welcome to join."

The high elder Mossbeard spoke, "Does anyone here offer a solution to the fogginess of this situation?"

The Creature rose and spoke to the Headbricker leaders, "Brothers of iron and stone, it is well known that your children are strong and courageous and not lacking in the knowledge of war, but I pray that you will reconsider the proposal. Fayatoch is an island full of some of the greatest warriors in our small corner of the world. It is a great honor to attend such classes, and with your children's wealth of knowledge, they will no doubt rise to the very top of their ranks and make your people proud."

The head clan chieftain rose and turned to his people, "Not even I could refuse that. My children are going whether any of yours do or not."

The headbrickers all rose and nodded their approval of the plan. "Then it is decided," the high elder Mossbeard replied reluctantly.

General MacArthur stood to speak, waiting for permission from the high elder. High elder Mossbeard addressed him, "Speak, son."

General MacArthur spoke, "My plan is dangerous, but will clear up a portion our predicament gaining us some insight," the high elder nodded for him to continue, "My plan is to infiltrate the opposing army," a few people muttered in doubt, but he went on, "since they are so desperate for recruits it will be easier. Me and a few of my highly trained students would be honored to undertake this task," he finished.

High elder Mossbeard replied, "Do you have a plan written out that you can give to the council to look over?"

"I do," General MacArthur replied, sitting down.

High elder Mossbeard replied, "Your plan will be approved, but first, I desire to see a more detailed presentation before you rush across our border and get people killed."

"Understood, sir," replied General MacArthur.

"Alright, no more interruptions," high elder Mossbeard said in frustrating tones, "Let's move forward. Honeysuckle is that all?" Honeysuckle nodded, "It is agreed to start sending the children to Fayatoch. General Alderman, will you oversee this course of action?"

General Alderman replied, "Yes, I would be glad to."

The high elder Mossbeard addressed the Creature, "Sir Creature, please give us your wisdom. I hear you have a proposal."

The creature passed Honeysuckle on his way to the rock and nodded in respect.

"My friends," the Creature began, "our country, though grand it may be now, has never been as glorious and unified as when a king sat on its throne. The seat of Biro, the stone must be filled if we wish to preserve this land."

This news shook the unsuspecting crowd, but he went on, "The days are getting longer, and dust falls thick upon Orfhlaith's (Or-la's) grave. Live in our past rather than the present, we simply cannot; forward we must move." The Creature paused so his words could sink in,

He continued, "I have prayed to Our Father, and He has given us a worthy king; only it is a youth who needs training and guidance. I firmly believe that this child will be a strong ruler. We should not crown the new king or even reveal it to the child until the training in Fayatoch is complete and all the children are home and prepared for the coming war."

The high elder gave the Creature a long, judging glare before he spoke, "Please raise, all who support this proposal." Every being present stood in agreement, sharing their respect for the Creature. There would be a king in Mossland once again.

The Creature spotted Daniel, who had been standing outside the doorway in secret on the high rock, and gave him a steady stare that meant 'go home'. Daniel nodded back in compliance and disappeared from the doorway, and made his way back to the room in silence. He sat opposite Aoife at the table with his head in his hands. Aoife did not ask what had happened or what was said.

After the meeting, when everyone went home, Daniel could not sleep. His thoughts were keeping him awake and eating him alive. Slowly, he crept out.

As fast as lightning could strike, he bolted into a run toward Firewhip Hill. Faster and faster, his heart pounded within him as he ran onward to Firewhip Hill. He had to tell someone; he couldn't just keep it inside. He knew someone who could listen; someone who would. Slowing to a steady pace, he entered the bear clan's village and walked to a small hut all the way down by Marigold. He rapped gently on Aoife's window so as not to wake the whole house. He knelt down so he could see whoever opened the window.

A sleepy-eyed Aoife, bundled in a large blanket, peered out. "Daniel, what's wrong?" she asked quietly.

"I need a good listener for a mite," Daniel explained in a whisper.

"Isn't this a better job for Demid?" Aoife asked as an excuse, "he is far closer to you than I."

"He didn't come down for the celebration. He was needed at home," Daniel replied, "besides, he's more of a talker than a listener. This world is full of people who want to be heard and try to drown out everyone else; what it needs is more people who can listen. Right now, I need someone who can listen."

"Rowsheen is a good listener," Aoife replied with a smile, rubbing her tired eyes. She couldn't help but tease him a bit.

"Don't tease me now, Sister," Daniel scolded, "you never have before, and I'm being serious now."

"Sorry, Daniel. I'll listen, but make it quick. Little Macintyre is asleep, and I needn't be up so late," Aoife apologized.

"Don't ask me the details, but a war is coming," Daniel spoke. Aoife bit her tongue hard to keep from interrupting him. He continued, "The youths, you and I, are being sent away to a place called Fayatoch for battle training. I don't know how soon."

Aoife's heart fell dead inside as a lifeless heap within her. "You're sure," she managed to whisper.

"Dead sure," Daniel replied, "and you mustn't tell a soul."

"I won't," Aoife replied, nodding. Daniel stood up to his full height, dwarfing the hut in size, then stepped silently off into the trees. Aoife stayed at the window to watch him leave, believing all she had heard and wishing she had not.

Chapter 9:
The Children Are Gone

The following words are not mine, but those of Aoife, who is telling this story, but were retrieved from her personal diary years after the war ceased, when she disappeared.

Water lapped at the boat's hull as I, Aoife, held on to its red, wooden rail and gazed at the shoreline; I could just barely make out my father, Honeysuckle the bear, waving goodbye to me. I was on the first ship headed for Fayatoch. The ship was full of children above ten years; fifty in number. There were all kinds of youths from Mossland. Many different beings were present: Rosians, giants, headbrickers, treebeings, fairies, and elflings.

A brisk breeze made me pull my blue cloak closer, and a thin arm hooked mine and pulled it tight. The arm belonged to Kate, who was just as glad as I was that we had made it on the same ship.

"I never thought I'd like the sea, but it is quite beautiful," Kate spoke, "so what do you think it'll be like? I think it will be exciting, what about you?"

"I think I'm going to be sick if this boat continues rocking madly about," I gave a long, sarcastic moan while wiping a loose strand of red hair behind my ear.

"You'd better get used to it. We'll be on the sea for two weeks." Kate replied, flashing her laughing, mocking grin at me.

"I'm going overboard," I said with a fake groan and smile. All I wanted was a nap, "You wanna push me."

"Are you kidding? Who would I talk to?" Kate teased with a jolly chuckle. "Your shadow, I suppose, unless you talk those young men over there," I replied with a mocking smile.

"Now I am pushing you over, ready or not," Kate said, poking me in the ribs. I returned this gesture by tickling one of Kate's long, blue wings, which made her jump.

I had a mixture of feelings on that day nearly a lifetime ago. Such a blend of nervousness, excitement, wonder, and sadness that I could hardly tell them apart at the time. The next chapter of my life had begun, and I was not ready, but are we ever truly prepared for our life's biggest tests?

The voyage to Fayatoch was a long one. Well, long for me because I got seasick a lot. A small storm on the fifth day scared me out of my wits. Despite my complaining, I stopped feeling sick on day seven and got used to the constant movement and my daily tasks. The captain's name was Acosta, and he was not overly fond of there being fifty youths aboard his vessel, but he soon found that giving them jobs kept them out of his hair and entertained them for the most part.

The captain was an interesting figure, and I was quite suspicious of him having been engaged at one time in piracy. His face was tan and quite oval-shaped, and his nose was tall and long, matched with light, grey, green eyes. His mouth was small with pale, thin lips, and his hair was light brown and long, tied back with a thick, black cord. He had a short beard of a few inches long, hiding his chin from view, with a small mustache and no sideburns, which was surprisingly curly in comparison to his hair.

The captain's attire was more formal, of course, than his crew. I will try to describe the three main aspects of his dress that never appeared to change from day to day. First, his black slacks were baggy and often were tucked into his boots that went to his knees (a traditional length for boots at the time), and the boots appeared to be made from the hide of some scaly animal. Second, his shirt was white and airy and fell to his waist, where it was tucked into his black slacks and secured with a black leather belt embellished with shiny jewels, and over his shirt he wore a black coat with a split tail with what appeared to be silver buttons plaited with gold.

Lastly, at his side, he hung a long sword that dragged the steps when he climbed them. I thought the sword to be a claymore (a large broad sword), but after consulting a colleague, Dermid (Leo's brother), on the matter, I found myself to be mistaken because a claymore was traditionally between four and a half feet long. I would like to describe his hat, for it was unusual to me at the time, with three points that made it resemble a black triangle from the top looking down. I asked Larry, one of the sailors that I was working with one day, why the hat was shaped so, and he told me that it allowed water to drain off in the instance of a storm and showed me by pouring a cup full of seawater over his hat; the results were just as he had explained.

The crew consisted of twelve men ranging in age from twenty-three to forty-seven. In the course of the voyage, I was able to find out their nicknames because none of them would render me their real names: Nicky, Shortnose, Peston, Fullbeard, Stickleg, Stinky, Larry, Broomstick, Tub, Bob, Terry, and Sharpeye.

Chapter 10:
Chores and Lore

All the children were delighted to be aboard a real ship and found the chores given to them as sheer play. Since there were so many children to watch, Captain Acosta had assigned several to each of the crew, excluding Peston, the youngest, and even a few to himself. The captain seemed utterly frustrated with Peston's lack of knowledge about the sea and how to work on a ship. Larry, one of the older sailors, had to manage and watch Peston even closer than the Mossland youths.

The first week, I was assigned to work with Larry, along with Daniel, Dermid, and Rowsheen. Larry was happy with the extra hands and used the opportunity to get the ship's spare supplies in proper order. The first day, he taught us how to properly wind up ropes. Larry was the oldest sailor present and by far the most experienced in sailing. Rowsheen, Dermid, and I picked up the trade of being a sailor and maintaining a ship quickly. Peston even got on Rowsheen's and my nerves for than a few times.

Larry wore long tan slacks that were very loose and held in place by a stiff belt, and a long red shirt that was tucked into his slacks below his large belly. His hair was white and grey with touches of black that once appeared to be dominant. He walked about barefoot on even the coldest days without a care; this puzzled us. Larry was very patient with us, which we greatly appreciated.

"Naice 'n tight litt'il ones," Larry instructed us with the ropes, "Be sure ta place 'em orderly."

"How long have you been working on this ship, Mr. Larry?" asked Dermid in his polite, curious way, standing tall above everyone else. Daniel could almost reach the mast if he stretched and stood up tall. His short sandy blond hair blew in the wind, and he squinted his soft green eyes against the blare of the sun reflecting off the waves. He was tall and lean, almost as thin as the mast itself. His skin was quite pale except for splotches of red sunburn on his face, arms, and head.

Dermid was a friend of Daniel's from the Horseland prairies and Leo's half-brother, and the two relished each other's friendship. Dermid was an elfling and much smaller than Daniel, with sandy, brown hair and skin that was a shade or two darker than Daniel's, who was quite fair. They often argued about silly things just to make the rest of us laugh and were always finding something new to amuse themselves.

"Well, that's a hard question," Larry began, scratching his grey, bristly beard and tipping his head to the sky, "I guess I was about your age, son. That was many long years ago."

"What made you want to sail?" I asked, hopping up on a barrel of cider to let my legs rest. Larry had finally given us a rest time, and I wanted to hear a story.

"Well, I lived on the coast as a lad and saw the ships 'n sailors come to dock," Larry answered, "It was a happy time. I've never seen a better. When I was not nearly old enough, I left home and joined the crew on the first ship I came to, and I've been traveling the world by ship ever since."

"It wasn't this ship. Was it, Sir?" Rowsheen asked after being silent for some time. Rowsheen quietly pondered many things, only speaking up once in a while when she had something profound to say.

"No, Lass," Larry sighed, "It was the great Scottish sail Freya; the most glorious ship in her time, but those blasted natives blew it to bits in 28."

"You were alive in twenty-eight, Sir," Daniel asked in disbelief with a puzzled look on his face.

Of course I was. I'm no spring chicken," Larry answered, "besides, it was a glorious age."

Larry had us organize and repair everything he thought needed it, which was everything from repainting to replacing parts of the ship that seemed unnecessary to us, but we were rewarded for our work by the many stories he told us of mystery and legends about his home country, and my favorite, myths of the sea.

At night, as we were rocked to sleep by the sway of the ship. In our hammocks, we thought about these stories Larry and the other sailors told us and tried our best to store them in our minds to tell our families when, or in my mind, if we arrived home someday. The 'if' plagued my mind. We never talked about home if we could help it. No one admitted to being homesick, at least for the first few weeks at sea; it was a deep sting inside of us and a wound not one of us wanted to address.

In the early mornings before the darkness had left, Rowsheen and I often would slip out of our hammocks and out of the children's cabin onto the deck and peer into the dark sea. We wouldn't really talk, but just be and sit or watch the waves in silence.

I loved the way the ship's lanterns, which outlined the vessel, reflected on the water. At that time, the only other person up was shipmate Terry, who snoozed a lot during the day and steered the ship at night. He had gotten used to our early morning raisings, and when he saw me, he just gave me a stern look that meant "if you fall overboard, I'll tie you to the mast."

During these early morning times, I would try to remember home and what I cherished most. I realized how much I had taken it for granted, and how much I longed to go back. It was a comfort to have Rowsheen present. Rowsheen was strong and capable. She carried a lot of weight and was always responsible. I always wished to be as strong as she was, but I knew that a cold darkness of Depression often plagued her, and I did not know how to help. I felt helpless to be of any assistance as I was dealing with my own demon, Anxiety. The only way I could go was forward, I had decided as I stared into the dark waves.

The third morning was dreary and wet. Water flowed wherever it pleased. Lightning struck in the distance ever so often, scaring me nigh out of my skin. Larry was ever determined to get his ship in order and clean despite the heavy rain.

That morning, he had us below the deck in the hull. Daniel and Dermid were winding large bundles of rope, and I was mending some of Larry's trousers. It was dark and musty in the hall, the only light coming from a lantern hanging on a nail on an old dusty wood beam.

Daniel was seated on the dusty, wooden floor, leaning against the beam, holding the lantern, while Dermid sat on an apple barrel at his side, kicking and wiggling his short, thin, dangling legs at will. I sat on a stool in front of them, trying to get as much light as possible to make sure my stitches were accurate. Every time the ship rocked to my left, my stool slid into Daniel's outstretched leg, which nudged me back as the ship rocked to the right. Dermid was sick and moaned as the ship rocked to and fro.

"Gotta go!!" Dermid gagged, running up the wide stairs to the deck, tripping on the last step. His green trousers disappeared from our view, "Ouch!" Sounded from above.

"Hhhuummmhumm," Daniel laughed under his breath, trying not to give away his amusement, but the hint of red in his cheeks gave him away.

"I'm next," I said, bracing my feet on the floor as the ship rocked again. My stomach sloshed and growled within me. I did not want to do anything. Another heavy wave of nausea washed over my whole frame.

Daniel laughed at my remark, then put on a serious face. I knew from experience that it was extremely hard for him to go from a funny mood to a serious mood quickly, so I knew he had something important to say.

"Aoife, do you remember what I told you before we left Mossland?" he asked.

Of course, I remembered well what he had told me. Honeysuckle had pulled me aside a few days before our departure and explained everything to me: the coming war, threats, everything. He wanted me to know this, so I did not take the experience lightly and knew what to expect when or if I returned to Mossland. I was grateful for this, but I kept my mouth shut because the rest of the parents had told the youth that the elders had decided to pay for all the youth of Mossland to attend the warrior school, and it was a rare opportunity.

"Yes, Daniel. I remember well, and I haven't told an earthly soul," I said, searching in his big, icy, blue eyes for the reason he had asked me.

"I talked about the war, and about us going to Fayatoch," he looked me in the eye to be sure I was listening, "There's more. I got that information by eavesdropping at the door to the meeting hall as you remember me leaving. Well…there is going to be a new King, Aoife. They have chosen a new King. I mean, the Creature has. It's one of us on this ship because we're on the first ship to Fayatoch. At least, I think. It's a child, and the child doesn't know and won't know till our return to Mossland."

"Ooollllee, mummm, blaaww, yyuckk," Dermid whined, stumbling down the stairs and holding his belly.

"You okay, Dermid?" Daniel asked, our conversation concealed itself, and we did not venture further than that.

"I'mm okkayy, hummmph," Dermid covered his mouth and ran up the steps again into the driving rain.

"I don't think he's okay," Rowsheen said elegantly, stepping down the rough, slippery, rocking steps in her usual graceful manner with three bowls of soup in her arms.

"I'm not okay either," I added, wiping water from my face that dripped down from the ceiling.

The warm aroma of potato veggie soup rose to my nose, bringing comfort and warmth. My cold fingertips timidly grasp the hot bowl of soup. I held the bowl to my face to warm my poor, numb nose and cheeks.

"I've got y'all's lunch," she said, handing Daniel a bowl of potato veggie soup. She set Dermid's soup on his apple barrel and started up the stairs.

"Thank you," Daniel and I said in unison.

"This is delicious," I called after her as she cleared the steps above, in appreciation.

The bowls were made of dark, soft wood with light veins running through it. The soup was made by Shortnose, the ship's cook, and contained lots of veggies, potatoes, and meat, almost resembling a stew by its thickness. The soup was warm and comforting as it ran down my throat, warming my whole body from the inside out.

Dermid tarried on deck for a while, encouraging me to ask Daniel for more information.

"What was the meeting like?" I asked him, breaking the silence as I lifted another spoonful to my lips to blow on.

"What do you mean?" he asked me in return to my unexpected question.

"What else did they say? Who spoke?" I asked him with curiosity, then added, "Please, if you don't mind."

"The high elder Mossbeard spoke for the most part, then your father Honeysuckle spoke for a while about us going to Fayatoch, General MacArthur spoke about infiltrating Ekland's army. Oh, and the Creature spoke about getting a new king to rule Mossland," He answered, digging into his soup, then added with a mouth full, "I'd like to help infiltrate the army."

"Interesting," I exclaimed, under my breath, then asked, "Did anyone else talk?"

"Oh, yeah, and Queen Oona," he answered, searching up the steps for Dermid, then coming back down, "She creeps me out and I don't know why."

"Aoife, you haven't told anyone that I left to listen, right?" he asked with a stern, questioning face.

"I knew that you wished me not to, so I did not," I replied honestly, "Yeah, she kinda creeps me out too, and I cannot place why."

"I mean, I guess I shouldn't have challenged Shaun to let me go," Daniel reasoned thoughtfully, "Our parents didn't tell us the details, and it probably was for our good, but I'm glad I went. It just wouldn't have seemed right for all of us to be sent out of the blue to Fayatoch. A few, maybe."

I held my tongue about Honeysuckle telling me while forcing another big spoonful into my mouth. I knew it would hurt Daniel not to have been told the truth by his parents when mine told me, and I wanted to fully understand the circumstances. A sense of gratitude welled up inside me. I was grateful for my parents, and I missed them. My father would always answer questions I had and explain things that I did not understand.

Swallowing a mouthful of thick soup, I reasoned, "Every child on this ship knows something is out of place. Most probably think as much, if not more than the truth."

"Yes, but we don't need to be the ones to bring their worst fears to life," he replied thoughtfully and added, "I think it's better for them to think that it's just them who has suspicions."

"You told me, and I am grateful," I reasoned, setting my empty bowl down on the wood floor beside my stool.

"I had to tell someone; it was too much to hold inside, which is strange because I normally have no trouble keeping secrets, but this one was rubbing on my conscience," he admitted, leaning back against the wood post and crossing his arms. He rarely ever talked this much to me, and I wondered why he did not trust Dermid with it.

"Thank you for telling me. At least now I know what is coming." I said, then whispered in an airy voice, "War."

Chapter 11:
Am I Worthy Of This Dream?

Oh, life on the sea,

carry me away, to somewhere beyond the day.

Let me dream of ships and waves,

Crashing waters, and deep dark caves.

Let me see a glimpse of day,

As the waters carry me away.

The second week was quite different from the first. This time, I was assigned to Shortnose, the cook, and to my delight, Kate was as well. Shortnose was an amusing character that was rather short in stature and stocky in my opinion, and that of my friends. We were ever cautious to keep our assumptions to ourselves to be polite, for we assumed that short tempers were common among seafarers.

"Ol'right, littil' ones," Shortnose called from the stone as we sat in a ring on the floor peeling potatoes, carrots, and shredding and chopping meat, "No cuttin yer fingers. We dunt want blud in de sup."

Pausing to stretch my arms behind my head, I realized that I'd rather work for Larry and walk around the deck with a mop. My back and butt were beginning to get sore from sitting on the hardwood floor. I took a deep breath. I stretched a little and began again peeling the potatoes.

The soup, I knew, would be worth the pain. Shortnose was a great cook. He never ceased to amaze me with his ability to make excellent food with limited resources and primitive cooking supplies. His stove sat proudly in a sand box to protect the ship from heat and sparks.

Shortnose handed me a wooden spoon and directed me to watch the soup while he went to get more firewood, as if he could tell that I was sore and tired of sitting. It was cold and rainy outside.

Dermid poked Leo in the ribs saying, "Dawll! Dawl, Dawl," and pointing to Kate, who was washing dishes. That was the boy's way of saying that someone liked someone. They mostly used it to tease each other, and I could tell that Leo was blushing, "Quit that. She's my sister!" Among the friends closest to me, they would call each other sister or brother even if there was no kinship present, just to mess with people around them. To my friends, a friendship meant basically that you were either a sister or a brother and treated as such with teasing and poking. Dermid and Leo were half-brothers through their mom.

The soup smelled so appetizing that my mouth began to water and my stomach rumbled. This soup had chopped-up pork in it, which was a treat. Usually, we had fish to eat at least once a day.

The ship we were on was primarily a fishing vessel, so fresh fish were in abundance, and the ship did not stay but a few miles off the coast for the first week and went into port twice to trade fish for other types of food. I was unable to watch this go on because Captain Acosta was worried about spies, so he sent us below deck while the trading was going on, and until the ship was out of sight of the shoreline.

About the ninth day, I noticed that Kate seemed tired, and I was beginning to see a touch of grey on her blue wings, which was very unusual for her. That night in the girl's side of the children's cabin, which was separated from the boy's side with a heavy, red curtain, I creped to Kate's hammock on the other side of the long dark room lit only by the light of the stars coming from the large window, and a bit of lantern light outside the large window that covered nearly the whole back wall. She was awake, staring out the big window at the sea that reflected thousands of stars back at the heavens. I knew she could feel my presence as I drew near.

"Kate," I whispered, resting my hands on the edge of her hammock.

"Yes, Aoife," she replied quietly, rolling over and sitting up to make room for me to sit down.

I sat down and had to catch myself when the ship rocked suddenly, "You haven't seemed yourself lately. Like, kinda sad today, even through your smiles, you looked sad, and your wings have hints of grey at their tips. You, okay?"

"Humm," Kate signed with a soft smile that I was barely able to make out in the dark, but I could feel her happy light returning, "I miss home, Aoife," she breathed slowly looking down at her dangling feet then back into my face where I could feel her steady gaze, "You know this is the first time I've been away from home this long. I miss Mama and my siblings and Daddy."

I stared off into the distance for a moment, trying to find the right words to comfort my friend, when we both heard a soft step approaching the hammock.

"Mind if I join you?" spoke a small, soft voice that we recognized to be Rowsheen.

Rowsheen was draped in a large multicolored quilt that dragged the wooden floor like the train of a long dress. Kate and I made room on the worn, leather hammock, and soon all three of us were seated comfortably and swaying at the boat's will. Rowsheen had sat on the other side of Kate, and I suddenly felt thankful for having Kate and Rowsheen with me; they made me sad because of the reminder of home, and yet comforted at the same time.

Rowsheen spoke first in her sweet, the point way, "You okay, Katy?"

Kate nodded, then, realizing that we couldn't see her, well replied with an "I'm alright," but her answer was far from satisfactory for Rowsheen, who gave her a big hug. I joined in and squeezed tight.

We let go briefly. I could sense that Kate was crying. Kate sniffed and rubbed her eyes. I felt a tightness well up in my throat, and my eyes watered. To keep myself from crying, I began singing a quiet song that we all knew well.

"A Dream, A dream (Rowsheen joined me)

I have a Dream, (Kate joined us)

Whatever doth this dream mean?

A dream, A dream,

I have a dream,

Sweet and softly doth it seem.

Rock me gently dream, oh dream.

As I see the moon's gleam.

Take me far, oh far away, To somewhere beyond the day.

Am I worthy, do you deem?

Am I worthy of this dream?

Oh, oh dream."

The song seemed to linger long after we ceased to sing. The journey we were on truly felt like a dream as we rocked to and fro on a ship in the middle of the sea. I could never have believed that my life would be here if you had told me a few months ago. I closed my eyes and rested my head on Kate's shoulder, and I wondered if I was worthy of this dream.

Chapter 12:
Fencing on Waves

Slowly, I began to get used to being on the water with the chores and jobs. I did not, however, get used to the beautiful waves sparkling in the sunlight and starlight, and looking out into the horizon. I helped Sharpeye look for sandbanks and ships on the horizon up in the crow's nest. At first, I was afraid of being up so high; then I began to feel powerful and confident standing in the wind as it blew past my face and lifted my hair.

My cheeks and nose grew ruddy, and the wind chapped up in the crow's nest, but I did not care. It was my new favorite place to be. I smiled as the warm sun kissed my face in the morning. Sharpeye took breaks every couple of hours and swapped out with me after he was pleased with my knowledge that he had taught me about scanning the horizon for dangers. I got my own black three-pointed sailors' hat.

One day, while I was up in the crow's nest, I spotted a dark purple and black line of clouds on the horizon. I pointed it out to Sharpeye, saying, "Is that a storm?"

"Aye, it is littil' one," he replied, looking through a telescope, "Get down quick! Tell the Captain and get in the haul!"

I could only nod in reply. My heart squeezed, and a cold sensation flushed through my veins. I was scared. I hurriedly rushed down the rope ladder and ran up the steps to the captain, nearly tripping on my way up.

"Whatever is the matter, child?" The captain asked with a concerned look on his face.

"Sharpeye and I saw a large storm on the horizon to the North," I replied, almost breathless. A large lightning bolt cracked across the horizon, followed closely by a deafening, "BOOM!" I had never before in my life seen a lightning strike so close and so loud.

"Go get in the haul now," the captain said, looking at the purple storm through a telescope, "Don't worry about your friends. We'll make sure they get there too. Run along now. This is an experienced sailor's challenge."

The wind started to pick up, and the sky grew steadily darker as I quickly made my way down the steps to the haul. It was dusty, musty, and dark when I got down the steps, but I wasn't there for long. Shortnose stumbled down the steps as the ship rocked with a huge pot of soup and a ladle hanging from his shoulder.

"There you are, littil' one," Shortnose explained, setting the huge black iron pot down with a huff, "Everyone else will be joining us shortly. We'll have a nice time down here till the storm passes."

"That storm looked rough," I said worriedly as I heard the voices of the youths heading down the steps.

"Every storm can look rough, my dear," Shortnose replied, handing me a bowl of soup, "you've got to learn that the Almighty is bigger than any storm that could come our way. Yes, the bark of the storm is scary, and its bite on the sea can be bad, but we know who we serve, and the end is not so bad. There is a purpose and a plan for all of us, no matter how big or small. God has a plan for you, and He'll see you through it all."

Those words echoed in my brain and sank in my heart as Shortnose turned to welcome the other youths and get them some lunch. He was a comforting presence down in the haul, telling us stories and keeping us occupied with knot tying.

"A good sailor must know how to tie a proper knot!" Shortnose bellowed as his stocky form stepped proudly around us as we sat down on the floor in a crisscross. The ship swayed this way and that seemed not to bother him at all. His large belly jiggled under his long tunic as he stepped amidst the ship's sway.

Shortnose made us laugh and giggle as the fearsome storm raged above. I felt comfortable for the first time in a long time, and I felt safe and secure. I was grateful for him and the wisdom he had to share. He did not get upset at us for making mistakes with our knots; he just gently corrected us and let us try again.

The old ship never ceased to amaze me at how the great pounding waves didn't tear it to pieces and bury us beneath its glassy depths. The storm raged on into the night. Larry and Shortnose handed out blankets, and we made pallets on the floor of the haul. Rowsheen and Kate curled up next to me, and we were softly rocked to sleep by the sway of the ship.

The next day, the world at sea seemed different and less cheerful. There was a lot of damage done to the mast and top deck. Over the next few days, my friends and I assisted Larry in repairing everything.

Larry loved to fill our heads with scary stories of piracy in his youth that seemed to defy all logic as I knew it, but I treasured every one. His songs were pleasant and funny, and I also knew that I could never be caught singing them.

One bright morning, as Larry took us around the ship doing chores, Dermid, talking continuously as ever, asked Larry this question, "Have you done a lot of sword fighting in your time?"

"Have I," Larry burst out laughing, "Lad, it's my specialty."

"Could you teach us? If we get done with all of our chores in a quick manner?" Dermid sweetly coaxed with a smile, flashing his soft grey eyes.

"Alright, you've persuaded me. That is, if you all wish to appear on deck when the moon is out. I don't want every Peston, Tom, and Flinch wanting a lesson." Larry warned. Secretly, I thought he was flattered by the request.

I slipped silently out of my hammock that night and tiptoed to the big, red curtain and slipped through. The moon was bright and full, making the high waves visible and the outline of the ship's deck. I was dressed in my daytime attire of loose, tan slacks, a white long-sleeve blouse, and complete with tall tan leather boots. Climbing up the steps to the deck, I found Daniel, Rowsheen, Leo, and Dermid already there, and they had invited a friend of theirs whose name was Jessie.

"Alright, children. I want you all in a straight line," Larry ordered, marching up behind us with a large bundle under one arm and a lamp in the other.

To our immediate disappointment, the bundle only contained wood swords, but I was soon thankful for this. First, Larry showed us how to stand and step correctly before he ever gave us a wooden sword.

"Okay, now everyone grab a sword and spread out. You'll be copying me. Don't hit anyone yet!" Larry directed us to get into a stance, looking over his shoulder, and he watched us try to duplicate his moves.

"Daniel, watch your feet. Dermid, what are you doing?" Larry asked, looking perturbed.

Larry split up Leo and Dermid to opposite sides and put Jessie and me in between them.

Dermid was pretending to be stabbed in the heart, making all kinds of silly motions and frolicking madly about. He stopped instantly at Larry's words and stood very still, trying to hold a straight face. Larry walked over and leaned in close to be sure Dermid could hear him and harshly whispered, "Leave now, or do as directed, Boy! I won't have any of those shenanigans here. You can never be a man until you learn how to act as one."

"Yes, sir," looking down at his feet, ashamed of his actions.

"Anyone else, while I'm in the mood?" Larry asked, addressing all of us.

"No, sir," we all whispered one after another as he looked each of us individually in the eye.

"Good," he replied, "now let's continue."

Mr. Larry paired me and Jessie (the new kid) up for exercises. We were told that we were supposed to work mainly on foot stability and posture, and leave the actual fighting for another time. Over and over, we practiced, all the while glancing down at our feet to ensure we were taking the proper steps. Mr. Larry stopped us many times, correcting us and giving us formal lectures before we could continue.

"This is harder than it looks," Jessie whispered, trying to even up his balance. "Move your foot slightly to the left," Jessie whispered to me.

"Thanks," I whispered back, correcting my form and straightening up my posture.

We were trying not to attract Larry's attention. Finally, Mr. Larry was mostly satisfied with our footwork after the third session. In the fourth lesson, he let us do slow swings and attacks with the wooden swords.

Finally, he let us work on counterattacks in the seventh session. As instructed, Jessie lunged at me in slow motion, but instead of me blocking correctly as instructed by Mr. Larry, I accidentally tripped Jessie. I grabbed his cloak as he flew past me, slowing his fall onto his face.

Jessie jumped up as quickly as a rabbit. He did not seem embarrassed by his fall. I thought he was going to pick me up and toss me clean over the ship's railing into the waves below, but he didn't. I covered my mouth from an unexpected smile at his serious expression.

"Sorry. I didn't mean to," I apologized, looking down at my wooden sword that dangled from my limp, tired arm.

He just gave me an irritated stare and a hard knock on my left shoulder. Again and again, we practiced the exercise, resulting in me getting tripped up twice by my own feet, but I did not hit the ground because each time Jessie grabbed me by my shirt or belt and set me back on my feet.

After nearly two hours of basic moves and exercises, I tiptoed through the children's dorms, rolled into my hammock, and drew my knees up to my chest. My heart was beating fast, and my stomach felt sick. Larry was hard to satisfy, but that wasn't what was wrong. I was anxious about arrival in Fayatoch, wondering if I would do well as a student, and longing for my father's big, comforting hug. I was on my own now. He couldn't help me from where I was. These anxious thoughts swirled in my mind like a booming, destructive hurricane. I couldn't cry.

Reaching down from my hammock, I lifted my bag and drew it up into my lap. Reaching inside, I pulled out the necklace my father had given, slipped it over my head, and tucked it into my shirt. I let my head fall into my bag and prayed. I prayed that God would protect my Father and siblings back home, I prayed that I would be able to fall asleep, I prayed for strength and courage, for the government back home, and most of all, I thanked God that my friends were safe and that He was still leading me onward. "God has a plan for me," I whispered, letting hot tears drip down my dry, wind-chapped cheeks, "God has a beautiful plan for me."

Every night until our arrival at Fayatoch, we snuck out on deck and trained under Mr. Larry's watchful eye. Jessie and I were getting much better at our exercises, and we rarely stumbled. The late nights wore on us, making us a bit irritable, so Larry advised shorter night sessions and a bit of independent, daytime practice.

In our spare time, which would be about ten to thirty minutes each day, Jessie would catch me, and we would practice. During these times, Dermid, Leo, and Daniel would come and practice a little, and watch Jessie and I and make sure to tell us what we were doing wrong. They made many comments about our form.

Jessie was from Son's Hill in Mossland, close to where I lived. He was a very serious soul when he wanted to be, but he had his own sense of humor that took a bit to get used to, and he was driven to do and be the best at whatever he set his mind to. This meant that if he wanted to get better at sword fighting, he was going to do it as much as possible.

We were ever learning new stories and songs from the sailors. Kate would walk about all day humming a song that she did not know the words to and wishing that the tune was not stuck in her head. I would often learn the words to one of their sad songs just to bug her when I was bored.

"I cannot stand it, Aoife! I keep getting crazy songs stuck in my head, and you're no help because you're singing most of 'em," Kate whined with a tired, laughing smile.

Kate was always smiling and laughing, but I could still tell her moods apart from one another due to subtle differences. When she gets worn out, she often gets either frustrated or really goofy. Also, when she's tired, her laughter tends to be longer and more drawn out.

"Sorry, I like 'em," I halfway apologized with a yawn, "The songs I'm singing now I've been singing for years now."

"But they're sad," Kate fussed, plopping herself down against the grimy, wooden wall of the ship's kitchen, "Someone is always dying in your songs, and her true love is gone an' it's sad, Aoife." We'd been washing dishes for hours, and there was still more to be done.

"They're sweet 'n sad," I replied, stretching my soaked arms over my head.

Somehow, I could connect with grief, sorrow, and loss. Songs about death and love or heartbreak meant something to me deep down, as if psychologically it was comforting to know that people still love and care about people even when they're gone. I did not know how to verbalize that then or even begin to explain my feelings and tendencies and what made me tick.

What intrigues you, dear reader? What can or do you connect with deep down? What do you value? What makes you feel safe? Write them down if you can. I know these are hard questions that may seem unnecessary, but it is important in life to know who you are.

"I can't stand 'em," Kate fussed with a groan and a yawn, "You made me yawn!"

"So, I did," I replied, lifting another dish to scrub. My hair was a frizzy mess, and my sleeves had already gotten soaked in soapy water, which frustrated me deeply. "I'll sing a better song."

"Take me to the yonder hills.

Take me past my father's mills,

I'm a lookin' for the world.

Is it under that yonder stone?

Is it past the great unknown?

I'm a lookin' for the world."

"How'd that one get stuck in your head?" Kate asked, rubbing her tired, red eyes. We were both worn out and exhausted. Our arms were tired, and we were mentally and physically drained.

"I don't know," I replied. I'd had enough of conversing. Mentally, it took too much brain power to carry on a good conversation when I was tired.

"Guess what I got stuck in my head?" Kate laughed, flashing her blue eyes while splashing me with soap water.

"What?" I replied, trying not to get mad. My drained body had had enough. I tried to focus on the last few dishes beneath the sudsy water in the old metal wash tub.

"That song that Shortnose was a singin' earlier," she replied, drying the last few dishes I handed her.

"Oh, I know that one," I said with a weak laugh, "I think I have it memorized." Then I sang it in the sweetest voice I could muster.

"I'm walking on the starlit sky,

Past the moon, Past the tide,

Tell me not I cannot be,

With the waves under me,

I'll play all night,

I'll dance all day,

In this crazed, nature's play,

Come and dance my sailor true,

The waves are rushing over you,

I'll take your air,

You'll breathe no more,

The waves rush, and scream,

And roar.

Why won't you stay,

And dance with me?

I am the moon.

I am the sea."

"You didn't have to do that," Kate sighed, her tired body collapsing into a chair.

"I know," I replied with a weak smile, leaning on the washing tub.

Chapter 13:
My Own Blade Set

It was a beautiful day, and despite my longing for home, I was in good spirits as I helped Shortnose make breakfast. Potatoes seemed to be his favorite food, for they were in everything he cooked, and today he had set me in charge of peeling them for his stew. It was still early, the sun not quite showing itself above the horizon yet, as I fiddled with the potatoes and daydreamed about what Fayatoch would look like.

A vivid image of my father wrapping me up in a big hug entered my mind, and it was in that moment that I slit my finger with the knife. Red blood trickled down my hand, and if I had not been looking, I would have sliced right through it, for my fingers were so numb from the chilly morning that I felt no pain.

"Ooouu," I grunted to let Shortnose know that I had cut myself and placed my finger in my mouth.

"Slit yer finger did ya child," Shortnose said with a laugh, "That's what happins when little children don't pai ettention to what they're do'in."

"Sorry, sir," I apologized.

"I guess you won't do that again," he chuckled, "run down to Tub. He'll bandege it up fer ya, and hurry up there's work tu be dune."

Tub was the medic on board, and he was constantly frustrated with the youths hurting themselves by messing around on board.

Tub pulled out some bandages from his large black medical bag. He was tanned from the sun, and his clothes were worn and rough from hard work. He was a strong sailor with large arms and light red hair poking out from under his sailor's hat. He had a tall, crooked, sunburned nose with kind eyes and a pleasant smile. He wrapped up my hand quick-like.

Tub cautioned me about using knives and paying attention to what I was doing, but he also told me that he was glad that I said something and did not keep it to myself, and let it get infected and lose my hand. It sounded kind of dramatic to me, but also like something that he had had to deal with before.

On my way back from Tub, as I was weaving this way and that around all the youths trying hard to follow the person they were assigned to, I was startled by Sharpeye's yell from the crow's nest.

"LAND!!!" Sharpeye yelled, "LAND IN SIGHT!!!"

"What is it, Sharpeye?" Captain Acosta yelled up to him, "It better not be a group of splinter-isles again!"

"No, sir! It's Fayatoch, I'm sure it is!" Sharpeye assured him, hanging over the side of the crow's nest to yell down.

Quickly, I ran to the boat's edge and peered in the direction Sharpeye had pointed, but could see nothing. Captain Acosta strode toward me with his telescope in hand. The limp in his left leg slowed his walk and made him seem tired and weary. His leather jacket made a stiff, rustling sound as he lengthened the telescope and raised it to his eye.

"This might help, kid," said Captain Acosta, offering me his telescope after he looked.

I held the long, black, and bronze instrument up to my eye and spotted a small darkish shape on the horizon that lay past large, violent waves that crashed continuously and madly against the ship's hull. The captain's breathing sounded long and raspy above the deafening noise of the sea, and I was at once concerned for his health.

"I think I see Fayatoch," I said, making sure that I was loud enough to hear, but not yelling, "but it looks so small from here."

"You wait till we get up closer, kid," Captain Acosta replied with a heavy breath as I handed the telescope back to him. I glanced at his sword as he took another look through the long instrument, for I was curious about its design and origin.

"Fayatoch's one of the largest islands in this part of the world," the captain said, almost lost in thought.

His sword had silver and gold on the hilt and handle; then I recognized that it had words engraved on it. I was studying the engraving on the handle of his sword when he caught me glancing at his sword. My cheeks gave away my embarrassment and curiosity.

"We should be at Fayatoch in three hours' time, kid." He puffed, then, looking at me, he said, "How would you like your own sword?"

This question froze me, and I could barely breathe a reply. "I would love to have my own sword," I finally made out in a whisper.

"Good answer," he said and smiled, then turned toward his cabin and directed, "Right this way."

The thought of having my own sword made my heart swell. I knew they were expensive, and I never really had a hope of getting my own. I could hardly believe what was happening as I entered his cabin and followed him to a large maple chest by his map table, which was covered with instruments of the like.

The instruments, compasses, and tools I assumed assisted in his navigation of the sea, but I could only identify a few.

"What are all these instruments used for?" I asked, pointing to one, "I've never seen so many navigational tools up close."

"This is a pelorus. It is used similarly to a compass. It helps us find our heading, and it's very old. It can also help us determine the angle between two objects or ships. It helps us make sure we're heading in the right direction. And this is an Astrolabe; it helps us use the position of the stars and sun to set our course and adjust as needed," The captain said with enthusiasm, he did not seem bothered by my questions, "You can have this one," The captain said handing me a small compass, "It might just come in handy some time."

The captain dug in his pocket and withdrew a small ring of iron keys, and there appeared to be a purple ribbon attached to one small key. He selected the one with the purple ribbon and thrust it into the lock's dark mouth and gave it a rattle. The lock made a satisfactory clink sound, and he lifted the lid that was beautifully engraved with fruits and angels. Inside the chest lay packages wrapped in black and blue silks, bottles filled with colorful stones, a large black leather coat, and many different swords and knives. I had never seen that many swords and knives in one place before. My mouth hung open as I stood tree-still a few paces from the large chest.

"Ha, ha, humm," he laughed upon seeing my face, "Here you are, this one will suit you well." He handed me a long sword with a leather sheath and bone handle, "and they go with these," he said, handing me a pair of twin daggers with matching leather sheaths and leather forearm guards. I was stunned at the gift and very grateful.

"Now don't you go bragging. I haven't got enough for the whole ship. You best stow those in here," he said, handing me a large backpack. He turned to leave.

"I don't know what to say," I muttered, barely able to breathe, "Thank you, Captain," I managed to get out.

In that moment, I remembered Shortnose and said, "Oh, I'm afraid I've forgotten my work with Shortnose."

"You're welcome, kid. You're going to need a sword where you're going. Shortnose can wait. Goodness knows he's got more help than he deserves."

Then paused halfway out the door before leaving and said, "But I'll tell him I had

I job for you, so he does not send people searching."

"Thank you again, Captain," I replied. I could barely believe that I had my own sword and dagger set. I took a deep breath and pinched my arm to make sure it was all real. It was all real: the gift, the chest, the gorgeous weapons. It was all real.

Later, I snuck to the youths' dorms and I opened my new backpack, gazed at its contents, which appeared to be a handsome set of twin daggers and a dainty cutlass with a rich brown leather belt that held the sheaths of all three blades each in its proper place. The large sword was connected to the belt in two places, the first at the waist and the second at the loop that was meant to be tightened around the wearer's upper right leg. The daggers that hung at the wearer's hips had bone handles and brass guards with touches of leather work.

The cutlass had a bone handle as well, but instead of brass, the full hand guard looked as intricate as spider webbing and appeared to be made from silver with emeralds and rubies embedded in it. Then it occurred to me that the set was constructed where the cutlass hung on the right, meaning that the captain must be left-handed, as I was, because a swordsman wears his sword on the leg opposite his dominant hand. He had chosen the set for me because he knew I was left-handed, but how did he know that? I looked dreamily at the blades for a while.

I gently lifted the handsome set and drew the belt with its dangling blades around my waist and secured it with the brass buckle (I did not mess with the leg strap, having decided that I would figure it out later). I stared down at the belt and blades with pride. I knew that we would be arriving in Fayatoch soon, and I did not want to take it off, so I left it on. It was cold outside, so I pulled my cloak over me.

I was so happy about my new blades that I proudly walked across the deck and climbed the steps to where the captain stood looking at a map of Fayatoch's ports. I stood still until he noticed my presence and turned around.

"It fits as if it were made for you," he beamed.

"Thank you so much, sir," I cried excitedly, throwing my arms around his neck. He chuckled again and gave me a tight hug.

"You better take it off now and keep it wrapped up till your lessons begin in Fayatoch," he instructed me, turning back to his maps.

"Yes, sir," I said, turning to leave, "I will keep it safe."

"Remember, a blade is something to take care of but not to be kept safe; the blade is to keep its user safe," he advised me.

"Yes, sir. I will," I replied with a smile.

"You can thank me by listening to your instructors on Fayatoch and behaving yourself," he said with a laugh.

"I will, sir, thank you," I replied.

"Run along now. Shortnose will be needing you." He said, "And careful not to lose that."

The leather package was clutched tightly in my arms as I slid into the children's cabin to tuck away my precious possession. It was a fine day, and I could barely believe that it was real.

Chapter 14:
Arrival at Fayatoch

"What do you have for me to do?" I asked Shortnose upon returning.

"There you be my red haired elfling. Where have yu bin?" Shortnose asked as he dumped a load of potatoes in his large iron pot. "Oh, I remember Lass. The captain had a job fer ya. Didn't he?"

"Yes, sir," I replied, and added, "Aw, that soup smells amazing. I'm starving." I placed my head over the large black pot and breathed in the soothing aromas. I could have stood there forever.

"Get yourself a bowl then, Lass," Shortnose chuckled, "but stay away from the potatoes there not dune yet."

Thank you, sir," I replied, smiling and reaching for a wooden spoon and bowl. I ladled myself out a bit and dug in.

"U missed yer breakfist, didn't ya," Shortnose said, slipping in more potatoes.

"Yes, I did," I replied between spoonfuls of soup, wiping my mouth on my sleeve.

"Well, Lass," Shortnose said with a hint of regret, "You 'n yer friends, will be leavin' in a piece."

"Yes," I said quietly, laying down my spoon, resting my head on my fist, and staring off into nowhere. The past two weeks had been so fun that I hadn't thought much about Fayatoch; it had seemed very far away then. Slowly, I came back to reality and realized that I would miss the dear ship, the captain, and the crew.

"Awel don't be glum, Lass," Shortnose said, "When awel this is said and dune, you'll need a ship to take u home. We'll be right here four ya waitin pretty-like. Got it, Lass?"

"Yes, sir," I smiled with a hint of sadness in my heart. I also felt a little anxious about Fayatoch.

For the rest of the day, I helped Shortnose in the kitchen, scrubbing dishes and chopping veggies and meat because a thick fog had rolled in, forcing the ship to anchor a few miles offshore. After helping Shortnose finish the dishes for dinner, I walked across the dark, silent deck toward the children's cabin in the soft, lantern light.

The only noise to be heard was that of the slapping waves mingling with a hissing, cool breeze, the creak of the ship as it rocked, and the faint flap of a sail that hadn't been tied down all the way. Larry had given us our sword-fighting lesson before dinner in case the fog cleared, so I was free to go to bed early.

Tip-toeing to the cabin door, I opened it slowly, only enough for me to slip in, but the door still made a creaking sound upon opening and a faint thud when I eased it shut. I inhaled, looking into the dark cabin. The only light to be seen was from the cracks between the dividing curtains and the walls. I would have to walk through the boy's side to get to the girl's side.

With a deep breath, I decided that I would walk straight through the center row of hammocks to the part where the curtain was split at the center of the room and hopefully not wake anyone, but it didn't quite work out that way. I put one foot forward, feeling with my toe, then the next, all the while with my hands in front of me, feeling for objects in my way. About halfway to the curtain, I heard a rustle of blankets in front of me. I stuck my left foot forward and touched a leather mat with blankets on top.

Someone was sleeping on the floor. Then I remembered Daniel had complained the second day that his hammock was not big enough for him. He was stretched out right across the middle row; I was trapped!

"Could I step over him?" I wondered. Would he wake up, or was he up already? *"I'll step over him,"* I decided, trying to make out exactly where he was in the dark. I took a small step forward; I was on the mat. Then I lifted my right leg and started over, but he rolled and muttered something, so I hurriedly placed my foot on the other side, followed by my left foot, and stood still.

All of a sudden, as I was about to continue to the curtain, I heard him sit up and say, "Halt! Who goes there!!!" I had been caught. Then he said, "Why, Burnard Laycock, you've a lot of nerve coming back here. It'll be the gallows for you this time!"

He was just dreaming, I thought, very relieved, as he sank back down and muttered something else, I couldn't make out.

"Go to bed, Daniel, you're just dreaming about outlaws again," I heard a sleepy voice say that sounded like Dermid.

"Okay," Daniel mumbled back and turned over. That was close, I thought as I finished tiptoeing to the curtain and slipped through. I made my way to my hammock, dressed in my nightie, climbed in, and felt the gentle sway of the ship rock me to sleep. I laughed softly to myself. That certainly had been very close.

The next morning, I was awakened by a gentle nudge from Kate.

"Fog's gone. Come on, we've got to get our things together," she whispered.

I pulled the blanket off my head, looked around, and replied, "Kate, it's still dark; everyone's still asleep."

"I couldn't sleep, Aoife," Kate whispered, looking at me through her wild hair.

"And besides, everyone will be up soon."

"That's my line," I replied, rolling over. "Oh, come on, get up," she replied, hopping into my hammock on top of me to try and get me out. She was wearing blue slacks and a long green top that I had never seen her wear before.

I pulled my blanket back over my head and said, "Just try and get me out." As soon as the words left my lips, I knew I was in for it.

Kate replied, "Okay," and dug her hands into my ribs, making me jump, knocking both of us to the floor in fits of poorly compressed laughter. Surprisingly, we woke no one.

Deciding to go back to sleep was not interesting to Kate, who was up for good and wound tight with energy. Kate proposed that we go on deck, but I quickly shot down the proposal, remembering last night's close call, and suggested that we gather our possessions, and if we completed that before everyone was up, we could read each other's poems that we had been working on in our spare time.

In an hour's time, all the children were on deck with their possessions in hand. I stood with my leather sack hung against my back by Daniel and Dermid, my two favorite jesters, and by Jessie, who called me his sidekick in sword fighting. They had been quite a comfort to me on the trip so far with their constant jabbering and jokes. They reminded me of home.

A cool wind rushed past, making me shiver, and I saw at that moment the captain out of the corner of my eye. I did not glance in his direction because I felt his eyes on me, a sudden gloomy shadow seemed to rest upon my body and stick to my heart. A minute later, he turned and entered his cabin. Why was this time so full of mysteries that never seemed to unravel themselves?

The ship slowly made its way into the harbor, pushed along by a gentle breeze. The island was becoming more visible every moment and looked quite massive to my eyes. There were rolling hills covered with fluffy green trees and mountains with hints of tall, sharp rock at the peaks.

I could just make out tiny figures on the shore when I heard a screech. The screech came from a young elfling who was pointing to the water beside the ship. I ran to the rail and bent over it right before Jessie grabbed my collar and pulled me back. There was a body floating in the water, surrounded by a reddish black, stained current. The children fell dead silent. We slowly turned away from the railing and sat on the deck. The body had been decapitated. Its head was nowhere to be seen.

Kate walked over to me as I leaned against the rail and sat down. She was white as a sheet. I felt bad that I hadn't thought to cover her eyes, for she had never seen dead people outside of a decorated casket about to be buried or burned.

There was a mortician close to where I lived back home, and he had let me help him when he was shy of hands, so the body hadn't bothered me, but I knew it was very disturbing to Kate, who had never been to an execution or seen anything of the like. I gently eased myself down by Kate and placed my head on her shoulder. She gave me a weak smile; that is good, I thought, at least she could smile. For another hour, nobody spoke save in hushed voices until the ship docked at the wharf. Jessie stood close to my side as we waited.

The crew tied up the ship and extended the gangplank. The children waited on the deck while the captain spoke with officials from Fayatoch about the ship's business and the cargo. After a good while, we were told to follow Sir Masuda. I waved goodbye to the captain, who tipped his three-cornered hat to me.

Sir Masuda was an interesting character of an origin I could not decipher. He was shorter, I suppose, than most men, but too tall to be a dwarf and quite fit for his age. His hair was black, his skin was tan, and he had a small, pointed beard without a mustache or sideburns. He looked to be forty years old. He wore a long black robe with a bright red belt. In silence, he walked ahead of us with his hands crossed behind his back.

The wharf appeared to be old but was in good condition. As we walked off the wharf, I gazed at the landscape which took my breath away. In the far distance rose majestic mountains that had peaks so high that the clouds enclosed them from view, and their bases were covered in tree-rich carpet that continued to the sands by the sea.

In front of the trees stretched a long, winding trail that Sir Masuda approached. I was the second in line, behind Jessie and Sir Masuda, holding Kate's hand as we started down the trail that was only wide enough for one to pass at a time. The trees on the path's edges threatened to overtake the path in places and were unlike any I had ever seen, with leaves larger than my head. I couldn't help but wonder if any of them walked and spoke like the ones at home.

In an hour's time, as we walked along this spindly path, I noticed that the path was beginning to show a prominent upward slant and a winding habit. My legs were beginning to tire, and my breath quickened. *How long would we be walking?* I wondered. I started to feel sweat trickling down my back, and my hair started to itch.

Rowsheen had caught up with me and Kate, who were no longer close to the front. I was ahead of them. And that was when the trouble started.

Our path had long ceased to be packed with dirt and was now covered with spears of grass, and rocks ranging in size from a dinner plate to a horse, and oddly shaped. The trees on the sides of the path were sparse now, and the space between them was tightly packed underbrush, decaying foliage, and large rocks with an occasional boulder.

We had reached a large flat rock covering the entire path. I stepped up first and slowly made my way across. I had a small slide at the peak. I stepped off rather gracefully in my mind, wondering if that was the elfling in me finally starting to show itself. I turned around to assist Rowsheen and Kate if needed. Kate strode across the rock as if it were an afternoon stroll, and as she neared the end, she prepared to jump. Her left foot landed first on a slanted rock, making her ankle twist, and it flung her forward. Just before her knees hit, she reached out to me, and I grabbed her arms. Her ankle was twisted and sprained badly, so that I knew without even looking at it.

Back at home, Kate twisted her ankles, often saying that she had weak tendons, but what she did have was courage and stamina. Kate was always active and wanted to run, play, and keep up with the boys at home.

Rowsheen hurried across, and the three of us sat down and rested. How would we make it now?

At home, Kate was normally fine in a few minutes after spraining an ankle and would just stay off it for a few days. We didn't have that luxury. The space between the children hiking was great, and the boys were far ahead of us.

"How bad is it, Kate?" Rowsheen asked, tucking a loose curl behind her ear. She had a worried look on her face.

"Just sore," Kate replied with a smile. Kate always smiled, and she was not about to let a sprained ankle bring down her mood.

"I have a wrap in my bag," I informed, digging inside to look. After a minute, I produced the wrap and presented it to Kate, who pulled off her short boot and began wrapping it; Rowsheen promptly took the wrap after seeing how loose she had wrapped it, ceased the wrap, and rewrapped it nice and tight.

After replacing the boot, we stood with Kate between us and took turns, with one guiding her from the side and front because the path was very narrow. We took it slowly and steadily with many breaks.

Finally, after it felt like an eternity, we emerged into a clearing where the children who had gone ahead of us were seated on the ground. Relieved, we stepped out of the pathway and sat down to rest under a tree. Kate pulled off her boot and began to rub her ankle. The ankle was swollen and bruised. It was a miracle we made it that far.

Chapter 15:
Flowers At Midnight

After all the children had arrived, we were ushered to our living quarters. The buildings were built out of beautiful red cedar wood that interlocked at the counters expertly; I did not see evidence of nails at all in the woodwork, as if the notches were holding everything together entirely.

The buildings were configured in a square pattern with a beautiful, large grassy courtyard in the center. I saw rose bushes and zinnias in the courtyard as we passed, and it reminded me of my mother's garden back home. The building on the far left was the youth wing. This wing was filled with hundreds of leather-lined wooden cots. There were two separate large open rooms: one for girls and one for the boys. There were many large open windows, and the only thing that covered these open, glassless windows were white, silk curtains that draped elegantly over.

Sir Masuda paused for a short time to speak quietly with a man dressed the same as him before we were led into our rooms. I carefully placed my belongings under a cot on the right wall against a window facing the inner courtyard, close to the exit, for there were no doors, only curtains of the same white silk. The boy's windows faced the woods outside the ring of wooden buildings. Kate and Rowsheen did the same, choosing cots close to mine but against the inner wall to the left that separated the two rooms. I think they were nervous about the open windows.

A moment later, the white silk curtain covering the exit parted, and a lady with light olive skin and black hair entered, clad in a black garb like Sir Masuda's.

"Come, ladies," she smiled pleasantly, motioning us to sit on a cot near her. When we were all seated, she rested herself on my cot by the wooden cedar wall and introduced herself, "I am Lady Catherine, and I am in charge of your affairs. If you need anything, you should come to me first. I will be present for most of your training classes and at the daily meals."

Lady Catherine was pleasant and quiet. Her nose was stately and tall; her chin was nicely rounded. She stood about an inch higher than I and was of close proportions. I watched her eyes and mouth closely to ensure that I caught every word and gesture. I felt anxious about pleasing my instructors and doing my absolute best that I could.

She directed us through the dorms and showed us their purposes. The first was the youth's dorm where we were already. The second was the training room filled with weapons of various kinds. I was curious about the weapons and wanted to ask questions, but Lady Catherine seemed to be in a hurry. The third was a very large room with long wooden benches and tables for eating and teaching, and the fourth building we were told was the master's dorms, which we were not allowed to enter on any occasion.

In the center of the vast courtyard was a large stone pool surrounded by a lovely garden full of flowers, vegetables, beans, rice, and potatoes. After the tour, we were led back to the youth's dorm and presented with new clothes that looked like black tunics with loose slacks of the same color. We were told to change and wait until Lady Catherine returned to take us to dinner. I stepped behind the changing wall and slipped into the odd clothes. To my surprise, I found them to be very light and comfortable.

In the half an hour's time we waited, I pulled out my diary, a gift from Larry, and began writing on page one. I described some of the sea voyage, the storm that scared me, my new blade set that I could not wait to start trying, and the coming war that Daniel had told me about before the voyage. Was Daniel right?

Dinner was eaten by candlelight and consisted of black beans and rice. Dermid found the red pepper and began to cover his food. Daniel was in on the challenge and did the same, covering his food in a spicy red blanket. Sir Masuda gave them stern disapproving glances from the table's head. I was finally able to obtain the red pepper long enough to spice up my own food. There were five masters and fourteen apprentices at the table parallel to our table; only Sir Masuda and Lady Catherine sat at ours.

In vain, I tried to quiet my mind that night, but negative thoughts came crowding in. I told myself I would never be able to fall asleep with the setting sun coming into my window, paired with the girl's whispering, and the next thing I knew, I woke up in the dark with the curtain brushing my face from the wind. I had fallen asleep quite hard. A rustle sounded outside my window. I sat up straight and pulled back the curtain. The faint moon illuminated a dark figure who whispered my name. "Aoife," it said quietly, and again, "Aoife". "Yes," I said, and continuing, "who are you?"

"It's me, Daniel," he said nervously, "Aoife, I need to ask a favor."

"What for?" I asked, rubbing my eyes and yawning, "Where's Dermid?"

"Behind the bush that's shaking over there," he replied in a whisper, pointing to a bush on his right.

I glanced at the bush; it was indeed shaking. "What do you need me for?" I asked. Daniel shifted from one foot to the other before resting his right elbow over his head on the window frame. His left hand remained behind his back.

"I was wondering if you could give something to Rowsheen for me," he said. I could feel a wide smile of embarrassment covering his cheeks and knew his face was red as a fang dragon's tongue. I could not help smiling to myself. Daniel mustered up some courage and continued, "And could you please not tell her they're from me?"

"Of course I'll keep my mouth shut," I promised, and asked, wishing to know what gift I would have to bear, "What would you have for me to give her?"

"These," he said, pulling his left hand out from behind his back and presenting a bouquet of flowers that I could not make out in the dark, and handing them to me. I held them gently, breathing in their fragrance.

"She will love these," I said with a smile. My heart felt warm. Even though the flowers were not for me, the gesture was so sweet that it made me feel happy and content. Even in hard times, there are still good and kind acts.

"Thank you, Aoife," Daniel whispered, and quietly called, "Come on, Dermid! We've got to go! Why are you so loud? Can't you be quiet for two minutes? We're gonna get caught!"

They snuck off and I wondered if Dermid even knew what the mission was about. I slowly closed the curtain, fighting off an explosion of laughter. Even in this crazy time, there were still little acts of love that would melt the heart. I slipped off my cot, felt my long night gown hit my ankles, and tiptoed to Rowsheen's cot on the opposite wall and laid the bouquet on her small cedar chest. She would find them in the morning.

Despite my restful night, I woke early just before the sun and moon were to change shift. I lay quietly for quite some time, dreaming up silly stories before deciding to rise. I dressed in my new attire and put on my brown leather coat. I also straightened my belongings. All of my things were jumbled up in my bag, and I felt anxious about the coming day. Oh, what would befall me?

Lady Catherine entered our room suddenly, startling me. She called for us to rise and dress, although the twenty-five of us were all ready. Rowsheen had been up for a while and now sat holding her flowers in silence. Kate walked over to my bed and sat down beside me.

Kate moaned, pulling her ankle into her lap and rubbing it. She tried to give me a weak smile, shrouding her real emotions. I knew that she was worried about her ankle. I gave a long sigh, and I did not mind if anyone heard.

With a gulp, I stood and strode across the room with my shoulders back and a sweet smile on my face. I stood close to Lady Catherine, who was speaking to someone else. I held my hands behind my back and waited patiently.

"What is it, Dear?" Lady Catherine asked with a smile, "Do you need something?"

Softly, I explained the situation with Kate's ankle sprain and how bruised it was. I explained that I was concerned about her training for a few days. Lady Catherine simply nodded and left. She returned in a few minutes with a shoe box in her hand.

Lady Catherine had Kate take her shoe and sock off. She cleaned and dressed Kate's ankle and made her prop it up in bed.

"She will be resting for a few days," Lady Catherine informed me, "You seemed interested in the salves and bandages. Do you want to learn?"

"Yes, please," I replied excitedly with a big smile. I sat beside Kate for a while before we left for breakfast. A long yawn escaped my lips.

"You tired?" Kate asked, striking her laughing, mocking smile.

"I had a long night," I replied with a weak smile.

"We have to be brave," Rowsheen said, looking across from us, "We have to be brave."

"We will be brave," I said, happy to receive some comfort, "It's all we can do."

"It feels so gloomy," Kate breathed, and groaned, "This is going to be an adventure, and I'm stuck in bed with an ankle sprain."

"And I will come and bring you some breakfast in a little while," I replied, falling back on my bed with a groan.

Lady Catherine entered once more, finding all the girls seated by the entrance waiting for her. She smiled at our cooperation. Silently, she motioned for us to follow her. We walked in silence to the eating dorm, and she seated us at the youth's table just as the boys entered following Sir Masuda. With permission from Lady Catherine, I slipped out, brought Kate her breakfast, and hurried back.

Daniel and Dermid sat downside by side on my left, and Jessie plopped down on my right, to Rowsheen's disappointment, for she always wished to sit by me and Kate, and I knew their intention. Two masters emerged from the kitchen with more trays covered with bowls of porridge and began placing them before us. Sir Masuda prayed; we all stood in reverence. Daniel began to stir his porridge and leaned over to whisper, "Did she like the flowers?"

"She did," I whispered back with a smile. Daniel blushed, turning his whole head red.

The porridge was warm and sweet on my tongue and a little sticky. It also had berries and nuts in it.

"What are you guys talking about?" Dermid mumbled with a mouth full of porridge.

I turned to Daniel, "Does he know?"

Daniel shook his head, "He thinks you're my half-sister," Daniel replied.

"Oh, that makes a lot of sense," I reasoned sarcastically, "Why didn't you say cousin? It would have made more sense."

"Yes, but I have a family history of cousin marriages, and he knows it." Daniel explained to me, "And he would have got the wrong idea."

"Whatever you say," I replied with a smile, shaking my head before I dug into my hot porridge.

After breakfast, we were led to the training hall. Sir Masuda demonstrated several fighting techniques that we would be learning, and the other masters each had a class for us to attend, including Lady Catherine. Her class was mostly on strategy and balance.

We stood on bamboo poles that were a foot above the ground. It was surprisingly hard. Afterwards, we were taken on a long hike with weighted packs. Kate's ankle prevented her from walking, but Sir Masuda let her fly above us, so she was still able to attend the training. The pack was heavy but not nearly as heavy as the packs Honeysuckle had made me carry when he took me hiking and climbing at home, so I barely noticed its presence and sucked in the beauty of the mountainous forest.

Kate soared above me, looking down from above the tall, ancient, moss-laden trees, and would stop every now and again to rest in some branches. I knew this was her first time flying with so much weight on her back. Being already on top of a mountain, the hike was mostly along the mountain ridge, making the hike more comfortable, but some of the children appeared to be struggling with the amount of weight they were given based on their size.

After a few hours, I too was beginning to feel the weight and every rest felt relieving. By this time, I had made my way to the front of the line behind Daniel and Sir Masuda. Dermid was behind making sure I knew that his every body part was in pain. Dermid was continuing to whine to me, but making sure he was not loud enough for Sir Masuda to hear.

"Give me that!" I said, turning around and facing him, "If you're hurting so bad, I'll carry it for a little while."

Dermid looked past me in the direction of Daniel and Sir Masuda.

"They won't see," I reassured him, "They gave me less weight anyway. I can take it."

"No thanks," he mumbled, pulling the pack securely up on his shoulders and trudging on ahead of me.

"That sure made him stop complaining," Jessie laughed, moving in front of me. The pack did not seem to bother him at all. Mine was beginning to wear on me.

"Your ears work too good," I replied, stopping for a short break on a large, moss-covered rock by the path.

"My specialty, but to be blunt, I don't think you could have carried his and yours," he replied, leaning his back against a tall tree on the side of the path, "you're tough, I'll give you that. I know you'd try, though."

"I didn't think he'd say, yes, but you're right, it would've been too heavy for me," I admitted, rubbing my sweaty, sore neck.

"We all have our pride, don't we?" he replied, offering me his hand to pull me up.

"Yes, very true," I said, taking his hand. With what seemed like an effortless yank, he had me on my feet.

About an hour later, we stopped walking, having caught up with Daniel, Dermid, and Sir Masuda. They were at a mountain peak resting on rocks close to the cliffs. The view was gorgeous, overlooking the mountain green ridges and a great stream below. The cliff lookout was sheer rock with streaks of pink crystal.

The view of the mountain range almost took my breath away with a fluffy rug blanket of trees draped happily over it. I smiled and relaxed my shoulders. It was a relief to have the weight off my back and rest my sore feet. The breeze softly kissed my face and melted the stress away.

A moment later, Kate swooshed down, limped over to us, and sat down in silence. I walked to the cliff edge and gazed over the jutting, jagged rock face below. I felt excited and terrified at the same time. We rested there in silence, gazing over the view until every youth had caught up and rested.

When Sir Masuda saw that we were all present, he motioned us to draw near in a ring facing the rock cliff where he stood.

"Children, I would like to tell you a story with a hidden meaning," he said, standing tall with his hands behind his back and walking around us, "and you will be charged with telling me that meaning before nightfall. If you all fail, we will do this hike again tomorrow with double the weight."

My heart sank. Would we be able to figure it out?

"The moon gave off an eerie glow,

A man walked home in knee-deep snow,

Another man appeared at his side,

Strong was his head and long was his stride,

"Where are you headed?"

The first asked the second,

"I am going to the stars,"

Come with me he beckoned

"Thank you, but no."

"I am going home,"

Away to the stars

Would feel as bars,"

The first man walked home, and to his surprise, where his house had stood was a castle that reached to the skies,

The second man appeared once again at his side, with a smile on him quite wide, his white teeth he spied,

"This could be yours," he purred and hissed,

As he blew at the surrounding mist,

"Forgive, but no. My house was enough,

It was plain and a mite tad rough,

But it was mine to come home each day,

And enough to see my children laugh and play,

I know who you are, now please leave me.

Goodbye.

I focused hard on his words, trying to find the answer I thought he wanted because we could only give one answer each. We spoke amongst each other as we walked back to the children's dorms, weary of walking and longing for sleep. Ten children had already turned in false answers, and we prayed that someone would give him a correct answer during our regular dorm and courtyard classes on history, battle tactics, wound care, and sword fighting.

Daniel and I had puzzled and discussed the story on the journey back to the training ground, if that's what I'm allowed to call it, and together we decided on three things that the answer could be: the importance of prudence, the importance of a close walk with God, or the importance of contentment. Lady Catherine ushered the girls down a trail to the washing pool when we returned.

The water was illuminated by the early moonlight and warm from the day's hot sun. My whole body ached as I slipped into the water and looked up at the stars. I nearly fell asleep. What could the answer be?

The next morning, I slipped off my cot and dressed. Outside, the early twilight rays were beginning to lace the horizon, chasing away the shadows from their midnight play. Everyone was still asleep, exhausted from yesterday's hike. Well, everyone except Rowsheen, who was not on her cot. I slipped on my brown leather boots and made my cot up. I thought that Rowsheen might have gone on a morning run, so I slipped out of the children's dorms and tiptoed through the courtyard.

The courtyard was empty, or so I thought. I looked around until I was sure that Rowsheen was not there and decided to amuse myself with the fishpond in the center of the flower gardens. The water was clear and cold, full of tiny fish, leaves, and flower petals. I longed for something fun to entertain myself.

"Morning, child," the voice of master Masuda sounded behind me. I jumped.

"Good morning, Master," I replied, overcoming my shock.

"Do you have an answer for me, child?" he asked me to sit down on a large boulder.

"I have several that I have entertained for a time, but I'm not sure," I answered.

"Go ahead and give me the one you think is most likely," he urged.

"Contentment is hard to come by and difficult to maintain," I answered.

"Very good, but I would also add that everything will try to take that contentment from you and keep it from you," he replied.

"Does this mean that we won't have to hike again today?" I asked.

"Yes, you won't have to hike again today, but I sense that you don't deem this as much of an award," he replied.

"I do love to hike," I replied, dreamily pondering the memories of my father and me trudging up a mountainside. I was quite proud that my father took me on the adventures with him, "My father enjoyed it."

"Hiking is a good pastime," he said, turning to go with a smile, "I sense you will do well here. Keep a smile on your face."

A few minutes later, Rowsheen entered the courtyard panting from her early morning exercise. "Rowsheen," I called. Her cheeks were red and her hair wet with sweat, sticking to her cheeks.

"Yes," Rowsheen answered breathless, wiping sweat from her hot face.

"We don't have to hike today," I replied with a smile, walking in her direction, so I did not have to shout.

"You won't believe what I saw," Rowsheen exclaimed, her eyes wide and with a face full of excitement.

"What did you see?" I asked with a laugh. My heart was happy, and I felt a joy and sense of pride welling up inside me.

"A big, fat, wild hog with great tusks and black bristles," Rowsheen answered, spreading her arms wide to show the size.

"What did you do?" I asked, wondering if she had challenged it to a running race.

"I climbed a tree and waited for a while. It was so big! I thought it was going to tear me to bits!" she answered, "I've been up for hours. One of the masters let me help with breakfast."

"Wow, I'm glad you're okay," I answered, almost concerned, I knew if anyone would survive a wild animal, it would be Rowsheen, "I wish I saw it. We could have had some bacon."

Rowsheen, Kate, and I had a time trying to memorize all the new training techniques Lady Catherine and Sir Masuda had for us. Standing in the open courtyard, we practiced over and over again till we all collapsed in the cool, soft, green grass. When I finally rolled onto my stiff cot that night and listened to the wind blowing the trees in the courtyard, every muscle in my body was sore and tense; I was trying to relax them. I closed my eyes and breathed deeply. Slowly, I would slip off to sleep.

While I slept, I encountered a horrific dream. Five paces from me sat the place of worship, our church illuminated by an eerie orange light. I stood calf deep in black water; everything except the orange light was black, including the sky, the water, and the surrounding area. The water was full of dead creatures of every kind, revealed only by the reflection of the orange light that came from nowhere.

Many of the creatures are beyond my description, but I will relay the two that I remember. The first was a horse with legs like a whale's fins that were broken off, and the second was a massive head that dwarfed even the greatest giant with massive teeth. I awoke to the dark dorm and looked around as my eyes adjusted so I could make out the outlines of objects.

The dream troubled me greatly so that I was at a loss to fall back asleep. I rose softly from my cot, dressed, grabbed my diary, and walked out of the child's dorm into the training dorm. A soft early light shone from the moon to light my way. Upon entering, I pulled a candle from the high shelf by the entrance and lit it with a match.

With the candle, I walked out of the dorms, looking back to see if Lady Catherine had heard me, and started down the mountain trail to the cliff. I reached the cliff in under ten minutes, sat down on the rough rock, opened my diary, and began to pray. When I finished praying, I began to write down my dream. I heard nothing, but I felt someone approach. I turned to see Sir Masuda walking gracefully in my direction. I looked up but didn't close my diary.

"Something troubling you, my student?" he asked, and continued after noticing my open diary, "Well, there's no better cure than prayer on a mountain top," he said, looking off into the distance.

"How did you know I was praying?" I asked with a curious look on my face as I sat cross-legged on the cold, smooth, rocky ground.

"You're at peace," he replied, "I can see it in your face and in your actions. Did you not know I was coming when I made no sound?"

"Somehow I felt it," I answered thoughtfully, gazing off into the misty mountain range bathed in soft twilight rays.

"With prayer comes peace," he replied simply, easing himself to the ground a pace from me, "Sometimes it takes a lot of prayer. So, what has troubled you to come out here to pray?"

"I've been having dreams that confuse and concern me to some degree," I explained, "but prayer has certainly helped me to clear my head."

"And where do these dreams come from?" he reasoned.

"I'm not sure, I suppose. Part of me wonders if they're signs of something important, but I don't know what. And I've thought it could be fear and worry," I replied thoughtfully, sharing my fears, "I just don't know."

"And where does the fear and worry come from?" he asked thoughtfully.

"Not knowing what will happen," I concluded after pausing for a moment, "not knowing and being afraid of every possible outcome."

"And why does the future concern you?" he asked, and replied, "Because you wish to know? Only God knows. Do you trust him?"

"Yes, I suppose so," I replied with a look of guilt covering my face, and my head dropped.

"My Dear, trust in God takes time. Doubt is normal, but we mustn't stay there. We must pray and seek him all the more when worry comes, and then leave it in His hands. No amount of worry can change anything that is destined to happen," he replied.

I nodded, knowing he was right. Worry won't change anything; it would only seek to trouble me and distrust God.

"How should I go about curing myself?" I asked eagerly, awaiting his reply.

"Try meditating with a candle at least once a day, and while you meditate, pray and seek His face," he suggested, raising to his feet, "Now come, let's get back before the moon sinks and the sun rises."

"Yes, sir, thank you," I replied graciously, standing and following his quiet figure down the path in the moonlight. He didn't answer me, but I knew he could feel my gratitude. I would certainly try meditating and praying more.

Chapter 16:
A Deadly Bite

New children were arriving daily, and I was at a loss trying to stay with Kate and Rowsheen. The moon became my friend as I talked to it at night, as its bright rays often kept me up at night. Daily, I met new children, but the more I met, the more I longed for home.

The morning was not a training day but Sunday. The first Sunday I was there. We were permitted to wear our regular clothes to chapel, instead of our training outfits. It felt comforting to be once again in my own clothes.

There were many new children at the chapel meeting. A boy named Liam and a girl named Libby, twins from Besanti Argema, introduced themselves to me. I asked them where Besanti Argema was; they told me that Besanti Argema was close to Mossland to the Southwest.

Libby and I got along well. She had dark brown hair, light brown eyes, and fair skin. She was smaller than me in nearly every aspect. Libby liked to talk rather than work and hated the outdoor activities, but seemed as if she was glued to me, trying to survive every day.

Liam was often away with the boys, but always found the time to speak to me each day, and that surprised me because I seemed like an unlikely person to spark his interest. He had dark brown hair and eyes. He was a few inches taller than Dermid. One thing about him that impressed me, if anything at all, was the fact that he was excellent at training and fit.

Daniel had given me more flowers for Rowsheen as the boys passed the girls on the way into the dorms last night. I slipped them beneath my cloak and kept them hidden until I was sure she was asleep. The flowers he handed me were red fairy hair.

As I lay there pondering the events of the day, I fell into a deep sleep and encountered a dream that puzzled me. I stood in a great hall bedecked in fine blue curtains, marble pillars, granite floors, high ceilings, and large paintings. I was dressed in a long red gown and was holding Honeysuckle's hand, looking up at his furry head. The great door on the back wall opened, presenting a finely dressed man and child. They walked toward us and bowed in reverence as we drew near. Honeysuckle bowed, and I curtsied.

"So, this is the child," the man said, looking down at me and then to the boy, "this is Stephen. Stephen, this is Aoife."

"Nice to meet you, Stephen," I said politely with a smile.

"Pleasure to meet you, Aoife," he replied. I noted that the boy was taller than me, with kind eyes and light hair.

Honeysuckle looked at the man and said, "How long?"

The man looked at us children and said, "Stephen, why don't you show Aoife the garden.

I'm sure she'll love the pond lilies."

Stephen offered me his arm, and right as we were leaving, the man said, "How old is she?"

"Nine years," was Honeysuckle's reply.

"Then, when she is eighteen, it will begin," the man replied.

"So, it shall, and how old will he be?" Honeysuckle asked.

"Twenty-one. The perfect age for a King to begin ruling and have a lovely Queen at his side," his voice wavered out of my hearing as Stephen and I walked through the great door.

With that, I awoke pondering how confusing the dream had been and how real it had felt, almost memory like. And the boy, he looked so familiar. I turned over and drifted off to sleep once more.

It was still twilight when I woke up early and lay upon my bed in the pale light, not able to fall once again into sleep. There was something on the windowsill pocking out from beneath the silk curtain. I sat up, shivered from the cool morning, reached the object, and pulled it out from beneath the curtain. It was a lace-wrapped bouquet of fire daisies. I examined the bundle closely. There was a label around the lace band. I pulled back the curtain so I could try and make out the name. It was my name. My full name. No one knew my full name, save my adopted father, Honeysuckle. And that was not all. Attached to the label was a silver necklace with a ruby-embellished cross pendant, and the note read: To my Princess, Aoife Catherine McKelvey Beairclen.

The gift puzzled me; I didn't know what to think about it. Clasping the latch on the necklace and letting the pretty piece hang, I smelled the flowers and felt their soft petals on my cheek. I heard the swish and creak of someone rolling over and quickly slipped the necklace into the neck of my night gown. The gift flattered me, making me smile all over. What would the day hold?

We filed one after another into the training dorm. The dorm had been cleared for the Sunday devotion. We sat down on the wood floors, as directed, facing the master Joshua Matapang, the highest master of the training ground.

I was seated against the wall behind Rowsheen and Kate. We were listening to his devotion on Daniel chapter 1. The chapter was about Daniel and his friends in a foreign land, where they continued to serve God despite facing negative influences. God blessed them for their obedience by granting them great wisdom and understanding. I pulled my diary from my pocket and wrote down what the devotion was about, then looked at my new necklace. It glistened in the light from the open window; I quickly returned it to my hiding place. I marked the chapter in my bible.

My D3 diary, 05/15/34,

Devotion 1, Daniel chapter 1, Always serve God. Serve God despite the pressure of the world, even if the pressures come from friends or peers.

We were told that we mustn't work, but we were allowed to play as long as we stayed in groups. I decided to find a nice tree and take a nap in its shade as soon as I heard it. I was tired from not sleeping well. At home, Honeysuckle made my cousins and me take naps on Sundays. We would all find a tree together and curl up beneath it. I missed my bear cousins; they could be irritating at times, but I loved them dearly.

Kate wanted to knit, Rowsheen had a book she was dying to devour, and Libby was content to do whatever I was doing, so I suggested we find a shade tree for all of our projects. We finally selected a large magnolia close to the south stream, a ways down the trail to the bathing pool. We all gathered our items of interest and started for the shady trail on the wood line.

"Eeefaaa," Libby whined, clutching her blanket as we strolled to the trail.

"Yes, Libby," I answered, rubbing my eyes. My boots seemed heavy, and I couldn't wait to take them off and rest.

"Are there wild animals in there?" she said, looking suspiciously at the wood line.

I looked into the sparse brush around the trees and sighed. It would take time for Libby to learn about the outdoors. I softly and gently explained that I could see for a long time through the trees due to most of the underbrush being cleared regularly. I also explained that there shouldn't be many wild animals due to the number of beings in the area.

"Maybe a few, but they shouldn't bother us," I added, lifting my bag to my shoulder.

Kate gave me a look, rolled her eyes, and gave her wings a rustle before disappearing into the shaded trail behind Rowsheen. She did not prefer kids who did not know their way around wildlife, and Libby's whiny voice got on her nerves. Unlike Libby, the rest of us girls had grown up in a forest and were accustomed to working hard.

"Okay," Libby said, taking a deep breath and hooking my arm.

We walked down the trail. I felt a responsibility to make sure Libby stayed safe because she had no one except her brother, Liam, who seemed too busy to care for his sister, who knew nothing of the outdoors. In a few minutes, we had made it to the beautiful, dark magnolia beside the trail. Great, old leaves were scattered on the ground, leaving a crispy carpet.

Kate, Rowsheen, and I kicked the leaves to scare away any snakes before we settled down. I laid my soft brown leather roll on the ground and unclipped my side bag before lying down on my crunchy bed. Rowsheen and Kate rested their backs against the tree and began their pleasure tasks. Libby laid her blanket beside mine, copying my motions before lying down. She rolled a time or two before lying still on her blue and orange patterned quilt. I drifted off into a deep sleep, weary from my long week.

While I slept, I fell into a vivid, enticing dream. A lone, swift rider rode through the driving rain on an inky night across a tree-spotted plane. He was clad in dark brown and red, and kept looking over his shoulder. A long sword dangled at his side beneath his long cloak as his dark, wet stallion ran on.

The man kept one hand on the reins and one hand cradling a bundle close to his heart. On and on the stallion rode until they reached a small, dimly lit town. The stallion breathed hard, and his breath was visible as steam from a boiling pot.

The rider rode slowly through the sleeping town past the main street and many homes until coming to a humble inn that was grey and quiet. As soon as the rider stopped, a man and a woman emerged from the inn in silence. The man's torch illuminated the rider's face; it was tan, wet, and bloody.

The rider was young, no more than twenty, and his countenance was rough. His hair was light brown and fell to his shoulders, half tied back and half covering his face. His eyes were a greyish green, and his nose was tall.

The woman extended her arms gracefully toward the bundle, and the rider placed it in her arms. Then she disappeared into the inn. The man held the reins as the rider dismounted. The man motioned for the rider to follow the woman inside and led the sweaty, tired horse to the stables. Inside, the rider ate and rested.

The bundle the women tended was a baby, and she fed it and rocked it to sleep by a large fire. The woman was clad in a soft red dress with a blue and white flowered apron over the top. Her black hair was tied up, and her soft, light brown eyes gazed with a smile at the sleeping baby in her arms. The woman rocked the baby in a chair by the fire. The firelight softly illuminated the scene. The baby stretched and yawned. The baby had soft blue eyes and a soft fuzz of red hair.

In an hour's time, another rider appeared in front of the inn, but instead of seeing the rider, the man motioned for him to wait for a time. The man woke the first rider, who collected the sleeping baby and walked to the second rider, who was hiding in the shade of the barn, where the faint moonlight couldn't reach him.

"Larry," The first rider addressed the second, "Be fast, we haven't much time."

"Of course," the second rider answered, "I'll be there before sundown tomorrow and you'll meet us."

"No, just get there and leave," the first rider ordered. "I'll meet up with you when I can. Just stay the course."

"As you wish," the second rider whispered, taking the bundle and mounting his horse.

Slowly, the second rider rode off, only riding fast when he was far out of the town, riding off into the dark trails. With that, I awoke and gasped.

A long, green snake lay on my chest, staring into my face. He felt my body heat radiating from me. Slowly, I reached toward its triangular head and grabbed it tight. I did not snatch it fast enough. The snake slithered forward and sank its fangs into my throat. I pulled the wiggling snake off my neck and held it tight, breathing hard.

I coiled up its long body, but by then the noise had reached Libby beside me, who let out a horrified scream, but she wasn't screaming at the snake. Around me in an outline was a ring of black, bloody arrows. Kate and Rowsheen jumped up and ran to our aid. Kate took the snake from me, and Rowsheen tried to help me stand. I shook from head to foot, quivering like a great bag of water. My eyelids rolled shut as I collapsed within the ring of arrows. My world went cold and black.

Chapter 17:
Time, Time, A Friend of Mine

A darkness met my cold eyes as I awoke. I was lying in a few inches of water, still in my leisure attire. My neck ached, feeling stiff and cold as if it were foreign to my whole self. My whole body ached to move. I was frightened. Trying at last to sit up, I just sank back down and cried.

"Aoife, hold still. Don't move about," a voice ordered, sounding authoritative, but coldly unfamiliar to my ears as I sought a familiar sound. I tried to open my mouth to reply, but no sound came. I felt some more warm water pouring over my limp self.

"You will heal if you rest," the voice assured me, "It will take time, and you must be patient."

"What was wrong with my eyes? My mouth? My body?" my mind questioned, drifting off into an uneasy sleep.

The next few days, or as I was told, I was unconscious. The warm water bath they had placed me in contained crystals, herbs, and minerals that were believed would draw the poison from one's veins. When my eyes began to work, objects appeared fuzzy, and a great deal blurred, so much so that it made me sick to keep my eyes open for any length of time. The viper that bit me was a basilikgon; a vicious and dangerous serpent when provoked, indigenous to the island's forests and waterways.

After one week, I had regained most of my bodily functions and was allowed to once again attend Lady Catherine's classes. I found it ever difficult to balance, and practiced long and hard to keep up with the rest of the girls in a class that I had once found to be effortless. Kate and Rowsheen were ever ready to assist me in any way I needed help, but I graciously refused, knowing that I needed to get better, and the only way to do that was to retrain my body to do what it had forgotten. I did, however, begin to truly excel in her class on strategy, for I had to

Find smart ways to outmaneuver my opponents, where my balance and once commendable strength failed me.

"Aoife, Child," Lady Catherine addressed me one day during a short recess, "you are commendable at strategy; I have a few books I would like you to read in your spare time."

"Yes, ma'am," I replied, looking up into her face with earnest. I was not sure; I would even be able to read for with the balance problems from the snake bite, which had also come with a blurry vision when focusing on something up close.

Lying out a board on the courtyard ground, when the day was nearly over, I tried to walk a straight line. More often than not, while I tried to balance, I succeeded in falling on my face, but I continued, and day by day, I could see improvement. Kate and Rowsheen were ever there to help me if I required aid.

"You're almost there," Kate exclaimed, standing on the tip of the board to hold it down. From where I stood, she was merely a blurry grey and blue blob in the distance.

"You mean I'm almost here?" I replied, reaching the end where she stood. Turning around, I began to walk back down to Rowsheen, who stood on the other end. "Keep coming. Keep coming. Steady," Rowsheen directed as I stepped onward, heel over toe, heel over toe.

"What's going on here, walking practice?" Jessie teased, strolling over to where we were in his sweaty, soiled, black training clothes and plopping himself on the ground cross-legged, as if to stay and watch.

"Jessie," Dermid called, walking out of the boy's dorms with a long, wet, dingy rag over his head, "Where are you!"

"I'm over here, towel head," Jessie teased, waving his sunburned arm above his head.

"What are you doing?" Dermid asked Jessie, walking over to join us.

"Yeah, what are you doing?" Kate echoed, trying to get him to leave while watching my wobbling steps.

"Nothing at all," Jessie replied, lying back onto the grass.

"Oh sure," Dermid replied, wiping his towel across his tanned forehead to remove the beads of sweat that dripped down into his bushy eyebrows.

"Aoife," Jessie said, addressing me sitting up, "I think you should try a different form of rehabilitation."

"Rehabili… what?" Dermid asked, making his eyes squint. Jessie ignored Dermid.

"I'm all ears," I replied, stepping off the board and sinking down to the grass.

"I think you should try sword fighting with footwork," he replied, getting up on his feet. His hands and legs were covered in grass clippings.

"I'd need a teacher," I replied, standing and brushing a greenish-grey grasshopper off my training clothes. The lush green grass of the courtyard felt comforting to my hands as I sat down. I was weary from a rest. My head often hurt, and it was hard to stand at times. I felt fatigued and anxious.

"Say no more," Jessie replied, taking off towards the training room.

"Where is he going now?" Dermid whined, plopping himself down, "I just found him."

Jessie returned presently with two wooden swords and began to demonstrate. Step by step, I followed his moves to the best of my ability. I then repeated them thrice more till I did them to his satisfaction. Kate and Rowsheen stayed, watching with critical eyes. Dermid stayed to watch Jessie and make sure he was doing it right. Slowly, but surely, my feet began to remember the steps, but I was far from regaining my full balance and strength.

When I could finally walk a straight line, I began to get better at my sword-fighting footwork. I tried balancing on the knee-high stone wall just outside the training base to test how good I was. I continued this balance practice daily at the end of the day when my whole body was shaky from training and my brain was foggy from lectures. Each night, I collapsed on my bed in prayer and poured my heart out to the Lord for healing. I would be healed and be the best soldier in the army yet, I told myself through tears.

For weeks, my throat was swollen and tied tight in a white, cotton badge. The bite oozed pus and a mucous-like substance, so that I had to change the bandage thrice a day. Surviving the deadly bite, I was very lucky. The poison killed the skin tissue where the fangs had sunk in, resulting in two nasty, purplish-white scars that I feared would stay with me for life.

Chapter 18:
Rain, More Rain

Rowsheen Diary entry:

The training has been tough, Dad, but I'm really enjoying my time here. I really made Aoife irritated the other day. Someone gave me a cup of tea from the kitchen. It wasn't a tea I was used to. I was full of energy and wouldn't stop talking to her. Aoife is very hard to irritate, and somehow, I figured it out. In a way, I think she enjoyed being irritated since she was always surrounded by her sibling cubs. I guess there is not much to say at present, dear Dad. The other day, our teacher decided that we needed to learn how to get out of quicksand. You should have seen Dermid's face when he began to sink. I thought he was going to scream. He was terrified. It was even funnier watching Dermid try to pull Daniel out. He heaved and heaved, and Daniel was just as calm and patient as he could be. I'll write to you soon, Dad. Love your Rowsheen.

Description from Aoife:

The day was cool and damp when we started our wilderness survival test. Groups of four randomly selected children were chosen and sent to different parts of the island. The only two things that the masters made sure of were that there were at least two girls and two boys, or all boys, since the number of boys was greater than that of the girls.

Libby clung to me harder than ever and followed my every move. Everywhere I stepped, water seeped up around my boots. The bite on my neck was getting better, but I still bumped into trees once in a while and stumbled often. Daniel and Dermid were sent with Rowsheen and Kate, while Libby and I were sent with Liam and Jessie. We started out for the falls on Ledford's cliff about two miles East of the training grounds.

The test was a one-night survival in the wild. To pass this test, we had to meet several requirements: build a fire, find/build a shelter, catch, cook, and eat wild game, and make the long trek to Jem's Peak.

Jessie and I wanted to find a cave to use as shelter due to the coming rain, but Liam insisted on a spot in the woods.

"If it rains, we'll need a cave!" Jessie whined to Liam, standing up straight to make himself taller than Liam.

"I agree, a cave'll keep us dry," I insisted, stepping beside Jessie, showing him that I look at Jessie's side. I put my hands on my hips and stood tall.

"A shelter in the woods would make us look more ambitious," Liam reasoned, trying to sound wiser.

"WE'LL LOOK STUPID WHEN IT RAINS!!!" Jessie yelled, pointing to the dark rain clouds hovering over the treetops, "I'LL LOOK LIKE A DROWNED RAT!!!! YES, I'M WAKING UP THE WHOLE FOREST. I DON'T CARE!!! I'M MAKING MY POINT!!!"

We plugged our ears.

"Liam," I said quietly but firmly, "It looks like it's going to rain in the next few hours. I know that you're good at building shelters in the woods, but perhaps we can do it another time. There is the possibility of us getting hypothermia if we get wet and cold. Also, a fire is going to be nigh impossible in the rain, but easier in a cave. In case of better weather, you have the upper hand with survival, and I commend you on your drive to succeed."

"Okay, don't lose your grey whiskers, Jessie," Liam replied with a snicker, "We'll find a cave."

"WHAT GREY WHISKERS!!! Jessie loudly replied, standing on his tiptoes, staring hard into Liam's annoyed face.

"What if we set up our camp beside a cave and make a shelter to show that we thought ahead," I reasoned with a sigh. My pack was already seeming heavy.

"Good idea," Jessie replied, patting me on the shoulder, "let's do that."

"Hey, Liam," Jessie said, tugging on his shirt sleeve, "Let's do that. Please, Please, Pleasssseeee.."

"Okay, Jess," Liam replied, with a shrug, "You take the girls and find a cave by the cliffs, but make sure we're close to the waterfall; we'll need the water."

"Let's go… wait a second, what are you gonna do?" Jessie asked, suspiciously crinkling up his nose, as proved to be his usual habit.

"I'm going hunting," Liam answered, starting off into the brush.

"But how will you find us?" Libby frantically whined in terror.

"I should be able to find you and Jess anywhere," Liam reasoned, looking at Libby and Jessie. "Aoife, do you have everything under control, or do you want me to stay awhile?" He asked, looking at Libby and Jessie and then giving me a questioning look.

"Am I a child?" Jessie whined, sensing that Liam trusted me more than him.

"We've got it, thank you," I replied, wishing that Liam would give Jessie more respect. Jessie knew what he was doing in the wild, and I knew it well. He was also a lot more agile than I, especially since my snake bite.

Liam disappeared into the brush. Libby looped her arm in mine and looked up at me.

"You do have everything under control, don't you?" Libby said, taking a long, deep breath as though she were trying to anchor her trust in me.

"We all have everything under control," I replied, looking at Jessie so he could catch every word, "And Jessie's in charge anyway. Jessie, you're the expert tracker. You want to find us that cave?"

"Right this way," Jessie replied with a bow. Jessie held his head high, grateful for my confidence in his abilities. I pulled my cloak closer. The clouds had already blocked the sun, sending a shiver down my spine.

There were no trails for intelligent beings in these woods, so we took elk, deer, and well-trodden hog trails to the cliffs about a mile to our south. It took us around an hour to reach the cliffs through the woods. It was a long drop down a sleek, sharp rock face into white, frothy rapids below. We stood looking down for a while, thinking through the best plan for finding a cave.

Jessie grabbed my arm and pulled me a ways from the terrified Libby, and spoke in whispers, "There is no way we're getting all of us down there to search for a cave, and if we found one, even a good one, we couldn't get her down there. The clouds are rolling in fast, and Liam will be looking for our smoke signal. We can go upstream and see if the cliff drops down, or we can search the boulders on the cliff's edges for a cave."

"How much time have we got before the rain starts pouring?" I asked Jessie. I trusted his opinion on the matter.

"A few hours at best, and we've got four hours till sunset if the rain doesn't start," Jessie approximated, studying the sky.

The look of the dark purple clouds above the tree line frightened me a bit. The wind blew softly and innocently across my face, *"The still before the storm,"* my brain screamed within me.

"I think going upstream and finding a cave close to the water would be best, but do you think we should chance it?" I asked with a questioning, concerned look.

"I think we should," Jessie replied, with a nod.

"Alright," I whispered, turning to walk to Libby. Libby was huddled on the ground with her head between her knees. Libby was very book smart and capable in a king's court, but not terribly outdoors smart or brave.

"Come now, Libby, we are going to find a nice, dry cave before the rain starts," I said with a smile, extending my hand.

"Okay, Aoife, you know best," she said, taking my hand and pulling herself up. She seemed to trust my opinion.

We walked on through the unforgiving, mangled brush for an hour more. The sun began to dip in the sky. As we walked, the cliffs became higher and the gorge became less deep as if it was rising slowly to meet us in warm greeting. We came to a large waterfall arrayed in a thick, foggy gown with steep, rugged, rock bodyguards on either side of her. Moss and vines hung thick on the tall rocks, cloaking her bodyguards in a wet, green, velvet coat.

"I'm sure this is a great place to make camp," Jessie exclaimed, peering down the cliff into the frothy water below. "I'm going down," he declared, studying the edge for footholds.

"Come, Libby. Let us prepare for the night." I said, motioning her towards the thick, unfriendly woods.

"Coming," she whispered, catching up with me. "Let's get this over with."

I looked back to see Jessie's sturdy figure disappear over the edge. Libby and I gathered limbs and dry brush for a fire, tied bundles together, and carried them to the cliff. The sun was sinking fast as Libby and I finished gathering brush and wood for our camp.

Libby helped me pile wood for the fire in silence. I had carried a small bundle of dry grass and a couple of pinecones to help me make a fire. It had been hard for us to find dry wood from all the wet ground, but we had managed to find enough that was somewhat dry. Softly, I took a deep breath and prayed before I struck my steel and flint for a spark. I had to repeat several times until I got a tiny catch. Softly, I blew upon the tiny flame until the grass had caught, then I fed it to my small sticks and pinecones and blew and blew until my head spun, but I had a fire.

Libby was seated on the rock beside me, tying strips of linen onto long poles for torches. We worked to tie bundles of wood and small limbs together and finished the torches. She had made eight already when Jessie popped his head up over the cliff and scrambled over.

"Found an overhang with a cave. How's everything coming along?" Jessie asked, quite out of breath from his climb.

"Well, we've got the wood and fire," I replied softly. The anxiety lessened when I was working with my hands, and I felt a little better.

"Love the fire," Jessie shivered through his teeth, hanging over the bright flames. His copper armor gleamed in the orange light. The firelight glistened on the beads of sweat dripping down his face and glued his bangs to his cheeks. He looked relieved to be back and have the fire to get warm. Even though it was cool out, I knew that the sweat was due to the hard climb.

"I'm taking supplies down, Aoife. I could use help." He said, looking at me with a questioning look through his shaggy, dark, brown hair that had worked its way loose from his black tie band.

"I'll help," I replied, looking at Libby, who was finishing a torch. She didn't complain, so I stood and helped Jessie decide how many bundles we could hold.

One bundle at a time, we tied together into larger bundles that each of us would carry down. Three bundles had been assigned to me. Jessie lifted my bundle so I could slip my arms into the loops. We also took torches to light our way. The sound of rushing water was almost all I could hear.

Jessie shone the torch down the cliff and showed me the course we'd be taking; it wound this way and that down the steep cliff before making it to its final destination. Jessie stepped down firmly and helped me down the first large step, holding my hand in a firm grip. I gripped the slippery, rough rock wall with one nervous, shaky hand, while Jessie held our flaming torches to light the way.

We made our way slowly down, ensuring that every step was sure. I slipped twice, but Jessie planted his heavy boot on mine just in time to stop me. When we finally reached the overhang, water was beginning to fall. The overhang was low, not enough to even stand on one's knees, and the cave went deep into the cliff. We took off our bundles and quickly formed a fire with one of the torches. I held the torch toward the cave so I could see a small portion of the deep cave. Quickly, me and Jessie pulled off our bedding from under our cloaks and placed them back in the cave. The fire burned brightly as we warmed our hands.

We had to start back up the cliff for Libby, but the torch wouldn't last long in the coming rain, so we would have to feel our way in the dim light. We started up the steep ridge, climbing over boulders and reaching for handholds. When we had made it about three-quarters of the way up the ridged rocks, rain started to fall heavily upon us. Not even our good cloaks kept it all off.

We went even slower. The water was running down the cliff side, now pooling in our rough path.

Despite the predicament, Jessie seemed to be in good spirits, clinging to the cliff wall behind me.

He started to sing a dancing song that our parents danced to during holidays called 'Life is Only a Past-Time'. It reminded me of home, watching the grown bears of the clan dance in harmony and wishing that someday I too would have a chance to join them.

I could see the happy blaze of firelight from the sweet old memory and smell the fresh scent of evergreen from the happy fir trees overhead and the whining of the Sweet Whistle being played by my Uncle Furey. I was a mixture of happy, content, and sorrowful at the same time, a feeling that Honeysuckle called 'wind' because you weren't sure where it came from, how to help it, or if it needed anything at all to be done about it. I longed for Honeysuckle's great furry arms and the strong scent and sweet taste of his wild honey.

"Sing my Lady, dance with me,

In the rain, under yonder tree,

Forget your woes, forget the time,

Life is only a pastime,

(I joined in, trying hard not to fill my mouth with water.)

Sing my Laddie, dance with me,

In the rain, under yonder tree,

Stay all day, stay all night,

Stay till the moon bears blue light,

Life is but a passing star,

Way away, Far, Far, Stay here where we are,

My little rose of wonder.

Sing my Lady, dance with me, (Me and Jessie stopped singing and stood still. Another person was singing with us, and the person continued.)

In the rain, under yonder tree, (It was a low, sweet voice.)

A dark figure was coming down the trail toward us and stopped in front of me. It was Liam with Libby hanging over his shoulder, wrapped in a wet cloak.

"You stopped singing," he said playfully.

"I GOT A SHELTER!!!" Jessie yelled through the driving rain with water running down the tip of his nose and face not fully covered by his cloak.

Another pour of water gushed over us. I quickly latched onto the rock wall; the handholds I could find were slick and sharp.

"So, I hear," Liam replied with a laugh, "I got dinner." His wet hair hung matted, and water dripped down his golly countenance as he spoke.

"Can we just get out of this rain?" Libby's muffled voice pleaded from somewhere within the dark bundle draped over Liam's shoulders.

Jessie turned around and we sloshed back to the overhang. All the water was finally beginning to seep through my thick headbricker cloak and dampen my padded, steel armor.

Jessie climbed into the overhang first on his hands and crawled to the far side so we all could fit. I followed his lead. Liam bent down and pushed the wet bundle of Libby in front of him before crawling in himself. I started unwrapping Libby. Surprisingly, she was not as wet as I had thought she would be, but she was shivering and pale from her trip down the cliffside.

"Look what I got," Liam said, reaching into his drenched cloak. He pulled out a large skinned scea (A bird native to the island that was often used for meat). "This one was hard to find," he said, fitting it on the cooking stand that Jessie had brought.

"I'm not starving," Jessie said, piling more wood on the flames.

"How so?" Liam asked with a playful, curious smile.

"I found something good as well," Jessie replied, pulling a bag from his bundle of supplies full of golden, fairy fruit (A brightly colored berry found near rivers and streams that were highly prized).

"You little devil. How did you find golden hoppers?" Liam asked, reaching into the bag for a handful.

"I'll never tell," Jessie replied, popping one in his mouth.

I reached into the bag of golden hoppers and found a big ripe one and held it to my nose and breathed in the soft, tangy fragrance before popping the tart berry into my mouth. They were ripe. *"Golden hoppers grow in small patches in hard-to-reach places, but they are the King's fruit; the breath of royalty,"* I remembered Honeysuckle telling me on a warm spring day as we searched for the golden hoppers, and they loved the cliffsides and rivers.

The scea bird carcass was beginning to cook on the outside, giving off a tempting, meaty aroma. I spread out Libby's and my bed rolls deep within the cave to keep my mind off the cooking meat that made my mouth water. The cave was not too big, but it was the right size for what we needed. There were slight traces of rat and bird, but that was to be expected in a cave so close to the water, and Jessie had told me that he had searched deep within the cave for certain unwanted animals like cliff crayals, teriflys, muckals, or granges.

I shivered as I untied Libby's roll and stretched it out wide. My cloak had kept most of the storm off me, and I was very thankful for it, but the rain had blown sideways, wetting my face and the hair around it. Libby was huddled by the fire when I returned. The firelight danced on the mossy, rough rock walls, casting strange shadows as it pleased. We were all thankful for the cave and the fire. Liam entrusted the scea cooking scea bird to Jessie and pulled his writing pad from his bundle that was drying by the happy flames.

"Shelter, Fire, Food," he whispered while jotting down notes in the dim light. "Did we miss anything?" he said, looking up at us. We pondered the question with great seriousness before shaking our heads.

We sat in silence for a while more when Libby broke the silence.

"What is that?" she whispered nervously, staring at the wall going into the cave from the overhang.

Staring back at us was a figure of a young maid clothed in queenly raiment, carved into the rock itself.

"It's just Saoirse (Seer-sha)," Jessie replied, turning the bird and licking his greasy hands.

Liam grabbed one of the torches, thrust it into the fire, and moved to the wall, examining the carving.

"The Child Mother of Dearbhla (Der-Vla), the great lost empire," Liam breathed, looking back at Jessie.

"Why yes, not many know that. Rumors say that she buried her kingdom deep in the earth so no invader would harm Dearbhla again." Jessie replied, pulling off some delicious meat for Libby and me to taste.

"Some would say differently," Liam replied softly, returning once again to his notes, but before he did so, he caught my gaze and held it; there was much more to that story.

We prayed over our meal and pulled strips of the meat off the carcass, then hung it back over the fire so the rest of it could cook through. The warm, unseasoned, greasy meat was delicious to my cold, tired body, and we were very grateful for it.

Chapter 19:
Twilight Tale

The carving of Saoirse (Seer-sha) rattled my thoughts as I lay on my left side on my bedroll, facing the dark north wall of the cave. The rock bit into my hip and shoulder, forcing me to plop onto my back and stare up in the blackness of the night at the rigged ceiling. I wondered how Libby managed to get any sleep at all, but she slept soundly on, without a care.

There was more to the story on the wall, I thought to myself as I remembered my history lesson from long ago. In the faint summer light that fell between the bright, rich green summer leaves above, I sat cross-legged in the ground beside Rowsheen and a blond-haired boy, Stephen, a few years older than me. I was no older than ten. The Creature sat in front of us, telling us great stories about the beautiful country of Dearbhla (Der-Vla). We often sat and listened to many stories as part of our education.

Saoirse (Seer-sha) was appointed to be queen of Dearbhla (Der-Vla) at the age of fourteen when her father, Prince Brian, and her uncle, the King Ogs, died in the great Battle of Ockland in the conquest of land. She was the only heir to the throne, and her mother feared that if the surrounding countries heard that a girl of that age was ruling, they would try to take advantage, so she called the elders of the country together, and they decided to give the young princes a new name for the safety of the kingdom. The name they decided upon was King Oberg the Protector to cloak the young queen as if her grandmother had had three sons instead of two.

She grew and gained wisdom from the many books and diaries of her forefathers, and the years of her youth slowly melted away, but the surrounding countries began to become suspicious when King Oberg the Protector refused to attend the gatherings of the Kings, host parties of nobility, or show off his knowledge to foreign advisors.

When Saoirse (Seer-sha) turned fifty, the age at which their children become adults, war broke out in Kallas, a city East of Dearbhla (Der-Vla) by the great sea. Kallas sent a message asking for aid to Dearbhla (Der-Vla), and Saoirse had to respond. Saoirse sent word to her generals, who gathered troops to be sent to Kallas by way of the river. Saoirse herself oversaw the arrangements and decided to travel to Kallas. Leaving her mother to oversee the country, she dressed up as King Oberg the Protector. In the past, she had done this often only to reassure herself that it was possible. Her generals begged her to stay in Dearbhla (Der-Vla), but none could sway her.

"My generals," she said, "If I do not come, they will think that Dearbhla has no King and no ruler. I must make an appearance." She did go to Kallas, but not until the generals had talked her into having her personal bodyguard pose as King for her.

Once in Kallas, she dressed as a female bodyguard and stayed close to her puppet King. The Prince of Kallas was very grateful for the troops and treated them with much hospitality as the tiny port city could offer. Kallas was not a rich port or a poor one. Because of the great port Dera to their North, they didn't receive the very wealthy merchants or traders, making them not as popular a destination as they would hope, but it did make them a strategic position for sea raids and invading armies since they were not able to hire an army for protection, and they were days from receiving aid from anywhere.

The invading force was sea-based. Ships from a pirate fleet were blocking any ships from entering or leaving the harbor until the city surrendered.

A drop of water dripped down from the ceiling onto my nose. What happened next, I thought. The stories flooded back to my memory. Vivid images that I had dreamed up as a child from the detailed descriptions of Honeysuckle and the Creature entered my memory as bright as day.

Saoirse's generals began driving off the pirates, but unbeknownst to anyone in Kallas or Dearbhla, it was the man who planned the harbor holdup, not a pirate. The man was called Kereru, and his plan was unfolding just as he had planned. Saoirse's (Seer-sha's) troops freed the harbor and drove the pirates off on the third night after arrival. The city rejoiced, and the Prince of Kallas proclaimed a feast to be held that night in King Osberg's honor.

Kereru and a handful of his specially hired troops infiltrated the palace during the feast celebration and held a sword to Saoirse's puppet King's throat in front of all the guests and declared that if the true heir of Dearbhla did not step forth, he would kill the fake king and burn the city. Kereru knew that Dearbhla had no King and sought to destroy Dearbhla's reputation among its honored alliances. Saoirse stepped forth and proclaimed herself to be the heir to please Kereru. Kereru laughed at the great feast and left with his troops. He had what he wanted.

Saoirse returned to Dearbhla with her troops. Word spread fast despite the people of Kallas remaining silent. Trade stopped coming from the neighboring countries, and one by one, all the alliances fell away, for no trust now existed; Kereru was building hatred against Saoirse's country one kingdom at a time. In a matter of three years, Dearbhla had to produce all of its own goods, and due to the lack of things that their country could not produce, like particular fruits and vegetables that were not indigenous to their lands. The country was now almost entirely self-efficient, but danger was on its way.

Kereru had been very busy running from kingdom to kingdom over the three years, but his methods were fruitful because he gained so much favor that he had entire armies pledged to his service. He is now prepared to march on Dearbhla. Saoirse had spies in the foreign kingdoms that told her of Kereru's work, and she was determined to save her kingdom from destruction.

When Kereru marched his army to Dearbhla, he found no kingdom; not a trace of Dearbhla. Nothing but ancient ruins and rubble. Dearbhla still lived, hidden, sheltered from the world, but safe. Saoirse spent the rest of her days building her kingdom richer than it ever had been, more concealed, but most of all, she found kingdoms far across the continent to ally her country with. Kingdoms like Mossland and Ekland now made a prosperous trade with Dearbhla and were true to their word.

"And so, ends the tale of Saoirse," I could hear Honeysuckle say. "*A tale is never at an end.*" I would say quoting him. "*Very true, my child. A tale is never over; for there is always more to every tale to be found in tomorrow,*" he replied.

"*There is always more to every tale,*" I whispered, slipping off my cot.

I made my way to the fire and plunged the tip of a torch into the dark, amber flames. It caught and burned bright. I crawled to the carving on the wall and inspected the fine artistry; it was Dearbhlarian style with roses and fruits, made by a fine-tipped chisel. Moss and vines grew around Saoirse's figure, or did it? I started pulling back the vines and moss.

There was more; the figure of a man and a small boy stood by her, clothed in kingly apparel.

"The tale did go on," I whispered with a smile. In the boy's breast plate was etched a warning in Dearbhlarian.

Though in darkness, we're unseen,

Rich in treasures we do gleam,

Count you worthy, we will tell.

But never will you know our dwell,

We move in silence, never seen,

We disappear as morning steam,

You leave us be,

We leave you free.

Never chase a shadow,

Never catch the dewy mist.

Heed ye not this warning,

You're at your own risk.

It was a warning that I had never heard before, so I pulled my writing book from my pocket and copied the complicated lettering, making sure that I had not mistranslated anything. I felt hot breath on my shoulder, but I didn't turn around; I knew who it was.

"So, you read and write Dearbhlarian?" Liam's hushed voice sounded behind me.

"Not as good as you," I whispered, jotting down the last Dearbhlarian characters and slipping my book back into my pocket.

"You know more than many would imagine," he replied, studying the lettering on the wall.

"Yes, William," I whispered, walking to the fire.

"There is more here," he replied, motioning me back to the mossy, stone wall. He pulled back some more moss on the opposite side that I had. There were more words etched in the rock. It was a song.

"It is a song about the Battle of Ockland before Saoirse's reign," Liam spoke.

"Read it to me," I whispered, propping myself by the fire and resting my chin on my hand.

He read the words softly, holding the torch close to the fine carving.

"Watch the wind come rolling in,

Upon a bright and pretty glen,

Sing my Lady, Sing my Lad,

In golden armor are you clad,

The ladies hang their hair of fine,

Out high windows like a vine.

They dance with steps as light as day,

May the night never carry it away,

Sing my Lady, Sing my Lad,

Look upon the bright, beau', and glad,

For our day has come in wealth and fair,

Take this for granted we do not dare,

Stand tall, my Lady, Pray, my Lad,

A war is coming be not sad,

You shall surly greave in time,

For this monstrous war is crime,

Weep my Lady, Goodbye my Lad,
The war is ended be ye glad,
You went not in vain,
Neither the blood of many slain,
But you never will, Dance with your Lady,
Upon the hill.
But there you'll sit in cave of stone,
Moss and vines yea overgrown,
By a river grave and fair,
Where the willows wash their hair."

"*Song of King Ogs,*" he finished in solemn silence. "Your Great, Great Grandfather," I breathed, looking into his deep, brown eyes.

"Aye," Liam answered, blushing at my knowledge before walking off into the shadowy overhang where Jessie snored in undisturbed peace, "How did you know?"

"Somehow," I replied with a soft laugh, "I knew the first time I met you. You told me that you both were from Besanti Argema. Well, that is not a place; Argema Besanti is a rare moth that blends in very well with its environment. Its appearance resembles a leaf, and the moth is on the flag of Dearbhla. I knew you two thought yourselves quite clever for using it."

"Not as clever as you, it appears, Aoife," Liam replied, "Or should I say, Princess Aoife."

Chapter 20:
An Unseen Terror

Libby and I woke up to Jessie shaking us, and the light of the torch in his hand casting dancing shadows on the walls. Though it was still dark, morning was coming fast, and we had to make the long trek to Jem's Peak. We rushed to tie up our bags and headed up the cliff in one long line.

Jessie took the lead with me behind him, and Liam with Libby riding piggyback behind me. The stone cliffsides were still damp from the night, making them very slippery, but we managed to reach the top just as the first rays of light were breaking through the sky.

"We need to reach Jem's Peak by noon, so you know what we have to do?" Liam asked as we stopped for a break at the ridge to rest and ensure that our bags and straps were properly tight.

"We're gonna have to run it," Jessie replied excitedly. We were finally in his area of expertise.

"That's right," Liam smiled back at me and Jessie. We hurriedly tightened down our packs for running. I made sure that my waist strap rested tightly on top of my hips and not too tightly on my shoulders, so it was easier for me to run comfortably.

Running with a pack was something I looked forward to doing almost as much as Jessie. My face was already red from our climb, and I hoped to be able to keep up, and I was glad to have our light packs on hand since I was carrying Libby's pack as well as mine. Jessie strapped Liam's pack on his so Liam could keep up while running, while carrying Libby down the rocky and uneven paths to Jem's Peak.

"Alright, Jessie, take the lead. Aoife, you're behind him. Let's go!" Liam instructed him, taking a deep breath and checking with Libby to make sure she was okay.

Jessie launched his sturdy figure down the path, and I raced to catch up with him, trying my best to watch my feet, so I did not trip on the many rocks in our path. We moved at a steady pace for about ten minutes before coming to a stop.

"Aoife, STOP!!" Jessie ordered from in front of me, but I stopped too late, tripped on a rock, and dove over the cliffside. Jessie snatched the back of my pack as I fell down the brutal cliff. I scrambled to find a handhold on the rock as he called down directions that I could barely hear over my beating heart. Once I got a hold of the rock, Liam had caught up and pulled me up the steep rock face. My legs were cut up and bruised, but I was so thankful to be on sure ground. Panting hard, I pulled off my pack with shaking hands.

"Please don't do that again," Jessie mused sarcastically, pulling bandages out of his pack and wrapping my cup legs.

"I won...," I started to say, but Liam stopped us.

"Quiet," Liam whispered sternly. Everyone froze. A faint rustle rose to our ears coming from somewhere up the cliff above us.

"Jessie, start down the trail-quietly," Liam whispered.

Jessie nodded, motioning for me to follow him. We hurriedly trodden on, trying to be as quiet as possible till we made it to the mountain ridge that ran the length of the island.

That's when Liam stopped us. "Slow down," he whispered, "stop fer a mite."

Jessie and I walked closer to Liam and Libby to possibly get an explanation from Liam, but Liam held up his hands for us to stop. We stopped and listened. A faint step sounded on the path behind us, then ceased. Liam motioned for Jessie and me closer. Libby went pale.

"Jessie, you and Aoife up that tree," he whispered, motioning to a large oak.

Jessie gave me a boost, and we climbed up till we could not easily be seen moving in and around the wide mossy branches of the ancient oak and covered ourselves in our grey-green cloaks. We watched Liam lift Libby and toss her effortlessly into the high branches of a large tree on the other side of the path before disappearing up its trunk. I marveled at how Liam and Libby blended their figures so well with the tree that it was nearly impossible to spot them.

I tightly clung to the trunk and balanced on a sturdy branch, trying my hardest not to shake. Jessie clung to a large branch above me in perfect disguise.

The footsteps became more apparent and sounded as if a person was directly below Jessie and me, kicking about the leaves and underbrush, but nothing was there. My heart beat furiously as the sound changed to the sound of a being climbing a tree, our tree. Twigs broke off, limbs snapped, and an invisible hand wrapped itself around my neck in an unsparing grasp. My whole figure grew cold and limp, my mouth could not utter a single sound, yet I could still see, hear, and feel, though I could not move. I felt my limp body being pulled downward off the limb and hung in mid-air as the whatever-it-was climbed down the tree with me in its tight, unfeeling grasp.

Where I hung lifeless, I could not see for my head rolled back, and all I beheld was the tops of trees meeting the sky in cheerful union, watching my current predicament in a calloused, mocking silence. Slowly, after some time, the beast turned its steps to the South, which tipped my limp head forward, where I supposed I would see my dangling, limp figure, but it was not so; all I saw was the place where my body should have been. Was my body cloaked in some unnatural enchantment?

Chapter 21:
Why Me

The beast that had captured me was, in fact, an I-HAVE-NO-IDEA! My thoughts rattled within my brain with an unpleasant clatter. I could not see the beast that had captured me.

It seemed as if the beast carried me for hours by the neck before entering a cave nearly hidden in the side of the brush-laden mountain and tossing me into a pile of bones and rubble by the rough, rocky wall. My body landed on its side, and to my delight, there was a silver and brass-plated shield lying sideways against the wall that acted as a mirror.

"I can see myself!" I screamed inwardly with joy, but just as I thought that, I heard more footsteps entering the cave. Something or someone was tossed in my direction. WHAM! Something landed behind me, knocked my limp body on my belly, and turned my head away from the shield.

"It's Jessie," I said to myself, staring at the back of his boots. I knew those heavy boots; they had stepped on me many times.

More footsteps entered the cave, and "Ouch!" Two more bodies landed on us. One directly landed across Jessie and me, and the other landed on top of Jessie's feet, where I could see its face; it was Libby. I figured that the heavy body that had landed on top of me and Jessie was Liam, partly because his thick arm was stretched across my face with his limp hand in my messy, unbrushed, tied-up hair.

"I hope Liam bathes when we get back to camp," my mind whined.

The rather smooth, ridged stone floor felt cold beneath my body, and the sound of a rushing underground river filled my ears.

"What can I do?" I asked my inner self. A small, peaceful voice whispered back in a soft, sweet tone, "Pray." So, I did pray. I prayed for my family over the sea and across the unfeeling, distant land. I begged mercy upon my country for the coming terror, I begged the blood of Jesus upon my friends and me, and I prayed for wisdom and guidance to lead me onward. Slowly, my mind was soothed and at peace, causing me to drift off to sleep without a care; "the Lord will take care of me."

I woke on a black, cushioned bed in an iron, stone cell; the only light came from a crack in the rough, stony wall. With a sigh, I drew my knees to my chest and leaned against the cold, damp wall. A thousand thoughts tortured my vulnerable mind as if repeating blows with a bludgeon (a short heavy club with one end made heavier, usually with a weight). Warm, salty tears trickled down my pale face, ran down my neck, and soaked into my red, cotton shirt.

"The Lord is with me," I whispered to myself, trying to clear my aching mind. "Think about home," I whispered again. The vivid image of Honeysuckle tending his garden popped into my head. I could smell the fertilizer and the fresh tomatoes, feel the soft, cool earth beneath my feet, hear the wind whistle through the trees overhead, and taste the fresh basil.

"I will live, and I will go home and help Honeysuckle tend his garden as I have done every year since I was a very small child," I decided, taking a deep breath. I would live.

Slowly but surely, that night, I fell asleep upon the black cot in an uneasy slumber. While I slept, I dreamed that our capture was just a test established by the masters, so they could place us in different categories.

I woke and looked around vainly in the dark, inky cell. Was my dream true, or was it just my mind's fabricated hallucination? As I pondered these thoughts, a dark, creepy nursery rhyme found its way through my memories and began to play in my head. It came in a soft, eerie voice that succeeded in calming my troubled head.

"Inky black,

The nursemaids hack,

To quell the voices on the sack,

In the woods, a timely shack,

With child two, San and Mac,

They slip from bed, travel forth

In the night, they travel North,

Never to be seen again,

On the dewy, hidden glen,

For now they reign,

In dreamland sky,

Never can you answer why."

Softly, I decided within myself not to sleep, but waited for the sun to rise. When the sun finally decided to meet the day, I rose from the cot and turned it over, examining the wood and looking for familiar details. The cot was a similar kind to the ones that filled the dorms and had just been covered with dark cushions. That meant that there was a small possibility that this was just a test.

Next, I set the bed back up and stood on it, trying to see out the crack in the ceiling. I saw cliffs and rocks warming in the bright, blinding sun.

"Not helpful," I thought to myself, climbing down and examining the walls. "Drip, drop," water dripped on my face from the earthy, stone ceiling above.

"Clink, clank," sounded chains sliding on the stone floor outside my cell, paired with the squeaky screech of an iron cell. A small, dark figure shaded the entrance of my cell. I scooted back on my cot, pressing my back into the rough, cold, rocky wall.

The figure set something down heavy on the stone floor, "Bang!" then slung the screeching, iron door shut, and the figure slunk off into the inky blackness.

Getting up off the cot, I examined what had hit the stone floor. It was a steel plate with what appeared to be my breakfast on it. Some sort of yellow porridge and a sliver of brownish-black, flat bread. The porridge was warm to my finger and smelled rich with corn. It was rather bland to taste, and the texture was rough and gluey to the tongue. The bread was quite dry and a bit burnt, so I ate it with the peculiar porridge, using it as a scoop. The first few bits awakened my hunger, and it did not take long for me to wipe the plate clean. A song the traders and merchants often hummed started to play in my mind.

"What to do oh, merry soul.
What to do, my lady,
I'm out of my own control,
Out of control lately,
The earth falls and flows,
And disappears in night,
Just as the wind, oh, blows,
It's always in the right."

"Why that song?" I thought to myself, then mused, "Perhaps I'm going crazy."

Chapter 22:
Plan, No Plan

"Clang, SCReeeeCH," the iron hinges of the cell door woke me in the night, "thud, clank," something hard hit the floor, "SCReeeeCH, clang," the iron hinges slammed tight again.

"OOuuaalll," the thing on the floor moaned and spoke in agitated tones, "ANYONE IN HERE!

I'd sure like to know!"

"Yes," I replied in an annoyed voice, realizing at once who it was, "we're in the same cell, Jessie."

"Aoife, boy, I've been on a wild ride," he replied with a long moan upon standing up. I could barely make out his outline in the darkness.

"You alright?" I asked, walking toward the sound of his voice.

"How am I supposed to know?" Jessie sarcastically replied as I ran my head into his outstretched arm.

"Oh, sorry, Aoife," Jessie apologized, then spoke seriously, "This capture is so strange. I think they would have killed us or turned us in for ransom by now."

"Jessie," I asked, concerned, "do you think this is a test?"

"Why would it be a... oh, that makes a lot of sense. Why do you think so?" Jessie asked, walking around the cell and bumping into walls as if trying to find a way out in the dark.

"The cot in this cell is exactly the same as the ones in the dorms at the training base," I replied.

"Same merchant that ships that kind in. OOuuuUU," Jessie reasoned before hitting his head hard on the uneven, rocky ceiling toward the back of the cell.

"Yes, I thought about that, Jessie, but why provide the cells with a cot?" I reasoned, trying to guess where Jessie was in the dark.

"Common courtesy," Jessie's voice came from behind me, "I see what you mean, but if this isn't the masters doing, then we have no chance, and we'd better get out."

"I agree," I replied, looking up at Jessie, studying the crack in the ceiling blocking the little light that entered the cell. I walked to the cell door to study the lock.

"Okay, I got a few ideas, WHOA!!" Jessie toppled off the cot, landing hard. "Well, don't try and catch me," he fussed, standing up.

"Sorry, Jessie, I was over here," I replied, then asked, "What ideas?"

"Okay, three plans," Jessie stated, "One, pick the lock, sneak out; Two, pretend to be dead, when the guards carry us out, we pounce; Three, uuuummmm.. I'll have to think about three."

"How about this," I whispered, "remember our lessons on illusion. What if we disappear?"

"I see where you are going. The benefit of the illusion," he replied.

Right away, Jessie and I got to work. The illusion plan was to deter the guards from our actual plan in order to escape unseen.

Step 1: Pick the lock. (Jessie's expertise)

Step 2: Memorize the Guards' schedule (Aoife's job)

Step 3: In two minutes, time lapse when the guards change station, open the cell door, steal the key to the cell door, reenter the cell, and hide.

Step 4: Search for captured friends.

Step 5: When guards find out that you're missing and go to search for you, sneak out of the cell and into the guard's quarters.

Step 6: If you have gotten that far, dress in guards' attire and find a map of the compound's layout.

Step 7: Sneak out of the compound unseen.

Step 8: Get to the Training base.

"That looks really simple on paper, Jessie," I stated in an annoyed tone. I did not want to get caught.

"It'll work, Aoife," Jessie replied with confidence, "We just have to do every step right."

"Ya, just do everything right," I replied sarcastically. "You got to trust me," Jessie said, "Or we won't make it out."

"I trust you, Jessie," I replied, looking over the plan again.

"Okay, watch the guards," Jessie replied, shoving a splinter of steel into the lock on the outside of the cell door. Several lanterns had been lit along the walls down the tunnel outside the cell door, allowing me to clearly see the guards. I counted three in black, steel armor posted in front of different cells.

Gingerly, I pressed my face up to the iron door to watch the guards. One of the guards in black steel armor twitched, then turned to the sound of Jessie fiddling with the lock.

"Jessie, STOP now!" I whispered, "We've been spotted."

"I've almost got it!" Jessie hissed between his teeth. The guard was now approaching fast. Jessie tried to pull his hands through the bars in time, but his wrist guard caught on one of the steel spikes on the cell door.

"AAWWWOOUAAAAAAA!!!!" Jessie screamed, the guard had come down hard with his heavy iron boot on Jessie's hand and wrist. I lunged at the cell door, trying to push the boot off his arm, but to no avail. The guard finally released Jessie, who fell to the ground with a moan, cradling his arm.

With one last spiteful kick at the cell bars, the guard said, "Try that again and I'll cut 'em off," then walked back to his post.

Jessie moaned again, rolling on his side and slapping the stone floor. I hurriedly pulled off my sash and belt and started towards Jessie.

"Don't touch it!" he moaned, rolling onto his back. "Please let me wrap it, Jessie!" I pleaded, sitting on his stomach, trying to keep him still, "Look, I know it hurts, stop being difficult!"

"AAhhaaaha, OOOowww," Jessie moaned as I wrapped his hand up in a splint using his empty dagger sheath, "OOh, that huurrts," he said in a voice that almost sounded like laughter, but I knew better.

The spike that caught his arm had left a deep puncture wound on the wrist and hand area, bruising it blackish blue and red.

"It could be broken, Jessie," I commented, concerned, laying my arm gently down on his chest. Sweat beaded up on his forehead, and I could tell he was in a world of pain.

"Wouldn't that be interesting?" he whispered faintly with a moan, then pulled himself up to sitting. "Aoife," he whispered into my ear, "we've got to get out of here."

Softly, I cradled his head in my lap and sang. I have him some herbs used for pain that I had on hand for my snake bite.

Oh, my child, let your eyes sink. You've run wild o'er the world,
And now it's time to sleep. The day is done, let it float away,

To somewhere beyond today.

Soft tears dripped down my cheeks and onto the cold, stone floor covered in earth and roots that felt cold against my legs. I breathed deeply, exhaling slowly and deeply. What were we to do?

Chapter 23:
Keys and Jessie Gone

Jessie's arm was badly swollen, and I couldn't coax him to move from the ground.

"At least the ground is cold," I thought to myself as I sat by the cell door with my head tipped back against the stone wall, pondering what to do next. Jessie had fallen into a light, agitated slumber a few feet away.

My mind hopped from one pressing matter to the next till my whole head spun. *"Clear your mind and you'll find an answer,"* I thought to myself, then sang out loud in a sound not nearly fit to be called a faint whisper, *"Life is only a pastime."* I hummed a bit louder, *"My little rose of wonder."*

"Quiet!" the guard closest to my cell boomed, making me jump nearly out of my skin.

Jessie fidgeted in his bundle on the cold ground. I caught a glimpse of his ghostly, pale face, and it scared me so, for he was ever so tough and tanned from the many hours he spent in the sun. I rose and walked over to Jessie; a plan was forming in my mind.

"Jessie," I said, kneeling down beside him. "What?" Jessie whispered, angry from being awakened from his uneasy sleep. "I'm going to get us out of here," I replied in a faint whisper. "Am I involved?" he asked, turning onto his side away from me. "No, I just need you to remain completely still," I replied. "Got it, still," he said, yawning.

A hard shiver rattled my frame, making me feel small and vulnerable. *"What would I do?"* my thoughts questioned, pelting me with one fear after another. A sense of true fear and despair weighs down upon my heart like a hundred boulders. *"It's just too much,"* I cried to myself as hot, salty tears dripped down my face, *"It's just too much. How am I expected to succeed? Why is this so hard?"* My body shook with sobs, and the tears continued to flow, but the more they did, the better I seemed to feel and the more composed. *"I can do this,"* I said to myself, *"I can do this."*

The guards were usually quiet and still. I had to find a way to get a key off one of them, but first I had to get their attention. When the guards changed positions, the one who had kicked Jessie was closest to our cell.

"Perfect," I thought, *"Time for acting."* First, I stood in the back of the cell where the dark hid me from view and did some squats and pushups to raise my heart rate. Next, I walked to the center of the cell and began coughing loudly and simulating choking. Lastly, I threw myself onto the cell floor, choking, wheezing, and thrashing about.

The guard shook the iron cell door harshly and bellowed, "WHAT en Terror's Name!!!" I continued to choke and thrash about, wheezing all the while pretending not to be able to breathe. "I DON'T Have the Patience for the likes of you," the guard muttered, jamming the key into the lock and yanking the cell door open.

Stomping up to me, the guard grabbed me by the neck, picked me up, and began to slam me onto the ground again and again. Blood gushed from my nose, and tears streamed from my eyes in response to the pain. The continual slamming was painful and disorienting, but I managed to grab his ring of keys and hide them in my shirt before he slammed me down the last time. I lay still, belly down on the stony ground to hide the keys, stopped choking, and began to breathe.

"BETTER!!" the guard yelled down at me, then stomped out of the cell and slammed the iron door shut.

"Ollemm," I moaned, rolling over to see if Jessie was still asleep, but he wasn't there. Looking around the cell frantically from where I lay, Jessie was nowhere to be seen. "He left the cell," my thoughts rambled. Hurriedly, I yanked the cushion off the cot, wrapped it up in my cloak, and placed it towards the back of the cell where Jessie had been lying. Jessie was on his own till I could manage to get out.

Chapter 24:
I'm a Soldier

Agitated, I paced the cell, wondering where Jessie was, if he had been found out, and if he had found Liam and Libby. I had to get myself out. It had only been a few hours since my charade, and my face still throbbed.

"I think my nose is broken," I whined to myself, trying not to rub it. I was waiting for the guard change so I could slip out unnoticed behind the guards. The guards changed position every four hours, and then it was the perfect time to act.

Finally, my wait paid off, and the guards started down the tunnel one after another. I had a little less than two minutes to get out. Hurriedly but quietly, I stuck one of the keys into the lock; it didn't fit. After frantically trying three keys, I found the right one and turned the heavy lock, pulled the cell door open. I heard the footsteps of the coming guards coming from the opposite direction from which the guards had left. Quickly, I closed the iron door and dashed down the tunnel in the direction the guards had left.

There seemed to be no end to the sparsely lit tunnel I had dashed down, just more and more rows of cells against the dark, gruesome atmosphere. After about thirty minutes of walking down the tunnel, I came to a flight of cold, indifferent, stone steps that led upward. Mounting the steps cautiously, I climbed upward for a time.

The light began to grow the further I climbed. The flight of steps ended at the beginning of a long hallway in which several rooms branched off. Loud voices issued from the room on the left. Tip-toeing forward, I peeked into the second room. Peeking in, I saw a rather untidy room half full of cots and half full of armored uniforms. I also spotted several sleeping guards sprawled out on the cots. I heard voices coming up the stairs, dove into the room, and made my way quietly to the side of the room with the armor.

Upon making it to the side with the armor, I noticed that there was a room behind it. Entering this room, I found long rows of uniforms hung along the walls, boots on shelves, and even a mirror. I quietly closed the door and selected a uniform that looked close to my size and hurriedly put it on. The uniforms were made to be worn with or without armor over them and were mainly cotton and leather with a tunic of chain mail. I put it on over my clothes in order to come off as a bigger person than I was.

The boots I had on looked nothing like the ones the guards wore, so I pulled them off and shoved them into my shirt to give the appearance of a larger chest and belly, and looked for a pair of boots that might fit. I found not one that was even close to my size, so I stuffed some rags I found into the toes and buckled them on as tight as I could. Looking in the mirror, I laughed to myself at the sight I was, but I also noticed that I had to cover my face and pull up my hair like the guards did. Finding a small box of ties, I slicked my hair back into a sharp ponytail at the back of my head and tied it tight in place.

Next, I scanned the room for a helmet. I did not find a helmet, but I did find a face mask used when in the woods and stuck it on my head. Placing it on my head, I decided that it would look too out of the ordinary and took it off, and wondered how I would not come across as a woman.

Leaving the room, I saw a stone fireplace on the opposite side. Trying not to clang too loudly in my new boots, I walked to the fireplace, brushed some ashes into my palm, and walked back into the room by the armor. Pulling my hair down, I brushed the ashes through, muddying my light red color into a blackish nutbrown. With the extra soot on my hands, I darkened my eyebrows and around several of my features to make my jawline and cheekbones appear more pronounced. Before leaving the room, I found a pair of good leather gloves and slipped them on.

Tip-toeing out of the room, I made my way to the door. As I reached to open the door, it swung open, and I was face-to-face with a group of surprised guards.

"I don't remember you, boy," one in a grey beard said suspiciously.

"A runaway, probably," reasoned another walking past.

"I'll take him to Boss," a towering one with dark features and a jagged, white scar across his chin said, grabbing me by my collar and forcing me down the long hallway.

"Where you from, kid?" the guard said in a deep, powerful voice.

"The sea," I replied in a nasally voice.

"A ship rat, aye. Aha, AHA," the guard replied with a hearty, deep laugh that reminded me of a headbricker laugh, then said, "I've done my years at sea. You met any pirates, kid?"

"No, but I've met some sailors that probably were," I replied, trying to move my legs as fast as possible to keep up with the tall guard.

"Ha, Ha. You know why, don't you?" the guard said, placing his hand over his heart in merriment. "No, sir. I do not," I replied politely, almost choked by his firm, calloused grasp on my collar.

"The Sabitons have gained control of many of the watersways and don't allow any such that call themselves pirates to access the ports, so many pirates have gone to pretending to be honest sailors in order to survive," he explained. The guard seemed rather pleasant and kind under his brash attitude and tone.

"The Sabitons?" I questioned in a breathless voice, then asked, "I thought their country was landlocked?"

"They'll make you think a lot of things if you're not careful," he cautioned, stopping at a door and giving it a loud knock.

"Yes," a voice on the other side boomed.

"We have a new recruit for the unit," the guard answered loudly.

"You're not going to turn me in?" I asked spellbound.

"I was a boy once," he replied, letting go of my collar, "This is your chance at a better life. I had to fight hard for that."

"Thank you," I quietly replied, looking down at my boots, very grateful.

"Send him in," the voice replied.

"Good luck, kid," the guard said with a smile that lifted the sides of his scar, making it seem as though he had two smiles before pushing me into the room and closing the door behind me.

An older, grey gentleman sat behind a steel desk in a high wood chair. "Come forward," he beckoned me. I stepped up to the desk and looked at the man with a serious face.

"What's your name, son?" he asked, sliding his chair back and folding his hands.

"Richard Longing, sir," I replied, using the name of one of my cousins.

"Richard Longing," the man replied, rubbing his eyes, then jotting it down in a big, green-covered book on his desk. Then he asked, "Any family?"

"Got a father on the mainland," I replied, folding my hands in front of me, which was true.

"Listen, son," the old man said, "Our soldiers usually go through a strict training that can last over three years, and it's highly competitive. Do you understand?" I nodded.

He continued, "However, these times we are in call for more in less time, almost no time.

Understand?" I nodded again, trying to catch what he meant. He went on, "Each new man is a chance for victory, so here is what I'm going to do, son. You'll stay here and train under me and earn a good rank if you work diligently and with sense. What do you say to that, son?"

"I'd be honored, sir," I replied through the pounding of my chest and the shaking of my legs. I had just been drafted into an army I did not know existed. I was going to be a soldier.

Chapter 25:
A New Name

I was to be a soldier in an army that I didn't know existed. What was I to do? Looking into the old man's face, I gave a weak smile to show my gratitude, but just as I did, the door slammed open and a hot-faced, out-of-breath guard stomped in and glared at me. This was a different guard; the one who stomped on Jessie's arm!

"That's the little rat we've been looking for, Boss!" the guard snarled, grinding his hideous teeth together.

"Now just hold on, Mr. Gray," the old man said. The guard grimaced.

He continued, "This young person had expressed interest in joining our order, and who am I to turn away such a promising find?" he walked to the window behind his desk and gazed out. "Those who start young in the business of war and take it to heart become the very greatest allies when grown and well-bred."

"Well, I hate to take your promising slice of cake, Boss, but that is a female," the guard snickered, "From our little Fayatoch exchange."

The old man gave me a hard stare, then addressed the guard, "If you'd know your history, you'd find that some of the very greatest world leaders have been women. My mind is made up, Mr. Gray. You give me any more trouble, and I'll have you transferred to the suicide ranks. Do you hear me?" (The guard nodded.) "Now leave us." The guard stomped out, leaving me a stare that gripped my heart with fear.

"Well, since the interruption is out now, let's start over, stall we," he said, sitting down once more and opening his book.

He asked, "Will you give me your name, or shall I give you one?"

"What you choose, sir," I replied, still overcoming the shock that I had not been stuck through with a saber, fed to some beast, or thrown in some deep, gruesome pit to rot like a maggot.

"Alright, have it yourr… wayyy…," he spoke, jotting something down in his book, then asked, "Eleanor Birdwhistle, satisfactory?"

"Yes, sir," I replied, not knowing anything else to say.

The Boss, as they called him, took some time writing down some things in his book, then jotted some things down on another sheet of paper. Handing the sheet of paper to me, I saw why.

Eleanor Birdwhistle: Training Class under General Fox

Born in Scantacy: Twenty years of age

He had made me a fake identity. I was speechless.

General Fox, as I was to address him at all times, started me on organizing his papers and tidying his office. I got a small room off the side of his office to live in. The room had nothing more than a cot and a wash pan. Tidying his office was a daily task, and if I completed it, I'd get several lessons on war, history, and battle tactics. He was hard to please, and I rarely felt like I was ever doing anything right.

However, being in the service of the general did have its perks; I was to be paid every Friday. A week passed faster than I could imagine, and still I found no time to look for Jessie or Liam or Libby. My hope of ever finding them dropped within me to what felt like a bottomless abyss. Day and night, I looked for opportunities to slip out and search; however, none seemed to present themselves.

The food the guards ate was hardly any better than the food I had been given when a prisoner, and I had never been one to complain of bad food. On the fourth day, GF, as I like to refer to him, presented me with a uniform. It was hardly any different than the one I had snatched from the guard's stash, but this one was smaller and slimmer through the shoulders. The uniform also came with boots that were closer to fitting me than any boots I think I'd ever owned.

GF explained to me that every uniform was custom fit to the soldier it was made for. I had never had any clothes custom-made for me, for that sort of thing was nigh unheard of unless you were making your own clothes. Most clothes I had ever owned were bought from merchants coming through on travel or hand-me-downs from friends or family.

The constant work and studying kept my mind off home and friends, but at night, when there were no distractions, the thoughts revealed themselves in a vicious, unruly form, making me sleep uneasily each night and drown my bed in sobs. The lessons that GF, however, are something that I look forward to with each dawning of the sun. Also, the new possibilities presented to me were exciting to my mind. To me, I was not just surviving, I was learning, something that would aid me in many ways in the years to come.

At the end of the first week, GF granted me an hour of free time that was to be spent learning how the guards of the prison worked by following them, asking questions if absolutely necessary, and not getting in the way. My time started when the guards changed position at the fifth hour past noon.

The guard who had taken me to GF offered to take me on his shift. I learned that his name was John, but all the guards called him Joll, a shortening of jolly, I was told, since he was rarely lacking a good mood and humor. I still had the keys I had successfully snatched from the guard and kept hidden. I took the keys with me during my spare hour, hoping to use them. Walking behind Joll down the musty, endless, dim halls, I tried to scan the cells on either side, but it was nearly impossible trying at the same time to keep up with Joll's steady pace.

At the end of my lesson, my head ached from the constant movement of my neck and the straining of my eyes. The tunnels all looked the same to me, winding this way and that as a wad of yarn that was so hopelessly entangled. I hadn't the slightest idea where my friends were.

The next day, GF made me recite what I had learned on my trip to the tunnels, and I told him what Joll had said about making sure one knew their way around before going alone, always expecting someone to escape, keep focused, and always stay alert. He seemed pleased with my answer, for he sent me again at the next guard change. This time, I focused on learning the tunnel passages instead of who was in the cells. My head still spun at the end of my hour, and I felt as if I was getting nowhere with trying to memorize the tunnels. I felt as though I was failing even when GF congratulated me on memorizing the bit of history he had wanted me to.

"What to do? Oh, what to do?" My head pulsated constantly, angry with having to wait to look for my friends, angry with myself for feeling weak, angry with Jessie for sneaking out when my back was turned, and most of all, angry that I was constantly fearful of everything. I was, as you could say, unable to control my emotions, which is a silly thing to say, for one

never fully has control over what he feels or what he wishes to feel.

The smelly tunnels became easier to navigate every day I went, and I also began to learn who was locked up, why, and where. When the twelfth day had passed since my apprenticeship started, GF began to let the guards teach me the important things about being a soldier. Each seemed to think the important thing about being a soldier was something different.

Sir Shallow was an old soldier who had served more years than any knew. His specialty was battle tactics. He was quite bent over and haggard from his many years of service, and his eyebrows were pure white, reaching nigh to his hairline. For hours on end, he would give me war scenarios, all the while shaking his long, grey beard and asking me to see what I would do, then he would tell me why his way was right. When he could tell that I was getting tired, he would pull out a game called *Live or Die* (a game that would sharpen one's mind, as he would always say). I was terrible at it, but he remained confident in my abilities to master the game in time. During these sessions, I would take a drawing pad with me and draw sketches of the battle layouts, forts with tunnels, and army groupings. In time, I felt my mind begin to sharpen and to understand some of what he was trying to bake into my head.

The next soldier who was charged to teach me was called Mr. Knight, a tall, muscular soldier who thought the most important thing about being a soldier was to be strong. He had a bald head partially covered with blue and red tattoos, and he was missing his two top front teeth. His nose curved down like a bird's beak, almost dipping into his mouth; he was also missing half an ear on his left side, and he had muscles that were as strong as iron. If he wanted to, I was sure he could snap me in half with one hand.

Mr. Knight took me to the soldiers' training room, where there were many instruments and weights of steel and stone for the soldiers to train. Some were for balance, building muscle, and improving one's fighting style. Mr. Knight taught me three days a week, leaving me sore and battered. During those three days a week, I lifted more weight than I ever thought it was possible for me to. I was ever happy to have his lectures after Sir Shallow, so I could rest my weary mind and get rid of my pent-up energy. The sword fighting scared me, for I wished not to get hit, even with the wooden practice ones. Every night, after I began to train with Mr. Knight, all I remember is collapsing in a heap in my room.

My patience wore thin as the days continued to end with no results from trying to find my friends. Bruises continued to appear on my arms and legs from training and walking into the sides of the tunnels out of pure exhaustion from my day, as my eyelids refused to offer any assistance to my troubled state. It had now been four weeks that I had been in this soldier school, and still I saw not where my friends were being kept. What was I to do?

Chapter 26:
Let it Be; There is A Way

Around midnight, I awoke in a cold sweat and shivered, but not from the cold but from the dream I had awoken from that I could not remember. Deciding that following back asleep was useless, I stood and dressed. It was still the wee hours of the morning, and the sun had not yet decided to paint the sky for the day.

Walking to the little nightstand that sat next to the small, barred window, I lit the lamp with a match and pulled on my clothes and boots for the day. After dressing in my uniform attire, I knelt by the window and folded my hands to pray. Tears dripped down my cheeks as I poured my heart out to the Lord. I stood with a peaceful heart and walked to the door, wiping the joyful tears from my cheeks.

"The Lord is in control," I whispered repeatedly to myself, pulling stray hairs out of my wet eyes.

Pulling the door open, I looked out into the darkness but saw nothing. Grabbing my lamp, I walked with determination into GF's office and out the other door. Walking hurriedly down the abandoned hallway, my heartbeat began to quicken with the clip clomp of my loose boots that I had forgotten to lace.

"DING, DONG!!!" the fortress clock chimed, making me jump, covering my heart with my hand. The clock's chime meant the guard's shift was about to change. Loud footsteps sounded in the guard's quarters as they prepared for their shift. Before I could move, the door to their quarters swung open. One by one, the guards filed out in a long line toward the stairs. They hadn't seen me. Since each one had their own lamp, I blended into them. Taking a deep breath, I stepped into the line and marched in pace down the long hall, down the stairs, and down the first tunnel. Down every tunnel, there was a guard's station, a room where an extra guard sat.

Mr. Grey had told me that they were essential to making sure that everything ran smoothly. Stopping at the guard's station, I went in as if it were my job to do so and hung up my lamp to show occupancy. There was no door on the guard's station, but there was a stool by the entrance. Sitting down, the line of guards had stopped, meaning that every position was filled and no one would be swapping with the guard at the guard's station for a while, so I decided to look around. The guard's station was quite large, containing a cot, a water pot on a hook, and a squat pot.

"What's that?" I said to myself, looking at the far wall. There appeared to be bars leading to a cell, but why would there be a cell in the guard's station?

Walking closer, I gasped; it was Libby huddled in her brother's big cloak. Before I could move, Libby spotted me and ran to the bars.

"Aoife," she whispered rather loudly. "SShhhh," I hushed her, reaching into my side bag for the keys I had stolen. Hurriedly, I began to try keys, but one after one did not fit. "Liam is here too," Libby informed me, waving her hand to a limp form in the corner of the cell, then asked a question that made my heart sink to my feet, "Where is Jessie?"

"He got out before I did," I answered, struggling with the keys, "I haven't seen him since."

"How long has it been?" she asked, pressing her delicate face up against the bars. "Since what?" I asked, looking her in the eyes.

"Since you last saw him," she answered, looking away. "A few weeks," I managed to faintly whisper. We both fell silent as I continued to fit keys in the lock. Of the hundred keys on the ring, I could not seem to find the right one. Time slipped away as I frantically shoved keys in the lock till finally the truth dawned on me; I wouldn't be able to get them out even if one of the keys worked for in a mere hour, I was expected in GF's office, and the guards would catch us all trying to escape, and we'd be in a worse situation.

"Libby," I whispered, handing her the keys through the bars, "I cannot stay, and I cannot explain, but I must go. If you and Liam get a chance to escape, take it, but wait till a guard change and be swift and head North through the tunnels. It's the closest way out. Use Liam's compass."

"What do you mean, get out if you can," she asked as I turned to go.

I turned back quickly and placed my hand on hers, "I got in the guard's service, but they don't trust me yet, so I cannot be safe sneaking around. I'll try and come back, but if I don't, y'all need to leave. Bye, Libby."

"Bye, Aoife," she whispered back as I grabbed my lamp and glanced back.

Taking a deep breath, I began to start down the tunnel, "Aoife, wait," Libby called. I ran back, wondering what would possess her to yell out, "Don't go that way. They'll know you were trying to help us."

"There is no other way to go," I replied with a worried countenance, approaching the cell. "Pull that hook," Libby ordered, pointing to a hook high up on the wall by the cell. I began to pull, but nothing happened. "Harder," Libby ordered. A section of the wall opened inward, revealing an old, winding stairway going upward. "Hurry," she whispered, "close it once you're in." I tripped into the passageway and closed the door.

"Now, where does this tunnel go?" I thought to myself, holding my nose so I wouldn't sneeze from the dust. I had a way out.

Chapter 27:
A Time to Choose

Climbing the tall staircase, I made my way to an old, rugged, cedar door at the top. Pulling the door open, I stepped into the hall where the GF's office branched off. Stepping lightly, I walked through GF's office and into my room. In the shadowy, early morning light, I paced about my little room before collapsing on my bed in tears and sobs that rattled my frame. I knew where Liam and Libby were, and I could not help them. Jessie was missing, and all I could do was pray.

That night, after another tiring day, I knelt by my bed and prayed till I sank into a deep slumber on the cold, stone floor. I awoke to someone shaking me, a hand over my mouth, and a voice that brought joyful tears to my eyes.

"Aoife, you're a hard one to find. How about we get out of this nightmare!" The voice belonged to Jessie. "Jessie, how?" I started, but he interrupted, "We have to go now! I know the way out. I can explain later, and you better do some too."

"I'll get us caught, Jessie," I replied, sitting up, "I work for the General in charge of the whole jail. As soon as I pop up missing, he'll have his whole regiment out looking for us."

"What am I supposed to do then?" Jessie asked, pulling my reluctant form towards the door.

"Liam and Libby," I said, snatching the door frame as Jessie lifted me off my feet and slung me over his shoulder, "They are locked up in the guard's station that has a secret entrance."

"What do I care?" Jessie replied, peeling my fingers off the door frame and hanging me over his shoulder as if I were a mere sack of animal feed.

In the pitch darkness, we caught the steady sound of footsteps coming. Stepping backwards, Jessie walked back into my room, sat me down, and closed the door without making a sound. The whip sound of someone lighting a match was followed by streams of light and moving shadows arrayed on the floor coming from beneath the door. I motioned beneath the bed to Jessie, and he quickly and quietly disappeared from sight. The only sounds that came from the outer room were those of rustling papers, coughs and grunts, and stomping boots. GF must be looking for a document, but why this late?

Breathing fast, I stood still, trying not to move. Not scared for me, but for Jessie. The footsteps started toward the door to my room; I nearly leapt onto my bed in haste as the doorknob turned and the old, wooden door creaked open. The door swung wider as I lay perfectly still, trying to calm my nerves. The person at the door gave a long, heavy yawn and closed the door before leaving the office altogether.

Jessie lurched from his hiding place as I slid off the bed, so I nearly fell on him. "Come on," he beckoned, grabbing the doorknob and pulling it open wide. *"I'll go,"* my mind decided fast, but only to see that all my friends were safe; then I'd return before the day had begun. Pulling at Jessie's arm, I got him to follow me in the dim light of the hallway to the door that led down to the guard's station, where I had found Liam and Libby.

Down the old, narrow stairway we raced with pounding hearts and gasping breaths. Coming to the trap door at the bottom of the set of stairs, we slowed down and cracked it open slowly. A guard slept by the exit way, propped against the wall and sitting on a stool.

"Wait here," Jessie whispered sternly, slipping out the door and pressing it three-quarters closed. My heart beat fast as I

watched the guard for any sign of waking. In two minutes'
time, Jessie reappeared, slipped back through the door, and
closed it shut.

"We just missed them," he whispered, pushing me back up
the stairs. I was spellbound, *"Had they escaped?"* I asked myself
as Jessie dragged me up the stairs by my forearm. The thought
felt both joyful and saddening at the same time. Had they
made it, or had they been stopped?

Up the stairs and into the hallway, Jessie continued to lead
me by the arm in a firm grip. In about ten minutes, I felt my
feet going down another staircase, then up a different one. We
were not heading back to GF's office.

Jessie continued to lead me onward for what seemed to be
ages, and I marveled at how he knew every turn and door in
the dim light. Finally, Jessie stopped at a lone wood door,
pushed it open, and pulled me through. With one firm snap,
Jessie lit a match to light a small lantern. The room was filled
with light, revealing many boxes and barrels of various kinds.
This was an old storage room. Rolls of dusty maps lined the
corners and the tops and sides of all available surfaces. "Aoife,"
Jessie began, picking up a heavy bag of items from the cobweb
and dust-laden floor,

"We have to leave, now, and there is no time to explain."

"But I think," I began before he cut me off.

"Aoife, this is important," he replied, laying his arm on my
upper shoulder with the bag swung over his other shoulder. I
felt a sharp pain in the back of my neck before everything went
numb and black.

Chapter 28:
A Long Ride

Opening my eyes to darkness, a musty odor hit my senses, and I swung to the left, then sharply to the right. An old cloak had been draped over me. Pulling it off, I found myself in a hammock. Lightning cracked, lighting up the room about me. I was on a ship in the middle of a storm. Looking to my left and right, rows of hammocks lined the room.

"Crack!" A flash of lightning was followed by a monstrous boom. Another flash lit up the room, and I spotted Jessie's hefty, brown-leather worn boots hanging out of the hammock to my right. Pulling the cloak over me, I curled up and squeezed my eyes shut. The boat continued to rock madly about as the night flowed on.

I marveled at how I had ever fallen asleep when my eyes opened to the early morning twilight. Sliding softly out of the hammock, I hit the floor and nearly fell back, not yet accustomed to the ship's constant sway. Tip-toeing forward, I glanced into the hammock Jessie had occupied the night before. Jessie was awake, staring at the rafters above. Catching sight of me, he slipped out and motioned for me to follow him. Out on deck, I looked over the deep, dark water only to see an empty horizon. It was a smaller vessel than I had been on before, probably used for fishing; I'd wager.

"Aoife," Jessie began, leaning on the railing, looking out into the sea beyond, "there was a lot more to our capture than we realized at first."

I held my tongue to let him continue. "The cave we were thrown into was on Fayatoch. The cell we ended up in was in Skysii."

"Skysii?" I exclaimed, looking up at him with questioning eyes. Skysii was a place I had only heard of in Lore. It was a rough place to live, I had been told.

"Skysii is a port city with over fifty miles of sea between it and Fayatoch," Jessie answered, solemnly looking into the dark water with a somber expression on his handsome face.

"How did we get out?" I asked, with a curiosity greater than hunger.

"Your friend, General Fox, is a spy for the Dearbhlarian army. They don't trust Skysiis. He paid our way out." Jessie answered, "He caught me snooping and questioned me. I told him about our being captured in Fayatoch and our training. He said that he was already arranging Liam and Libby's safe and immediate departure; he was under orders by the Dearbhlarian government to do so. He told me that you were safe and said that I needed to act fast before he was discovered as well."

"So, Liam and Libby are safe," I replied.

"First class protection," he replied, then continued, "I got a chance to speak with Liam a few days after I escaped. He said not to worry about him or Libby and that they would not be heading back to Fayatoch, but directly home. He's the one who requested our protection of General Fox."

"So, it was time for us to leave," I reasoned, wiping the salty sea spray off my face.

"Yes, it was," he replied, "this ship is not the fastest. We can expect a few good weeks at sea."

"How is your arm?" I interrupted with a concerned and caring expression.

"Still sprained, I think. Just been keeping it still," Jessie answered, then commented with a laughing smile, "if we keep getting stuck on ships, someday I might just buy one and have my own crew. I could use a first mate."

"Sounds fun. I'll check and see if I'm alive in ten years," I replied, with a big grin and quiet laugh. That certainly would be an adventurous time. It was nice to have a smile and a lighthearted conversation after everything we had just been through.

"Jessie?" I said quietly, rubbing my arms to calm my nerves.

"Yes," he answered.

"I'm scared," I said, dropping my head and crossing my arms in a self-soothing manner. Jessie wrapped me in a big hug. My throat felt tight, and big tears poured down my cheeks.

"I was so scared the whole time," I went on through sobs, "I thought you might be dead or hurt, and I was so alone, and I did not know what to do."

"It's okay, it's alright, it's okay, you're alright," Jessie consoled me, rubbing my shoulder and patting my head. I finished sobbing and relaxed, drying my eyes.

It would be okay. I would be alright.

Chapter 29:
A Wall of Death

On and on the ship moved to the flow of the water; up, down, and side to side. My neck still pained me at times, reminding me of how lucky I was to have survived the deadly bite. During this time, I focused on developing my sword and knife fighting skills. I still felt as though my skills were amateur at best.

"Don't back up," Jessie corrected as we practiced on a windy day on the deck of the ship. The wind blew his dark brown hair into his eyes and nose. His face was softly tanned from the sun's rays.

"Got it," I replied with a deep breath. Sometimes when I was tired, I could feel a touch of the weakness I had felt when I had first gotten bitten by the snake. I felt my cheeks getting red from the heat. Sweat dripped down my neck and spine.

"Alright, let's try daggers again," Jessie decided, pulling forth the wooden practice daggers he had made, "Ready, set, go!"

Close combat was quicker in coming to an end, but it was never my specialty. Back and forth, our wooden blades clanked and hit. Trying a new strategy, I pinned his arms with one of mine, then pointed my dagger into his chest. With that, he knocked my feet from beneath me and grabbed my shoulder.

"BOOM, CRACK, BOOM," a deafening lightning bolt followed by thunder struck close to the ship, scaring us out of our skins.

Still dangling in midair, I turned my head around to see a massive black and purple wall as far as the eye could see heading toward the ship.

"Training session over," Jessie said, hurriedly setting me on my feet, gathering up the training materials, and pulling me below deck. The ship rocked, creaked, and rattled as I tried to stand amidst the chaos of the sailors rushing to and fro. Jessie asked the captain if any more hands were needed, but none were. In one big pound, the rain wall hit the ship, rendering all other noises inaudible.

Clinging helplessly to a large support beam, I tried to keep my feet level with the floor beneath me as the ship was thrown this way and that. Jessie seemed to be enjoying himself as he slid around the room to the rock of the ship. He was gathering up all of our things and stuffing them into his grab bag.

"Why in the world is he doing that right now?" I thought to myself amidst the roar, crack of the thunder, and the pounding, relentless rain. All I could think about was hanging on for dear life.

Jessie slid towards me and grabbed the beam as the ship tilted to its right. He had our bags slung over his back. "Lllloooovvveellly wwwhhheeeaaatheeerrr!!!!" Jessie mused, raising his voice so I could hear him over the noise.

Slowly, I nodded my head in response. I was nearly scared to death. He did not see me nod, so he swung himself over to my side of the pole and yelled in my ear, "LOVELY WEATHER WE'RE HAVING!!!!!!!"

I pushed him away, nodded my head, took my bag, and swung it over my shoulder. "HHIII," I gasp as the ship violently tips to the right again.

Cold, salty water gushed down the staircase into the room and seeped through the ceiling onto our heads. Jessie grabbed my collar so he could yell in my ear again, "THIS SHIP IS GOING TO SINK!! WE HAVE TO GET ON DECK!!! FOLLOW ME!!!"

Jessie grabbed my arm in a death-like grip, and when the ship began to tilt right again, we jumped for the staircase and clung to the rough wooden steps as it plunged violently to the left. More water gushed down the stairs, drenching us to the bone.

Clinging tightly to the stairs, we crawled up through the endless river of water. Finally pulling ourselves onto the slick, water-covered deck, we fought our way to the railing. The deck lamps were still lit, but there was no one to be seen. The ship had been abandoned.

Looking down into the violent waves below, we saw the remnants of the row boats that had been dashed to pieces against the ship's side. I breathed hard and grasped my hand over my heart as the rain continued to pound, and I clung to the railing. Jessie had ceased trying to talk to me; now, he was just pulling me in the direction he so desired. In what felt like an eternity, Jessie dragged my near lifeless form up the stairs to the bridge, and, clinging to the wheel, he began to steer as I lay on the deck clinging to his ankles. The ship lunged forward and backward this way and that as the wind whipped viciously at the tiny vessel.

"CRASH!!! BOOM!!!" The ship struck something hard in front, throwing Jessie clear over the wheel and banging my head into its wooden stand. Rubbing my pounding head, I crawled to the place where Jessie lay motionless.

"You're still alive," I whispered as I turned him onto his back and checked his pulse. A large red knot was beginning to swell up on his forehead. Placing my hand over the back of my head, I felt something odd, so I drew my hand in front of my face; it was streaked with blood.

The ship had ceased to move forward but continued to rock and creak. Lightning struck loudly, illuminating the monstrous, savage waves on the horizon. Looking over the small, miserable shipwreck, I realized the inedible truth; slowly but surely, the fierce waves were pulling apart the ship, and we could not stay on it to get pulled into the vicious waves below.

Standing upon my knees, I pulled Jessie's limp body over my shoulders to balance out the weight (something Mr. Knight had taught me to do), and I forced my shaky legs to straighten. Clinging to both the railing and Jessie's arm, I met the stairs and began down.

Taking a deep breath, I laughed to myself, *"No one gets to do what you're doing, so exciting; right!!!?"*

"Yeah, right," I replied to my thoughts as the ship made another vicious lunge, causing me to sit down on the last step. Breathing hard, I stood and began to walk to the bow of the ship. Reaching the bow of the ship, I laid Jessie down and peered over the side of the ship, but could not make out what we had hit, so I snatched a lamp off its stand and hung it over its side.

Rain poured and pounded over us as I strained my eyes to see. Lightning struck close to the ship, nearly stopping my heart, but also showing me the reef we were stuck on.

"A reef!" My heart dropped; I couldn't possibly keep Jessie and me alive till the storm stopped on a reef beneath roaring waves. Pulling Jessie back from the bow of the ship, I made my way to the captain's cabin.

"The captain's cabin should be dry at least," I thought to myself, walking with the sway of the ship. A violent wave of water crashed over the ship, making me snatch the stair railing, and the cold water revived Jessie.

"Aaaaahh!" he yelled, rocking himself around, nearly knocking me off balance.

"What!" I hollered back, setting him down on his feet.

"Oh, nothing... Just wanted to yell out what I'd been holding inside! What did we hit?" Jessie asked, rubbing his head and pulling his cloak straight.

"A reef!" I hollered over the endless crash of violent waves.

"Oh, great!" Jessie sarcastically hollered back, walking underneath the stairs and out of the pounding downfall.

Jessie grabbed my cloak and hollered in my ear to be sure I heard him, "Do you think it's grounded on the reef!!!"

"Yeah!! But I could be wrong!" I replied, wiping my eyes on my shirt to clear the stinging saltwater.

"The captain's cabin should be dry," Jessie reasoned, fiddling with the lock, "It's stuck." He commented, giving the door a heavy shove with his shoulder. The door swung inward.

Stepping into the dark, musty cabin, Jessie and I fumbled around for a lantern. "You got a match?" he asked me.

Locating one, I replied, "Yes," and then fished in my side bag underneath my drenched cloak, "Here is one." With one whip of Jessie's hand, the place where we stood filled with light.

"Who's dere!" A deep voice demanded from somewhere in the room.

"Hello," Jessie replied, swinging the lantern around the room, "I am Jessie Gabriel... and this is Aoife Beairclen. We are passengers on this ship. Who are you?"

A moan sounded at the other end of the room, past the captain's deck covered in charts. Jessie grabbed a firm hold of my shoulder, pushing me slowly behind him as he moved toward the moan. Holding the lantern out at arm's length, the light revealed a man lying on the ground with a firm hold on his heart.

"Captain Greiner," Jessie exclaimed as we ran to his side and knelt down, "What happened?"

"What'd u expcit. A captain goes down with hiz ship. HHhooo," He took a deep breath, "But sume times de crew won't trust its captain to du hiz job. Dat's why I got a hole in me chest."

"What kind of weapon makes such a wound?" I asked, searching for a clean rag to press on his wound.

"Oh, jut ai musket, Ole," he replied with another long moan.

"Musket?" I asked as Jessie helped me put pressure on the captain's wound.

"New wepin… A kinda handcannin… Ahh," he replied, trying to get the words out right, "It's getting mor…sightly so they say for men o war." The captain tried to take in a deep breath, but failed, choking uncontrollably.

Quickly, Jessie and I tried to roll him over, but before we could, the choking ceased, his head tilted back, and his eyes held an upward gaze. I stretched out my blood-stained hand and closed his eyes. The captain was dead.

Chapter 30:
I Cannot Say

Jessie stood in silence; he wiped his hands on the curtain that hung from the window. Lightning still flashed out of the broad window in the captain's quarters, but the storm was calming down. He picked up the lantern and walked about the room as if searching for something. With a deep sigh, I stood and walked to the door of the cabin.

"Where are you going?" Jessie asked, turning around from the shelf in the room's corner. "Just to wash my hands," I replied, placing my hand on the brass door handle.

"Wait a second. I'm coming with you," Jessie replied, stuffing some papers into his sack and staring towards the door. I nodded, turning the brass handle and stepping out.

"Huh!" I gasp. From the darkness outside the door, a rag swung over my head, gagging me. I struggled and fought, swinging my assailant over my head onto the slippery deck with a thud. "That trick really does work!" I exclaimed out loud.

"GOOD FOR YOU!!" Jessie shouted from the top deck, "Could... USE... A... HAND!!! Jessie was sword-fighting a giant man with a sword greater than I had ever seen before.

"Coming," I breathed, drawing my sword that Captain Acosta had given me. This was the first time I was using the sword in combat. I raced up the dripping steps with the long steel blade in hand. Back and forth, Jessie and I fought the great man together, jumping out of the way of his slashing sword, then rushing forward to strike. Back and forth our swords flashed and bit as our hearts beat to the terror clash until the great man blocked both our swords with one swipe and punched Jessie, who fell back.

With one swing of his great arm, I was knocked back. Jumping back up on my feet, I plunged my sword into his belly, but he just roared and swung his sword again, not missing his mark. The lightning struck and the thunder boomed, but I did not hear it. I don't remember feeling much at that time. Nausea and pain had made my whole self numb as I stumbled. My whole self went cold as I collapsed onto the grimy, wet deck.

Over me jumped Jessie, plunging his sword into the great man's chest. The floor beneath me shook as he toppled over. Jessie's face appeared over mine, and his lips moved fast as if he were trying to talk to me, but I heard nothing. In frantic motions, Jessie pulled off my cloak and began to wrap it tightly around my leg, even pulling off his belt to secure it firmly in place. My thoughts tried to make sense, but everything felt dull except the now extreme pain from Jessie applying a tourniquet to my leg.

All I could think was, *"Dear Lord, protect us, we can't do this alone,"* as small raindrops pelted down onto my sweaty, cold face, *"We need you. Lord, I trust in you."*

"SPLASH," something heavy slapped the water over the side of the ship, jolting me awake. The sun was shining, and seagulls fussed in the distance.

"Jessie?" I called, sitting up straight. My head pounded and my lips felt dry. I was lying against the wooden wall beneath the stairs.

"One minute, Efie," Jessie's voice replied from above the stairs.

Pain shot up my leg as I tried to move it. Pulling the blanket off my leg, I was shocked at my discovery; from the knee down, my right leg was all but gone! My stomach made a lurch, and my head began to spin, *"Lord, what am I to do?"*

A soft, firm answer replied back, *"Trust in the Lord with all your heart; and lean not on your own understandings. In all your ways acknowledge him, and he shall direct your paths."*

"Aoife?" Jessie asked inquisitively, "You okay?"

"I dunno," I replied, breathing hard and trying to keep my spinning, light-headedness from showing. I felt weak, and I was sure that I was ghostly pale.

"You're fit to be a pirate now, alright," Jessie joked, obviously trying to make me feel better, "One-legged Efie, terror of the South Seas and first mate to Captain Gabriel, the finest captain to ever sail!"

"Okay," I clapped at his joke, trying to show a bright smile to appease him, but the sickness in my stomach was terrible. "I can wait some time to become a pirate, Captain Gabriel, but you might want to use your middle name if you plan to be a pirate."

"Oh, I'm not gonna be a pirate; just you," Jessie replied with a smile.

"Okay," I replied, looking off in the distance over the side of the boat. Something caught my eye, "There's land!" I replied, starting to stand.

"You stay still," Jessie ordered, "I'm working out the details as you speak. If you want to help, there are some boards that I could use help tying together."

"Yes, I'd like to help," I replied weakly, but still earnestly.

"You gonna get there yourself, or do you need help?" Jessie asked, half concerned and half with a laugh to lighten the mood.

"Help would be nice," I replied, wondering how long it would take me to get there myself by crawling.

"Okay," Jessie replied, taking my hand and tossing me over his shoulder like a rag doll. He set me down by the railing where a big raft was being pieced together. Crawling around like I was crippled, I worked the thick rope in and around the beams, lashing them together. At that moment, I was grateful for the tedious rope work I was taught as a child.

The stump of my right leg felt heavy and stiff as I crawled over the raft, securing everything together, but surprisingly, there was no blood leakage on the clean and new bandages. On Fayatoch, we learned how to care for serious wounds. Jessie and I had taken extensive classes in that area, but I had dropped out early due to the snake bite.

"How did Jessie get the blood flow to stop?" I wondered, thinking that my leg should be hurting much worse than it was now, and at least leaking some blood or fluid.

Jessie, ever critical of my work, continued to bring rope and boards from the ship to piece together his raft. Tying ropes here and there, he was preparing to winch his raft down into the water.

"Jessie, how long was I out?" I finally built up the nerve to ask, securing the last beam after we had been at it nearly all day.

"About a day and a half," Jessie answered, setting up his pully system that would safely put his raft in the water.

"What did you do to my wound?" I finally blurted out. I needed an answer.

"Do you really want to know?" Jessie asked as he finished securing another beam to his raft.

"Yes," I answered weakly with earnest.

"So first I applied a tourniquet, and when the blood stopped for a second, I pulled skin from the edges and stitched and pulled and tugged, and I cauterized the area I was not able to close, and…" Jessie looked at me with questioning eyes, "Do you really want to know those details?"

"I want to know how you did it and where you learned how to do that," I replied with amazement."

"They put me in advanced classes on how to stop blood flow from a major cut or amputation and how to perform a repair. I'm basically a doctor, but don't tell my dad. He would not believe me," Jessie admitted, "I told them at Fayatoch that I was really interested in being a medic and they ran with it and I'm grateful."

"Me too," I replied with a soft smile. Jessie's willingness to learn had probably saved my life. "Thank you," was all I knew how to say in reply.

Jessie and I continued to work on the raft, which was coming together well. Moving about was not great for me; my leg throbbed, and the hot sun was already pounding down upon us. I was thankful for the small breeze that made it bearable.

"Can you lift the other side of the raft?" Jessie asked, heaving from the other side. Sweat beaded up and dripped down his forehead, plastering his bangs to his face.

Crawling over to the other side of the raft, I sat down. I heaved with my arms trying to get one side of the raft over the boat's railing. Finally, I managed to get my side leaning over the rail, and Jessie was able to get the rest without my help.

Attaching the pully ropes to some barrels, Jessie pushed the raft off the side. The barrels lifted slowly, letting the raft continue its descent. When the raft was about halfway down to the water, Jessie secured the rope that was attached to the barrels to the main mast. This stopped the raft's descent. Lowering stuff down on ropes, Jessie filled the raft with food and supplies till finally it was my turn to get on the raft.

"Your turn, Aoife," Jessie informed me, attaching a rope to my belt, "Just push off on the side of the ship and you'll go down slowly."

"Got it," I replied, trying my best not to look worried, for I wasn't worried about being let down on a rope. I had done that many times, but the pain in my leg was making my face pale, and my body felt weak and drained. Jessie dropped me over the side of the ship. My descent was smooth, and I did not have to push off on the side of the ship, but thrice before dropping onto the raft.

Pain from my leg stump throbbed, making my face all the paler and sicker. Jessie swung effortlessly down the side of the ship, landing with a thud on both feet as if he had jumped it.

"Wahoo!!" Jessie hollered, scaring away the seagulls that had perched themselves on the ship's railing.

"Wasn't that fun?" he laughed, and then his expression changed when he saw my face. Without question, he opened a bag and fumbled through until he pulled out a small bottle.

"It's for the pain," he replied, taking off the top and passing it to me.

I nodded, taking the bottle and drinking a few sips. It tasted terrible. I tried to hold in tears from both my pain and my frustration at myself for not speaking up sooner.

"I gave it to you earlier," Jessie replied, with a solemn expression, "You were in and out of consciousness for a while, so you might not remember. It can also make you sleepy. I'm sorry I forgot to ask if you needed anything for the pain. I was just so focused on making the raft to get off. I'm sorry."

I softly cried as Jessie loosened the ropes, and we took our descent down into the cold, blue, salty waves. Jessie pushed off the ship with an oar he had found, and we started our voyage to land. He passed me a blanket, and I curled up on the bogs of gear and fell asleep.

"Better make it stylish," I said as I woke up after taking about an hour nap. I felt a smidge of joy flutter back into my weary heart. *I really am going to be a pirate,* my thoughts sang back to me, and for the first time ever, I felt okay with that. *I'll just not be the stealing, pillaging kind,* I informed myself with a smile that I knew would stay.

"Make what stylish?" Jessie replied, and a wave sprayed him with sea foam. The raft floated in the frothy, flowing waves full of debris from the ship and large patches of green and brown algae.

"My new leg," I replied, sitting up from my makeshift bed.

"As stylish as you want, as soon as we make it back to Fayatoch or Mossland or even Ekland for that matter. Any civilization we can find or come across, I'll take it." Jessie replied, "And yes, I know that Ekland is landlocked other than a river and a huge lake, but that's not the point I'm trying to make."

Whatever that pain medicine was, it was working, and I know it was working because I was able to smile at his joke. I still felt pain, but it was so much better than it was, and I was so grateful for it. Jessie steered while I rested. Finally, I experienced some relief and was able to rest. The cool breeze felt so comforting and soothing on my skin.

We had a bit of trouble trying to stay off the reef that the waves seemed to push us toward, but finally, with a lot of effort on my part, we steered around the reef and headed toward the long strip of land on the horizon. Our survival looked adamant or sure.

Chapter 31:
Take Me, Tie Me

"Splash!" Jessie jumped out of the raft into the waist-deep waves and began pulling the raft ashore. We had made it to the strip of beach. The only help I could offer was pressing the oar into the sand to try to move the reluctant raft forward. The waves splashed and rolled over the shore, pushing us forward for a mere moment, then pulling us back out. Finally, Jessie managed to pull the raft up on land. I looked at the thick, dark, and endless line of trees with dread. Where were we?

Slowly and with apprehension, Jessie chose a place to camp. It was getting late in the day, and the shadows were getting longer and more prominent. I was concerned because I knew nothing about the island and what it had to offer.

"I'm going to get firewood," Jessie informed me as we began to set up the camp.

"You okay here?" he asked, showing concern.

"I'm fine," I replied, pulling myself up on a cane, "I'm a pirate, remember."

"Alright, it's time for more pain medicine," Jessie replied, handing me the bottle he carried in his pocket. Then he turned and headed down the beach.

"Okay," I replied, looking at the bottle in my hand. I took a small sip and started looking around me. I had to get the camp looking right by the time Jessie returned, or that's what I wanted to do. If I was being honest with myself, Jessie would not have minded if I had done nothing at all and rested.

"Just do it one step at a time," I told myself with a dry laugh. Slowly, I began to get things in order. First, I set up a ring of stones for the fire, carrying one stone at a time.

It was troublesome work with one leg trying to balance and carry something at the same time, but somehow, I managed to get a decent fire ring. Often, I crawled where I needed to go; it felt safer than hopping or, rather, easier to manage.

"Alright," I said to myself out loud, "Step two: hammocks." Humming an old poem of mine, I stretched out the bundled-up hammocks that Jessie had brought from the ship and began to secure them to the two trees that Jessie had placed the gear around.

"Blow wind blow,

Please blow for me,

Blow me far across the sea.

Take me away,

Far away,

To a land beyond the day.

Shake the leaves and lift my hair,

In times of sorrow, gloom, and fear."

The song began to put me in good spirits, and the pain medicine had somewhat alleviated the pain. I still had some pain in my leg and a mild, persistent headache. Taking my mind to another song Honeysuckle used to sing, I managed to keep my mind quiet and my heart at ease.

I stopped there for a yell shot to my ears (Jessie's yell), then all was silent save for my beating heart that sounded louder than booming cannons in my ears.

The brush rustled as if something was coming my way. Propping myself up against a tree for balance, I drew my sword and breathed deep; all my fear melted away, and a new sense of confidence took its place as I looked down on my sword's edge. Whatever was coming, I was ready!

Raising my sword high for whatever was coming, the noise stopped. An eerie silence melted over the whole area, only broken by the endless slap of waves on the sandy, rocky shore and the occasional screech of the seagull. Keeping my eyes fixed on the dark forest in front of me, I caught a slight movement and reached quickly to cover my neck, but I caught the sound too late. A dart bit into my shoulder, going through my shirt, and I ripped it out as fast as I could. The forest shook with the sound of many bodies walking out toward me.

A slight dizziness mingled with the dart's sting began to shoot through my body and blur my vision. My world felt cold and black.

My senses awoke to the pungent odor and sizzle of fresh meat. Opening my eyes, I beheld a bright, blue sky devoid of all clouds save for a stream of black smoke billowing up to the sky.

"But I want the cookie! Mama, pleaseee!" I heard Jessie whine out loud. Rolling my head to the sound of his whine, I saw Jessie tied to a pole, quite unconscious. "He must be taking in his sleep," I whispered to myself, sitting up and looking around me.

There were dome-shaped homes all around, some nestled on top of one another, made from what appeared to be palms, grass, and tar. I saw no person in sight, but had the feeling that I was being watched. "Most of them," I wagered, "Are probably at the fire."

Jessie was bound hand and foot to a pole planted deep in the ground about a giant stride from me. I, however, had only my hands bound in front of me and was lying on a mat beside a pole. "Yeah, I cannot run away if I wanted to, huh," I told myself.

Rolling onto my stomach, I wriggled toward Jessie. Just as I was nearing Jessie's pole, a piercing trumpet blared. *"That doesn't sound like a native horn!"* my thoughts yelled within me. Scrambling around the pole, I pulled at the knot in the rope that bound Jessie's hands fast.

"Oh, come on!" I irately muttered, "Do I have to pull it with my teeth? Yes, that might just work."

"What did you say, Clad?" Jessie mumbled, picking up his head, then dropping it back down.

Gripping one part of the knot with my teeth, I managed to get some slack and pulled it off Jessie's hands. "Jessie, come on," I nudged him. No response. I suddenly felt a plunge of dread in the thump of my heart; all the noise had ceased.

Quickly, I threw the ropes back over Jessie's hands. The hum of loud voices began to rise, mingled with the thud of many feet on the ground. Not bare feet, no, that's not what I was hearing; I was hearing booted feet and the sharp clang of armor.

"Wait... I know that horn," I whispered to myself, "I've heard it before, but where?"

The noise grew louder, and a long line of armed soldiers marched into view, the likes I had never seen before. Their armor was plated with intricate engravings. Silver and brass work had been used to form trees, grape vines, birds, and animals. The shade of the soldier's skin was a dark olive; their hair was dark, and their voices harsh and brass to my ears. I couldn't make out their language.

Their leader, with a high plume of red sticking out of his helmet, appeared to be having a debate with the leader of the village. Straining my ears, trying to catch even one familiar word, the armored leader motioned to one of his men, who handed the tribal leader a heavy bag that appeared to be full of some form of money.

The armored leader pointed to me and Jessie, and several of the soldiers stepped forward. Two grabbed Jessie and headed out the way they had come, and the third grabbed my bound wrists and threw me over his shoulder.

"Well, I'm riding in style," I thought to myself as I was being totted out of the little village. *"I ought to get the award for most captured student when I get back to Fayatoch,"* I thought to myself with a comical sigh.

Marching past rows and rows of huts, big and small, we finally got to the edge of the village, where there were horses tied to trees. *"There are enough horses for every soldier here, and all the horses are black. How peculiar,"* I thought to myself, surprisingly just trying to amuse myself. *"That must be the road they take,"* I thought again, noticing a rather narrow horse trail quite overgrown on the side by vines and branches.

With an effortless toss, I was slung up to a soldier already mounted on a horse, and off the horse went trotting quickly down the horse trail, trying, obviously, to shake me to bits with the quick trot on the uneven ground.

It seemed like hours, to me, that I was on that horse looking for anything familiar, but I could see none. Even the trees were of different breeds that I was unaccustomed to; they had sharp thorns growing out of their stems, most of which were larger in width than my hands. The trees had monstrous and rather furry leaves, some big enough to hide me behind, and their bark gave off the shuddering appearance of snake scales.

"I'd never learn how to run in a forest like this," my mind mused, continuously looking for signs of similar things. Even the sky appeared foreign and cold with clouds of an unfriendly, eerie gray. The horse trotted on, sometimes slipping into a full gallop for a while, trying to keep up with the horse in front of it, never showing any sign of tiredness or wear.

Suddenly, I began to notice little black mushrooms in patches along the path's edges.

They almost appeared to be moving. "Those mushrooms are so peculiar," I accidentally said out loud. The rider grunted, looking back at me. I pointed to the mushrooms. A look of terror washed over the rider's face, who yelled something loud in a panicked voice several times. All the horses took off in full gallop straight ahead. Glancing back, I caught Jessie a few horses back, bobbing up and down as limp as can be.

"He's going to have a sore neck tomorrow," I whispered, trying my best to hold on. Looking down again at the mushrooms, I gasp. There were twice as many crowding the path and five times as many as they had been, making it more and more narrow by the second until a yell sounded from ahead. The riders pulled at the horses' reins, coming to a deafening halt; the mushrooms had overgrown the path ahead.

"What is wrong with the mushrooms?" I wondered, seeing that no rider or horse would go near them. Stopping at a halt, the riders jumped off their horses, grabbed what appeared to be matches, pulled small torches out of their saddlebags, and lit them in a hurry. I was left up on the horse watching the mushrooms. The riders waved the torches at the mushrooms; the mushrooms jumped back!

The horse I was on snorted and stomped nervously as the mushrooms got closer to his hooves, then, rearing up high in the air, I flew off the horse's back but landed softly into a patch of giant mushrooms. It was almost as if the mushrooms had caught me. The rider, now only worried about his horse having not seen or heard me fall, because the landing was soft and I had not screamed. The rider showed the mushrooms off the other side of the path.

Looking closely at the mushrooms, I noticed that they lit up a bright purple below their stems whenever they did something, and they made a squeak sound when they communicated. Suddenly, I got a weird sensation of moving. Looking around, I was indeed moving. The mushrooms were taking me into the forest.

"My friend is still with them," I whispered to the mushrooms, knowing that I could do nothing to get Jessie with one leg. All the mushrooms around me lit up their stems as if sending a message to the other mushrooms. The rider of the horse turned sharply around at that moment and noticed that I was not on the horse, but thankfully could not see me on the other side. The mushrooms continued moving me out of sight further into the woods. The rider sent out an alarm, but by then I was far out of their reach.

Besides my aching neck and stump of a leg, I was quite comfortable riding on a troop of mushrooms.

"Your forest is so pretty," I whispered, noticing how differently it looked now that I was inside it. Their mushroom stems lit up in a very light, happy violet, and they all gave off a happy squeal. On and on, the mushrooms moved further into the forest at a surprisingly quick rate.

"Where are you taking me?" I asked, wondering if they understood what I was saying and if they could, in fact, answer me. A few of their stems blinked on and off at the sound of my voice, but other than that, they gave me no indication whatsoever that they understood my babbling.

The forest was growing denser and more diverse in its tree species, but still none that I recognized. The sky still appeared unhomely to me, graced with an eerie red glow that became more apparent the further we went. The scale trees, as I decided to call them, reflected the red glow most peculiarly. The forest was indeed frightful, but I had the old sense that it was familiar to me in some way. Surprisingly, I felt at peace and let my body relax.

Pressing on, we began to pass large rocks and boulders. I had the urge to sing a song to calm me down, but something inside me said no, then a faint hum of an all too familiar song rose to my ears, and the soft babbling of a loud stream. "I know that voice," I breathed softly to myself. There was indeed a stream for its faint chatter grew louder and, in the distance, I spotted steam arising from its merry banks. The song grew louder, and a little stone cabin appeared by the stream's chatty bank.

"Merchant Buckles!" I exclaimed, recognizing that old, familiar, jolly face.

"Little Aoife Bear Queen?!" he exclaimed, lifting me off the bouncing mushrooms, "What brings you to this hidden and mercy-forsaken corner of the world? And what in heaven's name happened to yer leg? Yer a one-legged bouncing pirate! It's not safe in this part of the world if you don't know what you're doin'."

"Well, it's kinda a long story, but a friend of mine needs saving, and I'm not sure the mushrooms understand what I'm saying," I replied, watching their stems light up.

"Oh, I'm not entirely sure they understand anything or just have a funny sense of humor. This morning, I asked them for Feverfew, and they brought me Jewelweed. Completely different plant, and I know they grow here," Buckles replied, pouring me a cup of tea from the pot that was brewed on the fireplace.

"So, they're going to get my friend?" I asked nervously, sipping the strong, spicy tea that reminded me of the kind he used to sell Honeysuckle for the cold wintertime weather.

"You bet your boot," Buckles replied, sorting through a box of maps, "They're smart little fellas. They should have 'em here in no time at all, but in the meantime," he said, diving into a barrel of goods, "Ah ha. In the meantime, this should help you get around." He said, presenting me with a wooden peg leg, "This one is made from maple and dipped in the nectar of the fairies and hardened in dragon's breath."

"How much will it cost me?" I asked with a smile, admiring the fancy piece of equipment. It was covered in straps, belts, and latches that would be used to hold the device in place.

"Not a cent of money," he replied, handing the leg to me, "but there is one favor I'd require."

"I'm at your service," I replied, looking at the peg leg over, wondering how to possibly get it on, when a knock sounded at the door of his cabin.

They're back with your friend, I bet you," he replied, opening the door. There lay Jessie, tied up in vines from head to foot and still trying to fight the mushrooms to get loose. The mushrooms tossed him on the ground, where he landed with a thump.

"Thank you very much, general," Buckles thanked the lead mushroom and handed him a shiny jewel. The great mushroom general gave a nod in return and led his great troop of hopping, laughing mushrooms away.

"What be you friend's name?" Buckles asked me from outside the door. It was still difficult for me to get around on one leg.

"Jessie," I called back, trying to stand up.

"Well, I think you'd better untie Jessie," Buckles replied, coming back in, "I think he wants to rip me head off. Let me help you get that leg on."

It took Buckles about twenty minutes to help me get the leg on and tight. Merchant Buckles steadied me and helped me stand up and take a few steps outside. Jessie, who was flopping this way and that, gagged and tried to free himself.

"Jessie, hold still," I replied, trying to cut him loose with the knife Buckles had handed me.

"How did you get tied up in vines?" I asked with confusion, for the armed soldiers had used a rope on me, finally pulling off his gag.

Breathing hard, Jessie replied, "It was those evil, blackish, purplish mushrooms. They wouldn't let me go, so they jumped on me altogether and bound me tight."

"They were trying to bring you here," I laughed, cutting off the rest of the vines. "They were helping rescue you."

"Where's here?" Jessie asked, looking around. Jessie jumped up, brushing himself off, looking confused, agitated, and jumpy.

"My hiding place. Thank you very much. And you never saw it," Buckles answered him sternly helping me up onto my foot; well now feet.

"You look familiar," Jessie replied, trying to place Merchant Buckles.

"Merchant Buckles at your service, Son," Merchant Buckles replied. "And I hate to break up the introductions, but the young miss owes me a favor, and the sun is almost directly over us."

Merchant Buckles waved toward the stream that babbled on. "I'm coming," Jessie replied, standing and starting to follow, stumbling all the way.

Merchant Buckles coached me the whole way on how to use my new leg. Deep down, I thought that it would take me ten full years to learn how to use it properly. Merchant Buckles stood close and caught me several times when I stumbled and almost fell. I just could not seem to trust the peg leg. Step by step, I learned to put more weight through it, and it hurt to bear weight with the tight straps.

"Try to keep up," Buckles called to Jessie, rounding the corner of the stream past some trees. Jessie seemed like he was still in a brain fog and agitated from whatever the natives had given him to knock him out.

"Hey, where'd you get a leg?" Jessie asked, trying to keep up.

"Merchant Buckles," I replied, trying to balance myself with help from Merchant Buckles. Trying to balance on the new leg was like learning a foreign language to me.

"Are you alright?" I asked Jessie.

"My legs are asleep," Jessie complained, catching up to me around a bend in the path that led along the babbling stream's edge. Jessie limped along on tired legs, trying to keep up.

A faint mutter caught my ear; it was not from Jessie. "Shh," I whispered to Jessie, trotting behind me. He stood stone still, then crept quietly forward, not making the slightest sound. He heard the sound too.

"Are you coming, or are you?!" Merchant Buckles yelled back to Jessie from ahead. We continued forward, still wary of the noise that appeared to be getting louder.

The heavy pounding of water on rock vibrated the stone-laden ground, getting louder the further we went into the dense forest along the stream's edge. The muttering grew louder as well, although now I could tell that it was laughter, but not any form of laughter I had ever heard before. It was high-pitched, joyous, yet it ran like a consistent rhyme or drumbeat, with the same notes being played over and over again, threatening to go on indefinitely.

Merchant Buckles was waiting for us as we rounded the next bend, "Behold Wama's Hidden Weir!" he said, raising up his arms in dramatic display over the great natural wonder.

Our eyes beheld a great waterfall that seemed to be nearly swallowed by the land around it.

Water thundered down into a deep, dark watery hole, making contact with rock at the bottom, probably some hundreds of giant strides down. Around the edges of the deep hole grew shrubs, lichens, and moss of nearly every color I thought possible, all working to shroud the great, majestic beauty from view.

"Eluding every map in our world for centuries, living only in lore and myth, but I... found it!" Buckles exclaimed in excitement.

"So, what do you need Aoife for?" Jessie asked, folding his arms across his chest.

Merchant Buckles stood still for a moment before replying, while Jessie waited impatiently, "There are many places in this world that I have ventured, and sadly, on these journeys I have made many an enemy of the guardians of great treasures, the main being the entire water nymph population. Which is why I need someone who they will accept to get down into the underwater caverns that are full of the precious jewels I came here to find."

"How do you become an enemy to the entire water nymph population? I mean, I didn't even know they existed," Jessie asked.

"Oh, they exist all right and are very territorial. You either respect their rein, or you are never heard from again," Buckles explained, looking down into the great hole in the ground, then turned around and asked, "What do you say, Aoife? Is this a good move for you, oh future queen?" Buckles gave a dramatic bow to Aoife as he finished talking.

"I am honored and will gladly take on this momentous task," I replied quickly, walking toward the steep edge of Wama's Weir. I was stepping slowly on my new leg.

"Future what?" Jessie called after me over the thundering water.

Ignoring him, I pulled the chain around my neck off that had so faithfully held my parents' rings for years and thrust it out over the ledge and dropped it. Next, I unbuckled my sword and laid it on a stone by the Weir. I then walked back five paces, took a deep breath, raced forward, and leaped over the side. At this point in time, as I am falling, you may think me to be a downright fool for plunging over the edge of the deep Weir into the unknown darkness, but I, in fact, knew more than Buckles himself on the history of the weir.

How did I come by the history of the mythical weir, you ask? The Creature himself taught extensive history lessons on mystical places of all sorts, including how to deal with beings of all kinds. Step one when dealing with water nymphs is always to acknowledge their presence with a gift before entering their territory. They will likely give you far more than your gift was worth in return for you giving them proper respect. Failure to do so shows that you have no knowledge of them being there, which angers them, or you know that they are there but just don't care enough to acknowledge that, which can end up sealing your untimely demise.

The rings around the chain were worth a lot to me, but I know that that is not where my family is, and I would rather live to make them proud than hang on to them and let it be the end of me. Meeting a hard landing in a shallow rock pool did not scare me, for I truly knew the great mystery of Wama's Weir. The caves below the surface were said to contain air and other gases that billowed up and out of the great hole, slowing one's descent. Plunging down, I was beginning to feel exactly what it meant as I began to feel lift slowing me down drastically. When I finally dropped lightly into the water pool below, I had been falling for about seven minutes. Swimming toward the edge, a hand grabbed my shoulder. I prayed that my gift had been accepted.

Bright, glowing, scaly beings popped up all around me in the dark, murky water. I tilted my head down in respect and nodded thrice and remained silent. The Creature had taught me everything in such a circumstance.

One nymph fitted a breathing mask over my nose, mouth, and ears. At the same time, another motioned for me to hold on to his shoulders. I was going to meet their King. One final breath above the water, and the nymph dove under the murky, black film.

The deeper the nymph swam, the more I could see. Crystals that glowed in red and orange hues were scattered along the rough, rocky walls of the underwater caves and caverns. Deeper and deeper the nymph swam while the others followed behind. The mask they had given me was unlike any I had ever seen before, as it acted as gills, filtering air bubbles out of the water. Down, down, and down some more until I guessed that we had been going down for at least twenty minutes, then the cave began to curve slightly upward, and the crystals changed to green and blue hues.

Up we went into a great, grand cavern that glowed with more colors than I had ever seen before. Water nymphs lined the rocks and ridges of the great cavern above the water's surface and in the water.

"This has to be the throne room," I decided in my head, finally able to breathe above the water again. I was led to a large, empty rock half-submerged in the glowing water to sit and wait.

The nymphs that had brought me in hurried off as if they were trying to find someone important. I waited in silence, trying to pull any important information from my memory on the topic of nymph etiquette, but the only thing that came to mind was an old seaman's poem about nymphs that Honeysuckle had sung to me when I was just a little girl.

I could hear his own dear voice above the splashing and laughing of the jolly nymphs,

"Dark diamonds of pearl,

Ye gems of the deep.

Ye search for survivors,

In recks of great fleets.

Your voices are merry,

Your ways true and bright,

I see you dance about,

In the watery moonlight."

"Will I ever see a nymph?" I remember asking him. "Of course, you will, you little elf," he would reply with a laugh,

217

"I'm sure you'll go everywhere and find things you've never dreamed of."

A soft hush fell over the merry crowd till nothing could be heard save the lapping of the water at the rocky walls of the cavern. I remained still but sat up straight and looked down at my hands; I knew the importance of reverence. On the far side of the cavern, two nymphs lit torches, illuminating a gold throne that sat out of the water just enough that the top half was visible above the glowing water. A great nymph adorned with jewels of all kinds, holding a great spear, sat down on the throne; the nymph king.

Chapter 32:
The Nymph King Loughlin

Two great warrior nymphs appeared at his side, appearing like they were prepared for anything. The nymph king raised his spear up high, then swung it down, making ripples across the water. The nymphs that had brought me in helped me down from the rock and toward the throne, stopping about ten feet in front.

One of the nymphs handed the king my necklace. He nodded and fastened it around his neck. "He likes it," I thought in relief. He then pointed his spear at me. I dropped my head in respect. The king nodded to the nymphs at my side, who brought me closer to the throne.

"I am King Loughlin of the river nymphs," he exclaimed in a voice deeper than any I had ever heard before, "Who are you and why are you in my realm. Speak!"

"I am Aoife McKelvey, daughter of the departed Biro the Stone, and adopted daughter of Honeysuckle Beairclan," I began, trying not to shake, for I had never told a soul of my true father, but part of me knew that I had to answer honestly, "I have been sent by an acquaintance to acquire of your caverns crystals."

"Biro the Stone," King Loughlin replied, rubbing his chin, "Biro was a good friend of mine, a good king. You resemble him, Child. You're on someone's errand, yes, but why are you here?"

"To pick up where my father left off if I am able, your Majesty," I began with a respectful nod, "You and your great people are grand allies of might and power, and I am afraid that your honorable friendship has been neglected of late. Forgive us our grave mistake."

"There is no mistake, Child," King Loughlin replied with a hearty laugh, "I have been getting letters and gifts from your advisor since the passing of your father. In fact, they come quite regularly, and I have also received writings in your name."

"May I enquire as to the name of the advisor, my King?" I replied nervously, wondering if Honeysuckle had been keeping relations with the old allies.

"Theodore Weatherly, the Creature guardian of Mossland and keeper of the Great Tunnels, and a personal friend of mine, Child," King Loughlin recalled, "He tells me much about you, and he has quite a skill with the pen. You are most welcome in my kingdom, always, Child. Since you are the daughter of Biro the Stone, I will treat you as my own daughter."

"Thank you, your Majesty," I breathed, not quite believing that my professor had been the one maintaining relations for our country with the nymphs, "I am very grateful and appreciative of your kind and generous welcome."

"I will grant you the crystal your acquaintance desires and more for them sending you here, but I have one request of you," King Loughlin replied. "One moon from now is the Stellar night. Your father vowed to see it when the war was over, but never got to. It is the night where a thousand stars appear in our sky brighter than any other night of the year, and I would like you to fulfill your father's oath in his place."

"I will fulfill it with great pride and honor, my King," I replied, "May I, in your good discretion, oh King, settle one small matter before?"

"You may, and when you return, I will have a feast prepared in your honor," King Loughlin agreed.

"Thank you, your Majesty," I replied.

The water nymphs led me to an air-filled cave that led to the ground above. Stepping out of the cave, I shielded my eyes from the bright light. Waiting for my eyes to adjust, I sat down on a lichen-covered rock.

The rock moved and shook beneath me. I jumped up in a start, and my peg leg nearly slipped out from under me. "Well, hi!" I exclaimed with a laugh, looking at the great, purple mushroom that appeared green due to its lichen camouflage.

The mushroom squeaked in delight, light flashed up its stem, and it began to hop down a little path as if beckoning me to follow. Down the path we went through the eerie wood, hopping along the way. The mushroom turned around every now and then to make sure that I was following it, then delightedly squeaked and hopped on. After about an hour's time, I spotted Merchant Buckles' cabin.

The mushroom gave a squeak, then hopped away into the dense wood, leaving me by the cabin. "Merchant Buckles! Jessie!" I called as I was entering the cabin.

"Out here, my Lady and Queen," Merchant Buckles called from somewhere behind the cabin.

"Boy, am I glad you made it out," Merchant Buckles called as I rounded the corner. Merchant Buckles was tied up to the great tree by the stream.

"What happened?" I exclaimed, rushing to untie him, but my peg-leg tripped on a root, causing me to fall flat on my face.

"Jessie! Jess, my boy, she's back and safe as ever, just like I told you," Merchant Buckles called, "You can untie me now."

"Where!?" I heard Jessie call from a distance.

"Jessie tied you up?" I asked to untie the knot that bound his hands behind the tree.

"Well, yes and no," he replied, standing up, "I know my mouth got me most of it."

"Aoife," Jessie called, emerging from the woods, "You're okay."

"And what about me, crystals?" Merchant Buckles asked, walking toward Jessie and me. Jessie looked as if he were going to flatten him.

"The nymphs agreed to give you the crystals you desired and more, but I have a few terms of my own," I replied.

"Anything you want, my Lady," Merchant Buckles replied with a bow.

"I need safe passage in your ship to Fayatoch, the delivery of a message to Sir Masuda, and several messages to home, and that one tenth of the crystal goes to Sir Theodore Weatherly, the Creature of the Deep Tunnels," I replied, "I deal that is a fair trade."

"I'll do better than that and give him twenty-five percent," Merchant Buckles replied with a large grin on his face.

"So, it's a deal?" I asked, stretching out my hand.

"Deal," Merchant Buckles replied, shaking my hand.

"So, we're going back to Fayatoch finally," Jessie replied with a long breath of relief.

"You are," I replied, "The nymphs wish me to stay with you for one moon's time, and then I'm returning."

"What?" Jessie objected, "If we're going back, we're going together."

"If I don't stay and honor my promise, there will be no ship to sail in and no safe waters from here to home," I replied, determined to find a way to get Jessie to go with Merchant Buckles.

"What she says is true, my boy," Merchant Buckles added, "If you do not honor the nymph people, they will not honor you."

"Then I'm staying till you leave!" Jessie shouted loud enough for the entire forest to hear.

"I will be readying my ship, my Lady," Buckles informed, walking toward a worn and overgrown forest trail, "Have your letters ready before sunrise."

"I shall," I replied with a gracious smile, "Thank you, Master Buckles."

"Look, our parents sent us to Fayatoch for war training and safety in case it was to happen early," Jessie reasoned, "Why do you think they sent all of their daughters as well as their sons?"

"I know," I replied with a nod, "There we were out of harm's way. That's why I was sent and why I did not stay home. My father never intended for me to see war. Did Daniel tell you about it?"

"Yes," Jessie replied, "Daniel told me, but anyone could have guessed the same. Aoife, me, you, Liam, and Libby got a real taste of the true world we live in. We got more experience in the last few weeks than we could have ever learned at Fayatoch. If any of the kids sent to Fayatoch ever see war, we will be the ones who are most prepared. Look, Liam wrote to Sir Masuda about what happened, so there is no reason for either of us to hurry back. One month's time shouldn't spring this war into action, and if it does, then our next is to journey home."

"You make a compelling argument," I replied, wondering if King Loughlin would accept another guest at his table.

"Listen, you can think it over all you want," Jessie argued, "but there is no way you can force me onto that Hoot's ship. So, I'm staying. Whatever you decide."

"How much do you like water?" I asked with a laughing grin.

"What?" Jessie asked, his face a puzzled look.

All that evening and night, I stayed by the fire in Buckles' cabin and wrote letters. For my father, Honeysuckle, I bundled up my diary notes and writings along with a simplified and condensed version of 'my adventures' as Jessie called them. He, too, was writing home. For the Creature, Sir Theodore, I was writing him a thank you for maintaining the country's alliances, a full report about my meeting with the water nymph King Loughlin, and a full report about what I heard in Skysii, and other rumors and little bits of information I had acquired concerning unrest or violence. To Sir Masuda, I wrote simply that we had been delayed in returning to Fayatoch and should arrive in a moon and a half's time.

The fire flickered on as my eyes began to fall in the early dawn when I finished writing my last letter. Stretching, I stood and shook Jessie, who was fast asleep.

"Come on," I whispered, "Buckles will be leaving shortly."

"Good," Jessie moaned back, covering his head with the blanket, "more sleep for me."

"We need to help him leave," I explained, "and bring him our letters."

"Oh," Jessie replied, getting up with a yawn, "we have to help him leave."

Down at the docks, we loaded the last of Buckles' things onto his little ship. In the bay, water nymphs presented Merchant Buckles with more crystal than he had ever imagined getting, and in return, Merchant Buckles traded beautiful silks and cloth, steel armor embellished with silver, gold, and bronze, arrows, bows, and other assorted goods from his cargo.

Before Buckles left, I asked him for a small piece of jewelry from his merchant's collection. He graciously agreed to give me some jewelry, presenting me with a beautifully engraved bracelet set with fair jewels. I smiled and tucked it away in my bag. It was a prayer bracelet, and I had been wanting one for a while.

"The fair Lady Aoife," Merchant Buckled said with a smile, bowing and tipping his hat as he left, hanging onto a rope standing on the deck, "Soft spoken, godly, meek, strong, delicate, tough, sensitive, loving, caring, wise, resilient, and frugal."

Jessie waved goodbye to Buckles' ship as it sailed away, as if relieved that he was not on it. I smiled a soft, sweet smile. I breathed a sigh of relief and felt at peace within. A soft breeze blew my hair around my face as soft and light as a fairy kiss.

"I'm going home soon," my heart sang within, *"Soon, I'll be going home."*

Chapter 33:
Nymph & Crystals

Jessie and I walked to Wama's Wier to join the nymphs. Pain shot through my leg with nearly every step; something was not right, but there was nothing I could do at the moment, so I gave a silent prayer: *Lord, I cannot heal myself. I asked forgiveness for my sins. I give my all to you, and I thank you for all of your blessings. I know you have the power to heal. Please guide me and help me to continue on.*

In Jesus' name,

Amen.

Looking down into the great dark hole, Jessie exclaimed, "You're trying to kill me. Even if I survive the fall, they'll eat me!"

"That would be sirens," I replied, tossing the bracelet Buckles had given me into the Wier.

"But I heard that mermaids ate beings, too!" Jessie fussed, looking down into the inky darkness.

"Well, it's a good thing then that we are a thousand miles from the nearest mermaids," I replied with a weak smile.

"Isn't a mermaid the same thing as a nymph?" Jessie asked, puzzled.

"No," I explained. "Mermaids are half human and half fish. They also live near humans and can be aggressive when disturbed. Water nymphs do resemble mermaids, but they are not part human or fish. They are closer to a fairy or dryad and have scales that look like dragon scales. There are also different kinds of nymphs; these are water nymphs."

"Where do you get all of this information?" Jessie asked, "You know the Creature of the Deep Tunnels? His name is Theodore Weatherly."

"I think I've heard of him," Jessie replied, scratching his head.

"I am one of his students," I replied, then exclaimed, "Alright, it's time to jump."

Jessie and I stepped back from the edge, and taking a deep breath, we both took a running jump.

Down we fell on the rising steam-like fog till we finally dropped into the eerie, black water below. Trying to stay above the water, I listened for Jessie, who emerged with a gasp. A scaly hand gripped my shoulder.

"Who is this?" a voice from behind me asked in questioning tones.

"This is a friend of mine," I replied nervously, "I pray he is welcome." There was a long silence as more nymphs arrived. The nymphs talked among themselves in their own language of the deep till they had come to an agreement.

"Any friend of yours is a friend of ours," the head nymph guard announced with a nod.

The breathing masks were fitted on Jessie and me, and our journey began as we dove below. Down, down, and still the deeper we went through the tunnels of glowing crystal. The light from the crystal bounced off the nymph's colorful scales, making them appear to glow as well.

The journey was about halfway through when a sickening feeling crept inside my gut that gave way to a throbbing sensation in my stump of a leg. My thoughts and senses seemed to scream all at once, *"Infection! Infection! Infection!"* *"Oh, dear,"* was my heart's reply as it dropped within me.

On and on, our party dove deeper through colder water. My leg, or what I had left of my leg, ached all the more, bringing with it a gruesome headache. The journey seemed to be taking longer than the one I had first been on, and it seemed to me that we should be heading up now instead of down. I judged that we had been underwater for at least two hours when my first journey had taken no longer than half an hour. I tried to put these thoughts out of my mind and just enjoy the journey, but somehow, they were still there, pulling at my nervous fear.

On and on we went through tunnels with crystals of all kinds imaginable and beyond. Time seemed to make no sense to me anymore. Cloudiness crept into my vision and senses. My whole body no longer hurt; it was numb. I closed my eyes but got no comfort. Slowly, all my senses went numb and cold, causing me to drift into an unconscious sleep-like state.

While I was unconscious, I had a dream in which I saw something that I would say was strange. I was lying in an open, animal pasture littered with bushes under a dull, cloudy sky. Sitting up, I looked around me at the tall, brown, dead grass.

Presently, I stood and began walking toward a pond in the distance. While I walked, I noticed that I was wearing a long, brown dress and my feet were bare, causing me to feel the soft, damp grass beneath me. Cold, wet mud began to seep up around my feet as I was nearing the lake. The water was clear, allowing me to see what it held: an animal carcass, a few fallen logs, and a handful of red fish.

"Aoife, Aoife," A voice called from the far side of the small lake that was surrounded by a barrier of lilies, tadpoles, and high fairy grasses of many kinds.

"Aoife! Aoife!" the voice called louder.

"Coming!" I ran in the direction of the voice through the tall, scratchy grass around the lake. I knew that voice; it was my Macintyre, my little brother.

"Hurry," little Macintyre called.

Rounding the corner of the lake, I saw little Macintyre wrapped in a cloak and holding a basket of eggs.

"What's wrong?" I asked, lifting my little brother out of the high grass.

"You left me," he whined, looking into my eyes, "Why did you go?"

"Father wanted me to go to prepare for the war," I replied, "but I'll be back in no time."

"Promise," he exclaimed, looking up at me with his deep, dark brown eyes. His soft, dark, thick brown fur blew softly in the quiet whispering breeze.

"Promise," I replied with a smile, feeling tears rise to my eyes, and I could barely choke out the words, "You have my word."

"Okay," he smiled, then asked with a serious expression, "You bring me back some treats?"

"Yes," was my reply with tears brimming in my eyes and spilling down my cheeks. I knelt down and squeezed him tight. Oh, how I missed him and my family.

With a jolt, I awoke from my dream with a start. I was lying in a small, rock pool of warm water in a large, air-filled tunnel. In the water beside me and on top of me lay small crystals of every kind I could imagine.

All the pain I had had was now gone. My foot itched within my boot, but as I sat up to scratch it, I jumped; It appeared as though I had two full legs. Reaching down, I pinched the alien leg to see if it was truly my own, "Ouch!" It was my leg. Noticing steam rising from my shirt, I realized how hot the water was that I was lying in.

"Lay down and rest," a nymph girl with silvery scales ordered me as she pulled herself up onto the rocks around the pool, "New leg needs time to bond."

"New leg?" I asked, laying down in the warm, steamy rock pool that was surprisingly comfortable and soft.

"Me Erena. I grow you new leg," she replied, setting a net full of crystals beside the pool, "Go bak to seep." One by one, she lined the crystals up around me and down my new leg.

My whole body was tired; in fact, I felt completely exhausted. Carefully placing the crystals, Erena sang and hummed in her own language.

"What song are you singing?" I asked curiously.

"It is called in your tongue *A Gem of Day*," Erena replied.

Then she continued, "The words go like this."

"A gem, a gem
Within the Sea,
The crushing waves surround thee.
You are worth the sweetest prize,
To my heart,
To my eyes.
I'll search for you and only when,
I find you at journey's end,
I'll sing for joy,
I'll dance all day,
For my prize,
The gem of day."

"That's a beautiful song," I replied with a soft, weak smile as I closed my weary eyes.

"Me father wrote dat song for me mother," she replied continuing her task, "You find that your new leg hav scales instead of skin, but day will match in color."

"Scales?" I asked, puzzled.

"Scales stronger, skin weak," she replied before hopping off the cave rock and back into the water-filled cavern.

Sitting up, I pulled up the end of my pant leg to see what she meant, "Well, it certainly looks like skin," I thought to myself, but rubbing my hand on it, it felt like snakeskin.

When Erena finally decided that I was well enough rested three days later, she allowed me to join the nymph feast.

In a great hall-like cavern on a massive floating table woven of willow branches, fairy grasses, flower vines, and sea grasses sat every kind of food known to the sea and beyond. Erena kept a close eye on me wherever I went, and I was grateful that the water was so thick with water nymphs that it was hard to swim around. Looking this way and that, I tried to locate Jessie and finally spotted him dead asleep on a large, flat rock by the cavern wall as full as could be.

"You need to eat," Erena directed me towards the table, "Go eat."

Doing as I was told, I swam up to the table and looked at all the different kinds of food.

"Seaweed soup good for you," Erena commented, filling me up a great shell-full, "Eat."

"Thank you," I replied, digging in even though I had no appetite. The soup was good, and a bit salty, but I enjoyed every bite. The soup had aroused my appetite. I found at least seven different kinds of seaweed in the soup, each with a distinct flavor. One type tasted almost like meat. Once I had finished the soup, I decided that I had had enough to eat, but Erena had other plans.

"Eat this," Erena directed, filling my shell with a whiteish, custard-like mush that had a savory, fishy flavor.

"Thank you," I replied once again, this time eating more slowly. I had finally gotten the hang of holding onto the table with one hand to keep me above the water and eating with the other hand when Erena put a whole roasted fish in my shell and handed me another shell full of sweet water to drink. She didn't bother to tell me to eat it; I knew what to do.

Within an hour after I had finished off the fish, Erena thought it wise that I would rest again, and I was grateful for it because my stomach could fit no more.

"Aoife, Aoife," Jessie whispered, shaking me awake in my crystal pool.

"What?" I moaned, rolling over.

"We have to leave," he replied, trying to pull me out of the pool.

"Why?" I replied, sitting up, "Jessie, you don't look so good. Are you alright?"

"No," he replied, whispering, "They won't stop feeding me. I'm gonna burst!"

"Oh, come on," I replied, rubbing my eyes, "How bad could it be?" "I abut to throw up," he exclaimed, placing his hand on his stomach.

"Well, not on top of me," I replied.

"How long do we have to stay here?" Jessie whispered.

"A few weeks. Why?" I asked.

"Because I can't stay here if they're gonna feed me like that," Jessie replied, "Man, that water is hot."

"They stuck me in a hot spring," I explained, "Jessie, I'm sure that the feast will end soon."

"You're sure," Jessie replied, giving me a hard stare.

"Sure," I replied, standing up and stepping out of the crystal pool.

"Why'd you put a boot on your peg leg?" Jessie asked with a puzzled look.

"It's not a peg leg. They somehow grew me a new leg," I replied with a shrug.

"That's impossible," Jessie skeptically replied, wrapping my leg to see if it was made of wood, "Well, it's not wood." Jessie pulled off my boot to inspect the new leg, "Wow," was all he said, looking for scars along the incision line around my knee, "This is amazing. I've never seen or heard of this kind of medicine. You can barely tell where the scales begin and end on your leg. Their medical capability is extraordinary! I would love to learn from them, but seriously, when are we leaving?"

"The morning after Stellar night," I answered, pulling my other boot off the water drain out.

"I don't suppose you know when that is," Jessie questioned, lying down on the rocks.

"At least two or three weeks from now," I replied, trying to judge from what the king had told me.

"I'll never make it," Jessie replied coldly, "Unless I can hide that, is." Jessie looked at my water pool and climbed in and lay beside me. He lay his head on my shoulder and yawned softly.

"You don't mind, do you?" he asked with a pitiful look on his face.

"I don't mind," I replied, closing my eyes. I trusted Jessie with my life, and to be honest, I was lonely in a strange place. Jessie fell asleep almost instantly, and I slowly drifted off to sleep.

We awoke about eight hours later to, "Get out of dere," It was Erena, "You not supose to be here."

"I just wanted to see how she was doing and keep her company," Jessie retorted as Erena pulled him out of the pool and led him to the tunnel where he was supposed to be staying.

The next few weeks went faster than I had ever imagined, and finally, it was the day before Stellar night. Erena had many exercises for me to ensure that I could walk and run properly, and when I had finally passed them all, I was able to attend Stellar night.

We had breathing masks put on us once again, and the nymphs swam us out into the bay after sunset. Jessie and I sat perched on a boulder with the waves lapping at the sides. The sun set softly over the horizon in beautiful shades of red, yellow, and orange, and then slipped into purple, pink, soft lavender, and finally a dark blanket of blue hues melting into the night.

"Princess Aoife," King Loughlin addressed me, lifting his muscular arms from the dark water that reflected the gorgeous sky as a mirror, "Behold the wonders of the night sky on Stellar Night!"

Looking up, I beheld the most beautiful sky full of more stars than I could have ever imagined. I gazed up and then down at the sea reflecting the bright heavens like never before. I was awestruck! I had never seen something so magnificent before. The great wonder almost brought tears to my eyes. *"Oh LORD, how majestic are your ways in all the earth!"* I prayed.

"Your Majesty," I addressed the King, "I am truly grateful that you wished me to see this great miracle of God's creation."

"Your joy is all the thanks I require," the King replied, "and tomorrow I will see you and your friend safely to Fayatoch."

To be honest, I stared into the heavens, sitting upon the boulder in the midst of the sea, till I fell asleep beneath God's bright heavens. I awoke in the shade on a sandy beach.

"Jessie, Jessie," I called, sitting up.

"What!" he answered me about five giant strides away, lying on the sand, "Wait! Where are we?"

"Fayatoch," I answered, seeing a figure dressed in a long black robe walking across the beach to meet us, "We're finally home."

Chapter 34:
Hope

Stepping into the training dorms once again, I felt a relief that I had not felt in a long time. "Everything is going to be alright now," I breathed to myself as I collapsed on my old cot by the window set with white silk curtains. I had been away for utterly too long, and I was so grateful to be back at Fayatoch.

"Aoife! Aoife," voices called entering the girl's dorms.

"I'm not here," I whispered to myself with a smile.

"Get up and tell us all about it," Kate demanded, trying in vain to pull me up.

"You can't just leave us like that," Róisín whined, "We were worried about you."

"It's good to see you too," I replied with a laugh, sitting up. "And so we're on the same page, I did not plan to go and be gone that long. And I don't plan to ever do that again."

"So, what's the most exciting thing you did?" Róisín bubbled with a laugh, tucking one of her rose petal curls behind her ear.

"Well," I began thinking over the entire journey. "A pirate cut off my leg, and a nymph grew me a new one. I was captured by a monster, the Skiskies, natives on an island, men in armor, and mushrooms rescued me. Merchant Buckles made a deal with me. A lot happened." Sadly, saying that only started the questions coming, and I talked and explained for over two hours about my adventure. That night, I wrote down everything I remembered from my adventure, and over the next few weeks, I consulted Jessie to make sure I included everything that had happened.

"Oh, come on," Kate mused, poking me in the ribs when I explained about my leg, "Tell us something real." She obviously did not believe me.

"That was real," I replied, pulling up the end of my pant leg over my boot, "Look, it's not skin; it's scales."

"It looks like a dragon's scales!" Róisín exclaimed, running her fingers across my skin.

Over the next few weeks, I began to really see the benefits of the nymph leg. It really did not seem to wear out when the rest of my body was exhausted. Just as Erena had said, the scales were indeed strong. I figured that out when I took an accidental slide down a long, steep slope. The leg did not appear to have any damage, even when the rest of my body was scratched and bruised from the fall.

Lady Catherine had a lot of catch-up work for me, which proved to fill most of my spare time, and I enjoyed it for the most part; I was happy to be back. Months passed, and winter set in for Fayatoch, bringing chilly mornings and brisk nights. The silk curtains were replaced with animal hides and secured down to keep the wind out. Despite this, girls pushed cots together in sets of two to three so they could huddle up at night, and Sir Masuda changed the usual evening workout into a morning one to get everyone's blood flowing.

Kate, Róisín, and I were tasked with dishwashing for the morning and night, which we did not mind, for there was always water heated for such occasions, so it kept our hands warm, but the soap dried our hands out, making them raw and red. At night, I would lather my hands with lotion and ointment and slide on my gloves to heal my hands.

"I done lost my warm layer," Róisín whined to Kate and I. "Now I'm cold!" Talking about the few pounds she had lost from the workouts. We both died laughing.

Several things had changed from the last time I was at Fayatoch. The most noticeable change was that I never felt relaxed in the woods and forever kept watch on Róisín and Kate when we were out there. The second change was that Jessie stayed within ten feet of me wherever we went away from the training grounds. And finally, the third change I noticed was that I often found myself thinking about the upcoming war rather than training.

Winter flew past faster than I could keep up with it, and a nice cool Spring took its place in the balance of seasons. Finally, when I found myself alone to rest in the courtyard between the training dorms, I reached into my pocket and drew out three letters that had been delivered to me from the docks. Merchant Buckles had gotten safely to Mossland with all of that crystal.

Opening the leather-tied envelope with Honeysuckles' handwriting, I drew out the letter and held my breath as I read it.

Dear Aoife,

I am so proud of you, and I pray for you constantly. Little Macintyre is getting bigger every day, nearly up to my waist. I miss your help in the garden and with projects, but Little Macintyre is stepping up to the plate and doing a great job at it. Buckles said that you left your necklace on his ship, so I'm putting it in this letter. I am hurrying to write this because Buckles is leaving in a few hours. I plan to read your stories tonight, and I am very grateful for them and you're your safety. Remember to pray, my precious child.

Love you, baby,

Honeysuckle Beiarclen.

I tipped the envelope upside down; my necklace chain with my family rings that I had given to the nymphs dropped into my palm. "They gave my necklace back?" I whispered to myself in awe.

Opening the second letter, I pulled out a thick wad of papers that were packed tight and wrapped with leather from the creature.

Dear Aoife,

Yes, I have been keeping up with the country's allies. It was of necessity that I did so to preserve our nation's respect among the peoples and beings of our world. I am truly grateful that that meddling Buckles did not get you killed and overwhelmed to hear of your safety.

I am in haste, deciding to bring you children back in two years' time unless things get worse.

Aoife, don't forget who you are. Learn well the lessons they have for you, and whatever you do, protect Róisín. Her country will need her in due time.

Greatest of Hopes,

Sir Thoedore Weatherly, the Creature of the Deep Tunnels

The next four pages were notes that he had written about beings and countries of all different kinds for my reference.

Chapter 35:
Terror in Daylight

Ships often arrived at the docks with merchandise for the island and more children from Mossland for training. Sometimes the masters took us to the docks with them to watch and assist them if needed. The ships that docked in port belonged to merchants from nearly every corner of Unifa, bringing fascinating wares, many of which I had never laid eyes on.

There were many different styles and sizes of ships, I noticed when I was able to go. I went mostly to get writing paper and pass off letters for Honeysuckle, my dear Father, and possibly receive one from him, always stuffed with pictures from my younger siblings.

The hikes down the mountain to the docks were becoming easier for me when I thought of all the excitement happening at the docks. I also longed, dear reader, for the letters. Often, I felt homesick even though this was my home away from home. I relished the few trips we were granted and sometimes even went in my spare time.

I also was beginning to enjoy Sir Masuda's rigorous mountain hikes; they made me feel confident in my abilities, and the morning air was sweet. The hikes also reminded me of the many hikes my father had taken with me when I was back in Mossland. It was almost as if I could feel his presence.

One morning at the docks, as I was following Master Masuda, I saw a ship carrying only dry goods and looked through the articles of clothing as Master Masuda was talking with the merchant of the ship. I came across a necklace that was round before tapering into one chain with a cross at its tip.

It was a rosary, a necklace used by Catholics over the seas for prayer and devotion. Honeysuckle had owned one as long as I could remember, and it reminded me of him, so I decided to purchase the necklace. I was admiring the wooden beads when I felt a bushy beard tickle my neck. It was the merchant. He was an old, charming man with blue eyes and a long, bushy, white and grey beard.

"What can I do for you, young miss?" he asked me with a merry grin that lifted his whole beard.

"How much do you want for this, sir? I'd like to purchase it." I replied, pointing to my newfound prize.

"The rosery, oh, five shillings," he replied.

I reached into my side purse and counted out five shillings and handed the money to him.

"That there is a fine necklace, miss. Came all the way from Vatican City," He said. "Would you also want a devotion book. Tells you how to properly use it. And only three shillings more."

"Yes, I would," I quickly replied, and he fumbled in a dark brown wooden box with dark blood-red leather hinges till he emerged with a red leather book with gold lettering on the front. I handed him three more shillings.

"This contains all the prayers and mysteries for the devotions," he explained with a smile that made it while his grey and white beard rose, shaking my hand. "And before you go, I have an endless selection of dresses and fabrics for the young ladies."

I spotted Master Masuda walking further down the docks. I did not want to get far behind him. I knew that we had to start traveling back up the mountain soon.

"Thank you, sir, but I must be going," I replied with a smile. I concealed my purchase in my side bag as I started towards Master Masuda's direction.

He was speaking to another merchant about his price of fish for the training dorms. I ran my hand down a soft, purple, velvet coat hanging on a makeshift rack that the merchants set out, and wondered if I still had enough money to make another purchase when I heard a great, "BOOM, Crack!" A ship anchored at the next dock over was smoking and on fire.

"BOOM, CRACK, BOOM, CRACK, BOOM, CRACK," it sounded again. I hit the deck, and the clothing rack fell over me. I was hidden under a pile of fancy, woven cloaks and coats. Five more ships in the harbor began smoking and sinking. Two that I could see were sinking fast; their men were trying in vain to get them to shore. The island was under attack!!!

Master Masuda was calling for the children and leading them hurriedly up the path. Three great black ships plated with metal accents came into view. The merchants were ordering their men to cast off and man the cannons. More shots came, one after another.

On and on they boomed, shooting their cannons at the docks and merchant vessels. The merchant vessels returned fire at random, only succeeding in tearing the main mast off the lead ship. A few merchant ships were able to get away.

As the large metal warships inched closer, I knew that I could not remain in my hiding spot. The ships would be at the remaining docks in mere moments! Slowly, I pushed and wiggled my way out from under the large clothing rack and stood on my feet. Despite feeling as though I was frozen in place, I managed to run ten yards, but I was still twenty yards away from the wood line. I wasn't fast enough. Rough hands grabbed my arms from behind. I shrieked and yelled, fighting to get loose. I jumped backward, jamming the back of my head into my assailant's face. He loosened his grip just enough for me to turn around and knee him in the crotch. He let go, and I ran hard to the path's mouth that led up the mountain. I didn't get there. Someone grabbed me, lifting me in the air before covering my mouth and nose with a handkerchief. Everything went black.

I woke up on the dingy, musty wood floor in the brig of a ship in one of its black iron cells. A brig is usually the name of a vessel that was square rigged and two-masted, with additional differences, but for war or pirate ships, the brig was a term for where the prison cells were located below deck, and I appeared to be in a brig, again!

It was dark; the only light I saw came from a crack in the ceiling above. Loud voices sounded from the deck above, deafened only by the endless roar of cannon fire. I shivered from the surprising cold and saw my breath turn white. The cell was empty save for an iron bench against the back wall, a bucket by the cell door, and a knee-high pile of hay on the right wall by the bench, or so I thought.

"BOOM, CRACK, BOOM," the noise of the splintering ships and yelling men thundered in my ears. The ship shook madly, being slapped about by hostile waves, a clear result of a few missed cannonballs. I crawled to the iron bench and clung to it with one arm while trying to cover my tortured ears with the other.

"BOOM, CRACK," the ship was hit. The noise of cannon fire slowly died down, leaving only the angry shouts on board. I shook myself trying to get free of the shock my body was in, but it was all in vain.

When I finally woke, it was dark, but the shock in my body was wearing off. The cold had crept in, numbing my hands and face. I remembered at that moment that my cloak was in the cell by the door. I had forgotten it during the cannon shower. The ship was still rocking furiously about, so I crawled, feeling the ground beneath my hands.

"Ouch," I ran my head into the iron door when the ship lurched to the side. The hit wasn't hard, but I cried anyway as I rubbed my head and finally located my cloak. It was a real comfort to wrap the cloak about me and lie against the hay. I drifted off to sleep in the chilly cell.

Despite the chill of the night, the ship's endless creaking and rocking, and my bruised head, I managed to fall into a deep sleep. I awoke before my eyes and limbs were ready to, so I knew I would have to wait for a minute to let myself wake up fully if I wished to move. I realized at that moment that I felt warm. A loud snort sounded behind my head. I jumped to my feet, wheeling around, my cloak wrapped around my face. Another snort followed by a snoring sound made my heart almost stop within me. I slowly freed my face of the cloak, dreading to see what was there. It was a large, scaly, grey-green, Fang Serpent.

Fang Serpents were long dragons without any wings that inhabited the warm, slimy cliffs of Unknown, a peninsula protruding into the South Sea. I had never seen one of these creatures before. Many travelers and merchants told stories to children about the beasts and drew pictures, but it was hard to believe that a giant four-legged serpent existed when you'd never seen one in anything but pictures.

The Fang Serpent lay in a ring with its great, spiny tail wrapping all the way to its head, and was snoring softly with smoke steaming out of its nostrils. Why had I not noticed the great serpent before? I clutched my cloak and tried to remember everything I'd been told about the creatures.

Merchant Buckles passed through the Mossland around the river Merigold nearly every year with exciting stories of his adventures. Once, he told me a story about a time when he encountered a Fang Serpent on his journey through Unknown for rare gems said to be found in the caves there. He had said, "' It was my last moment,' I thought as I stared the beast in the face. 'The beast had me cornered against a cave wall when I remembered that dragons hate spritelings, so I pulled a spriteling-made cloak from my bag and wrapped meself in it."

"What happened then?" the children who gathered around said spellbound.

"The beast walked closer and sniffed the cloak, then turned and walked away. And I have never gone looking for gems in Unknown since that very day," he told me.

"Why do fang serpents not like spritelings?" I asked.

"It's because spritelings are poisonous to fang serpents. The spriteling blood will kill them, and they know it, so they try not to eat anything that smells like a spriteling. If I didn't have that cloak, I wouldn't be here today." Merchant Buckles explained as he told his adventure tales.

I could hear his voice in my head as I stared at the creature, but I didn't have a spriteling cloak. "Keep thinking," I told myself. The tinker Cardello came to the New Year festival every year, and I remember that he told a story about a spriteling princess who tamed a fang serpent and kept it as her pet. He told us that many years ago, in his travels, he saw a group of spritelings in Unknown that actually rode the wingless creatures like horses. Okay, so they could be tamed, but this was not much help to me with a hungry fang serpent.

An elder from the Horseland prairies, called Mr. Edmund Hender, claimed in his tales that they disappeared and magically changed their scales to blend in with their surroundings, so they could sneak up on their prey and take it by surprise. Well, that could explain the reason why I didn't notice the giant serpent. The question was, why was I put in the cell with the great beast?

The hay began to rustle; the creature was stirring. A great puff of smoke bellowed from its nostrils as it stretched and opened its yellow eyes with deep black pupils. I backed up till I was against the rough wood wall by the black iron bars. The creature walked toward me with curiosity, sniffing my clothes before curling into a ball at my feet and falling asleep again. I stood frozen against the wall as the great creature snored, winding its long tail around my legs.

The amount of time I stood there, I do not know, but it felt like hours. I woke up in the dark once again, noticing my incredible hunger for the first time and the soreness of my neck that had been tipped forward for hours. I remembered that Daniel had given me a bag of jerky he had gotten from home as a thank you for delivering flowers to Róisín. It was quite a large bag, I realized, as I struggled to pull it from my side bag. When I finally retrieved it, I found a large piece and stuck it in my mouth. Tasting the chewy, tangy venison made my mouth water.

"Aarrfffs," the creature sniffed, woke up, and moved its head to my lap. I could faintly see the creature's eyes in the pitch-black of the night. On Captain Acosta's ship, there were always lights on deck at night, but this ship seemed to have none.

"Ssshhhiiirrrmmm," the creature whined and puffed warm steam into my face. I drew a handful of meat from the bag and felt where its face was with the other hand, and dropped the pieces in. It felt oddly satisfying to eat with the serpent. I did it just like I would feed my little siblings at dinner, *"A bite for you. A bite for me."* I softly whispered, rubbing the serpent's smooth, scaly head. We continued to eat the jerky, all of it. First, I put a piece in my mouth, then a handful in the fang serpent's mouth, until the bag was empty and we were satisfied. Then we drifted off to sleep.

I was no longer terrified of the fang serpent; rather, it was a comfort to me and a companion now.

I awoke to the sound of the iron door opening, "Creak!" The fang serpent was still sleeping curled around me, so I could not see who had opened the door, and they could not see me. "Thud," something hit the floor, and the door slammed shut again and locked.

I lifted myself up to see what it was that they had thrown on the ground. It was a great salmon, at least five feet in length, clearly meant to feed the fang serpent that must have been forgotten during the ship's raid on Fayatoch's central harbor. Why would they raid the harbor? Surely there were other harbors and ports with finer goods closer to civilization. I pondered this along with how I could possibly escape.

As I was pondering my escape, loud footsteps came down the stairway and stopped at each cell, looking for something. I sank down out of sight and lay my head down on the fang serpent's tail. I could not be seen from the door of the cell, or at least that's what I hoped.

"Georgi!!" The man yelled.

Another set of footprints came down the stairs and answered in a deep voice, "Yes, Captain Grenon."

"Where's the girl you were told to get?" the voice of Captain Grenon asked, sounding perturbed and irritated with Georgi for some reason.

"Is she not here?" Georgi asked with an inquisitive tone as if he was sure that he had done what was asked of him.

"No, she is not, Georgi," the captain replied, and asked sternly, "Where did you stick her?"

"Right in here, Sir," Georgi replied, turning to the cell with the fang serpent and me hiding. When he saw the serpent curled up on the hay, he jumped. "EEaaawww! What is that?!" he asked with fright!

"That my unfaithful and utterly stupid sailor is my new fang serpent for interrogation purposes. Now tell me, are you sure that's where you stuck the girl?" he asked with increasing irritation in his voice.

"Yes, Captain," Georgi answered with hesitation, then asked, "Just how important was that girl anyway?"

"That girl, Georgi, was the daughter of Biro the Stone, late King of Mossland, and we were paid by King Micra the cold-hearted to deliver her to him unharmed. Do you understand me, Georgi?"

"Yes, Captain," Georgi replied with a shaky voice.

"Camber!! Flecher!!" Captain Grenon yelled.

"Captain!! Please No!! Captain!! I'll make it up to you!!!!" Georgi begged for mercy.

"I'll pay you tenfold!!"

The Camber and Flecher came up behind Georgi. They were tall and rough.

"Get rid of him, boys," The Captain ordered.

Georgi begged and wailed as they carried him up the stars. His shrieks soon ended, followed by the sound of steel and a loud splash.

"Bash!!" the captain yelled.

"Yes, Captain," Bash said, coming down the stairs. "Why'd you send Georgi to the depths? Not the best upstairs, but he was a good worker." Bash asked with some concern.

"I know Bash, but he finally struck out of luck," the captain replied.

"What'd he do, just out of curiosity, Captain?" Bash asked.

"He stuck the royal kid in the serpent's cell the day before last," the captain explained.

"Oh, no worries, Captain, that kid was part spriteling. It wouldn't touch her." Bash replied, leaning against the cell door, "He's quite tame, too."

"I know, Bash," the captain replied.

"Then why'd you tip Georgi over?" Bash asked.

"Because if he did it once, he could do it again, and the kid or sailor might not be half spriteling the next time," the captain explained.

"Speaking of which, where is dat kid?" Bash asked, turning around and peering in through the iron cell bars. The fang serpent lifted its head and gave a puff of smoke as if warning him.

I held my breath.

"I don't know. Somehow, she got out, so she's on the ship somewhere. I want your men to search this ship up and down," the captain ordered.

"What if the kid jumped?" Bash asked.

"Unlikely, most kids from Mossland don't swim, and we're too far out to sea," the captain said. "Hurry up, Bash. The sooner the kid is found, the sooner my mind can rest."

"Aye, Aye, Captain Grenon," Bash replied on his way up the stairs.

"Hi, Beast," the Captain whispered through the bars. "You haven't touched your breakfast. Don't you worry, you'll be out of this cage and on deck soon. You're a part of my crew now."

The captain turned to go up the steps and then whispered back, "I call you Jonny, boy," then disappeared up the stairs.

I let out a deep, pent-up breath of air and melted into the floor. *"I am the daughter of Biro the Stone,"* my thoughts mused, *"I knew that, but I am also half spriteling. I really wish I knew as much about myself as other people seem to."*

"I've got to get out of here," my thoughts screamed inside of me louder than booming cannons.

I pulled myself from the sleeping fang serpent's curled bundle and listened for footsteps on the stairs. I heard none, so I made my way to the iron bars. I rattled the lock as loud as I dared, feeling the hole with my fingers.

The lock hole was about the size of a small pen knife. My pen knife might fit, I thought, reaching into my left boot for the concealed pocket. I pulled out my shiny black steel pen knife, which had been a gift from my Headbricker cousin Ben, and I slid the blade into the lock. Just then, I heard the door above swing open. I yanked the knife out and dove into the hay pile by the iron bench.

I heard footsteps and voices coming down the stairs.

"Bash, we've looked everywhere. Are you so sure that dragon didn't make a meal of the kid?" a high voice whined.

"I don't see no dead dragon, Tar. If that dragon got one bite of that kid, it would die, and besides, I don't see no bones," Bash reasoned.

"But where do we look now, Bash?" Tar asked,

"Look below deck and in the captain's quarters. Mmumm, get a party and search the hull as well; we could have missed the kid there. And check the kitchen; kids like to eat a lot," Bash answered, scratching his head.

"Alright, Bash. I'm goin'," Tar said, mounting the stairs. His large, heavy boots gave off a loud thud with every step up the creaking stairs.

The hay was sticking to my back; it hurt, but I didn't dare move because Bash was searching the brig for me. I heard him open cell doors, and there was a pause before he pulled the heavy iron doors shut. I counted the number of slams. There were fifteen cells besides the one I was in, and in my mind, they were empty. I noticed a jingle as Bash went up the stairs; he had the keys on him.

Slowly, I rose from the hay and tried to fiddle with the lock again, but I couldn't focus. My stomach growled, and I turned to the raw salmon that lay by the sleeping fang serpent. I needed something to eat. I looked at the fish's gills; they were red, which meant the fish was fresh. Running my pen knife along the side, I shaved off a portion of the scales and cut off a hunk of flesh. The salmon was incredibly fishy and chewy, but I didn't mind. It didn't take much of the fish to satisfy me, and the salmon was delicious, but I decided that the sooner I got out of here, the better, because I knew that I could not live completely off fish, which seemed to be the fang serpent's main diet. Again, I fiddled with my pen knife to no prevail. The fang serpent stretched and rose. In one swallow, the great fish was gone.

The fang serpent walked about its cage, circling its perimeter and rubbing against my legs, pressing me into the iron bars. He clearly wanted out. After a while, he, or I should say Jonny, began to puff and roll on the rough wood floor. I sighed, slipping to the floor. I couldn't get out, and I couldn't hide here forever. I was trapped.

Chapter 36:
A Tunnel, A Pirate, Oh My

After the peppering of cannon fire at the docks, the masters met secretly. I obtained this information from Libby following my capture. Libby did not go to the docks that day due to a pounding headache.

Description from Libby:

About an hour or so following their departure to the docks, Lady Catherine woke me and took me to the underground cellar beneath the courtyard. All the other children were there except seven.

Five of the seven had been at the docks, and the other two children were on the beach on the other side of the island. The missing children include the following: Dermid, Wiliam, Aoife, Selah, Alice, Kate, and Rowsheen. Kate and Rowsheen had gone with a group of children to the beach on the South side of the island for a relaxing day off training.

Rowsheen's diary entry, Capture at the Beach!!

Kate and I decided to take a stroll on South Beach. We were searching for shells that we wanted to make into necklaces and send home to our families. About noon, we had grown tired of our search and settled beneath some palm trees in the shade. I fell asleep for some time in the warm shade.

I awoke with a start to loud voices drifting across the beach. I shook Kate awake and motioned for her to keep silent. Hacking sounds filled our ears; they were searching the woods for something or someone. Kate pointed up. She could fly us to safety, or at least splitting up would give us a greater chance of staying hidden.

The voices got closer. Kate couldn't take off under the trees. I motioned to a small clearing deeper into the woods. She nodded and silently slipped into the brush. Her bare feet moved soundlessly along. I scanned the beach for a hiding place to keep low and still. There were high dark rock formations that jutted out into the crystal blue water about fifty yards to my left. The sun was high in the sky.

Another boatload of rough-looking men landed on the beach even closer than the first. I had to get to the rocks. I glanced back in Kate's direction; she was nearly to the clearing. The sound of Kate's wings would deter the men long enough for me to get to the rocks.

"Steady," I told myself, watching Kate for the right time to move. "One, Two, Go!!" I screamed inwardly as Kate flapped her great wings, carrying her upward above the trees. I took off at the first flap I heard, not looking back. I reached the rocks and scrambled over them, panting. I looked anxiously over the rugged rocks to see if I had been followed. No one had seen me. Something crashed to the floor of the forest. I prayed that it wasn't Kate.

"Ole!!" I slipped on a wet rock and fell hard. I was far from the water; what had made me slip? I placed my hand on the hard, grey rock beneath me; it was red with blood.

Kate's Diary entry:

The day of our capture began like many of the holidays on the island. We buddied up and decided upon a destination. Rowsheen and I got a day at the beach approved by the masters. We had been asking them for this for weeks now, and we had been planning the beach trip since last winter, when all we wanted was a relaxing day in the sun to collect shells and enjoy ourselves.

Aoife left Rowsheen and me for a day at the docks, I guess she wanted to shop, so we spent our day in leisure at the South beach on the other side of our dense, rich green, vast wooded island without her. We played the morning away on the rocky and yellow sandy beaches and slept beneath the large, shady palms at noon. I collected a ton of shells! And I was dreaming up a design for shell earrings to send my mother and sister back home.

Rowsheen woke me, and my ears were filled with the sounds of loud voices and swords slashing through the brush. I was terrified! Rowsheen and I decided to split up, so I ventured into the brush where I could possibly take off. The sharp underbrush bit my bare feet and pulled my feathery wings, but I was determined to make it to a place where I could take off and get help.

Finally, I had made it to a good enough clearing, so I stretched my wings and stood tall. I heard shouts from the men; they had seen me. With a few powerful strokes, I was off the ground, not daring to look back. I had barely passed through the trees when a large black net entangled my wings, forcing me down. I crashed down through limbs and briers before hitting the ground hard. My whole self shook from the shock. I was nauseated by the pain in my ankle, and my wings felt bruised and battered from the fall. Everything spun around my head before encasing me in inky black.

Continued entry Rowsheen:

"Blood?" my thoughts screamed! I looked around the jagged rocks; the body of a decapitated sailor lay on some rocks below me. I stood shaking from head to foot. The sailor had been killed very recently because the blood I slipped on was still bright red.

The trail that led back to the training grounds was a long way down the beach past the rough-looking men. Another boatload of men landed, but this time it was within ten yards of the rocks I was hiding behind. There were five men aboard the tiny boat. They were dressed like rough seamen and each carried a weapon. Well, all except for a young sailor who was dressed rather nicely for a young shipmate. He appeared to be giving orders to the other men. He stared in my direction. I gasped, ducking quickly behind the docks. It was Liam!

His cold stare froze my heart. Was Liam a pirate!? Had he seen me?

Daniel, as we are aware from Aoife's writings, was not at the docks or the South beach but at the training grounds resting.

Description from Daniel:

On the day of the children's capture, I was sick in bed with a stomachache and body aches. Dermid had dared me to eat something in the forest. I thought the plant was edible, but after vomiting a few times, I learned from the master's that I had two plants mixed up in my head. I was given medicine and sent to bed.

I immediately sensed something was wrong when no voices accompanied the sounds of footsteps on the training dorm floors. The children hardly made a whisper. I began to get nervous and tense. Dermid had not come to fill my head with stories about his new beau, Aoife had not come to check to see how I was feeling, and the children were silent.

My head pounded and my body ached. I longed for the tea Aoife had promised to bring me back from the docks. The sound of a heavy foot fell on the threshold. I recognized the sound of the step as Benant, one of the apprentices. The curtains parted as he entered.

"Daniel, is that you?" Benant asked. "Good Spirit, did no one come for you, Brother?!"

"What is wrong, Benant?" I asked, sitting up with my hand on my head and the other on my stomach.

"My dear brother, come with me, and once we're safe, I'll tell you all," Benant said, taking my arm and helping me up off the cot. My legs felt weak and wobbly beneath me, and I took my bucket with me.

He pulled me hurriedly behind him into the courtyard on the far side. When we got to the far side, he reached his hand into a small hole in a big grey boulder covered with moss and furry lichens. A door opened in the rock.

"After you, Brother," Benant said, nudging me toward the opening, so I ducked down and entered.

Benant jumped in behind me and swung the door shut behind us, sealing it tight. We were in a dark rock tunnel lit by two lanterns on the walls, lighting up the hollow pathway. I was able to stand because the floor dropped at an incline by the entrance and continued to wind downward. We walked in silence, each holding a lantern to pierce the thick blackness.

The tunnel got wider as we walked on, going deeper with every step. After we had walked for nearly an hour, Benant stopped and turned around as if he was checking to see if anyone had followed us. After a few minutes, he walked to the left side of the tunnel and reached up and grabbed a rock that jutted out of the wall.

With a hard pull on the rock downwards, a small, invisible rock door swung outwards. I entered first, and the cold, hard rock ceiling brushed the top of my head as I ducked walking in. I was in a large rock cavern lit by the light of lanterns hung on the walls. Master Mark was waiting there for Benant.

"Daniel, I thought you were with the others," Master Mark exclaimed through his crooked teeth, making his shaggy grey beard shake.

"I was down with stomach pain, Sir," Daniel replied, still looking pale and feeling nauseated.

"Aw, yes," he said. "Well, the past can't be helped. We can only look to the future."

We continued down another dark tunnel on the north wall of the cavern for a short time before Master Mark and Benant lifted a hidden door in the floor. A ladder led down into the thick blackness. Benant went down first, followed by me, and lastly Master Mark secured the door behind the three of us.

We walked into a dimly lit cavern with grey walls. All the children sat in groups along the rugged walls. I looked for Dermid and Wiliam, but I didn't find them. Lady Catherine was at the far end of the great cavern, pacing back and forth. Her long black hair was a scraggly mess.

Benant walked alongside her, speaking in hushed tones.

As I approached, Lady Catherine waved her hand to Benant and walked to the other side of the cavern. The children were silent for the most part, and many were asleep on blankets piled on the rocky floors. Benant's back was turned. He seemed to have found something interesting in the grey rock ceiling because he stared at it intensely.

"Benant," I addressed him upon reaching his position in the dark cavern, "forgive my curiosity, but I do not take this matter as a drill or a test. I pray you tell me all as you promised."

"Let us rest in comfort first," Benant said, guiding my arm toward an empty pile of blankets by an underground pool. The water reflected the light bouncing waves on the cavern walls. We sat down, and Benant stared intently into the water.

"There was a vicious attack on our harbor early this morning. We received word a few hours ago," Bentant explained, not taking his tired eyes off the water. "We don't know all the details yet. Sir Masuda sent the word. He is keeping the children who were at the docks in a bunker close to the beach while he investigates. The last message we got was to watch for intruders. This island is a peaceful place, Daniel. It is always neutral in war. We have defenses, but we haven't needed them on this island for a hundred years."

"What defenses do we have?" I asked, wiping water off my forehead, the dripped from the ceiling.

"We have a fleet of our own ships, bunkers scattered all over the island, and our own personal army hired from Sabatoy that guards the borders and waterways," Benant answered me.

"Why have I not seen any of them before?" I asked.

"The army is Sabatoians; they can disappear in the sunlight and prefer to, but they are brilliant in every way. They search all the ships before they are allowed to come into port and guard the docks." Benant explained.

"Do you have any idea why we were attacked, or could you even tell me?" Daniel asked, looking hard into Benant's uneasy face.

"I don't know, dear brother, and I wish I could tell you. Come, let's tend to that stomachache." Benant led Daniel to the supplies and whipped up a cup of herbal tea for him.

"Thank you, Brother," Daniel said, sipping the warm, herbal tea.

"Not to worry, Brother, I will be thanking you in time," Benant replied, leaving Daniel to himself.

Chapter 37:
Misdirection

"Screeeeech, Thud, Screeeeeech," the iron doors of musty, rough cell opened to receive new cotenants, then closed. Kate landed stiffly on the dirty, rough, wooden floor.

"Ooowwwa," Kate moaned, rolling on her side, covered in sand from the beach. Her wings were badly bruised, and her ankle had twisted in the fall. Slowly, she pulled herself to the pile of hay in the corner and collapsed, exhausted and in pain.

Meanwhile, Rowsheen studied the body of the unfortunate soul on the rocks below after she had seen Kate's unconscious body being carried away to the Main ship.

"I need a disguise, my good man," Rowsheen whispered to the dead sailor as she stooped down, "I hope you don't mind."

Rowsheen borrowed the sailor's coat, hat, and boots for a disguise. She pulled her long, curly rose petal curls into a knot at the back of her head and pulled the hat on tight before smearing mud on her face and hands to blend in with the other sailors and drew on the large, black, tall, and rugged leather boots. Rowsheen was now quite a ruddy sight in her brand-new attire and hoped it would fool the canty pirates.

"Oh, dear," Rowsheen whispered to herself, peering over the rocky hedge at the row boats on the shoreline. Pirates were everywhere, searching the forest and shoreline with their swords and weapons drawn. How would she get into one of the boats? A group of pirates by the boats that appeared to be the brains of the operation waved the search party in.

"This is my chance," Rowsheen thought, scrambling over the rocks and walking toward the boats with the mass of pirates.

She blended in well while walking to the boats and helped in shoving the closest boat off before hopping in and averting her gaze from the other pirates. In the boat with her, there were five pirates: two at the oars with their backs turned, two in the front facing ahead, and one in the back beside me. They were not all that she had pictured them to be; rather, they were rough, dirty, and barefoot, but they did not look like the monsters she had pictured them to be. However, the weapons they carried would strike fear into any heart. The weapons she was able to recognize were the elegant cutlass, the rapier, and the boarding axe.

The waves grew and rose as the boat continued to move forward, fighting the fierce waves of the sea. Water splashed and dripped over the sides of the creaky, wooden boat. Rowsheen stared into the deep waves splashing the sides of the little rowboat. She was sure that she could not turn back now because she was too far from shore to swim back safely.

Rowsheen tried to keep as quiet and inconspicuous as possible for fear of exposure, but even that could not keep her from listening in curiosity to their conversation and commenting.

First pirate in the front of the boat on the right: "Come on, boys! You be slower 'an slimy sea urchun."

Pirate on the left rowing: "I always thought it was pronounced 'urchon'".

Pirate on the right rowing: "I always fancied it was 'urchen.'"

Pirate in the front of the boat on the left: "The correct pronunciation is 'urchin' and it's spelled ur-c-h-i-n."

First pirate in the front on the right: "No, it's pronounced 'urchun' you uneducatid seabag."

Pirate in the front of the boat on the left: "Uneducated seabag? I graduated from the phourth grade, thank you."

First pirate in the front of the boat on the right: "Well, I graduated from the third grade."

Pirate in the front of the boat on the left: "Exactly, that means dat I'm smarter dan you."

First pirate in the front of the boat on the right: "The tird grade is greater dan the pourth one."

Pirate in the front of the boat on the left: "Is not, the third comes befour the phourth."

Pirate in back by Rowsheen: "Dair at it agin, aye," he said, nudging her with his elbow.

Rowsheen in reply: "Aye."

Pirate in back by Rowsheen: "Hey, yur new arnt ya."

Rowsheen in reply: "Aye, transferred."

Pirate in back by Rowsheen: "Transfurrd. Wat fur?"

Rowsheen in reply, trying to sound like the pirates: "Dunno, the ship was a mite crowded though. Day wer getting on each oters nerves."

Pirate in back by Rowsheen: "I seess."

The boat was now in deep water, coming alongside one of the great lead vessels. The vessel was a rather large, lofty vessel of fine sailing stature. Ropes were thrown down from the deck and attached to the rowboat. The rowboat began moving upward until it reached the deck. Rowsheen followed the other pirates from the rowboat, moving onto the deck and ducking out of the way, for there must have been a hundred pirates on deck securing row boats, opening the masts, and doing other such jobs. Rowsheen's feet hit the wooden deck with a thud, and she gripped the main mast as the boat tipped to one side.

"Has it truly been that long since I've been on a ship?" Rowsheen asked herself as she tried to stand amidst the crazy confusion. She looked up to see the overseer overseeing the men's work and barking orders.

"I'd better do something," Rowsheen said to herself. Rowsheen looked frantically around and saw a group of men taking barrels down to the hull of the ship.

Ducking down, she dashed to the barrels, heaved a small one onto her shoulder, and started down the stairs after another worker. Her eyes began to adjust as she entered the musty hull. Another overseer was checking the barrels as they got stacked and could not see Rowsheen behind the worker in front of her, so she ducked down and went behind the stairs. In a few minutes, all the barrels had been stacked, and the overseer mounted the steps after the last worker and closed the heavy hull doors.

"AChooooo," Rowsheen sneezed, stuffing her face into the baggy elbow of the pirate's coat. The only light streaming from the cracks in the ceiling above revealed the thick dusty air, then she thought to herself, "Now what?" Rowsheen scanned the hull she had gotten herself locked in. The hull creaked and moaned, jostling this way and that. It was quite a large hull because it took Rowsheen a good ten minutes to walk from one side of it to another. There appeared to be hundreds of barrels of different sizes, and crates stacked along the walls.

Rowsheen walked past more barrels, trying to find something useful. She found many things she'd expect to be on a ship, such as rope, stacks of lumber, crates of silk, and barrels of gunpowder, but what she needed was a way out and a way to find Kate. Close to the very end of the hull, where the seams met old, musty sheets, battered and torn, hung from the supporting beams and ceiling. Rowsheen ventured on looking behind the dusty sheet after sheet till she looked up and saw that a newer sheet had been nailed to the ceiling covering a few square feet of area.

"Why are you there?" Rowsheen whispered, pulling an empty barrel under the peculiar sheet that she had found. With one big pull, the sheet ripped off two of its nails, revealing an iron door on the ceiling.

"There's my way out," Rowsheen whispered, standing on her toes, reaching above her head. The ship jolted, knocking Rowsheen off the barrel and headlong onto the foul, musty floor. "OooUU," Rowsheen moaned, pulling herself up, then whispered, "That's not gonna work."

Rowsheen was not the tallest being in Mossland, but she was stubborn. Carefully and quietly, she gathered barrels amidst the tossing and turning of the ship and stacked them up like a pyramid beneath the iron door. After completing her pyramid of barrels, Rowsheen took a deep breath and began climbing, trying to maintain her balance as much as possible. Upon reaching the top, she studied the door to see how it opened, then pulled the latch and pushed upward. The door gave a small budge then sank back down.

The door was too heavy. "Come on," Rowsheen pleaded with herself, "You've got this." Lying her back on the top barrel, she pressed her feet against the iron door; it moved.

"Come on," Rowsheen grunted again, pushing with all her might. "CREAK," the heavy, iron door opened and swung upward, revealing the floor above.

"Anybody home?" Rowsheen whispered, sticking her head through the opening. The door opened up beneath a desk. Crawling through the opening and out from under it, she saw what struck her as very odd or out of place. She was in an old, musty room complete with a fine wooden desk, a tall, urban bed, a large window with heavy, embroidered curtains, and other select furniture, including a globe stand, a wall-sized map of Unclia, and several large chests. The room was rather small for all it contained, she thought.

Something on the desk caught her eye, so she strode across the room. On the desk lay books, charts, instruments, and notes. "What's this?" Rowsheen whispered to herself, pulling a piece of crumpled paper from beneath a steel paperweight. Walking over to the window, Rowsheen read the scratchy handwriting.

It read: *Receipt of Sale: 5th Moon of Summer 1234*

One fang serpent was sold to Captain Grenon for 500 gold coins of the WycKoff fleet from McGinnis South Sea Merchandise.

Signature of byer: <u>Captain Grenon of WycKoff fleet</u>

Signature of Seller: <u>Merchant McGinnis of South Sea Merchandise</u>

"A fang serpent!" Rowsheen gasp, placing her hand over her heart, "This Captain is crazy!"

"Stomp, clang," footsteps and faint voices sounded outside the door of the cabin.

Rowsheen quietly closed the iron door beneath the desk and ducked under the tall, wooden bed.

The door creaked open. "Set the course, Bash. You know the heading," a voice said, stepping into the room and shutting the door.

The floor creaked as the captain (as Rowsheen assumed) walked to his desk with heavy, hard steps, sat down, and began to sort through his papers as if looking for something.

Rowsheen peeked out from under the bed to see what he was doing. After twenty minutes, the captain pushed back his chair, stood, walked to the shelf, pulled down a large, heavy book, carried it back to his desk, and began to write in it.

Rowsheen soundlessly slid further underneath the bed, where she was sure to be out of view, and tried to quiet her pounding heart in vain. After about an hour of listening to the captain shuffle papers and books and staring into the dusty spiderweb-laden blackness, Rowsheen had to sneeze badly. She tried hard to rub her nose viciously to ward off a sneeze, but out the sneeze came, "Achoo!" The papers stopped rustling at the desk. The captain had heard her!

Chapter 38:
Cat Chase

Rowsheen wiggled as fast as she could to the other side of the bed as the captain walked toward her hiding place.

"Bang, bang, bang!" Loud knocks sounded at the door.

"Come in," the captain replied in annoyed tones.

Bash entered and said, "Progress report, Captain, there is no sign of the little miss aboard."

"And you tell me this, why?" the captain remarked. Rowsheen slipped out from under the bed and dove into a pile of laundry heaped by a large chest and froze.

"What I'm saying, Captain, is what if she were put on a different ship. I mean, it could happen," Bash reasoned nervously, wringing his hands.

"No, Bash, I do believe that she is on this ship," the captain replied, "what else do you have for me?"

"The Boss wants to see you," Bash replied, "he's on the mainland."

"Take us to Wearoff," the captain replied, bending down to look under the bed.

"What you lookin' for, Captain?" Bash asked.

"Nothing," the Captain replied, sounding rather irritated, "the next time we're in port, buy a cat. I swear, there are too many rats on this ship." The captain pulled on his cloak, and Bash handed him his sword and his three-pointed hat and walked out, slamming the door behind.

Rowsheen popped out of the pile of laundry and sucked in air. "Uggh, that was not worth it," Rowsheen gagged, pulling herself out and dusting herself off. Quickly, Rowsheen walked to the desk and opened the black book that the captain had written in and turned to the last entry.

07/54/34

Good morning, behind the wheel, the sea is not too rough. The kid from Mossland is still missing somewhere aboard the ship. The kidnapping that the Boss ordered was performed successfully.

Note to self: Find someone else to work for.

"Kidnapping?" Rowsheen asked, lifting her head, "Kate could be on this ship."

"Clip, clomp," footsteps sounded outside the door. Rowsheen dove under the desk.

"Captain, Captain, I got your tea," a voice sounded outside the door, "I'm commin' in."

The door creaked open, and a pirate stepped in with a silver tea set in one hand and a feather duster in the other.

"Boy, it's dusty in here," he said, setting the tea set down on the desk and beginning to dust the shelves. Rowsheen peeked her head out to see the pirate. He had striped grey and white trousers and a blue coat with brass buttons.

"Achooo," he sneezed into his sleeve, "we need another cabin boy." Rowsheen ducked back under and huddled into a ball.

"Bash!" A voice yelled from the door.

"What is it, Camber?" Bash said in an unphased voice, still humming his song and dusting the shelves. Camber walked through the door, leaving it open, and walked over behind the desk and leaned on it while conversing with Bash. Rowsheen's mind left their conversation and went to the open door.

"I can get out," she thought to herself. Crawling out from under the desk, she began to walk towards the door. "Hey, You!" Bash said, referring to Rowsheen, "What are you in here for?"

"Just getting the laundry, Mr. Bash," Rowsheen replied, not turning her back and taking a scoop from the pile. "Carry on then," Bash replied, turning his attention back to Camber and the shelves.

Walking out the door, Rowsheen scanned the deck. Men were mending the sails, winding up ropes, swabbing the deck, and painting the rails and other such parts of the ship. An officer who appeared to be in charge stood on the stars giving orders.

"Excuse me," Rowsheen asked, walking over to the stars a few yards from the entrance of the captain's quarters.

"Yes," the Officer replied in an annoyed tone.

"I was told to fetch the captain's laundry. Where should I take it?" Rowsheen asked, pulling her hat over her eyes.

"To the kitchen, and hurry up with that," he said, motioning to the other side of the ship close to where she had gone down to the hold. "We need to have the ship shining before the captain returns, or it will be the brink for all of you."

"Yes, Sir," Rowsheen replied, tipping her hat still further down over her eyes and starting across the deck. "Hhhii, Thud," Rowsheen gasp aloud, landing on her back on the deck. She had slipped where someone had been swabbing.

"Oh, well, that's just great. The captain's clothes are all over the deck," the pirate who was closest to her complained. Rowsheen quickly looked in the direction of the head officer. He had his back turned. Hurriedly, she picked up all the laundry and dashed to where she thought the kitchen was.

Bounding through the kitchen door, she saw who she thought to be the pirate in charge of the kitchen and said, "I have the captain's laundry as I was ordered, Sir." He had his back turned, working on something at a small table.

"Set it down by the big pot and hand me that roll of twine on the peg by the door," he replied, continuing on his project.

Quickly and carefully, Rowsheen set down the pile of laundry by a large, iron pot and snatched the twine off the peg by the door. Walking swiftly up behind the old, stocky pirate, she reached to set the twine by his arm. In a split second, the pirate grabbed Rowsheen's wrist and turned to face her with a suspicious glare.

"I did not order the captain's laundry to be brought," he whispered, holding her wrist in a grim, unflinching grasp.

"One of the officers must have told me to then," Rowsheen replied, trying to remain composed, breathing in his foul breath that fumed from beneath his large, burly, grey beard.

"I know every sailor on this ship...and I don't know you," the pirate replied in almost a whisper. Rowsheen felt her heart freeze within her and could not find words to reply.

"I'd say you were from another ship, but you're wearing Georgi's clothes and he's no longer ticken," Rowsheen began to struggle to break loose, pulling hard. He grabbed her other arm and swung her into the support beam, knocking her hard onto the ground.

"Fletcher!" the old pirate hollered, laying his sword across Rowsheen's throat.

Loud footsteps boomed into the room, and an ugly, massive shadow blocked the light that issued from the door. Looking up, she saw the largest, meanest-looking pirate she had ever seen. He stood too tall for the ceiling, so he had to bend over.

He had a long, white, gristly scar that ran from his ear down his neck and disappeared down the collar of his tattered, sweat-stained, white, sailor shirt that was rolled up past his elbows.

"Stole away, Fletcher," the old pirate said with a hideous grin, pulling his sword away from her neck and going back to his business.

"Got it," Fletcher replied in the deepest voice Rowsheen had ever heard.

Rowsheen was paralyzed with fear. Reaching down, Fletcher grabbed Rowsheen by her neck and dragged her out of the kitchen. When on the deck, Fletcher straightened to his full size. He was so tall that Rowsheen hung inches off the ground as if she were a hunting prize, kicking her legs back and forth with both her hands on his clenched fist. Fletcher seemed unfazed by her kicks and struggles as he climbed the steps to the top deck, where the head officer gave orders.

"Mr. Drum," Fletcher said, addressing the head officer who had his eye in a spy glass surveying the shore.

"What is it, Fletcher?" the officer replied in stern, annoyed tones.

"Stole away, Mr. Drum. Crimp found 'im in the kitchen," Fletcher explained, shielding his eyes from the sun's powerful glare.

"Throw him overboard," the officer replied simply.

"Shouldn't I give 'im to the Captain's new pet. I mean that's why he bought 'im, right," Fletcher suggested in his incredibly dark, deep voice.

The officer turned around and looked up at Fletcher, "If that makes you happy, by all means, do what you want."

"Yes, Mr. Drum," Fletcher replied, giving a quick bow with his head and turning to go down the stairs. The stairs creaked from his immense weight, and the tips of Rowsheen's boots touched the steps on the way down.

"Fletcher, wait," the officer called, hurrying down the steps, "let's wait till the captain gets back. You can put the stole away in another cell till then."

"Okay," Fletcher replied, turning toward the stairs that led down to the brink, and asked over his shoulder, "Anything else, Mr. Drum?"

"No, as you were," the Officer replied, mounting the stairs up to the top deck.

Fletcher went down the stairs to the brink and threw Rowsheen into one of the iron-barred cells and locked it tight. "Enjoy your stay, stole away," Fletcher called to Rowsheen before disappearing up the stairs.

"Rowsheen," a voice called from the cell on the other side of the brink.

"Aoife," Rowsheen called back, "how in Osgood's name did you get here!?"

Chapter 39:
Bones under Hay

Aoife replied to Rowsheen, "Hush now! They don't know I'm here."

"They've got you in a cell, don't they?" Rowsheen asked, rubbing her sore neck.

"They put me in this cell on accident, and looky what's in here with me," Aoife whispered, pointing to the napping fangserpent in the corner.

"What is that?" Rowsheen asked, squinting to make out what it was.

"Oh, just a fangserpent," Aoife replied, scratching its scaly head.

"Fangserpent!" Rowsheen exclaimed.

Rowsheen picked at the lock while Aoife watched from the far cell. "How did you get out of the cells in Skiski?" Rowsheen asked Aoife, pressing her face against the bars so she could wrap her arms around to pick the lock.

"Well, that time I pretended to choke and swiped the keys off the guard," Aoife replied, laying her head on her arms on the cold, dirty, plank ground.

"If you could offer any assistance, Firebolt, I'd be surely grateful," Rowsheen commented, taking her big, three-cornered hat off.

"How would you like to be the lucky owner of my pen knife that I can't get to pick a lock?" Aoife replied, rolling on her side. "Love to. Toss it over," Rowsheen replied, holding her hand out to catch it.

"Here you go," Aoife replied, flinging her pen knife into Rowsheen's open palm. Loud footsteps thundered down the stairs.

Rowsheen pulled her arms through the bars and hid the pen knife in her shirt.

Aoife hopped up to take a dive into the hay pile and snagged her pants on a loose nail, pinning her to the wood floor. The footsteps clomped down the stairs. Aoife scrambled to lose her pants from the nail, but her nervous, jittery fingers couldn't be felt past her pounding heart that echoed in her ears louder than a cannon roar.

Rowsheen turned her head to see Aoife pulling frantically at her pants, then spotted the legs of the pirate ascending the stairs. With one firm hit, Rowsheen threw herself at the iron bars, rattling the cell, and plunged herself onto the wooden floor, kicking and pounding.

"Bah," Bash scoffed at Rowsheen, banging his fist against the iron cell, "Ain't no soul ever gotten out of that cell, in that ain't about to change."

Rowsheen continued her mad fit until Bash turned to head back up the stairs; all the while, Aoife lay sprawled out on the floor of her cell, shaking.

Rowsheen tossed the pen knife back over to Aoife, who was still in the same place, frozen in shock.

"Come on, Aoife, get up!" Rowsheen hissed through her teeth.

"Just let me find my stomach first," Aoife replied, brushing a loose strand of hair out of her face and tucking it behind her ear.

"Hurry," Rowsheen ordered, pressing her face against the bars, "I want out."

Aoife finally freed herself from the nail, then collapsed on the hay pile with her hands on her upset stomach.

Rowsheen, irritated at Aoife's unmovable form, examined the cell door, walls, and hinges for weak spots.

In a stressed moan, Aoife rolled herself behind the hay pile and landed on something hard. Standing up fast, she dug through the hay only to find a pile of bones.

"Disturbing," Aoife whispered, about to cover it back up when she spotted a sharp, splintered shard off a large bone, "this could pick the lock."

Listening in case another pirate was coming down the stairs, she moved herself to the cell door, wrapped her arms around the outer frame, and began moving the shard this way and that in the lock. Back and forth, back and forth she continued until, "click, scccrrreeeecchhh." The lock turned, and the cell door swung open. The fangserpent lifted its head and gave a low gurgling sound. "You can come too," Aoife said, motioning for it to follow her. The fangserpent stood and walked slowly out while Aoife held the door open. Closing the door shut as quietly as she could, Aoife led the fangserpent to Rowsheen's cell.

Rowsheen was lying on the ground of her cell, staring up at the ceiling. "Rowsheen," Aoife whispered, shoving the piece of splintered bone into the lock.

"How did you get out?!! Why did you bring that thing?!!" Rowsheen asked frantically.

"Quiet," Aoife whispered, remembering that Rowsheen was not overly fond of large animals,

"I'll have you out in a minute."

"What's that?" Rowsheen asked, pressing her head up to the bars to see what Aoife was using to pick the lock.

"You'd rather not... I'll tell you later," Aoife replied, turning the lock. "Click, screeech," the hinges creaked as the door swung open.

Rowsheen stepped out quickly and helped Aoife shut the door quietly. "Okay, we're out," Aoife whispered, scratching the fangserpent's head.

"You haven't thought of anything else, have you?" Rowsheen criticized folding her arms.

"We have Tame," Aoife answered, "that's our way out."

"What do you mean?" Rowsheen replied, stepping away from the fangserpent who was trying to sniff her boots.

"He can swim and turn invisible," Aoife replied, giving him a pat on the head.

"You better be right, but first we have to find Kate," Rowsheen replied, looking into the other cells along the walls.

"Kate?" Aoife asked worriedly.

"The Pirates... Liam was with them, Aoife," Rowsheen began. "Okay," Aoife replied, nodded, and took a deep breath, "We can't stay here and talk. We need a place to lay low until we can find Kate and leave."

"The hull should be directly below us," Rowsheen reasoned, "look around for a hatch."

"The hull is not directly below us," Aoife disagreed. "This ship has many levels. When they were shooting cannons, I could hear them going off above and below me. Most likely, below us is where the crew sleeps."

"Do you have another idea?" Rowsheen asked with her hands on her hips, looking around and feeling a bit stressed.

"Yes," Aoife replied. "Snatch the key ring off the hook, find which one fits the lock, take it off the ring, put the ring back, get back in the cells, wait till dark, get up to deck, and get Tame to jump overboard with us on his back."

"Look for Kate," Rowsheen added.

"We will look, but I don't think she's on this ship," Aoife replied with a frown. Where had they taken Kate?

Chapter 40:
When You Can't Be Seen

Aoife searched nearly the entire floor looking for the ring of keys while Rowsheen searched for Kate. Aoife walked with her hand on Tame's neck as she scanned the walls for the ring of keys. She searched for a long time with a beating heart, wondering who was about to come down the stairs, until she determined that the ring of keys was not on that level of the ship. Plopping herself down beside the rough wooden wall in disappointment, Tame sniffed Aoife's face and puffed smoke in her auburn red messy hair. Tears dripped down Aoife's cheeks. She was overwhelmed and scared.

"Do you know where it is?" Aoife asked Tame through tears, scratching the scaly sides of his face. Tame made a low, whining sound, then plopped his great head down into her lap as if trying to soothe her quiet sobs. Then something happened that she had not expected; Tame disappeared! His head was still in her lap, but she could see nothing of him. Aoife wiped her tears on her sleeves and focused.

"How did you do that, Boy?" Aoife asked Tame, her eyes still puffy and red. Tame grunted back and licked Aoife's whole face in one swipe.

"UuulLL," Aoife moaned, wiping the saliva off her face with her sleeve. When she finally opened her eyes, she still did not see Tame, but his head was still in her lap... Wait, she could not see her lap. It had disappeared. Looking down at her arms, they were still visible.

"I wonder," Aoife mused, laying her arms down on Tame's head. The rest of her became invisible as well! Aoife took a deep breath, scanned her whole body again, and experimented a few times.

Rowsheen searched painstakingly around nearly the whole level of the ship, staring into cells, causing a great ruckus among cell occupants, but she did not find Kate. Finally running down the last row again, she spotted an ancient, cedarwood door on the back wall.

Anxiously, she pulled on the door, hoping to get inside, but it did not budge. As she was about to shove again, voices sounded on the other side. Rowsheen looked around frantically for a place to hide, but saw none, so she planted herself on the left side of the door, flat against the splintery, wooden wall. The door opened all the way, pressing Rowsheen into the rough wooden wall. Two men dressed as rough-looking sailors with ruddy complexions stepped out.

"Well, Garrison. A marvelous job as always," the first spoke, who looked to be the younger of the two, with fewer wrinkles and dark, unruly, sandy blond hair tied back in a long ponytail with a black strap.

"Don't flatter me, Tom. The sooner I take a swim, the sooner you will," Garrison barked. He had deep-set dark-brown eyes and a square, clenched jaw; he was bald and wore small, hooped gold earrings in each earlobe. His bald head appeared to be sunburned with scars streaking his scalp.

"Pleasure doing business with you, then," Tom politely replied, tipping his three-pointed hat and walking off in the direction of the stairs.

"Bah," Garrison mocked with a heavy sigh and slapping the top of the door frame as he entered the room and slamming the door shut with force.

"Garrison must be the jail keeper!!" Rowsheen's thoughts screamed within, "Aoife is looking in the wrong place for the keys, and that pirate is coming straight towards her!!!"

Aoife only looked towards the stairs for impending danger, since the steps were so creaky that she could hear them at any moment. As a result, she didn't notice Tom approaching on her left.

"SHAKING SEABAGS GOING TO THE DEPTHS," Tom cursed under his breath after tripping over Tame's invisible tail. Aoife's heart raced. She had not seen him coming, and he could not see her. Muttering curses and contempt, Tom stomped up the stairs, making as much noise as he possibly could.

Rowsheen waited outside the door for what felt to her like an eternity till Garrison left for his noon meal. Slipping inside the ancient, wooden door, Rowsheen searched for the keys in piles of paper, in drawers, on shelves, and everywhere else she could think of.

Aoife was ecstatic about her new knowledge that she could turn invisible, too, so she decided to take it for a test run. She thought to herself, "It worked on that sailor. I need to find the keys, or at least another way out."

So, Aoife sat on Tame's back and held onto his neck. Tame caught a whiff of fish and started up the stairs in his invisible state. Aoife clung tight as he rattled up the stairs, just about shaking her off. The scent of fish was coming from a barrel beside the railing, so Tame went right for it and began digging in. Aoife's stomach rumbled; she wanted a snack too.

Looking around the deck, it appeared as though most of the sailors were taking a short noontime break. The only sailor Aoife could see was sitting on the ground by the captain's wheel, eating an apple. Slipping off Tame's back, Aoife was now visible. The voice in her head screamed at her to get back on Tame, but her stomach's call was far stronger. Moving slowly towards the kitchen door, she stooped and picked up a three-cornered hat and slipped it on.

Slowly approaching the door, she peeped in, looking for a chance to get something to eat. Just as she was about to slip in, however, a voice called her name, "Aoife!" the voice called from above.

Looking up with one hand on the hat, Aoife spotted someone tied to the mast; it was Kate!

"Kate," Aoife's thoughts shouted with joy and anger at the same time, "Of course she is tied to the main mast!"

Climbing up the net to the place where Kate was tied, Aoife's heartbeat quickened. The barrel of fish that Tame had been eating out of was now empty. Where was he? Finally reaching Kate, Aoife pulled out her small pen knife and began to cut Kate free.

"I am surprised you don't have a gag," Aoife joked, trying hard to cut through the thick rope. "I did, I just got it off. Me and Rowsheen were on the beach, and then this group of Pirates..."

Aoife cut her short, "Tell me later." Finally, cutting through the last rope, Aoife helped Kate onto the net ladder. Her blue wings were ruffled and untidy. Climbing off the net later, an invisible nose butted Aoife's back. "Come on, Tame. Let's go," Aoife whispered. "Who's Lame?" Kate whined following behind Aoife.

Rowsheen stepped out from behind a fish barrel, scaring Aoife and Kate. She motioned them to get down behind the barrels.

"I'm so glad we found you, Kate... I couldn't find the keys, Aoife," Rowsheen whispered. "We need a new plan."

"Why don't we leave now?" Aoife whispered.

"Where is your dragon?" Rowsheen asked, looking around her.

"Right here," Aoife replied, reaching into midair and petting invisible Tame's head.

"Dragon?" Kate replied spellbound. "Can't explain now, but get on," Aoife ordered, feeling the place where Tame's back was. Throwing her leg over, Aoife disappeared from view.

"Come on," Rowsheen ordered, pulling herself and Kate onto the dragon's back. Aoife grabbed a fish off the ground that Tame had forgotten, waved it in front of his nose, then tossed it overboard.

Tame leaped over the railing toward the roaring waves below. Aoife, Kate, and Rowsheen held on for dear life as they plummeted down past the steep, steel sides of the massive battleship into the icy waters below. Gasping for air, Aoife looked behind her to see a drenched and pale Kate and Rowsheen as they emerged from the icy, unfeeling water. Tame swallowed the fish, licking his lips, and began to swim towards the shore. Aoife's stomach rumbled loudly, reminding her of her missed lunch.

"I'm hungry," Aoife informed herself with a whisper.

"You're hungry, in a time like this?" Rowsheen gasped as she held the back of Aoife's red shirt.

"Um… hum," Aoife replied with a nod, letting go of Tame's neck and ringing out her wet locks.

"I got a banana," Kate replied, fishing her hand into her dress pocket.

"The same banana that you found on the beach!!" Rowsheen exclaimed, looking behind her to see for herself if it was real.

"Oh yeah," Kate replied, passing the banana to Aoife.

"I'd feel bad if I ate your banana that has been through so much with you," Aoife exclaimed, refusing the banana.

"What if we all split it?" Kate replied, peeling the mushy fruit.

"I don't kn..." Aoife began to decline, but that was as far as she got because Rowsheen had shoved the poor banana into her open, unsuspecting mouth.

"Thank you," Aoife mumbled with a mouth full of soft banana.

Tame swam onward over the rushing, cold waves. The sun beat down on Aoife, Kate, and Rowsheen. Aoife splashed water on her head to cool herself down. The heat worried her. She did not do well in the heat. In the past, she got headaches and fatigue when she was in the sun for too long. She was also worried about Rowsheen, who was used to the dense and damp forest areas of Mossland. Aoife lay her head down on Tame's back, closed her eyes, and drifted into a light slumber.

Aoife awoke to the soft, cool breeze of an Island's dark, shadowy night on a bed of light, smooth sand. Her head throbbed with the pain of a severe headache. Aoife let out a soft moan.

A quiet voice spoke, "Aoife, you alright?" Rowsheen asked, feeling for her in the dark.

Aoife moaned again, "Just a bad headache," she replied. Rowsheen inched over and patted her back until Aoife finally fell fast asleep.

Chapter 41:
"We are as far as we can go!"

Kate awoke in the misty twilight before the sun's rays had begun to show themselves to the slimy tongue of Tame bathing her face. "Uuuggghh. That's disgusting!!!!" Kate hollered, "Aoife, help!"

Aoife rolled on her side, stood, and staggered toward Kate and Tame in the dim light. "Come on, Boy. Get off," she spoke, pushing at Tame's shoulder. Aoife looked down at her body, all covered in dry, sticky sand. She felt tired and overstimulated. Aoife tried to brush the sand off as best as she could.

"He was trying to eat me, I think," Kate exclaimed in a shaky voice, fussing over every little thing. "I don't think he would, Katy," Aoife replied, wondering how she could possibly explain.

"How do you know he won't eat me? Ouch!!!" Kate asked, backing up and picking up her left foot, "A crab pinched my little toe!"

Aoife covered her mouth to conceal her chuckling, "You okay?"

"Yeah, but man, that little crab pinched hard, Aoife," Kate replied, holding her foot while bouncing on one leg and rubbing her sore toe.

"I said I did not think he would because...do you remember that old Merchant Buckles? He said in one of his stories that spritelings were poisonous to fangserpents, and your kind is pretty close to the spritelings. Actually, cousins, if I remember right." Aoife explained, sitting her tired self down on the cool, fine sand and scratching Tame's scaly neck.

Rowsheen had been up for an hour already, walking up and down the shipwrecked beach searching for anything that could be of help to them. A song her father had always sung to her played ever in her mind.

"I wish you were here, Daddy," Rowsheen whispered to herself as she walked where the waters lapped at her boots.

In the misty twilight, Rowsheen tripped over something hard, half in the water and half out. Getting up out of the wet sand, she brushed off her knees and turned around to see what she had tripped over. It was another decapitated body. Rowsheen jumped, startled. It was one of the pirates from the ship; she recognized him as Garrison, the ship's jailkeeper. Trotting through the uneven, wet sand, Rowsheen hurried back to camp.

"Where's Rowsheen?" Aoife asked, glancing around their little camp, "Katy, have you seen her?"

"No, I woke to your dragon eating my face," Kate replied, splashing salt water on her face, "Ouch, that stings! I got salt water in my eye, Oww!"

Aoife noticed something in the water that froze her heart.

"Kate, stop, close your eyes, and walk away from the water," Aoife ordered, pulling her shoulders. Kate turned around, covered her eyes, and ran away from the water.

"What is it, Aoife?" Kate asked, looking back.

"I'll tell you later," Aoife replied, turning her gaze away from the severed head that bounced up and down in the wavy froth. Aoife expected Kate to protest, but the white, pale look on Aoife's face seemed to do all the explaining necessary; Aoife had seen more than just the floating head; a ship was entering the harbor.

"Let's go find some breakfast," Kate suggested, catching sight of the ship and walking toward the endless wall of dense trees and underbrush awaiting them.

Aoife followed; she was glad that Kate had not asked for further explanation. For she knew well that Kate was tough, but when Kate got worried, nervous, or anxious, she had trouble digesting food. Her stomach would be upset for a week or more, and she would eat very little, losing what little weight she had on her slim frame.

Rowsheen ran faster, trying to shake the scared feeling that gripped her fast. Stumbling on Tame's tail as she entered camp, Rowsheen fell headlong into the fine sand.

"Aoife! Kate!" Rowsheen yelled, cupping her hands around her mouth.

"Over here," Aoife called, trying not to draw too much attention to her voice.

Rowsheen followed Aoife's voice into the thick underbrush with Tame's massive, scaly, green form close to her heels.

Aoife snatched Rowsheen's hand and pulled her into the deep underbrush, beneath a tree where Kate was already waiting in perfect silence.

"What is it, Aoife?" Rowsheen asked quietly.

"There is a ship in harbor," Aoife replied with a nervous glance, "They are probably waiting for the fog to clear before they land."

"Then we need to get out of here fast," Rowsheen replied, standing on her feet.

Aoife pulled her back down, "We will, but we have to first destroy our footprints or they'll track us wherever we go.

"How do we erase all the footprints we made?" Rowsheen asked in disbelief, hoping for a logical answer.

"I'll do it," Kate replied, sitting up straight, "If I fly low over the sand, it will be as if we were never there."

"Can you do that before the fog clears, and still have time to get away?" Rowsheen asked, concerned for her friend.

"Oh, yeah," Kate replied with a confident grin.

"Wait!" Aoife nervously voices feeling around the brush as if she had lost something important, "Where's Tame?"

"Aoife," Rowsheen replied, "He was right behind me a few minutes ago."

"If he turned invisible in the forest," Kate began, "It's likely that we won't find him."

"He'll be fine," Rowsheen assured Aoife, "Maybe he'll catch up with us later."

"What do we do in the meantime?" Rowsheen asked, looking at Aoife's determined face.

"We start towards the mountain behind us. It's nigh impossible to track footprints on rock," Aoife explained, "And Kate can catch up with us in no time."

"Are your wings alright?" Rowsheen asked, and Aoife gave a questioning look at Kate.

"My ankle is sore, but my wings are fine; just a bit ruffled up," Kate replied, straightening her feathers on one wing and then the other.

"Alright," Rowsheen said with a determined voice, "Let's do it now!"

Rowsheen, who blended in perfectly with the surrounding trees, followed Kate to the beach to make sure it was safe, then hurried back to the brush where Aoife, high up in a tree, was watching the ship in the distance. As soon as Rowsheen nodded to Aoife that the beach was safe, they made for the mountain in the distance, making fast time.

Kate reached the shore and spread her wings wide over the sand. With two great flaps of her great blue-grey wings, she was in the air. Hovering close to the camp, Kate erased all traces that they had made there, then rose high above the trees and started toward the mountain.

Meanwhile, Aoife and Rowsheen were making good time. This was their specialty. In what felt like no time at all, they were already near the base of the mountain, looking up into the high, earthen-covered rocks above. The base of the mountain is crowded with ferns and mosses of many different species.

"I like the mountains that gradually rise better," Aoife commented dryly, looking for a better way up the rugged incline.

"Hum, hum, ha," Rowsheen laughed to herself and started up a ragged, deer trail that led up the slope. "This way goes up," she called back.

Kate was now hovering over the canopy of trees by the base of the mountain, looking for a sign of Aoife or Rowsheen. She was beginning to get worried when she spotted movement in a tree not far away from her. Looking closer, it was the size of a small being wrapped in a dark, green colored cloak.

"Aoife is climbing trees. Probably looking for me," she thought, for Rowsheen being the color of a tree could never be spotted.

"I'll surprise her," Kate decided, flying lower so Aoife would not be able to see her. Then she burst into action, flew around the tree fast, grabbed the person from the tree, and landed on the leafy, rich, black-soiled earth.

"Hi Aoife!!" Kate laughed, setting the person onto the ground.

"GET AWAY FROM YOU FLYING MENOUS!!!" a boy's voice yelled from inside the cloak. Kate froze solid; that was not Aoife!

Chapter 42:
Oh, Great Fairy

Rowsheen and Aoife trekked up the old, rugged deer trail that ran on the steep mountainside. On either side of the thin trail grew tall, thorny underbrush, and all kinds of birds, bugs, and forest life made noises within them. The air smelled sweetly floral and fresh as they ran. Both

Aoife and Rowsheen were grateful for the sweet-smelling air after being on the nasty pirate ship.

Aoife kept her head down, watching the trail for snakes, roots, and rocks. Rowsheen blazed the trail ahead of her when loud voices rose to her ears. Turning around, Rowsheen caught Aoife's arms and motioned for her to be still. Aoife nodded, indicating that she too heard the voices and pointed to the underbrush. Trying to be as quiet as possible, Rowsheen and Aoife plunged into the thick underbrush and got down low. The voices got louder as if they were coming closer, down the trail.

Aoife pulled her cloak over her head and inched lower, only an inch from Rowsheen's shoulder. She heard a small rustle in the grass beside. "Just a field mouse, or a small rabbit," Aoife figured, brushing a whisp of grass out of her face.

Loud footsteps thundered around the bend in the trail, passing the place where Aoife and Rowsheen crouched quickly. Rowsheen straightened up to see who the footstep belonged to, but only caught a glimpse of what appeared to be two men in rough, animal skin clothes walking at a fast pace down the mountain. "Aoife, I think they're headed down the mountain. We should be fine," Rowsheen whispered, kneeling down by Aoife. Aoife did not reply. Aoife did not move.

Kate, in her horrified terror, snatched up a long stick and tried to deepen her voice, "Stay where you are! Who are you?" she asked, holding the stick at arm's length.

"I am Jad, and I do NOT appreciate being snatched out of my tree!!!" Jad replied, whirling around, snatching the cloak off his head. He looked like a human boy; tan, deep-brown eyes, sandy, brown hair, with a small, wide nose, and ruddy cheeks.

"Sorry. I thought you were someone else..Did not mean to disturb you," Kate half apologized, I'm looking for my friends.

"What are you, an overgrown fairy? I have never seen anything like you around here," Jad asked with critical eyes.

"I'm a butterfly child," Kate replied, "and no, I'm not from around here."

"Then what are you doing here?" Jad asked, folding his arms across his chest.

"I kinda washed up on shore with my friends and we're trying to get to the top of the mountain to see where we are," Kate explained, hugging her long stick closer to her body.

A look of fear came over his face. "Where are your friends now?" Jad asked seriously.

"Probably close to the base of the mountain, why?" Kate asked, curious about what he had to say.

"That's fairy territory! They are vicious creatures!!!!!" he nearly yelled with excitement, grabbed Kate's arm, and pulled her after him, rushing through the trees and underbrush toward the looming mountain in the distance.

Rowsheen looked down at Aoife as she was playing a bad joke on her, but she still did not move from where she had knelt down, head on knees. Rowsheen felt something small and sharp pricking the back of her neck. Reaching back to slap the 'bug' off, Rowsheen lost her balance and collapsed into the thick underbrush beside Aoife.

"What will they do to my friends if they find them?" Kate asked Jad as they ran toward the mountain.

"Probably take 'em hostage first," Jad replied, jumping clear over a stream that blocked their path.

"Hostage?" Kate asked, using a flap of her wings to get her across.

"Yeah," Jad replied, picking up speed again, "they hold 'em till they get a ransom."

"Where do they hold 'em?" Kate asked, trying her best to keep up with Jad, for limbs and vines kept catching and grabbing at her wings.

"Dunno," Jad replied, "no one has left their territory alive to tell."

"What kind of a ransom?" Kate asked as her heart pounded within her and her feet pounded nonstop on the forest floor.

"That depends," Jad replied with a funny laugh.

"On what?" Kate asked, worried about her friends.

"On what mood they're in; of course," Jad replied, "Could be a frog's tongue, or a merman's tooth, or if they're in a really good mood, they might just decide to keep 'em."

"Keep 'em?" Kate started to feel sick.

Jad stopped suddenly, stone still, and motioned Kate to kneel.

"We are as far as we can go," he whispered. Reaching into his pocket, he pulled out a chunk of hard, blued cheese and tossed it a ways from him, then knelt down. The brush rustled and parted, revealing tiny, armor-clad, forest fairies, each with a weapon in hand and no more than six inches tall. Their wings were neatly folded behind them.

The group that emerged from the brush stood in a semicircle as more and more came to join them, till there were well over a hundred present. They marched about in perfect lines, every movement in unison till they were in position, then turned and stood solemnly in rank.

Kate's first instinct was to laugh, but she bit her tongue hard at the stern look on Jad's face. This was obviously no laughing matter.

Aoife awoke softly to the chatty murmur of a bubbling brook. She was lying at the edge of the book, her hair almost dipping into the water, on a soft blanket of prairie grass. Dark shadows loomed from high, rock walls on every side of her. The only light came from the blue sky above. She was inside a gorge.

Rowsheen opened her eyes to the laughing, merry chatter of a ring of maid fairies. They were dressed in all colors of long, flowy dresses hemmed with lacy flowers. Their eyes were sharp and bold, their ears slightly pointed, and their hair twisted and braided this way and that with flowers and vines. Their wings fluttered this way and that.

Rowsheen tried to straighten herself up, but she was tied in place to a thick, maple tree, with hearty, strong vines covered in a snowy-white bloom. The fairies saw her open her eyes and began to dance about and sing.

> *"We have the tree of flowers,*
> *We'll dance about for hours,*
> *We'll grow her in the snow,*
> *We'll tie her in a bow,*

And we'll never let her go,

Oh, never let her go!"

The second verse, as the first, was far from comforting to Rowsheen.

"The other we hid deep within a hole,

Soon we'll call the Prince to come and get his mole,

He'll give us gems and fancies for his lovely prize,

But we will not let him go, for he is not wise,

We'll drop him in the hole, place a lid on top,

We'll hide his gems and fancies in the belly of the Lopp,

In the belly of the Lopp!"

Nor was the third any brighter.

"Evil men, oh pirates,

Oh, the mighty tyrunts,

Kill and tear each other apart,

For they know not the word, smart,

We'll knock then about, oh yes,

We'll show them who's the best,

They'll lose their eyes, then their toes,

And last of all their measly nose,

We'll set them loose inside the bog,

And arouse our friend, oh humble Mog."

Round and round the fairies danced and spun, singing their cruel songs over and over again till Rowsheen thought she was going to puke.

Kate breathed hard as she watched the line of armored fairies part for a fairy clad in gold armor patterned in intricate flowers and wildlife. The fairy marched up to Jad, then turned and approached Kate with a low bow, "Oh, great Fairy of the blue realms above, I am the Governor King of this provenance. What does your unexpected visit mean to your unworthy children?" Kate was stunned.

Jad replied, "She is..."

"Do not speak for the Great Fairy, Peasant," the Fairy cut him short, holding his long spear to Jad's neck.

"Would it please you, oh Great Fairy, for me to terminate this worm?" the Fairy asked Kate, preparing to run him through with his spear.

"Oh, no! It would not please me!" Kate objected, placing her hands over her mouth in horror, "He is helping me."

"He is your servant?" the Fairy asked, leaning on his spear with the tip pressed into the ground. Jad quickly nodded at Kate, giving her an intense stare.

"Uh, Yes. Yes, he is. And we are here to...find my two other servants...who I sent ahead of me to... tell you of my coming." Kate ended her statement firmly, trying to sound authoritative.

"Ah. Yes," the Fairy began, "I'm afraid we have mistaken your servants as intruders. This will be corrected right away, and may I have the privilege to ask on what errand you have come to visit?"

Kate knew she would have to think up something fast, "The... errand in simply to come when you would expect me not so... to teach you that you must always be ready..at any time for me to come."

"I see," the Fairy replied, rubbing his tiny, bearded chin, "It will be in our highest honor to have you join us for a starlight feast in your honor." Kate looked at Jad for an answer, who nodded furiously.

"Yes... I... I mean, we would be delighted to attend your feast," Kate answered with a nod of her head.

Aoife's head spun as she tried to stand, then sat back down. The colors of the rich, green grass, the dark, reddish-black, rocky canyon walls, morphed and melted together in a spinning cascade. Aoife held her head in her hands and tumbled back down on the ground. Pain shot through her neck where the snake had bitten her so long ago.

"Why, why, why, do I keep getting captured, and why does my bit keep paining me?" Aoife mumbled out loud, rolling to and fro. Aoife finally just lay still and took some deep breaths to calm her body down.

"The pain medicine!" Aoife remembered suddenly. The pain medicine was the bottle that Jessie had given her months upon months prior, and she still had it in her side bag for emergencies. Aoife took a sip and lay still, and continued with deep breathing and relaxation techniques she had been taught at the training grounds for managing her chronic pain from the snake bite. In about an hour, Aoife could see clearly again and sit up without dizziness.

Rowsheen struggled trying to pull loose from the thick, tight vines as the fairies chanted their mean songs endlessly. When another fairy, clad in odd, silver armor, ran up and whispered to the other fairies one by one, then ran off again.

"The Great Fairy,
Oh, beloved canary,
We'll release her tree,
We'll untie her bands of Vie,

We'll feed her rosy tea,

We'll lead her to the Dee,

Because her Lady,

The lineage of Crady,

Has come to see,

Our little home in Scree,

We'll pull the mole,

Out of her deep hole,

We'll throw her ropes of Vie,

We'll lead her to the Dee,

Her Lady will be pleased,

And we will throw a feast,

And we will throw a feast!"

With that, the fairies untied the vines that held her fast and pulled at the hems of her pants for her to follow them. Rowsheen obeyed at once, walking slowly to make sure that she did not step on any of the tiny, bouncing fairies.

"Where are they taking me?" Rowsheen could only wonder as she straightened her clothes and brushed the dirt off.

Aoife tried again to stand, and this time was successful. Walking to the high canyon wall, she tried to make out if she could climb it, but decided that it was too high without a rope. Leaning her back against the rock wall, Aoife began to doubt if she would ever get back to Fayatoch's training ground, or even Mossland, for that matter.

Taking a deep breath, something bumped into the side of her head. Looking up, she saw a group of fairies letting down vines to her. "I am about to do something stupid," Aoife whispered to herself, tying a vine around her waist, planting one foot firmly against the hard canyon wall, and taking one long, deep breath.

Kate held her head high and her shoulders back, trying to make a good impression on the little fairies who were leading her high up the mountain past large boulders and steep cliffs. Jad walked stiffly behind her. The fairies seemed to terrify him, and Kate could not understand why, for her, they seemed rather cute and amusing.

Finally, after what seemed like an eternity to Kate, they reached a large opening on top of the mountain with a great, ancient tree resting in its center. Rowsheen sat perched on a low stone to the left of the tree, surrounded by more fairies than Kate had ever seen in one place before. "We have your tree," the Fairy King said to Kate, "and we have your Princes, and she will be here shortly."

"My Princes?" Kate asked, not understanding what he meant at all. "Yes, the Red-haired Princes. There is quite a large bounty on her head," the Fairy King replied, leading Kate to a great marble table fashioned with stone seats beneath the great tree.

Aoife held the rope tight; her legs were beginning to wobble, but she could not turn back now, for she was at least three-quarters of the way up. Finally pulling herself over the ledge, Aoife collapsed onto the ground, breathing hard. "Sir Masuda did not cover that lesson yet," she whispered to herself. The bouncing, happy fairies tried to coax her to her feet.

"Stand up, come forth,

We will travel North,

The Fairy of all,

Has come to call,

Now up, arise,

Prince's prize,

The fairy waits at the Dee,

The fairy waits for you 'n we!"

Aoife stood, wondering where the little fairies were taking her as they pulled at her boots and cloak, leading her down an old 'n worn path.

Chapter 43:
A Tea Party

Aoife stumbled onward, trying to figure out where they were taking her, *"The songs are riddles,"* Aoife reasoned, *"Then they are taking me to Dee? To the Fairy? Where is Dee?"* But there was none to answer her questions; she would just have to wait and see this fairy for herself.

"We are nearly to the Dee,

There she is,

There she'll be!"

The little fairies bubbled, pulling at her boots to try to get her to move faster. Trying her best to keep up with them, Aoife stepped a little faster. Rounding the bend in the path on top of their mountain, there appeared a clearing in the thick brush. Aoife did not notice the Great Tree or the Marble Table at first because she was watching her feet, so she did not step on any bouncing fairies.

"You're alright!" Kate breathed, embracing Aoife in a tight hug. Aoife squeezed Kate's slim, bony frame. She had missed her.

Rowsheen would have done the same if the fairy children were not climbing all over her and pulling at her rose curls. Pulling Aoife's boots, the fairies led Aoife to a seat at the marble table. Sitting down, the fairies presented her with a blue, crystal cup of steaming red-tinted tea.

Aoife brought the crystal teacup to her lips and breathed in the sweet aroma of a tea that she had never smelled before. Taking a small sip, Aoife found the warm, steamy tea to be slightly bitter, tangy, and sweet. Aoife took a deep breath and continued to drink her tea and eat the dainty foods of many different colors presented to her.

The sun was beginning to set over the horizon, bathing the mountain top in radiant orange, blinding yellow, and rich, pungent red streams of light. The forest life began to sing their song to welcome back the shadows long. It was as if they meant to say...

The sun sank low and finally disappeared from the horizon, and as the pleasant, timely shadows began to appear, the tiny fairies lit up their crystal lanterns, covering the mountain top in a spectrum of bright, glowing, crystal lights. Aoife pushed away her crystal teacup and lay her weary head on her arms and closed her eyes. Rowsheen bundled up her cloak and rested herself on the ground by Aoife.

Jad tried his best not to yawn. *"The fairies had invited Kate to a starlight feast, not a sunset tea party,"* Jad thought to himself. *"Their stay was not yet over. They were supposed to attend a fairy feast, which usually happens at midnight."*

"Kate," he whispered, trying to get her attention.

"What?" she whispered back.

"You can't fall asleep," he whispered in her ear, "You're a goddess, remember, and there is still a feast to attend."

"I'm tiiiiirrreeeddd," Kate whined.

"They'll kill us if they find out," Jad hissed.

Kate gave a hearty laugh as if she were utterly amused. "But they're so cute. How could they hurt us?" Kate asked, watching the fairies dance around the glowing lanterns.

"They'll eat us! They will," Jad exclaimed through his teeth, "Find something to keep you occupied."

"Alright," Kate sighed, sitting up and walking over to where Aoife sat, nearly asleep with her head resting in her arms.

"Aoife, Aoife," Kate shook her, "Wake up."

"Yes, Boss," Aoife replied, straightening up and stretching.

"I need you to tell me all you know about fairies," Kate whispered.

"Long version or short version?" Aoife asked, rubbing her weary eyes.

"Long version, please," Kate replied with a nod.

"Forest fairies are very territorial and will protect their land at all costs. Some families are more forgiving, like the ones we have at home. The ones here are called Nevsee because they are rarely ever seen and never leave a trace or mark at the beginning or end of their territory. Which is why it is very easy to wander into dangerous fairy territory without knowing it."

"What do they eat?" Kate interrupted nervously.

"Most eat fruits, plants, berries..." Aoife thought, Kate cut her off, "What about meat?"

"Yes, they'll eat meat on special occasions." Aoife replied softly, "They roast it; I think."

"What about us?" Kate whispered in her ear.

"Well, probably not you or Rowsheen," Aoife replied, "but the rest of us besides you two, sure."

"What about a feast?" Kate asked with a concerned look on her face, "They invited me to a starlight feast."

"A feast at midnight, most likely, or a feast when the stars are at their brightest," Aoife replied, "You've got a few hours. Eat what they give you. Be polite. Act like… well… whatever they think you are."

"I was the only one invited," Kate recalled, staring off into the dark, blackness of the night, "Do you think they'd allow me to bring someone along?"

"Maybe," Aoife answered, tipping her head back and yawning, "Ask if you can take someone with you. They'd probably let you if they think you're some kind of deity."

Aoife lay her head back down and sank into a deep sleep.

"Jad," Kate called, sitting down beside him at the round table, "You seem to know more about fairies than any of us. Will you come with me to the feast?"

"You'd have to announce it," Jad replied, looking around, "because they're not just going to let just anyone in."

"I shall," Kate replied with a sigh and a long yawn. She had to stay awake, and this was certainly more adventure than she had bargained for.

In the span of a few hours' time, the fairies ran this way and that, till finally the Fairy King arrived to announce that the feast was ready.

"You Majesty," the short Fairy King announced, "Your feast is prepared. Right this way to Klunder's Hall."

"My King," Kate began, trying to sound decisive. "I am taking my servant with me to our feast."

"Very well, your Majesty. Anything you desire," the King replied with a long bow.

"Right this way."

Kate and Jad were led quite a way down a rocky path through the woods behind tiny fairies carrying small torches in their left hands. Kate thought the dark night with a sky dotted with stars was the prettiest she had ever seen.

"The Hall of our late King Klunder the Courageous, Your Majesty," the King announced as he presented a long, low, rectangular, white-streaked marble table set with tiny chairs and covered with more food than Kate thought she had ever seen in one place. Kate and Jad were seated on the right and left of the King at the table's head on stones rather than the tiny chairs to Jad's relief.

"Thank you, Oh Great Fairy," The King began, "for this unspeakable honor. And now may you meet your people." The King clapped three times. A great thunderous cheering sounded at all sides of the table as fairies began to appear from everywhere and sit down at the great table digging in to berry puddings, and rabbit roast, acorn raspberry pies, pine needle tea, and all sorts of berry and leaf teas, egg 'n nut custards, mouse and hummingbird cakes, and still more that Kate could not identify.

Kate felt overwhelmed as more and more food was heaped on her plate; she had always been skinny and had a hard time on Church eating days when she wanted to try all the delicious food. *"How am I ever going to eat all of this?"* she wondered, digging into the enormous pile.

While Kate and Jad pushed to clean their plates, Rowsheen and Aoife slept soundly at the round, marble, mountaintop table. While they slept, both Aoife and Rowsheen had terrible dreams.

Aoife stood on a battlefield strewn with dead soldiers, clutching the long sword that Captain Acosta had given her. The stench of death crept to her nose, making her grimace. Drums beat in the distance, quickening the beat of her heart. The sun faded behind unfeeling, cold clouds above, mingled with a chilly, biting breeze.

"Aoife," a voice called, running toward her.

"Jessie," Aoife replied, turning around. Jessie's face was smeared in dried blood; his hands were bloody and bruised, and he looked as if he had been rolled in dirt.

"Daniel is on the southern ridge," Jessie blurted out, grabbing Aoife's arm, "He needs our help!"

Aoife ran behind Jessie, barely able to feel her legs beneath her, over the strewn battlefield as fast as she could run.

Hideous war calls sounded over the ridge as they were nearing. Horns blew and bellowed over the endless drumbeats.

As they reached the ridge, Aoife's heart sounded like thunder in her ears, nearly drowning out the horrid drums. Aoife caught a glimpse of Daniel in the distance; he was surrounded on all sides by enemy soldiers, yet he fought on, aided only by a single, tall, muscular warrior in piercing black armor with a long, slim sword.

"Must be Dermid," Aoife's thoughts decided as she drew her sword. Jessie drew his sword in unison as a swarm of enemy soldiers came thudding toward them.

"For Mosssland!!!" Jessie yelled, slashing through the first soldier.

Aoife swung her sword to meet that of her enemy. The sword felt oddly weightless in her grip as she fought, moving her feet to the rhythm of the drums while ducking below swords and jumping over debris. When she finally caught an opening in the seemingly endless flood of enemy soldiers, she dashed forward toward the last place that she had seen Daniel.

An unexpected root took her footing when she was within ten giant strides of Daniel, flinging her headlong onto the muddy battlefield. Stunned for a moment, she glanced at her sword lying on the ground in front of her; she did not recognize the sword because it was not the one Captain Acosta had given her.

A screeching yell sounded from across the battlefield. Looking in that direction, Aoife spotted a cannon, and it was pointed in Daniel's direction!

"Daniel!" Aoife hollered, and it was at that moment that Aoife woke up to Rowsheen shaking her.

"Aoife," Rowsheen whispered with a concerned look on her face, "that must have been quite a nightmare. You woke me up hollering. It was like you were calling someone, but I couldn't make out who because your head was buried in your cloak. You're all sweaty!"

Chapter 44:
An Old Face

"Just a bad dream, Rowsheen," Aoife replied, rubbing the sweat off her face with her cloak, "I'll tell you later."

"I had a bad dream too," Rowsheen replied, shaking her head, "Oh, it was awful, and yet it felt so real."

"Were you on a battlefield?" Aoife asked with a shiver, trying to collect herself.

"Yes," Rowsheen replied with surprise, "I was on a white and black speckled stallion in front of an army of soldiers of all different kinds; headbricker, tree being, rosian, bear, giant, and fairy. I was leading them into battle."

"Were there drums beating in the distance?" Aoife asked wide-eyed.

"Yes, I think so," Rowsheen replied with a shrug, "at least before the army started moving forward, I heard them; very eerie."

After the fairy feast, the fairies escorted Jad and Kate to the edge of the fairy territory, where Aoife and Rowsheen were already waiting.

The fairies begged Kate to come again anytime she wished. Walking away from the fairy territory, they all felt a sigh of relief.

"Thank you, Jad," Kate began, "my two best friends would still be stuck in that pickle if you hadn't helped me rescue them." "Yes, thank you," Rowsheen and Aoife graciously echoed.

"Thank yourself for snatching me out of that tree," Jad replied, putting a smile on Kate's face, "You sure got my attention."

"Kate," Aoife whispered, bumping her shoulder, "You've got to fill me in later."

"So, why are y'all in Daj anyway?" Jad asked with a puzzled look.

"We're trying to get back to Fayatoch," Rowsheen replied with a questioning look on her face. "How far is Fayatoch from Daj?"

"Just a few hours' boat ride from the East coast," he replied, pointing in the direction he spoke of. "My village is down that way, close to shore."

"Could you show us the way?" Kate asked, staring into the dense jungle.

"Yes," Jad replied with a grin, "but first I need help with my chores that were interrupted."

"Chores?" Kate questioned.

"We'd be glad to help," Rowsheen quickly voiced, cutting Kate off.

"I got trap lines all up and down the island," Jad replied, pointing in several directions, "It often takes hours to check them all, and I could use some help catching up."

"Got it," Aoife replied, "Just point me in the right direction."

"There is a lake about half a mile in that direction," Jad directed, pointing to Aoife's left.

"I have five beaver traps set along their mudslides. Meet back in this spot in an hour."

"On it," Aoife replied, disappearing into the dense forest.

"I've got several fish traps set along a brook about a mile that way," he replied, pointing to Rowsheen's right.

"I'll be back in an hour," Rowsheen replied, disappearing into the brush.

"What else?" Kate replied with a shrug. She was not fond of seeing little animals trapped.

"I've got boar traps this way," Jad replied, "If I got one, it'll take the two of us to carry it out."

"You should've gotten Aoife for this job," Kate replied, "She has done more with hogs than I have."

"Nah," Jad replied with a laugh, "You'll do fine."

Aoife trudged through the now sticky and hot jungle in the direction that Jad had pointed. In about twenty minutes, Aoife found the Lake sitting concealed in the forest of tall trees and vines. Walking around the lake, Aoife started looking for Jad's traps at the water's edge when, suddenly, a great splash sounded in the water beside her. Aoife fell back onto the shore in shock.

Trying to calm herself, she whispered, "There's nothing there. It was probably just a beaver trying to scare me off," she reasoned, standing up. The splash sounded again now at the other side of the lake; something was struggling to get loose in the reeds at the edge of the water.

"Well, at least one of his traps caught something," Aoife told herself, running around the lake to the other side.

Getting to the trap, Aoife saw the oddest sight; the trap was moving, but she saw nothing inside it, so Aoife grabbed the trap and began to pull it out of the water when a puff of smoke blew into Aoife's face.

"Tame," Aoife scolded, "What have you been doing?" Tame turned visible, wagging his long tail that was caught in the trap.

"Well, you don't look hurt," Aoife replied, cutting the trap off, "but you do owe a friend of Kate's some money for a new beaver trap."

Tame jumped on top of Aoife, happy to be free of the trap. "Comm'on, Tame," Aoife replied, "We have to check the rest of these traps for beavers."

Rowsheen marched through the dense jungle toward the brook, stepping over snakes, vines, and logs all the way.

"I'll never live in a jungle," Rowsheen said to herself out loud, "Too many snakes."

Rowsheen ended up with more fish than Aoife or Jad, and Kate ended up with beavers or hogs. After meeting back when the hour had passed and Aoife explained once again what Tame was, the tiny group headed through the grueling jungle to Jad's village by the shoreline. Jad stopped close to a house built nearly as high as the tree beside it.

"Jad Maust!" a woman's voice called from inside. "Where have you been?"

"Coming, Mother," Jad replied, disappearing into the house built up high on stilts. "Be right back," he assured Kate.

"Well, now that we're here," Jad announced, winking his eye at Kate, "My family is inviting y'all to dinner."

"I'm still full from the fairy feast," Kate groaned in a whisper to Rowsheen and Aoife.

Aoife at once found her way into the kitchen, helping Jad's mother with washing dishes. Rowsheen offered to set the table, and Kate... well... Jad took Kate on a walk around the village before dinner.

In the evening, a few hours before the sun would sink beneath the horizon, Jad's family began to arrive. His older sister showed up with her husband and child, his little sister, two of his cousins, and, of course, his mother and father were there as well. After dinner, Jad insisted that we (Kate) stay to play a popular ball game on the little island. Kate came close to winning several times. She'd played this game at home in the summertime. Kate was a very competitive player, and often was the only girl playing with a giant group of boys.

Aoife cringed when Kate fell flat on her tail. "The last time I watched her play," Aoife recalled, "she jammed one of her fingers, and she claims that it still hurts now and again."

Aoife walked away from the game toward the shore, her heart felt heavy, but she was glad to see a bright smile on Kate's face once again.

"Why do I have so much on my mind at such a peaceful time?" Aoife whispered, slipping off her shoes so she could wade in the salty water as the sun dipped still lower in promising shades of orange, purple, and pink. Yet Aoife knew the answer; she did not want to fail her country or her father. The future felt like an anxious, painful lump in her heart, and she felt somehow unable to shake it loose or forget it. Tears streamed down her face as she knelt in prayer: *Lord, I can hold onto this no longer. I give it to you. I give you my worry, my pride, my regret, my anxiousness, and my pain. I surrender my all to you. I lay it all down at the foot of the cross. Let thine will be done. In Jesus' name. Amen*

Aoife pulled her notebook out of her side bag, surprised that she even had it. Aoife drew out a pen and wrote these words:

> *Life is full of ups and downs,*
> *Bundle of joy and creasing frowns.*
> *Each and every distinct.*

We know one from the other.
The sister of pain and frustration,
Known for her tears and grueling exacerbation.
But she also brings growth and challenges,
And hope to last,
Through her trials, till they're past.
The brother comes next with a sunrise of joy,
Glittering gold like a shiny new toy.
What comes with him is rest, healing, and peace.
But even his glory must cease,
For we cannot be challenged under his hand,
Nor can we grow under his span.
Both brother and sister are needed in life,
They both jump about like mischievous sprites.
Each needs the other to keep life exciting and fresh,
In this world, wrapped tight in flesh.

"Well," Aoife replied, looking over her poem, "It's not as good as one of Kate's, but it's sure good to me. Tame nudged Aoife's arm and licked her face. "Hey, Tame," Aoife whispered, "Where have you been?" Tame answered by blowing a puff of fishy smoke in her face.

"Where have you been?" an old, familiar voice asked, walking toward Aoife with a smile.

"Liam," Aoife replied, standing up, "What are you doing here?"

"I've needed to talk to you for a long while," Liam replied, looking up at the sky. "And frankly, I've had a lot more than I bargained for trying to travel down here." "Why did you come?" Aoife asked with a puzzled look on her face.

"To say that my father has passed away," Liam whispered, dropping his head.

"I'm very sorry," Aoife replied, wondering about the purpose of his journey.

"My older brother reigns in his place, and he has given me the freedom to decide when and if I want to marry and who," Liam continued.

"That's very kind of him," Aoife cut in.

"He gave me that freedom, and well it hit me that I should give you that freedom," Liam went on, "We did not have that freedom when we were little, but I want us both to have it now, so whatever happens I want you to be happy."

"Thank you," Aoife replied, "But you could have told me that in a letter."

"Yes, well," Liam began, "I also don't feel you're safe here, and I was going to take you home."

"Not safe," Aoife laughed sarcastically.

"Jokes aside, you've been captured twice!" Liam retorted, crossing his arms, "How can I be assured of your safety?"

"You cannot," Aoife replied, "because we are not guaranteed tomorrow over the next sunset, and with all this danger coming, how am I any safer at home or anywhere?"

"You'd be safer in Dearbhlaria," Liam replied with concern in his eyes.

"Thank you, Liam," Aoife replied with a smile, "I trust that I would be. I kinda need to stay here. This is where my family expects me to be. But I do have one question for you."

"Anything," Liam replied.

"Rowsheen said she saw you with the pirates," Aoife began, "What does that mean?"

"I paid them for a ride to Fayatoch and got a lot more like I said before than I bargained for," Liam replied with a sigh, "I saw Rowsheen hiding from the sailors on a beach at Fayatoch's South, but there was not any port or base in miles so I demanded they take me around which they would not do, and I found out later that it was because they were attacking Fayatoch's main ports with their many other ships. I got a glance at the list of all the youths they had caught and saw you on it," Liam continued, "Later, I learned that you had escaped and went searching for you here on Daj. Told the fairies that I'd pay them handsomely if they'd help me find you. They were no help."

"Oh, that's why," Aoife smiled with a shake of her head.

"What?" Laim asked.

"The fairies called me the redheaded Princess and said that there was a bounty on my head," Aoife replied with a grin, "Few people have ever called me that or know that I'm a princess."

"So, you don't wish for me to take you home?" Liam asked. "You would be far safer."

"Not right now at least," Aoife replied, "but thank you very much for everything."

"You're welcome," Liam replied, walking down the beach where he disappeared as if he had never been there at all.

Tame ran up to Aoife and puffed smoke in her face.

"Are you ready for a swim?" Aoife asked, scratching under his chin. Tame wagged his tail excitedly. "Then we will be off soon," Aoife replied, standing up.

"Aoife," Rowsheen called, emerging from the path that led to the village, "Kate wants you to play one round on her team."

That night, Rowsheen, Aoife, and Kate camped out under the stars on the white sandy beach.

"Aoife," Kate asked suddenly, "Do you think we'll ever come back here?"

"It's certainly possible," Aoife replied, rolling off Tame's back, "Why do you want to?"

"Yeah," Kate confessed, "It's so beautiful here and the people are so nice." "Too many snakes for me," Rowsheen cut in, "but the views are very nice."

"So, we can come back here?" Kate asked.

"The island is only a few hours from Fayatoch," Aoife replied, "assuming that Sir Masuda doesn't ground us for the rest of our training time; you might just be able to come back."

Rowsheen awoke before dawn and woke Kate and Aoife. The little group then began their journey over the waves back to Fayatoch, mounted on Tame's back. They were off long before the first rays of light began to flicker across the sky.

"Too bad we couldn't say goodbye this morning," Kate whined, running her hand through the cold water.

"I thought we said goodbye last night," Aoife replied, shooting Kate a wink.

"I remember," Kate assured her, flipping her long hair over her shoulders, "but I don't see why we had to leave so early."

"Did you see the color of that lobster at dinner last night?" Aoife asked in annoyed tones.

"Yes," Kate replied with a loud laugh. "You afraid you're gonna look like that?"

"Not the shape, just the color," Rowsheen replied with a smile, "Aoife, what's that over there?"

"What did you see?" Aoife replied, slowing Tame down and turning her head.

"Like some wood or ship wreckage floating," Rowsheen replied, pointing in the direction she had seen it in, "and I thought I saw something on it."

"Tame," Aoife whispered in Tame's ear and pointed to the floating debris, "Let's go over there to check it out."

Tame swam about five giant strides away from the debris but would go no closer.

"It looks like a body," Aoife announced, turning to Rowsheen as if to say, *Let's go now, we've seen enough.*

"Wait," Rowsheen replied, "I saw him breathe."

Chapter 45:
Future Eyes

What has the sea brought me,

A pearl of precious prize,

The sea hasn't brought me fancies,

Just a set of future eyes.

"Him?" Kate replied, wishing they would turn away.

"I'm going to check it out," Rowsheen replied, slipping off Tame's back and into the water.

"Not without me," Aoife retorted, slipping into the cool, salty water. With a deep breath, Aoife pulled her arm forward and back to propel herself quickly through the water while fluidly kicking her legs.

"I can't get my wings wet," Kate whined, not wanting to stay alone on Tame.

"Just stay there," Aoife replied, treading water, "We'll be back in a minute."

Aoife and Rowsheen pulled themselves up against the great chunk of debris. There was a young man dressed as a sailor lying seemingly unconscious in the center of the debris, clinging to a beam. He had sandy blond hair and a tan, slim, ruddy complexion for his large, bony frame.

"He's breathing," Rowsheen announced, climbing onto the debris and feeling his pulse, "Aoife, I need help getting him off."

"I don't think it can hold all our weight," Aoife observed, watching it move up and down in salty waves.

"It will," Rowsheen reassured her, holding out her hand and helping Aoife up.

Together, Rowsheen and Aoife pulled the sailor off the beam and laid him on a solid plank to push over to where Tame was impatiently waiting. The sailor's eyes opened for a moment, and he whispered, "Mermaids to my rescue?"

"No, I'm a Rosian," Rowsheen replied to him, steadying the beam in the water. Rowsheen wiped a strand of hair out of her delicate face and tucked it behind her ear.

"A Rosian," he whispered, weakly falling unconscious again, "In the water?"

Rowsheen, Kate, and Aoife managed to get him on Tame's back, and they continued their journey across the bay. The hours slipped by slowly, and soon the sun began to grow intense, so much so that they took turns swimming in the water behind Tame while holding onto Tame's tail.

Kate and Aoife swam behind Tame while Rowsheen stayed to keep an eye on the sailor they found.

"This water feels so nice and cool!" Aoife exclaimed, tipping her head back to get her hair wet.

"Yeah, I could stay here all day," Kate decided.

"Guys!" Rowsheen exclaimed, "He's waking up!" Aoife and Kate swam around Tame's back to where Rowsheen sat.

"Who are you all?" he asked, rubbing his eyes and unruly sandy blond hair.

"We're youth from Mossland currently training at Fayatoch," Aoife replied, placing a hand on his shoulder so he did not slide off Tame into the water.

Rowsheen cut her off, "We found you on the wreckage of a ship about an hour South of here."

"We're traveling back to Fayatoch. We're about an hour away. Where are you from?" Kate asked with a curious and judgmental look. She did not trust him at all.

"I'm from Dawnland. The names' Cal, Cal Bowen."

He replied, "I gotta get back there… They're under attack!"

"From whom?" Aoife asked with a shiver. A strange, eerie feeling came over her. She felt her heartbeat quicken and grip cold. Sadly, she already guessed the pirates were to blame.

"Pirates!" Cal answered, sitting up with his hand on his head, "They've been polluting these waters for years, and recently they've gotten a lot stronger, like they've learned to work together or something, like they all got one big boss!" Cal seemed to get increasingly irritated when he talked about the pirates attacking his homeland.

Aoife swam to Tames' head and whispered in his ear, *"A little faster, please, boy. We need to get back as soon as possible."*

Tame gave Aoife's face a big lick with his great, bluish-grey, slimy, wet tongue. Somehow, he seemed to understand what Aoife wanted and why she was so worried. He gave one smoky sniff back to Kate and Aoife, who were still in the water. Kate and Aoife climbed on Tame's back with Cal and Rowsheen. Tame shook his scaly head and shot forward in the deep, bluish-greenish-emerald water, picking up the speed over ten times faster than he had been going.

The wind filled their faces and hair. Kate's long, straight hair shot into Aoife's eyes and mouth. This did not get better, even with Aoife ducking and closing her eyes. Aoife kept her head down and eyes covered.

"Sorry, Aoife," Kate apologized, trying to keep her hair under control and her wet wings back, "This speed is going to tie my hair in a knot!"

Aoife, who was just amused by it, felt a sudden urge to look behind her. Just over the horizon was a ship!! Her stomach dropped, and her heart once again grew anxious and cold as if in a violent, claw-like grip.

Chapter 46:
Run, Swim, Scat

Can a ship on dry ground sink?

Can the clouds rain black ink?

Can a thinker help not think?

Can a pirate but not reek?

And a ship of rock not sink?

"Kate, a ship behind us!" Aoife yelled in a whisper tone, nervously shaking Kate's shoulder with vigor.

"That's the ship..." Kate's lost the rest of her words, her tongue felt paralyzed, and her mouth was dry. "That we were just on!" Aoife replied in horror after finishing her sentence.

A great wind picked up behind them, aiding the ship, which changed course in their direction! A sense of fear fell upon the whole party. Panic filled their faces.

"I think they've seen us!" Cal nervously shouted, looking behind, "Okay, okay," he breathed, "We need to be quiet and move quickly!"

Tame was beginning to get tired, and Aoife knew he could not go on that fast forever. Aoife scanned the horizon, looking for something; anything! All at once, she spotted some jutting isles far South. Aoife climbed over everyone to the front and patted Tame till he slowed to a stop.

"What are you doing?" Rowsheen asked frantically, "We can't stop!"

"We can't go on like this forever either," Aoife replied, directing Tame to the splinter isles to the South, "I have a plan." Tame started for the splinter isles as fast as he could swim at this point.

"We can hopefully lose them in the splinter isles there," Aoife replied, pointing in that direction.

"Can we make that?" Kate asked, looking pale. "Well, I guess we'll find out, won't we. Aoife, I'm gonna check it out." Kate rose into the air with a few great flaps of her massive blue wings and started toward the splinter isles.

The ship was not close enough to fire, but it was gaining fast! Kate flew ahead of us and hovered over the splinter isles in the distance that rose into the air like tall, jagged mountains in the middle of the sea.

"I think they're gaining too fast!" Cal nervously observed, looking behind us every few seconds.

"Kate's flying back!" Rowsheen shouted, pointing to Kate, who was flying back against the wind.

Aoife felt a shiver run down her spine. The sky had darkened above them, painting the once clear water an eerie emerald green. Dark purple clouds mounted the horizon, blocking out the sun.

"We got a storm coming," Aoife informed in a breathy whisper, wondering what else was coming their way, *"Lord protect us and keep us safe."* Aoife prayed, closing her eyes.

Kate flew over beside them and shouted so she could be heard above the quickening wind, "There's an island in the middle, large enough for us to rest on! I can take someone to ease Tame's load!"

"Rowsheen," Aoife addressed her, tapping on her shoulder, "Go with Kate. We'll be right behind!"

"You go. I'm not," Rowsheen retorted, trying to force Aoife to go. "I'm too heavy for Kate to carry over," Aoife whispered to Rowsheen, "Please go."

"We don't weigh much of a difference," Rowsheen replied, looking up at Kate, "but I'll go," she replied, standing up on Tame's back and jumping to Kate, who caught her and started off the island.

"We're too far away!" Cal exclaimed, watching the ship move ever faster behind them. His panicked expression frightened Aoife, for she knew that he had had far more dealings with those evil men than she had.

Aoife looked back at the ship, then down into the water, "Cal, swap places with me. I have an idea."

Cal moved behind Aoife, who placed her hands firmly on Tame's scaly mane, "Cal, hold on and hold your breath."

Tame plunged under the cold, emerald water till they were completely submerged. Aoife steered Tame North under the cold, refreshing water. The ship passed overhead, and Tame popped up on the other side behind the ship.

Cal and Aoife gasp for air. "Slow and steady, Boy," Aoife whispered in Tame's ear, "Just float and rest for a while. I need you to disappear, Boy." And Tame did disappear, Aoife realized that he could not move quickly when he was using all of his energy to stay invisible.

The sailors on board appeared to be confused and disappointed. They looked this way and that around the ship as if scanning for us. The ship continued South toward the Isles for only a brief span of time before heading West out of the direction of the coming storm.

"I think we'd better head to the islands now," Cal suggested, pointing to large purplish-gray clouds on the horizon.

"Yeah, that sounds like a good idea," Aoife replied, nudging Tame in that direction. Tame turned visible again and started at a steady pace toward the splinter isles. The closer they got, the more eerie the water seemed. Just below the waves lay the carcasses of countless ships, almost camouflaged into the sand and reef far below.

"This doesn't look like a good place to sail," Cal observed, looking down with a shiver as they passed around a tall, mountain-like splinter isle that jutted out of the sea.

Tame swam up to the sharp splinter isles and placed his front claws on the wet, slippery, brown rock covered in green and rust colored slimy sea grass.

"Hold on!" Aoife advised Cal as Tame began to ascend the great cliff. Aoife clung to Tame's mane and neck and clamped her knees tight as Cal held onto Aoife. Tame climbed higher and higher till he was almost vertical against the rugged, grassy rock cliff. Finally, Tame reached a ledge and climbed onto it. Aoife and Cal slid off Tame's back as he shook the water off his scales like a wet dog. Kate flew down to the ledge and set Rowsheen down.

"The... ship... phew…," Kate breathed heavily before she could reply, "seems to be heading the other way. Wow! I think we lost them!"

"BOOM, CRACK! BOOM." Lightning lit up the sky, followed by ground-shaking thunder. The sky grew darker, and eerie shadows started to appear around the isles.

"We can't stay here," Cal breathed with a grave and serious expression on his face, and he was right; Aoife and the other acknowledged that they would need to find safe shelter and fast.

Chapter 47:
You're crazy!

Jump into a rosabush,

Feel a wild pain.

Stand up to stormasea,

Join de past slain.

The next thirty minutes were just a blur to Rowsheen and the others as they scurried around trying to find shelter and whatever twigs or brush could be found on the little splinter isle for a sustainable fire. The shelter they found was just a small, sad little overhang in a tight, precarious position; right on the ledge, not ten feet from the cliff drop-off, but to these weary souls it was a warm, comforting palace.

Rowsheen squatted by the crackling fire and rubbed her hands together over the bright, heartening flames. She felt exhausted from the day at sea, and the weariness made her eyes start to fall so that she had to shake her head every few minutes to keep them open. The pounding, deafening rain beating down just a giant's stride away gave way to a cold mist threatening the tiny fire and giving Rowsheen a chill.

Inside her head, Rowsheen was fine. All her thoughts were of getting back to Fayatoch, and then some even drifted to going back home. *"I can't think about that just yet,"* she scolded herself. A sickening feeling welled up within her about home, "Something is not right," she whispered to herself, "or something very wrong will happen soon."

Aoife curled up beside Tame and hummed a little song she remembered Honeysuckle used to sing when it rained,

Drip, drop, oh drip drop, oh drip drop, oh rain.
Know that I love thee,
Don't carry disdain.
Drip, drop, oh drip drop, oh drip drop, oh rain.
Some say you're a soldier,
Or a monster of gain.
Drip, drop, oh drip drop, oh drip drop, oh rain.
Yet I see your purpose,
I don't ask for restraint.
Drip, drop, oh drip drop, oh drip drop, oh rain.
Continue, my ally,
I shall not complain.
Drip, drop, oh drip drop, oh drip drop, oh rain.
Water my fields,
Let green grasses reign.
Drip, drop, oh drip drop, oh drip drop, oh rain.
Know that I love thee.
Don't carry disdain.

Several hours before dawn, Aoife awoke with a sudden start. Aoife strained her ear trying to figure out what had woken her, but everything was silent, an eerie silence. It was as if the place was void of noise altogether, save for the soft, hushed, cool whisper of thick floating mist as it drifted into their snug little burrow.

"What woke me up?" her thoughts still rattled, being unsatisfied with the aspect of mere chance, but all at once she knew exactly what had woken her up, *"Rowsheen is awake; she must be!"*

Aoife's thoughts decided as Aoife rolled over, trying to go back to sleep. Her thoughts were too noisy, banging around in her head for Aoife to get any more sleep, so Aoife was quiet as the drifting mist slid out of her blanket and pulled on her cloak. Her boots were still on because she dared not take them off.

Crawling out from under the ledge, the ten-foot cliff offered little comfort because this morning it felt unforgiving and slick. Looking up above the ledge, Aoife spotted Rowsheen high up the cliff getting her morning exercise. Rowsheen's exercise routine included weight training, running, squats, and jumping. Rowsheen appeared to be using large stones as weights.

In less than a second's thought, Aoife pressed her hands firmly on the rock ledge and jumped. Before Aoife knew what had happened, her hands slipped, her teeth clanged into each other as her mandible (bottom jaw) smacked the rock ledge, and she fell down onto the cliff beneath her. Her chest hurt as if the air had been knocked from her, and her arms were bruised. The rock was a lot slicker than Aoife had realized, making her hands slide straight out from under her.

Kate woke to the sound of Aoife's crash and ran to see if she was okay, and Rowsheen hurried down the mountain as she caught a glimpse of the crash out of the corner of her eyes. Aoife stood up straight, holding her arms and stating that she was alright.

"I'm alright," Aoife replied as Kate rubbed Aoife's shoulders, "I'm never doing that again. I'm definitely done with stunts for today. I did not realize how slick the rock was."

"I could have told you it was slick," Kate replied with a laugh that made Aoife feel embarrassed and hurt.

Aoife, trying to prove that she was alright, shook it off by starting to pick up their camp, but when Kate and Rowsheen weren't looking, she pulled back her sleeves to reveal red abrasions all down her forearms, where the rock had met her skin.

A sleepy-eyed Cal, who had slept through the whole ordeal, was filled in by Kate and Rowsheen, only to Aoife's embarrassment.

"You guys are crazy," was Cal's only reply as he rolled over, covering his head with the blanket they had loaned him.

"Come on," Rowsheen beckoned, tying up the last of the supplies they had been given on

Daj, "We need to get to Fayatoch by noon!"

The sea had been stirred all night by monstrous winds and colossal waves. Dead fish, plants, limbs, and rubbish floated along the surface of the water, making some areas hard to negotiate. And on top of the floating rubbish, the foul scent of death rose to their noses in horrid displeasure. Tame did not seem bothered by the dead fish; in fact, he seemed quite happy eating his fill of slimy sea creatures that had floated to the surface.

In a day's time, they managed to make it to Fayatoch. The weary crew walked slowly down the once familiar sandy beach toward the dock, yet now there was a difference; it was strewn with wood from ships and the dock. The dock appeared to have been shredded in the cannon fire, and it looked like it was under repair, with piles of new timber stacked and only a few merchant vessels docked.

As Aoife neared the sight of the dock, she spotted a lone, tall figure standing by a pile of timber. The figure shielded his eyes from the sun and then ran to meet them. It was Daniel running with full force to meet them. When he had barely come to a stop, he wrapped Rowsheen in a big hug, then quickly hugged Aoife and Kate to hide his embarrassment. Aoife just flashed him a laughing smile, which made him blush bright red.

Chapter 47 (Part 2):
Repairs

The next week was a blur of excitement as Daniel filled them in on his side of the wild tale while Dermid interrupted him to tell the good parts, and Jessie disagreed, whispering to Aoife what really happened. The dock, of course, had to be rebuilt before any training could be done, so Aoife, Rowsheen, and Kate had not missed anything. Cal stayed to help rebuild the dock and sent word back to his country of what had befell him and when he would be able to return.

Board by board, splinter by splinter, and nail by nail, the dock came together. They worked hard, dismantling the broken and splintered boards and beams and replacing them with sturdy wood and metal. Aoife felt as if she were growing stronger with all the lifting, digging, and throwing.

Jessie seemed to have changed; he looked older and more mature, yet he still kept a remnant of his playful nature. He was able to make jokes as he once did; however, it was far less often and less funny in Aoife's mind. Aoife thought that his jokes seemed darker than before.

"Aoife," Jessie asked taking a big bite of a thick meat and tomato sandwich as they sat on the edge of the dock with their legs dangling off during their break, "I'm so very glad you're back safe and sound," he paused for a moment, "because I simply cannot deal with Dermid and Daniel without you."

"Thank you," Aoife said with a smile, then gasped aloud for Dermid had snuck up behind her and gave her a shove, sending her over the side, but he wasn't quick enough for Jessie, who grabbed Aoife's arm in one hand and bashed his sandwich over Dermid's head with the other.

Daniel, Kate, and Rowsheen, who had just walked up with their lunch and saw the whole thing and laughed and giggled till their stomachs hurt as Dermid peeled Jessie's smashed sandwich off his head. Jessie, who assumed Dermid was through, reached down to pull Aoife up, but he was badly mistaken as the sandwich-pasting Dermid gave one hard, blind shove and sent Jessie and Aoife splashing into the salty water below.

Jessie and Aoife popped up in time to see Daniel lift Dermid from behind with one strong arm and toss him off the other side.

"You've been avenged," Daniel informed them with a laugh, walking away as if to say that his job there was done.

"Aoife," Jessie called, swimming over to her where she was treading water.

"Yeah," Aoife replied, taking a deep breath as another wave swept over.

"Well, now is as good a time as any," Jessie replied, looking into her light-brown eyes.

Then, he whispered, "Aoife, I love you." As he said those words, he kissed her wet, salty forehead and then swam off to shore.

It took two months in all to be completed, but in the end, it was grand, standing proudly in the midst of crashing crystal-blue salty waves.

Cal had a long, tearful goodbye with Rowsheen before he boarded the ship to take him home. He thanked her for rescuing him, and they promised to write to each other as often as they could. Cal also promised to visit Mossland someday to see Rowsheen's country, and in the same way, she promised to visit Dawnland someday. After their sad goodbye and the finishing touches were put on the proud dock, everyone made their way back to the training grounds.

With almost three months lost, training and lessons started back in full force. Aoife was placed in the healer division and began to learn many things about wound care. Kate was to train in the fliers' division, Rowsheen and Daniel were sent to the Generals' training, while Jessie and Dermid were sent to train to be Captains.

These training courses had been placed in would take over a year to complete. The once close friends would see little of each other over the next year as this war was becoming all too real to them.

Chapter 48:
Time Flies, No Reason Why

Time flies, no reason why,

Where to begin this silly Rhyme?

It's been a day,

And that's not all,

My eyelids are about to fall.

When things feel uncertain,

When the road is rough and tiresome,

I look above where my Savior stands, amidst the brewing storm.

He holds my hand and guides my way,

Through winds and tempests dark,

I shall not fear; he is my joy,

My hope and solid rock.

I may feel pain, and my frame feels weak,

He wipes away every tear on my cheek.

There's nowhere I can go that I'm out of his sight.

In me, he placed love, and in me, he placed light.

I see my path as steady; I see the future as bright.

To him I look; on him I lean,

Over this path with things unseen.

Aoife felt unrest within her soul as she lined up, side by side, the other youths that had been training with her for nearly four years. How could all the mere children that had arrived on the ships from Fayatoch now be ready soldiers to fight for their country? It all seemed too fast. Clad in their black and white training uniforms, they now marched in perfect order, flawless ranks.

Rosian stood at the head of the great force. She has been selected as the general of our training ground force. Five hundred students marched on an open field to practice tactics and stance side by side with the next training force, with their own general and so on.

Kate marched side by side with all the flying beings in their force, while Aoife stood with the beings that would tend to the wounded; they were often called healers. We had been training and learning in small groups, and now we had to learn how to be a fully functioning army. For seven weeks, the individual forces practiced marching, turning, and taking orders. After the marching was over, we would practice setting up camp in perfect order with the ranks all in place.

"Tomorrow," Aoife whispered to herself, lying in the tent with all the healers, "we will march again in full armor and practice running with it on."

And the big day came. All the youths woke to the horn before dawn and helped each other get into their armor. Aoife helped a friend of hers in the healing troop to lace on her armor. "Aoife," she asked her as she was tying her hair up tight, "Are you worried?"

"Ella, I would be lying if I said no," Aoife replied, pulling on her chain mail, "but I have peace in knowing that God protects us." Aoife felt proud looking at herself in a makeshift mirror that rested against the tent wall. Her rosy cheeks glistened as she put on oil after washing so she would feel clean and fresh.

"Aoife, Aoife," a voice called outside the tent. Aoife recognized the voice belonging to Jessie. Aoife felt a bit of nervousness welling up within her.

"I think someone's here to wish you good luck," Ella teased with a sweet, laughing grin. The sides of her rosy lips rose to meet her ruddy, round cheeks. Her dainty, elegant nose sat comfortably between her round, blooming cheeks. Her face was softly framed with wisps of dainty, light brown, fine hair. Ella's eyes were bright green with hazel tints that seemed to glow.

"Coming, Jessie," Aoife whispered under her breath. Aoife had finally chopped her poor hair. Aoife had very thick, coarse auburn red hair. The sheer weight of her hair irritated her scalp and made her chronic headaches worse. Finally, she had summoned up the courage to cut her hair a couple of inches above her shoulders, and she loved it. Aoife felt beautiful looking in the mirror at her new face with a framing bouncy look, and the best part was that her scalp did not hurt much anymore. Aoife carefully pinned her hair back for training as was mandatory.

"Hey Jessie," Aoife replied, slipping out of the tent with a beaming smile. Somehow, she felt more confident and secure in herself. "Good luck out there today."

"Thanks, I'm sure I'll need it," Jessie replied, giving Aoife a big, unexpected hug, then running off. Aoife felt her heart jump as he ran off towards his troop. His slim, muscular frame disappeared amongst the endless rows of tents.

Aoife turned to go back into the tent, but stopped at the sound of her voice being called. One armor-clad Kate was flying in quite a chaotic manner directly toward her. Landing with a thud and almost knocking Aoife over, Kate shot Aoife, her big, wide, excited smile mingling with her bright, laughing, blue eyes while breathing hard.

"Kate, you look great!" Aoife laughed with a smile. Aoife half thought Kate would suffocate under the weight of the armor.

"I got to have more practice flying with this heavy stuff," Kate replied with a chuckle. "Man, it's hot. I'm sweaty already. I gotta fly in this too!" Kate laughed, wiping wisps of hair out of her face and tucking them behind her ear.

"I'm sure you'll do awesome, Katy," Aoife replied with a smile. "How do you have your hair fixed?" Aoife asked, wondering how she had managed to tie up her thin, long, straight, fine hair.

"In a bun," she said, pulling her helmet off, "I can't seem to make it low enough, so my helmet tilts to one side. It's funky!" She said, laughing and giggling at her predicament. She always claimed that it was hard to get hats or headpieces that fit correctly due to her head shape being funny.

"When do we have to be in formation?" Aoife asked because she was not sure if her timepiece was right.

"In about five minutes," Kate replied, sticking her helmet back on and trying to get it to sit straight.

"Well, see ya later," Aoife replied, giving Kate a hug. Aoife squeezed her bony, slim frame. Aoife said a silent prayer of protection over her.

"See ya later," Kate replied, squeezing her back. Kate gave a jump and flapped her wings, making her slim armor-clad frame rise from the ground and into the blue sky.

Clad in full armor, all the units lined up on the large, green battlefield. All Aoife could see was the soldiers around her as she walked in sync with them.

"One, two, one two, one, two," she repeated to herself, breathing heavy. Her armor felt hot and heavy. Aoife was very grateful for the slight breeze, and she knew that she was not the only one.

"Halt!" the command rang out over their unit. All stopped still. In ten minutes, when all the units were in order, the commander yelled, "Run on."

Two minutes passed, seeming like an eternity to Aoife, "Baaaammmp." The horn blew, and the soldiers started forward, but they were not in sync, so the instructors lined them back up, and they started again. They tried running with the armor five more times, then the troops marched for another hour.

That night, everyone passed out in exhaustion. Aoife felt a terrible headache coming on, and within an hour, she crawled out of the tent and threw up. Shaking and terribly nauseous, Aoife rubbed her pounding head and pulled her thick hair to try and release tension.

"Ella," Aoife whispered, shaking her weakly and looking terribly concerned at Aoife's behavior.

"What's wrong, Aoife?" Ella asked, sitting up in the dim-lit tent, "Are you terribly sick? Is the snake bite bothering you again?"

"I got a really bad headache, Ella," Aoife replied, lying on the ground, "I can't even walk. I need help!"

"What can I do?" Ella asked as she helped Aoife get back on her cot. Aoife moaned and tried to get comfortable on her cot, but no position allowed for any comfort.

"Kate Granger is in the fifth Butterflychild unit on the Southside of camp. She has a bright blue tent with coral flaps and drapes that I'm sure is not regulation, but you can find it easily," Aoife breathed. "She knows how to treat this."

Ella quickly dressed and left for Kate. Aoife moaned and rolled this way and that on her cot. She had had these headaches before, but not in a long time and not this severe. Stress often made her headaches worse, which made Aoife afraid of being in stressful situations. Ella found Kate without trouble and explained what was going on with Aoife. Kate nodded and pulled a bag from her things, and a kettle.

"I need this filled with water," Kate directed Ella. When Ella got back with the water, she found Kate stoking the fire in front of the tent. Kate poured a cupful of the herbal contents of the bag into the kettle and placed it over the fire.

"What's in that?" Ella asked with a puzzled expression on her face, "How can silly tea help Aoife? She needs medicine."

"Herbs are medicine. They are just old medicines that have somewhat been lost with time. It's a mixture of Feverfew, Butterbur, Peppermint leaves, Ginger root, Willow bark, and green tea. All of them together work well against a bad headache or, in Aoife's case, an irk," Kate replied, placing more wood on her fire.

"What's an irk?" Ella asked, resting her chin on her fist. Ella seemed confused, so Kate elaborated.

"A headache that can put you down for more than a day at a time. Most can't walk or stand with it. I've had some myself," Kate replied, "I took an herbal remedies course a year ago and made the blend up for Aoife."

"Why aren't you in the healers' unit if you know this much about remedies?" Ella asked, "You could do much good."

"Yes, but I can't stand blood er suffering er death, and the one person I couldn't help would torment me more than all that I could help, but I can help Aoife." Kate replied, stirring the tea, "It's ready now."

In about ten minutes, Kate and Ella got Aoife to take a few sips of the tea, and in half an hour, Aoife was lying still and her irk was mostly relieved. Kat got her cold compressed on her head and neck, and Aoife fell asleep.

For the next six weeks, the units marched and ran in armor in the mornings, then they practiced fighting in full armor in the evenings. They were growing more confident. The youths collapsed on their cots every night and dreamed of it being over. Their wish would be granted all too soon.

Chapter 49:
The Mournful Moon

Daniel crept back from the river after his bath quietly through camp so as not to wake anyone up. The moon shone full and bright, illuminating his path in the dull darkness. Walking through the camp's center, he paused at the commander's tent because he heard loud voices inside. He crept closer and listened, placing his ear to the tent's dark leather side.

"They'll be here in a week!" a deep voice scoffed, "Do they think we can train them overnight?"

"Have patience. Just be glad they did not come a month ago," a calm voice answered. Daniel recognized this voice as Sir Masuda.

"They need more time!" the deep voice retorted, sounding increasingly irritated.

"Perhaps they are more ready than we know, Loane," a soft voice, Daniel recognized as Lady Catherine. "They're not our youth."

"They have been for the last five years," Loane replied, "They're good, but good enough to fight a war..." Daniel did not want to hear anymore. He covered his ears and ran off, nearly plowing a tent over on his way back to his own.

Daniel ran through the camp with no specific direction till he had to stop for air. To his left, he heard laughter, and his weary heart seemed to pull him toward it. A group of youths sat around a fire, sipping tea and sharing stories in the light of the full moon. Jessie, Dermid, and Aoife were among them, and Kate was nearly asleep on Aoife's shoulder.

Daniel walked up and sat down by Kate and Aoife in silence. Jessie was telling the story of the time he and Aoife had been fighting pirates on a ship in the middle of a lightning storm. Jessie was using dramatic hand motions and sound effects to tell his story and capture his audience's attention as best as he could.

"And the ship rocked this way and that while the foaming seawater splashed over the sides of the ship! Lightning CRACKED and BOOMED!!! Lighting up and maddening scene..." Jessie dramatically went on, whipping his hands this way and that to illustrate the sword fighting and cracks of lightning.

Daniel finally decided to tell Aoife what he had heard. Daniel tuned Jessie out and whispered to Aoife, "Aoife?"

"Yes," she whispered back softly so as not to wake Kate or interrupt Jessie. Aoife softly turned her head and sensed that something was deeply bothering Daniel.

"Don't say anything, but I think we're going home," he said quietly. His left knee was jumping up and down with nervous energy as he tried in vain to sit still.

Aoife straightened up so fast she nearly knocked snoozing Kate off her shoulder, "You're sure," she breathed, feeling a ping of homesickness in her gut.

"Yes," Daniel answered with a pale, painful look on his face.

"What's wrong?" Aoife asked, "You don't look happy."

Daniel leaned forward and whispered in her ear, "The war is coming, the one I told you about over five years ago; that's why they need us home."

Aoife's countenance fell as she tried to summon up enough courage to reply, "Have I not commanded thee: Be strong and of a good courage. Be not afraid, neither be thou dismayed; for the Lord thy God is with thee whithersoever thou goest. Joshua 1:9. Joshua was going to fight, and God was within him. He will be with us."

"He shall," Daniel replied, standing up. "Good night," he said, walking away.

The moon, the Daniel, seemed to hang low in a sad, mournful look as if it were dreading the war as much as he was.

"Be with us, Lord," Daniel prayed, "Please be with us." Daniel felt an answer come to his heart, "I will never leave you nor forsake you," Hebrews 13:5.

Aoife smiled at Jessie, depicting how brave he was in his story, *"Thank you, Lord, for the good things that you give me in life, like great friends, loving parents, loving siblings, a place to call home, and most of all for you, Lord, my Saviour. Amen."*

Chapter 50:
Whisked Away Beyond Today

In about a week's time, the ships arrived to take us back home. Everyone packed their things with nervous energy. Both Aoife and Kate had upset stomachs, and Daniel looked nervous and worried.

Aoife stood with her bags on the pier, elbow to elbow with youths who once arrived as children on that very pier. The bun in her hair pulled, telling her that she had tied it too tight; it was starting to give her a headache, but she tried to forget about it, telling herself that one last look upon Fayatoch was more important to her at that moment. She felt very small and alone amidst the great multitude, yet the great feeling of getting to see her family again welled up in her.

Suddenly, she felt a tap on her shoulder. Turning around, she saw Jessie in his travel clothes with a great bag swung over his shoulder. He looked solemn and nervous. Aoife thought that Daniel had probably told him what he had heard.

"Bye, Aoife," he whispered, embracing her with a big hug. Aoife noticed that he looked so grown up. Where was the boy she had traveled to Fayatoch with that long ago?

"Bye," Aoife whispered back. Jessie leaned in and kissed her cheek before disappearing into the crowd. Aoife stood still, as if she was frozen in place, staring into the crowd where he had just disappeared.

Aoife stood there for a long time as youths shoved this way and that on the crowded dock. The sun was rising high in the sky when the first sails were spotted on the horizon. By now, all the youth had grown weary of standing and sat in crowded groups. Aoife sat with her legs dangling off the edge of the great pier, watching into the deep, blue water rise and swell with every wave.

She was weary of the training, the coming war, the rumors; she even felt scared of going home after being away for so long. *"What if it's not the same?"* her thoughts cried inside, *"What if I can't live up to what they expect of me? Lord, please heal me. Please grant me peace."* Warm tears dripped down her cheeks, blurring her vision, but lessening the weight on her heart.

"Hey, Aoife," a soft voice whispered behind her. Aoife recognized the voice as belonging to Kate, but she also felt a sense of sadness mingled with different emotions.

"Hey," Aoife replied, wiping her tears off on her sleeve. Aoife took a deep breath and sat up taller; she did not want Kate to see her tears because Aoife was sure that she would break down crying again if Kate hugged her.

It was Kate, arrayed in her flowy, long, blue, ankle-length dress that matched her bright wings. Plopping down her bags, she sat down beside Aoife and let her bare feet dangle off the edge of the pier. Aoife just stared into the blue waves with foaming white caps lapping at the support beams for the dock.

"You happy about going home?" Kate asked with a soft smile, straightening the greyish-blue feathers on her right wing. Kate tucked her thin, light brown hair behind her ears.

"Yes, but I'm kinda also nervous," Aoife replied with a weak smile. Her stomach felt upset, like her headache and nausea.

"Yeah, me too," Kate replied, drawing her knees up into her chest, "What if everything's different? What if I don't recognize my siblings because they've grown a lot? What if we're not as close as we were as siblings?"

"There's no way of knowing. How's Jad?" Aoife asked, trying to change the conversation, "You mentioned you two were writing."

Kate's countenance fell.

"We stopped writing," she whispered. "We didn't see eye to eye on... somethings."

"I'm sorry," Aoife replied, giving Kate a hug and rubbing her slim shoulder and wing. Aoife thought that her eyes looked sad and a bit sunken in.

"It's okay," Kate replied with a sniff, "It's sad to lose a friend, but I am going to be so happy to eat Mommy's food again!"

"Me too," Aoife whispered, watching a ship come closer and closer to the docks, "Isn't that Captain Acosta's ship?"

"It looks like it!" Kate replied with enthusiasm, jumping up and waving to the ship. The sailors waved back. Kate loved being on the ships.

"What do you want to do first when you get home, more than anything else?" Kate asked suddenly, flipping her hair around and plopping back down on the dock.

"Humm," Aoife thought long, then replied seriously, "I want to go to church and hear my Daddy sing."

Captain Acosta's ship came into dock first, and Sir Masuda and his helpers gave Captain Acosta the list of youths that would be traveling in his ship and which port in Mossland they had to be at. Larry was shaking hands and exclaiming about how much the children had grown up in a few years' time. Aoife, Kate, Rowsheen, Dermid, and Daniel were all assigned to Captain Acosta's ship along with many other youths.

Aoife pulled her old blade set from her bag, buckled it on, then stepped onto the gangplank. The familiarity of the ship sank in as she walked up on deck amidst the jostling and bumping of over thirty youths trying to go in every which direction in the same crowded spot. The ship seemed a bit older in Aoife's mind as she looked at the rails, decks, and sails.

"Look at the strong soldiers!" Larry beamed talking to the youths. Every youth wanted a handshake from Larry because they all remembered him giving lessons, telling wild stories, and teaching them how to sail.

After all the youths were on board, all of them were counted and organized by Larry, who ushered them below deck to show them where they'd be sleeping and where to put their belongings. In the hustle and bustle, Aoife seemed lost in thought and void of emotion. She was tired from all the training she had endured in the past few weeks. Deep down inside somewhere, a desire just to talk to someone who would assure her that everything would be alright pushed its way up into her thoughts and hung heavy in her heart like a stone that wouldn't move.

That night, Aoife lay in a hammock below the deck with the same feeling pressed against her chest. Slipping from her hammock, she knelt down and lit the lamp she had set by her bed. She then pulled her notebook from her bag and wrote her heart out, letting warm, salty tears drip down her cheeks.

"Terror, what is terror? True terror is feeling hopeless when looking into the merciless eyes of this world; no room for error, and not a glimpse of feeling in its eyes. How does one continue through such stress? Well, someone who has God on their side will always be victorious in his will. True courage through such terror, such trials, is putting your trust in the one who fashioned your very form in your mother's womb. So have courage and be strong! You're not alone, and despite your fears and endless tears, God had something

great in mind for you, so just hold to his hand and trust, for sometimes the ability to trust is all we need to grow."

With those last words, she breathed a sigh of relief, closed her notebook, and slipped it into her bag, but she did not climb back into her hammock; she just sat still. A soft noise had caught her attention; it was like soft, velvety whispers coming from somewhere above deck. Aoife was nervous about going up on deck without permission, but she shook it off and climbed the rocky, creaky wooden stairs to the deck.

Stepping out on deck, Aoife looked around for the sailor on night watch. She wanted to make sure whoever was on night watch knew that she was on deck. It was the rules. It was to make sure that if anyone accidentally fell over the side, someone would know to look for you.

"And what be you doin here, little missy?" Larry sounded loudly from behind her, making her jump in start. He had what appeared to be a cup of strong coffee in his right fist and a sea biscuit in his left hand. His sailor's hat was off, and his feet were bare as usual.

"Larry," she gasped with her hand on her heart, "I couldn't sleep."

"Many have dat problem under a full moon," Larry replied with a laugh, patting her shoulder, "Come up to de bridge and tell me why you're really out here."

Aoife climbed the stairs behind him and sat down on a barrel by the railing, "I thought I heard voices," she began.

"Of course. The nymphs are out, love," Larry replied turning the great wheel to the left with a huff and grunt as he turned the wheel.

"The nymphs?" Aoife replied in shock as memories about being in the nymph tunnels flooded back in her memories, "I did not know they were around here."

"Yes," Larry replied, with a laughing smile, "These waters are full of 'em, but don't you be hanging over the side, they'll snatch you right over it." Aoife stayed at the bridge as Larry told her about Nymphs and wild stories.

In the days to come Aoife tried to find small things to make her smile, like a being up before dawn to watch the sun rise or listening to her friends joke, yet she still felt a twinge of unexplainable, disheartening fear inside somewhere deep down that surfaced every now and then in bouts of tears, prayers and writing like an unwanted intruder tearing at her from the inside.

Finally, on a beautiful rainy day, below deck, she seemed to find a little joy playing cards with her friends. She was tired of working all the time with no play, yet any sort of play made her feel guilty that she was wasting valuable time. Her soul, however, longed to be filled with some remnant of joy and hope.

The storm raged on and on, growing worse as the night fell. Many of the youths sat huddled in piles on the floor listening to "BOOM, CRACK," over and over again amidst the pounding rain. This storm continued for weeks, and due to the youths being crammed together under the deck, a sickness arose among them.

Kate had the sickness first; she slept most of the time and had very little appetite. Aoife and Rowsheen worried that she was dehydrated because everything she ate or drank came up. They were also worried that she would lose what little weight she had on her tiny, bony frame. The second week, Kate was fairly better, but Aoife was now sick, and the ship tossing this way and that in the storm was not helping matters.

Aoife sat leaning against the stairs by Kate and Rowsheen, sick and nauseous late one afternoon. Kate and Rowsheen had nodded off while Aoife sat still, hoping the nausea would leave. One more roll of the ship and Aoife felt like vomiting. She crawled up the stairs that were shifting this way and that with the ship and out into the cool and moist, dark evening air.

Pulling herself up on the railing at the top of the stairs, she walked leaning this way and that to the side of the ship and rested her hands on the side. Aoife sank to her weak knees, but she made an effort to try to stand up. The cool breeze felt refreshing on her face as she breathed in the salty, moist air. Another wave of nausea fell over Aoife just as a great wave smacked the side of the ship.

The ship tilted madly forward, knocking already unsteady Aoife over the side of the ship. Splash! Aoife plummeted into the cold, salty moving water. She tried to get above the water for air and managed to get a few breaths. The cold water had snatched her voice, and she began to feel helpless when something grabbed her ankle!

Chapter 51:
Watery Rescue

Aoife kicked her leg to try to free herself from its grasp. It let her go. Aoife heard something surface behind her and turned around to see what it was.

Oh, watery grave,

Don't be my demise!

Let me live,

Answer my cries.

You're the cruel fate of many,

But not me today,

I've got friends in all places,

To help me today!

Erena surfaced, lifting her scaly head from under the water and staring at Aoife, who was struggling to stay afloat.

"Erena!" Aoife managed to blurt out as a wave washed over her, filling her mouth with cold, salty seawater.

Erena pulled Aoife up to the surface where she could breathe, "King Loughin wishes you to be present. There is much brewing in this world both above and below."

"I don't know," Aoife nervously replied, treading water to keep herself afloat, "They will find me missing and panic."

"We nymphs have our ways," Erena replied with a wink and a grin, "Bending time is not hard for us. They won't notice you're gone."

"Alright," Aoife replied confidently, still struggling to get a breath against the salty spray of the waves, "I'm ready to see King Loughin."

Erena fitted her breathing mask, then they plunged down into the sea below. Aoife was surprised at how well Erena could see under the dark, cloudy, cold water, but she knew her way. Down, down, down, down they went till Erena entered a large, lit cave under the briny sea.

The walls of the cave were surprisingly smooth and decorated with intricate art drawings and lit up with glowing shells, lichens, and sea mosses. Nymphs appeared everywhere, and the number of them grew as Aoife neared the King's court. King Loughin sat tall and proud on his throne and nodded his head in reverence when Aoife entered. Aoife bowed in reply.

"Princess Aoife, daughter of Biro the stone," the King addressed her, "there is a war brewing on the water as well as on the land. Are you aware of this?"

"Only a little, your majesty," Aoife replied, wondering what news she might have for her.

"Pirates are teeming in these waters," he began, "Ships from everywhere are wrecked and sunk to the depths; few have been saved."

King Loughlin and Aoife discussed the details of being allies in the war for nearly three hours. It was important to understand the extent of aid each country would receive.

"My people shall aid yours' by river and sea," the King spoke in low tones to Aoife. "This war is dangerous for both of us. You and your people are vulnerable on land and the sea, yes, but we, we are thought of as only legend by many beings, and we will be hunted and killed as the unicorn that was slain by mighty hunters to show their valor. Alone we can perish, but together we shall be triumphant.”

“What can we do, your majesty?” Aoife asked respectfully.

“Spread our existence,” the King replied, “We deserve to be respected as every respectable being.”

“I’ll do what I can,” Aoife replied, hoping that she could honor her pledge.

“We shall scout out the rivers and waterways and patrol the seas all around. We shall get word to you of all our findings,” the King decided, scratching his scaly beard.

“Could you send it to the Creature, um, Theodore Weatherly?” Aoife replied with hesitation.

The King agreed because he knew the Creature well. Aoife was returned to the ship, and it was as if no time had passed at all. They had not missed her, and everything seemed exactly as it was, even the time of day.

Chapter 52:
Nearly Home

Finally, the ship arrived at Mossland's shores. Standing on the deck side by side, watching the land grow larger and larger, Aoife and Kate stood leaning on the ship's dinghy red rail as they had done so long before. The last time they were joking and laughing with each other to soothe the loss of home, but now there was no denying the homesickness that had crept into both of them.

"Aoife," Kate whispered with tears in her eyes, "I want to hug mama and daddy again. I want to see my siblings."

"Yeah, me too," Aoife replied, tearing up and almost choking on the knot that was welling up in her throat, "and I want to hear my dad laugh."

Kate wrapped her arm around Aoife, and Aoife wrapped her arm around Kate. Aoife knew that if she tried to talk, warm tears would stream down her cheeks, so she remained silent and listened to the waves slapping the hull of the ship.

Rowsheen appeared at Aoife's side, placed her hand on Aoife's shoulder, and whispered, "One adventure is behind us and one... one is about to begin." Rowsheen stood tall and proud with courage and determination on her face and in her posture. She embodied the look of a King!